Home FOR A Hero

CHLOE ALAN

A FINDING HOME NOVEL

Dear Reader,

This story was a labor of love and the book of my heart. The idea for *Home* started as a conversation with a friend about the power of love and in finding that place you feel you belong. I began the first draft years ago, decided I wasn't a good enough writer to put the story on paper as it lived and breathed in my head and shelved it. Over the years, I've finished it, expanded it, and put it back on the shelf. However, the love I have for this story and the characters that have been talking to me for almost a decade wouldn't quit. With much re-writing, *Home For A Hero* is finally the book I envisioned. I hope you love Home as much as I do.

Callan and Vicky's journey is sweet, sexy, and suspenseful as they find their way to a happily ever after. This book contains swearing and pre-marital sex between the lead couple as well as discussion of the effects of PTSD. I understand stories like this are not for everyone and every book has its audience. If you choose to continue, I hope you enjoy!

Happy reading!
Chloe

*S*tupid, smug, Prince Charles and his too-punchable face. This was the third life-sized cutout Callan had had to replace in a month. In a town with only a handful of teenagers, you'd think he'd be able to figure out which of the punks liked to get creative with a sharpie. At least the added facial features weren't as X-rated as the last time. Callan grabbed the cardboard prince and tucked it under one arm. He'd stash Chuck in the storeroom of the hardware store until another could be printed and sealed, this time like a dry-erase board. The mayor would have one of her fits if Callan left the prince at his station in the main square under the billboard welcoming visitors to Home, Colorado to experience Real Romance at Home. He hadn't believed that was the actual name of the town when John had told him. But here he was, living in it. For now, anyway.

He marched across the park as the sunrise lit the corners of the newly renovated space. Why'd it have to be weddings? Marriage drove people crazy to begin with and the town wants to invite couples to have crazy weddings as a business?

He didn't get it. Callan didn't have to like the town's commitment to becoming a theme wedding destination. He only had to help make it work.

The soft thud of his work boots hitting the distressed boardwalk the town had recently put down made a pleasant drumbeat to his ingrained speed of one hundred and twenty steps per minute. Even with carrying the extra fifteen-pound, six-foot chunk of pressed paper.

He propped his load against the window of Pearce Hardware and took in a deep breath of crisp morning air and let it puff out in a white cloud before rolling his shoulders in a stretch, wincing at the pull of tight skin and muscles under his layers of cotton and flannel. The sun had begun to rise only an hour before, and he'd been walking the perimeter of the town for the majority of that time. He'd grown used to the regular schedule and quiet mornings, which kept his predawn scouting under the radar of most of Home's three hundred residents.

Except one.

"Good morning, Mr. Singleton."

He heard a soft curse before the older man stepped out from the recessed doorway of the empty storefront next to his. "Morning, John. I thought sure I had you this time."

Callan blinked away the unexpected sting of being called by his best friend's name. After pretending to be John for almost three months, he'd thought he was over the guilt the lie caused.

"Better luck next time." Why the man wanted to sneak up on him was a mystery, but it seemed to be a game of sorts. He'd almost had him once. Thankfully, Callan had stopped carrying a firearm or it might have turned out differently.

The barber shuffled closer and looked him in the eye. "Just 'cause trouble comes knocking, doesn't mean you have to offer it a place to sit."

"Yes, sir." Callan nodded. "And always drink upstream from the herd."

Mr. Singleton's mouth cracked wide, and his laugh cackled through the air, as paper-thin as the skin covering his reddened cheeks. "Yep, that's what my daddy always said too."

They'd been trading *wisdom* as a greeting most mornings since Callan had arrived in Home. They rarely spoke otherwise, but it surprised him how much he looked forward to a simple thing like seeing his neighbor an hour past dawn each day.

"Why don't you stop by later and let me shave that beard for you? Those big weddings the mayor is chasing could be a real chance for you."

"A chance for what?"

"Weddings are full of pretty girls in pretty dresses usually looking for someone to dance with 'em and make them blush."

"Don't brides have a groom for that?" he asked, trying to make light of the man's meddling.

"You're as stubborn as they come. Give me twenty minutes and I'll make your cheeks so smooth, they'll be begging for a lady's lips."

"Tell you what, at the first actual wedding Home calls their own, I'll think about letting you give me a nice shave but for now, dates aren't a part of my work orders." There were no ladies or dates in his plans, which was for the best. He didn't have time for the simple pleasure of a woman's lips on his skin, much less romance.

"You must not be trying." A weathered laugh tumbled out again, filling the silent morning with the sounds of the septuagenarian's humor.

"When you get a break, come by for a cup of coffee. I'll tell you about a date I had with a lovely actress when I worked as a set barber in Hollywood."

"I bet you have some stories," Callan said.

"I've had a life." A solemn expression crossed the old man's face. "Home's been good to me. It will be to you too. It's right you took over the shop and are keeping your land and business out of Blake's hands. Your dad would be proud if he were here. Blake won't be able to buy us all out with you here fighting for what's right."

"Thanks." Callan nodded and swallowed the growing guilt at lying to the man. John's dad should have been proud of the man *John* had become. Old Mr. Singleton had been good friends with Jed Pearce, the former owner of Pearce Hardware, and the father of the real John Pearce, the man Callan had been impersonating since arriving in Home months before.

He hadn't set out to lie about who he was and what he was doing in Home and certainly didn't enjoy that Mr. Singleton thought of himself as an uncle of sorts and was determined to remind John his father hadn't always been the town drunk and had missed him when he'd moved away.

"Good day." Callan accepted the small salute with a nod. He wouldn't open as early as his neighbor, but he had inventory to rearrange and a new display of china patterns to put out.

Callan was stuck between being helpful and neighborly and keeping his distance. The less he became personally involved, the better for his friend's future in Home. When the real John was recovered from his latest round of surgery and rehabilitation and had moved back to Home, Mr. Singleton would have a chance to redeem Jed Pearce's memory to the person that mattered. Until then, Callan would be John as far as any pushy Blake Corporation representative or friendly neighbor was concerned.

A small stream of customers kept him busy until Tyler, his only employee, showed up for his shift behind the register and Callan could focus on the wedding set facades and what supplies needed to be ordered to complete the remodel of the main chapel. Acting as store owner and foreman for his make-shift crew of independent handy-men and locals with construction experience was a new job for him but one that at least played to his strengths and let him spend most of his time outdoors.

By early evening, the setting sun turned blue skies to shades of purple and pink, and the afternoon heat turned cool. Tyler had gone for the day, and Mr. Singleton should be taking his walk down to Jo's for his predinner meet and greet with the regulars for news and conversation, and Callan was almost ready for his nightly security check.

Preparing to close, he moved the last of his construction crew's supplies onto a pallet—ready to load for the next day's work. The chime on the door announced a visitor. He wiped his hands on a rag and walked toward the front of the shop, spying the heads of three men over the tops of the shelves.

Damn.

His pulse jumped from the immediate spike in adrenaline. Steady, he thought with each step.

"Mr. Dewey, can I help you with something?" Keeping his voice even, he directed the question at the man whose homestead abutted John's on the outskirts of town.

"Listen to what these men have to say. That's all I ask." He pulled the worn cap from his head, working the rim between his fingers and motioning toward the younger man standing next to him. Callan had met him a few times. Blake Corporation's smiling face sent to charm the town, Grayson St. James.

"It's we who can help you, Mr. Pearce."

Callan ignored his outstretched hand. He had to be civil for John's sake, but he didn't have to be friendly. "Not interested in any help."

The third man stood back, his narrow-eyed gaze roaming the interior of the store.

Every instinct Callan had honed in combat hammered at him to keep an eye on that guy. The way the prick that hadn't been introduced assessed the room and kept his distance—he wasn't there to charm or dazzle residents with dollar signs.

"John, listen to him." Mr. Dewey stepped toward him, and Callan dragged his stare from the man he'd marked as the enemy. "They have an offer sure to get you to sell. You could open any kind of store you want, anywhere you want with what they're offering. Let's help each other here."

"Who's your friend?" Callan sent his question to St.

James, lifting his chin toward the man who had yet to speak. "Haven't seen him around before."

The man held Callan's stare, primed to meet the challenge head-on, but St. James responded. "My associate, Mr. Barnes, is riding along with me today as I deliver a few offers."

"Think it over, would you." Mr. Dewey's pleading pulled him away from his unspoken standoff. Sad desperation underlined the request.

Callan dragged in a deep breath. There was no immediate threat. Not the time. Not the place. He was John Pearce, hardware store owner. His only mission was to be there for his best friend. To buy him and the town more time to mount a defense against predators like Blake Corporation.

"Are you taking their deal?" he asked Dewey. His words were slow, and his heart hammered in his chest. Outwardly, he kept his stance steady and refused to swipe at the sweat causing his neck to itch. His brain knew he was fine, but his gut urged him to fight or flee.

"I want to. Blake's offering a package deal. Ten percent more for all of us if you, the Carlisles, and me, agree to sell and we all sign a contract before the end of the month."

"The end of the month, huh?" The same time as the mayor's wedding and the town's new business venture's first test. *What a coincidence.*

Dewey's, Pearce's, and Carlisle's land bordered three-quarters of Home. With those, Blake would own most of the property around town and Home would be swallowed up by the resort development the usurpers wanted even if they didn't get all the businesses to sell. The Mayor's plans would have no chance to get started if that happened. Much as he hated the destination wedding idea for this town, it was that or tell John he should sell out and move.

"There are some new, more favorable terms in this offer that include an increase in the offer for your store as well. Think it over." St. James held an envelope toward Callan.

"Time for you to leave." Callan forced the words through his clenched jaw and took the offered packet. He needed them gone. He'd leashed the desire burning in the back of his mind to inflict damage, but Barnes' presence was testing the extent of his control. He could not afford to have a flashback triggered just then.

"I'll be around." St. James turned on his heel, positioning himself between Callan and Barnes.

The three men filed out. The click of the door closing behind them broke through the warring signals of fight or flight and the anxiety his anger produced. He locked the door then raced toward the back exit. Pushing it open, he stumbled into the alley and sucked in a lungful of cool air.

He paced a circle, waiting for his heart rate to slow to a normal beat. He blew out a hard breath and bounced on the balls of his feet. This wasn't a new scenario. He'd been fending off aggressive offers to buy John's land for months. This one was an escalation but he'd handled it in a way that wouldn't hurt John's future in Home. That was what mattered. He hadn't punched the asshole or gotten lost in the past. He'd call it a win.

As long as Blake was still trying to buy the town by upping the money, everything was fine. Fielding the harassment so John could recuperate in peace and prepare Home for when Blake Corporation got tired of playing nice was the reason Callan was there. The town was no match for a company like Blake. Deep pockets paid for a lot of discretion and they wanted Home. All of it.

His pulse returned to normal and his shakiness subsided. A quick circle around the block would burn off any residual adrenaline. He paced up the alley that ran behind the buildings a few blocks and turned toward Main Street at the next open intersection between two buildings. Rounding the corner, the woman in front of him stopped him in his tracks. His brain stuttered at the unexpected sight.

Bent at the waist, inspecting a sign in the window of the bookshop, her phone in one hand, keys in the other, he didn't recognize her as being one of Home's residents.

She did a quick double take and straightened. "Whoa, where'd you come from?"

"Alley," he said gruffly.

One side of her mouth tilted up, revealing a dimple on her left cheek. She looked familiar, but he couldn't place her. He'd made it a priority to recognize all the current residents of Home. An awkward silence lasted a beat before she half-turned back to the window she'd been staring into and pointed at a sign. "Is there really free Wi-Fi in all these places?"

"Wi-Fi?"

She tapped on the glass of the bookstore's window and cocked her head, the force of her full attention on him. "Wi-Fi . . . You know what that is, right?"

"Sure." Smooth, Jackass. "I mean, yeah, there's Wi-Fi for customers. When it's working."

"That sounds about right." She sighed and pushed her phone into a back pocket of her jeans. His gaze followed her hand over the curve of her hip, fit and generous in all the right places.

"Oh, crap." One second she was about to walk away from him, the next she'd ducked behind him and wedged between him and the brick wall.

He immediately turned to assess the unknown threat that had caused her alarm. The only person in view was Mrs. Hanson, who rivaled Mr. Singleton in age and wisdom, walking into Jo's Diner a block down.

"Crap, crap, crap. I knew I shouldn't have stopped. Tell me when she's gone. If she sees me, I'm dead." The woman's hand brushed the back of his forearm, holding briefly before letting go. Callan's world zeroed in on that single connection before stuttering back to life. He peered down at her crouched against his side. Whoever she was, she'd fit right in with the crazy here in town.

"Who, Mrs. Hanson?"

"Yes, is she gone?"

"Yup."

The woman edged out from behind him and peeked around past his shoulder. "Thanks for the assist. It's hard to explain."

"No problem." His brain and body finally synced, and he sidestepped her reach. Oh, no. This couldn't be happening. He needed to get the hell out of there, PDQ.

Which is just what he did. No exchange of names. No goodbye. No nothing. Whatever she thought of his quick exit, it didn't matter. He'd come up with an excuse later. He double-timed it back around the block. Keeping to the shadows of the alley entrance next to the hardware store, he waited until he spied her white sedan cruising slowly down Main Street.

Her picture was all over the mayor's house. That's why she looked familiar. Dammit all to hell. She wasn't supposed to come back until her mother's wedding.

She was a complication.

He followed her progress along the street until she pulled into a parking spot in front of John's store. She looked right at him and smiled. She couldn't possibly see him hidden in the narrow passageway. Why was she waving at him like a lunatic? Maybe she was in real trouble this time? She nodded and beckoned him toward her. He took a step and stopped himself. What the hell did he think he was doing?

"Queenie Jones! What a sight for these old eyes." Mr. Singleton strolled toward the car and accepted a hug as soon as she stepped out. Of course, that made more sense. She'd know everyone in town and would have grown up around Mr. Singleton. He'd almost blown his cover over a pretty smile.

"Or, should I call you Vicky Alexander now. You being famous and all."

"Definitely not famous and Vicky is fine." The laughter in her voice matched the smile on her face. Callan couldn't leave his covered spot without showing himself. He'd have to wait out her little reunion. He wasn't prepared to face the one person John had warned him might not accept him at his word.

"I can't stay and chat, but I had to say hi. If anyone tells Mom I'm here before she sees me . . . well, you know how she can be."

"Run along, then. I'll keep it to myself for a bit."

"I know it'll be hard," she said with a laugh, "but thanks."

"It sure is good to see you." His light tone turned serious. "Your mother needs you right here, where you belong."

Her smile faltered as she took her seat behind the wheel. "I'm only here for a short visit."

"That's what they all say."

Callan watched her wave goodbye and resume her drive toward the mayor's side of town.

"You remember Queenie Jones, don't you?"

Callan flinched. Damned if the old man hadn't finally surprised him. He cleared his throat and stepped from his hideout. "Sure do."

"She'll be thrilled to see you. Night then." Mr. Singleton began to whistle the wedding march on his way toward Jo's.

John and Vicky had been best friends as children. John had told him about Queenie Jones, aka Vicky Alexander. Even after twenty years away, he believed she'd be the only one that might see through their lie. Looked like Callan wouldn't be lucky enough to avoid that test after all. The mayor's daughter, John's childhood best friend, and a political columnist for the *DC Chronicle*.

Every one of those titles was a threat to him and his mission.

* * *

The single stoplight designating Main Street turned red as she slowed. Vicky checked her watch and grimaced. Damn flight delays. Not that anyone was expecting her. Surprise was the best defense for keeping her sanity the first twenty-four hours of being home. A loud growl from her stomach reminded her ice cream and a latte weren't the filling snack she should have grabbed during her layover. Jo's would still be open for a meal, but someone was sure to call her mother before she'd even made it out the door then she'd catch hell for stopping to eat before telling the mayor she was home for a visit. She shouldn't have stopped at the bookstore, but she just had to take a peek at the signs. And maybe she was procrastinating. If Mrs. Hanson had seen her, she would have made a scene for sure. Vicky had made enough of one with Mr. Hot mountain-man. At least someone new had moved to Home.

Assuming he lived here and wasn't passing through.

But why else would he be walking in the alley between the businesses on Main if he didn't live here? Hot dude made at least one new resident since she'd moved away. There might be more, so her mom's fear about Home's declining population could be another exaggeration. She wondered if any other newbies were as drool-worthy. Maybe she should rethink her best friend's insistence that some rebound dating would help her forget her cheating asshole ex.

Stop. Focus. She couldn't let herself get distracted.

Cracking her window, she let a bit of the crisp air in. This had been her favorite time of year growing up—cool, dry, sunny days filled with canyon hiking trails, fishing, horseback riding, anything to stay outdoors as long as possible. But that was before her mother had been elected mayor and became obsessed with her place in Home's history—thereby making sure Vicky knew her place as well.

Joneses settled Home and we will take Home into the

future. Her mother was fond of romanticizing their family history and what she'd declared a duty to maintain. What future did Home really have? She never understood her mother's obsession with being so entrenched in town affairs there was little separation between something happening to the town and something happening personally to the Jones family. Leaving to pursue a journalism degree at NYU had been tantamount to desertion as far as her family was concerned.

No use opening old wounds before she even saw her mother. With everything new going on in Home and how busy her mother would be planning her own wedding, maybe this visit would be different.

She scoffed. She knew better than to lie to herself like that. Instead of a relaxing vacation, she was going home, almost unemployed, mostly broke, recently single, and completely miserable.

At least she'd be off Laura's couch and have some room to work. She could do a little digging to prove Blake Corporation wasn't doing anything illegal to satisfy her mother's concern and concentrate on finding a way to bring her editor a story to get her back where she belonged—employed, living in her own place, and enjoying the single life in DC. No cheating ex or public humiliation, no lawsuit and scandal, no questioning of her work ethics. She needed to keep that visual in her mind at all times.

She needed to bring something new to show the *DC Chronicle* and Stan, the most unapproachable editor on the planet, that she wasn't going to run and hide from one mistake. She'd get her name attached to something—anything—not related to illegal campaign finance contributions and Standridge Pharmaceutical's lobbyists, especially if they are personal friends of one of the paper's board of directors. That had been a once in a lifetime mistake.

The curved drive around the front of her parents' home was blocked with several cars heading up a line of others parked along the street.

Warning bells clanged in the back of her mind as she pulled into an open spot along the curb. Maybe she should have called first. She shouldn't have taken the time for an extra loop around town to steel her nerves, but it was too late now.

Outside, her breath came out in swirling, opaque puffs. The last rays of the sunset had disappeared, and the air felt colder than it had just a few minutes before.

The thin silk of her blouse was a poor shield against the forty something degree weather. She was shivering and her teeth were chattering by the time she made it to the door. She knocked and walked in, rather than ringing the bell, far too cold to care what she might be interrupting.

The house was eerily quiet and dark. Odd. The owners of the cars outside had to be somewhere. She pulled her bag over the doorstep into the candle lit foyer then kicked the door closed behind her.

"Surprise!"

Out of the center of the shadowy darkness, a bright laser of light pierced her vision and people jumped from every corner of the living room, dining room and den that opened onto the foyer.

Vicky screamed and stumbled back. Her overstuffed bag tipped over. The heel of her boot caught in the handle and she fell, landing hard on her behind, one leg sprawled in front of her, one bent underneath. Her butt burned where she sat on the side of her heel.

Momentarily winded, she squinted at the phone camera lights that flashed around her. Someone had the blessed sense to turn the actual room lights on.

"Oh my god, Queenie, what on earth are you doing here?"

The concerned faces of her mother and grandmother came into focus, along with friends and neighbors from town. Every one of them stared at her like she'd returned from the moon.

Not exactly the reaction she'd expected. "Nice to see you too, Mom. Don't worry, I'm okay."

Several sets of hands grabbed a different part of her to help her untangle and stand. Her mother hugged her and then stood back. Her grandmother stood in the forefront with a row of women crowded behind them, Vicky's kinder-garten teacher, her Sunday school teacher, the girl who worked the counter at the pharmacy, along with several new faces.

"Whoever the surprise party is for, you might want to slow down on the flash photos." She glanced from one familiar face to another. Her earlier feeling of apprehension stood on its tiptoes now, poised over her with a bat ready to bash her if she ignored it again.

"Surprise party? How did you know we were having a surprise party?" her mother asked with almost sincere innocence.

"Oh, I don't know, maybe the loud ass surprise you all terrified me with?"

Pressed into the foyer, the crowd hadn't allowed her any

further into the house except to place her luggage against the door so it wouldn't fall over again.

"Right. We weren't expecting you in town so early." Her mother's tone was bright, but the reproach zinged straight to its intended target.

"Obviously." Vicky matched her mother's sarcasm.

"We're having a surprise wedding shower, now move over Judith and let me hug my granddaughter," her grandmother answered, stepping between the standoff and opening her arms for a hug. Her mother eyed Vicky over the shorter woman's shoulder. She felt the weight of her scrutiny and tried not to squirm.

The crowd eased back some, but no one actually left the foyer. Most likely waiting to see what would happen. Instead of the usual twenty questions about her life and the guilt trip for not communicating more, a flash of speculation pinched her mother's features before she turned on a full-watt smile usually reserved for crowds.

"Oh, bountiful universe." Her mother clapped her hands and closed her eyes, her lips making the barest movement before she opened them again.

"Mom?" *I've stepped in something. Dammit, the credit card bill for a week in the Bahamas isn't looking so bad.*

"You're in time for the fun." She grabbed her hand and led her into the dining room.

"I know that look and I don't—"

A soft whistle from the back of the crowd interrupted her and everyone scattered to the various rooms. Caught in the shuffle, Vicky tried to hide behind the door, but was shooed away by two others already there. Finding a spot by the dining room window, facing the front of the house, she pressed in next to her grams.

"Who are we surprising?" Vicky whispered to her hideout companion.

"Ingrid. It's a double bachelorette party for her and your mom."

"Ingrid and Mom? Why?" Ingrid had already been married almost half a century, and Vicky's parents, though recently engaged, had been together only a few decades less.

"Shush." Grams waved a hand at her as the doorbell rang. Asking again why there was a need for a bachelorette party would only lead to a complex answer she wouldn't understand and likely give her an even bigger headache. Maybe this was one of those times when ignorance really was bliss.

She'd go with that for a while.

Vicky had to give it to seventy-six-year-old Ingrid. She handled the surprise better and managed to stay upright.

The partygoers led the bachelorettes into the formal living room and Grams's appletinis were handed out instead of punch. Vicky wasn't sure who pressed one into her hand, but she was grateful.

Gulping one plastic martini glassful helped dull the ache starting to beat the wedding march on her temple.

After the third, she was tapping her foot along with it.

Whoever had decorated for the party had a flair for all things phallic. From penis shaped balloons to dancing penis crepe paper, everywhere she turned there was another one-eyed monster staring her in the face. Please, God, don't let the same person have designed the cake.

"Here, you need one of these as daughter of the bride.

Your hair looks great in an updo." Sandra, the sheriff's daughter, pinned her hair back with something. "You don't want to miss what's next." Her wink and waggling eyebrows should have concerned Vicky, but she took a sip of her drink instead of questioning her.

Vicky's motto of go with it was starting to work. She didn't ask any questions and her glass was steadily refilled. If the rest of her time in Home was this festive, she might just be able to relax and enjoy her mother's wedding and forget all about the last few months in DC.

2

"*S*top!"

The hoarse-voiced command and tap on the shoulder stopped Callan in his tracks. He hadn't heard anyone come up behind him over the construction noise currently filling the mayor's back yard. *Getting sloppy, O'Shea.*

An impatient Vicky stood behind him, squinting against the sun. Just the person he was hoping to avoid by checking on his crew so early.

"Ma'am?"

"Stop. Please stop." Both hands held up to shade her eyes, she squinted up at him. Some kind of bracelet hung on her wrist. He stifled a laugh when he recognized what was on it—tiny plastic penises. What a party it must have been.

Keeping his face angled her way, he whistled to the other men in the yard and all the construction noise stopped.

"Thank you." She had to be feeling the effects of her evening. By the looks of her, she'd rolled right out of whatever bed she'd stumbled to and out to scold him. Disheveled, disoriented and probably in a lot of hangover pain, she wasn't looking for friendly conversation. That was a plus for him.

"Can I help you with something? If not, I have a job to finish." He watched as her relief at the quiet was replaced with irritation. She straightened and looked like she was ready to give him hell. This wasn't how his first interaction with her as John was supposed to go. If she didn't ask, he wouldn't tell. He wasn't ready for a reunion. He'd assumed she'd be sleeping her night of fun off for the whole morning. He was only supposed to be there for a short time before heading back to the store.

"Ma'am?" He kept his voice low and quiet. She was a sight—long shapely legs and smooth skin peeking out between man-sized wool socks and a pair of thin boxers emblazoned with a washed-out college logo. They only covered an inch of her thighs. The silky blouse she'd been wearing the day before was buttoned wrong, causing a large gap over her midriff.

"I don't care what you think you have to do. Please. Stop. Hammering. Now." Fingers pressed to her temple, she squeezed her eyes closed. "And don't call me ma'am." That's one hell of a hangover she's fighting.

"You don't look well. You should probably sleep it off," he suggested, burying any amusement at her party souvenirs.

Straightening, she lifted her chin and took a step toward him. "Take your hammer and your men—"

His reaction time was too slow. One moment she slapped a hand over her mouth, and in the next she emptied the contents of her stomach onto the ground, splashing his work boots. Bent over, with her hands on her thighs she didn't move except for gulping in a few more quick breaths.

"Maybe you should sit down. I'll get your mom."

"Don't." She grabbed at his arm—letting go when he paused. She peeked up at him through the hair hanging in her face. Her gaze traveled from his slightly yakked-on boots to his face.

"Do I know you?"

"No."

She studied his face for a moment. "I met you yesterday. You disappeared down the alley."

A breeze blew a few strands of hair into her face, distracting her from the conversation and suddenly she was grabbing something attached to a fly away curl. This time he couldn't hold in his laugh. Being saved by a condom hair clip was too much.

"Queenie, my poor dear. What are you doing out here dressed like that?" Her grandmother tsked and stepped between her and Callan. "Come on in and have some of my special breakfast tea. It'll clear up that stomach trouble of yours in no time."

"Don't lay it on too thick, Grams. No one buys the sweet old lady act, and you know it." He silently agreed. The elder Mrs. Jones had as much steel in her spine as any of the Jones women as far as Callan had seen.

"Now, now, dear, no need to be cranky in the morning. My special recipe will have you right as rain." She patted Vicky's arm before grabbing it in a not-so-little-old-lady grip for their walk toward the house. "You can go back to work now, John. We need St. Paul's completed by Friday so you can start on the palace next week," the older woman directed.

Callan watched them walk away. Vicky looked back over her shoulder, and he met her gaze for a moment. He shouldn't have been as amused as he was. He didn't want to embarrass her further. He could hear her grandmother giving her an earful as they walked to the door. That had been close. If she'd been one hundred percent, he'd not been prepared to convince her of his identity.

He should have gotten there earlier. He needed to haul more materials to the main staging area and finish the work there before moving on to the St. Paul's facade at the construction area the town had set aside for their work. He gave instructions to the crew to meet him when they finished and skirted the house and hopefully any more conversation and headed to his truck.

"Morning, John." Paul Evans, Vicky's father, called in greeting from the driveway. He must have stayed away from the night's festivities.

Callan waved a hello but only paused when he called his name again and walked toward him, holding something in his hands.

Another ancient machine part, he suspected. Callan knew construction, but mechanics was a whole different skill. *John's* skill. Not Callan's. No matter how many times he claimed ignorance, Mr. Evans insisted on asking for his input on whatever new part he'd scavenged for his collection.

"I think I've found something really special here, John. What do you think?" He held up the rusted hunk of metal.

"Possibly." He pretended to analyze the object.

The older man nodded and watched him over lowered glasses. What was he contemplating?

"It's funny how life tends to give us second chances. Maybe this is the time for yours?"

"Sir?"

"With Queenie. It's not easy losing your best friend at such a tender age. She cried for weeks after you left." He eyed Callan, "Never did understand why you didn't call or write. She took it pretty hard."

The weight of Paul's accusation hung between them.

"I guess I was just a dumb kid and thought I'd be better off forgetting than being reminded of what I was missing."

Callan hoped he didn't sound as rehearsed as he felt. He'd stated the truth as John had relayed it to him, but convincing someone the sentiment was genuine wasn't as easy as it had sounded at first.

"But you're back. And she's here now. You might be able to start up where you left off. A second chance at friendship."

"Uh, yeah." Callan's stammered, unsure what that meant exactly.

"Come by later if you want to see this baby cleaned up." Mr. Evans grabbed his new toy from Callan's hand and sauntered off toward the backyard and his garage-turned-man cave.

He watched the man leave a moment before turning to his Jeep. The new situation needed some thought. An investigative reporter, especially one specializing in Washington politics could be the absolute worst person for him to be around. Avoiding her would be his best strategy. How did one avoid someone in such a damn small town?

His reaction to her surprised him.

He didn't like surprises.

Surprises caused complications, which spelled trouble.

Callan had all the trouble he could handle.

* * *

Vicky sat at the French country farmhouse table taking up the middle of the breakfast nook off her mother's kitchen. Grams's special tea steamed in a blue ceramic mug. "You don't expect me to drink this do you?" Whatever was in it made her eyes water.

"No more sass out of you, missy. Drink up. It will calm your stomach and maybe take some of the sour lemon out of your mouth." Her grandmother's voice wasn't far off from the sweet old lady she acted but was full of bite when needed.

"I learned from the best," Vicky retorted. Her grandmother chuckled as she filled another mug and set it at the seat next to her.

"So, what's this John doing here?" Vicky tried for nonchalance as her heart hammered in her chest. Please say he's leaving next week. How could he look even sexier in sunglasses and a bandana? And how could she have made a fool of herself in front of the same man twice in less than twenty-four hours? She could only blame the appletinis for so much. This was what coming home did to her. Bad luck all around.

"He's building the wedding sets. Now drink."

"What's a wedding set?"

"It's the structure to set the theme for the wedding." Her

grandmother answered. "The old pavilion on the edge of the park has been turned into the main wedding chapel and facades are being built to turn it into a replica of St. Paul's cathedral. John and the others are hard at work on multiple facades and moveable pre-fab's for stages and sets for other themes. Your mother has been developing plans for all kinds of fantasy sets. Now finish your drink so we can get the day started."

Seriously? She wasn't ready to roll with her grandmother's enthusiasm for what sounded like an immense amount of work for no guarantees.

She eyed the mug suspiciously before taking a quick sniff. Blech. The smell of cinnamon was overpowered by ginger and anise with a little too much onion mixed in.

"Victoria Alexandra Mary Elizabeth Jones!" Vicky grimaced as her mother's voice preceding her through the swinging door to the dining room. "How could you carry on like that? In our yard, no less? Poor John, you'll have to apologize and have his boots cleaned."

Jesus, had the woman watched out the window?

"Me? Carrying on? You were the one with a stripper in your house last night, Mother dear. And what the hell was in those appletinis?" Involuntary defensiveness came pouring out, even though she'd told herself to go with it.

"Profanity isn't pretty, Queenie." She huffed and sat next to her and took a sip from the mug in front of her as if it were high tea. "It was a bachelorette party after all. The stripper was your grandmother's idea."

Vicky rolled her eyes and grimaced. Even her eyeballs hurt. Of course, she'd have to apologize and have John's boots cleaned. She knew that, so why couldn't she bite her tongue and agree? Any questions about John would have to wait. Her mother would immediately start matchmaking at the slightest hint of interest.

"How can you drink this stuff?" Vicky avoided any more mention of the man outside, the appletinis, and the under-toned, over-aged stripper that had finally arrived. Her mother's smile turned wistful.

"It reminds me of when I was pregnant with you. I was nauseous for nine months straight, and your grandmother made this for me to settle my stomach."

Gross. Vicky sniffed the steam and pushed the cup further away.

"You've been giving me heartburn for almost thirty years, the least you can do now is help me out with my wedding plans while you're here."

"I still don't see how this huge wedding deal is going to work." Her previous complaints about Blake Corporation trying to buy up land around the town hadn't included discussions about making Home a premiere wedding desti-nation. "I mean, I'm thrilled you and dad are finally going to tie the knot, but a business? And the whole town is in on it?" Was the business the reason her former hippie parents decided to get married?

"You don't have to see, you have to help. I couldn't have asked for better timing. I don't know why I didn't think of it before. Since you were going to come home for our wedding anyway, these extra few weeks will be perfect for another job I have for you. You're needed here in so many ways."

"So glad my ruined career is helpful to you." Doing a little digging on Blake to give her mom peace of mind wasn't that big of a deal. A couple days' worth of work, max. She'd have plenty of time to work on her own story-writing for her editor.

"Ruined, shmooined. You need to take a step back is all and try something different. I have the perfect solution."

Damn, the woman worked fast. *Please don't let it be another blind date with the hopes of grandchildren.*

"Mom, I'm not really—"

"We need someone to write a blog chronicling the wedding plans."

"Highlighting all the businesses in town and their expertise," Grams added from her seat at the other end of the table.

"Blog? On town expertise? For your wedding?" This was why she almost never drank. Clearly, her mind was too slow to keep up with an excited and wide-awake Mayor Judy Jones and her plans.

"Yes. Mine and all the other weddings we can do. You know, drumming up buzz and excitement so people from around the world will want to experience Real Romance at Home. This is exactly why fate put you here. Myra's place at the paper is waiting for you. It's the perfect cover for investigating Blake and gives you a job at the same time."

She laughed and clapped her hands together in front of her as if she'd explained the meaning of life.

"Mom. Stop with the fate stuff. I'm only here until you and dad get married, and Myra broke her hip, it's hardly fair to thank fate for those circumstances. Do you expect me to drop the slogan into every conversation?"

"It's our new brand, Queenie. Everyone in town is using it. It will put Home on the map. Your job at the paper will be an integral part of the plan. We need the marketing, and

I need you to give Blake Corporation the Standridge treatment. Someone needs to really dig in and find all their secrets. They're no good, Queenie. They have skeletons, I know it. And you need to expose them."

"First, the Standridge treatment landed me in a lawsuit and isn't going to happen again, and second, how do you know they're no good? And third, you want me to write for the paper too?" Blog, newspaper, and investigate Blake? A little much for a few weeks off. A few weeks if her boss agreed to give her another chance. If not? She didn't want to think about if not.

"Haven't you been listening? Your blog is going to be published in the *Home Daily*. Your position there will keep others from becoming suspicious. I know they're no good because of what they're trying to do to this town, and that's a fact."

"You do know what a blog is, right?" She asked, ignoring the emphatic accusation of the company's ill-intent.

"Don't get snarky, Queenie. You still owe me for nine months of vomiting. Anyway, we've got internet all over town, but our service isn't as clear and fast as it should be, so the paper will publish the same articles from the website."

"So all the signs around town offering free Wi-Fi are what . . . Wishful thinking? And suspicion from whom?"

"Nonsense, we do offer Wi-Fi at most of the establishments, and it's free to customers. It just gets bogged down when a lot of people use it at once, but faster coverage is coming to our little part of the state soon. As far as suspicion, you never know who Blake might have hired as a spy. Their representatives know way too much about us. Someone is telling them our business."

The dual conversation and paranoia were making Vicky's headache worse, and no amount of temple massage would help.

"I don't know what to say." Vicky sat at the table, the two women staring back at her with almost identical features, gave her images of herself in thirty and fifty years. Their similarities didn't stop at looks—these two had nerves of steel and could bulldoze their way over any obstacle. Just like she could. Or thought she could. Vicky had faced a heavyweight CEO with powerful friends, junkies selling information on prostitution and drug dealing to the junior staff members of congress, and even her editor on the day he had to fast for a colonoscopy. All of that done without being intimidated into stopping her planned story. Yet, she'd been ramrodded by these two women into double duty, launch Home's marketing plan and play investigator on the down low.

She needed to regain some of that Jones women confidence.

The stubbornness, though—she really needed less of that.

Then she'd be able to let go of whatever feelings of responsibility she might have about helping her hometown with its crazy plans—consequences be damned. Or, better still, she'd be able to give up on a job that might not want her.

Yes, less stubbornness would be nice.

"Now that that's settled, there's more." She patted her hand and her smile widened. "I've already booked our first client and the town has been working to put together their wish list."

"Besides you and Ingrid?" Or was Ingrid not really having a themed wedding? She'd have to go back to the beginning and have this conversation again when everyone was wide-awake and not so confusing.

"They're celebrities." She rushed on, voice pitched high with excitement, "They want to remain anonymous until the wedding day. No one knows their real identities except me, and I'm counting on you to advertise everything we're doing without really advertising the actual wedding. If you know what I mean."

"Wow . . ." Celebrities? In Home? She bit her tongue to keep the conversation snark-free. She didn't want to hurt anyone's feelings.

Her mother stood and wrapped Vicky in a quick hug. "All right, now, hurry up, we have to get this day going or we'll be behind schedule again."

"Whoa, hold up. How in the world did you manage to book a celebrity couple to come to Home of all places for their wedding? Who are these celebrities and why do they want to remain anonymous?"

"If I told you who they were, they wouldn't be anonymous. We made contact through a friend of a friend on vacation in Telluride and next thing I know, they're booked for the end of next month. Which is just enough time for us to get everything built and my wedding out of the way as a practice session for everyone involved. The plan is starting to work. We just have to keep it going and give it time."

"How do you know they're serious?" Vicky asked, not wanting to dampen the enthusiasm but concerned about the pace of what she was being told.

"I communicate with them over the phone and through

email. They want an out of the way place so the paparazzi can't get to them and like the energy of Home. The expanded royal themed sets we're building are for them. They appreciate Home's uniqueness and the personal touches the town offers. Trendsetters, I'd say. Not to mention our ticket to making Romance at Home a success. Now scoot."

And that was that. From the firm set of her shoulders and flat line of her mouth, Vicky knew no amount of questioning would get results.

"I'll go with it for now. But I want full-disclosure if you really want me to back you up. This isn't another nudist resort or llama farm you're building." Entertaining, but relatively harmless investments when they went belly-up. This new plan held the future of the entire town. Her mother really believed the risk was worth the envisioned reward. Vicky tried another tactic.

"If Blake really is doing something underhanded and wants the land as badly as you say, they aren't going to go away. You'll have to deal with them head-on. One wedding won't be enough."

"Don't worry. They aren't going to get away with bullying us into leaving so they can build over everything this town has worked for. Now that I have you here to help, everything will be fine." She leaned down and kissed her cheek. "As soon as they give me permission, I'll share their names."

"Promise?" Vicky wanted to hear it. Her own plan hadn't included being pulled into something that might blow up in their faces. Staying in Home meant there'd be no avoiding it or her mother's expectations.

"I promise." Her answer was sincere. "Do you?"

"Yes."

"Good. Then, when you're ready, I want to know what the hell happened in DC."

"What do you mean?" That weak response wasn't going to get her anywhere. She braced for the onslaught of questions.

"You know exactly what I mean. Last time we talked, you had a job and were living with what's his name. Someone you haven't mentioned once since you got home. I'm your mother. You can't keep it from me forever."

Vicky opened her mouth, an excuse ready to go, but a raised hand hushed her. "I don't want to hear anything but the truth. When you're ready to tell me everything, I'll be here. Whatever problems you're running from, you're better off being here, and I'm grateful. End of discussion."

Being there wasn't going to make everything better. If everything they suspected was true, Vicky had no power to stop it. Discovering the truth and being able to do something about it were two different things.

She rested her head on her crossed arms. Please let this be okay.

3

*B*y midmorning, showered and dressed, Vicky felt almost human again. She slid into the backseat of her mother's SUV. "You're going to be amazed at how much has been done in just a few months' time," she assured Vicky before switching to discussing hairstyle choices they planned on testing for the upcoming wedding photos. Thankfully, a subject that didn't require her input.

Through the window, Home's landscape changed from her parents' house on the edge of town to Main Street and the downtown business area. Calling the area downtown was a stretch, at best. They still had the longtime anchors that kept the residents fed, boozed, styled, and well-read if they desired, but nothing more than the necessities. No Starbucks or hip new eatery to revitalize a dying area.

The ambitious scheme to get it recognized by the state tourist board as a hot new destination was beyond anything they'd tried before. But the amount of people moving in were too few to make up for the number who'd left over the last few decades. They needed jobs and they needed a reason to stay. Vicky hoped it worked, for her mom to have invested so much into the idea and the town to follow, it was a significant risk, but she still didn't see how it would ever become a major theme-wedding destination. And to start with a royal themed wedding? The town council had big dreams.

She'd had big dreams once too. Now she'd settle for getting back the life she'd had at the *Chronicle*. She'd been doing well there. Her work was hers alone as Vicky Alexander—not Queenie Jones, the mayor's daughter. She turned her thoughts back to the town. Old insecurities wouldn't help her here and now.

Her mom parked as soon as they came to the small row of brick buildings making up the shopping and dining area. Adjacent to the newly expanded six-acre city park, the whole square would be turned into the main wedding staging area. She got out of the car and looked around.

"What's that little building over there?" Vicky pointed to what looked like a guard shack or small kiosk kind of building at the corner of the park facing Main Street.

"That's the welcome center." Her mom answered as if that made perfect sense.

Off in the distance she could see a fence that blocked where the old pavilion sat along with Home's first town meeting hall. What started as just an old cabin had been turned in to the unofficial meeting place for the town's founders before the official one was built. In her lifetime, it had been everything from a summer camp staging area to scout meeting room. Now they were turning it in to something for the wedding business. If the pavilion was being upgraded to a chapel, the other building could be anything.

"We'll walk. You need to see how things have changed."
She caught Vicky's gaze. "You couldn't have seen much last
night."

"Just the welcome signs. Oh, and the free WI-FI signs.
You really need to work on those."

"Yes, yes. It's all in the works. Now, come on."

The three women strolled down the wooden boardwalk
that ran the length of the streets that made up the small
business area. Many of the old stores she'd grown up with
were still there, intermingled with a few new ones. Everything looked fresher. Maybe the scheme had brought some
life back to the dying town.

"How'd you get everyone to agree to spruce up their
storefronts? These boards," she stomped lightly on the
smooth treads with her heel, "are beautiful." The boardwalk
and new paint gave the area a whole new look, inviting and
cozy with an old-fashioned feel. Someone had been busy.

"Incentive, dear. It's all in knowing the right incentive.
Premier destination weddings equal guests with money,
which equal customers for every business owner here.
Simple."

It might sound simple, but no one seemed to be
concerned step one was a premier wedding. She'd yet to see
how that was going to happen. Vicky kept her opinion to
herself—she'd been promised a tour of the wedding sets and
a full explanation after their hair appointment was done that
morning. She'd reserve her many questions until then.

They passed the Book Nook, the used bookstore and
unofficial town library, and the Stitch and Sew, a fabric
store, and paused at the entrance to Jo's Diner.

"Wow. Jo fixed the door." When Jo's grandfather opened the diner fifty years ago, he'd commissioned an artist from Denver to create a set of double doors inlaid with stained glass. The bright blues and tans of the western landscape design had glowed in the sunlight. As a little girl, Vicky thought it was the most beautiful door in the world, magical and sparkly when the sun hit it. One side had cracked during her senior year in high school. Jo's father hadn't bothered to have it fixed and the reflection had never been the same.

Vicky stopped to inspect the improvements. "It's exactly how I remember it."

"Everyone's been working hard. As I said, we're all in this together."

Vicky ignored the gloating. Someone had worked hard. She couldn't see where the crack had been.

"I swear I smell Mexican food." Cumin and chile scented the air as she opened the door to peek inside. The diner looked much the same as it always had—serviceable tables surrounded by a wall of booths covered in brown vinyl and a long counter lined with stools along the back leading to the kitchen.

It was a little early for lunch, but there were a few customers seated already.

"Oh, yes, Jo is working on a whole new menu—Mexican, Italian, French, vegetarian, and gluten free options." She ticked the list off on her fingers as she counted. She stopped and looked at Grams. "What was the other one?"

"Greek," Grams answered.

"Oh, yes, Greek. Tourists want variety." She tugged on her sweater. "Now come on, we don't want to be late."

"You can't serve the same things every night and give them a new name, you know."

"Daily cuisine specials is a brilliant idea Jo came up with on her own." She waved off her teasing, wiggling a perfectly manicured hand in her direction. "A weekly rotating menu so there's variety for everyone. I don't know if it's the thought of new customers or competition with the new part-time chef in her kitchen, but you wait and see. You won't believe how good her new menu is."

They reached Split Ends beauty shop. It literally was the split end, as Main dead-ended at a T-intersection with First Street.

"I can't believe this." Her mom huffed and opened the door, clanging bells with the force of a hurricane.

What? Vicky scanned the storefront, trying to find what had set her off. Painted a blindingly sunny yellow and with a big decorated sign, it matched the other shops in that it was all spruced up, newly painted, and bold. Nothing seemed out of place.

Then she saw it. The bride to be pulled down the small window sign warning No Penises Allowed. Vicky burst out laughing.

The bells jingled only slightly less violently when Vicky opened the door. Someone needed to tell Erline to lose a few of those or her customers would leave with a new hairdo and a migraine.

"What's the matter, Mom? I didn't see you complaining about all the penises at your bachelorette party," she said with a grin.

"This is business, Queenie. Not a bachelorette party." She shoved the sign into a trash bin at the checkout desk.

"Queenie?" The high-pitched squeal streaked from the back of the salon. No one materialized from behind the flowing batik curtain, but the voice was unmistakable.

"Rochelle?" As Vicky said the name, her once best frenemy from high school peeked out from her hiding place. She had plastic gloves on her hands and held them up, in a sign of apology.

"I'm getting set up, be out in a sec."

Her mom and Grams sat in stylist's chairs, and motioned for her to sit in the third. Two more seats were at a washing station. Overall, it was a much nicer salon than had ever been there before.

"Rochelle's running the place now. Erline sold it to her before she retired to Las Vegas."

"Really?" Vicky eyed the space but declined the seat. Whoever had renovated it had made the best of the small square footage. Natural light flooded in from the large front windows and the reconfigured waiting area allowed room for more chairs. The color scheme was bold—not a restful spa experience—but energizing in a unique way.

The bright interior matched the exterior. Thankfully, the yellow paint didn't carry to the inside, but the soft cream walls were the only subdued color in the entire place. Every accessory, from the chairs to the hairdryers was a different coordinating color. Once her eyes adjusted, the patterned tapestry hanging on the wall and the upholstery on the waiting area chairs brought the decor together into a semblance of order.

Rochelle finally emerged from the back, pushing a roller cart with her little bowls of goop on top and baskets full of tools on the bottom shelf.

Before Vicky could say hi, Rochelle wrapped her into a surprisingly fierce hug. "I'm so glad you're home," she said, a smile in her words. Vicky returned the hug, surprised at her affection.

"Thanks." Vicky turned a half circle and motioned toward the waiting area. "I love what you've done with the place. It's almost unrecognizable."

"I know! Isn't it great?" Rochelle's enthusiasm bubbled with every syllable, and Vicky couldn't help smiling in return.

Rochelle hadn't changed much since high school. Her height no longer stood out. Her long red hair was tamed and made more exotic looking with a series of highlights giving the country girl a city edge.

"Oh my goodness, Queenie, have I got the perfect color for some highlights for you." Rochelle picked up a handful of Vicky's hair and let it fall lightly through her fingers, inspecting the ends and tsking lightly. "And a conditioner treatment you'll love."

"I'm not really—"

"I only need a sec to set up, I can fit you in with your mom and grandma since they're only here for a wash and style." Rochelle rushed to the back, cutting off Vicky's protest.

"When was the last time you had your hair done anyway?" her mom asked.

"It's not that bad," she said, but looking at herself in the mirror, she couldn't deny she needed some work. Her wavy hair had gotten a little out of hand, and she'd missed her last two trim appointments because of deadlines. Leaning closer, she grimaced.

Rochelle rolled another cart toward an empty chair. "I've been working on this new technique for darker and lighter highlights—your coloring is perfect for it. It'll freshen up what you've let grow out."

A little pampering would be nice—but this was Rochelle offering. Still, they were grownups now and not high school rivals. Clearly, Rochelle knew what she was doing. Her mother and Grams trusted her. She was already mixing different tubes of goop in a bowl and the older women glared at her as if she were about to embarrass them.

"Okay." She managed a small smile and slid into the empty chair. *Just go with it*, she reminded herself.

"You won't be sorry. I promise." Rochelle immediately pulled a smock around her shoulders, a towel around her neck, and started painting sections of Vicky's hair and placing foil between small sections. "Not like the time I switched your shampoo for red stain before homecoming." Her throaty laugh echoed through the space, soon joined by Mom and Grams chuckling.

Vicky stiffened, but Rochelle patted her shoulder with one gloved hand. "Don't worry, once was plenty."

Having her blonde hair stained red at homecoming was bad enough, having it stained red when their team's colors were blue and gold, and the rivals' were red and white was worse. Vicky'd canceled her plans and her date ended up taking Rochelle to the dance. Eventually Erline was able to wash most of the red out and color over it. The next day, everyone expected her to easily forgive and forget—she was the mayor's daughter, and any retaliation would look like the mayor's kid getting away with being a brat and not taking a joke. She'd had to accept Rochelle's apology and move on, but the sting of the prank had lasted much longer. She shifted in her seat at the uncomfortable memory.

"Did you know Jimmy Norton's in jail for trying to sell fake uranium finds?" Rochelle asked, not changing the subject completely.

"Figures." He'd been a creep in high school for not even asking if she was okay when she canceled their date and, apparently, still was.

"You're lucky you didn't have to put up with his octopus hands all night at the dance too."

Yeah. Lucky me. Flashbacks of hiding in her room instead of celebrating with her classmates and the town made it hard to sit still while Rochelle covered her head in cold goo.

"How many from high school stayed here, anyway? Didn't everyone who could afford to leave do so?" Silence followed Vicky's question. She peeked at her mom through the foil hanging over her forehead. Her narrow-eyed glare pierced from ten feet away.

Vicky met her gaze with a silent, "what?"

"Not too many." Rochelle's answer was quiet, and so was she for a beat before launching into a detailed history of every one of their thirty high school classmates who'd stayed around. Where they'd been, currently were, and who'd hooked up with whom.

Another thing hadn't changed about Rochelle—once she started talking, she didn't stop. She could keep a conversation alive for hours without much more than a yeah or uh-huh.

"So how long have you had Split Ends?" Vicky managed

to sneak the question in while Rochelle worked on all three women's hair in turns.

"Oh, Mamma sold it to me six months ago. It was a mess. The salon I'd been working at in Denver closed and when Mamma decided to retire and wanted to sell the place, I knew it was what I needed to do."

Vicky listened to her explanation but before she could ask more questions, Rochelle bounced to another sore subject.

"Now, your mamma and the rest of the town are going to bring in all the customers I can handle. Isn't that right? It's great of you to come back to help after the big mess in Washington. We heard you might get arrested."

"I'm not going to get arrested—"

"And for what it's worth, that jerk of a boyfriend wasn't good enough for you anyway."

"You get DC gossip all the way out here, huh?"

"Well, it's not every day one of our own gets her couple status discussed in a gossip rag. You caused quite a stir in conversation at Jo's. There's even a bet going around—"

"She starts at the paper tomorrow," her mom interrupted. "Wait until you see her blog. You'll be her first story."

Her first story? That should be fun. Did she want to know what the bet was about? Probably if she'd get arrested or fired or called into congress for testimony. Or maybe just if she'd come crawling back to her little hometown with her tail between her legs, sorry she'd ever left in the first place. She absolutely despised being the center of gossip. It was one of the reasons she'd shied away from Jeremy. Her ex's microcelebrity status as a former most eligible bachelor of DC made her fodder for low-rent news, and that had made her real job harder. She was supposed to report news, not become it herself. She'd failed on that end too.

"Show her the new spa treatments you're offering," Grams requested, bringing her attention back to the present.

"Oh! You're going to love these," Rochelle squealed, and Vicky's stomach sank.

"Uh. Are you making something yourself?" Vicky's willingness to experiment only went so far.

"Oh, gosh, no. Don't have to. Remember Mr. Garcia from tenth grade Science? He and his wife retired and started growing lavender and a bunch of other herbs and they make some great products like all-natural soaps, aromatherapy sachets, and for me, a line of facial scrubs and masks." She held up a jar with a label that read Dom and Doll's Herbal Delights. "Your mamma is going to help them get an internet business going. Let me try the lavender and oats on you while you wait." Rochelle rushed to the back and returned with a bowl of nice smelling paste.

"I'm not sure." Vicky eyed the mess. "Have you tried it?"

"Uh-huh. It's great. Isn't it, Ms. Jones? Now lay your head back." A cool spoonful hit Vicky's cheek. Rochelle held a finger to her forehead, keeping her from moving while she spread it around and plopped another spoonful on her forehead. "It will soothe some of the redness and it should revive some of that old looking skin you're carrying around."

What? Old looking? She was only three months older than Rochelle. She bit back a snide remark. After all, it did smell nice and dried pretty quickly. Maybe she'd get out of there without any mishaps.

The clanging of the bells at the door officially cut off

Vicky's defensive response. Rochelle dropped her gloves on the cart and rushed away. Swiveling slightly in the chair and peeking under the foil folds hanging over her eyes, Vicky cringed.

Really? Here?

John stood inside the shop, talking to Rochelle. He smiled down at her and she leaned close.

Looking away, Vicky caught her mother and Grams watching her watching John and Rochelle. Rochelle was beautiful and there weren't many eligible men in Home. And why did she care if they were a couple anyway? She straightened and turned back to the magazine she'd been strangling in her lap as if the super-hot guy she'd embarrassed herself in front of wasn't in the room, until a squeal from Rochelle brought her attention back to the couple.

"You are the best, John. I owe you." She smiled up at him and her adoration made Vicky briefly lower her gaze as jealousy tinged her thoughts. "Don't wait too long to come collect." Rochelle winked at him and sashayed back to her station with a little more swing in her steps.

"You ladies have a good day." He said, his gaze meeting hers for a moment before breaking away.

A chorus of "you too" followed the jingling of the bells on the door. All eyes were on John as he walked out.

Raising a hand to her cheek, Vicky felt the mask now in a thick layer on her skin.

You have got to be kidding me. *Why, universe? Why me?*

Vicky's mother cleared her throat. "You really need to apologize for barfing on his boots. It's the least you could do."

Vicky shrugged at her directive and Rochelle's gasp. Could nothing be kept within the family?

"I tried, but he was too busy." She squirmed in her seat at the lie. She'd seen him standing by his truck and could easily have spoken to him after she'd gotten her stomach under control.

"Did you really puke on his boots?" Rochelle swallowed a laugh with a snort as she pulled a piece of foil out of Vicky's hair and checked the color.

"Mom's party hit me a little too hard, and he was making too much damn noise in the backyard. And it wasn't on his boots." The details didn't need to be spread around town any more than they already would be. His entire crew had witnessed it—Rochelle would hear a firsthand account from someone else. Vicky didn't need to talk about it herself. She changed the subject. "I thought there was a no penises allowed rule in here."

"The penis rule only applies to the actual cutting of hair. He can bring his in anytime." Rochelle's laugh was infectious, even over her mother's protests about propriety and class.

This coming from the woman who'd handmade penis bracelets and condom hair clips.

"I'm telling you, this color is going to work great for your complexion." Rochelle patted Vicky's shoulder before leading her to a wash station.

Please let her know what she's doing.

"Maybe I'll buy him a new pair of boots for his birthday." Rochelle went on as if her switch in subjects was perfectly natural.

The idea of being attracted to Rochelle's man irritated

her. It was the kind of situation that zoomed her back to high school. Damn hormones. As much as her breakup with Jeremy was good for an embarrassing tweet or two, the signs that they were headed for a split had been there for a while. They'd both been comfortable ignoring them and he'd been comfortable finding a woman on the side instead of just ending things with her cleanly. She'd been the fool and their little social world knew it. She'd blame her recent lack of any intimacy for her unusually strong attraction to a man she hadn't even officially met. Yes, a little desperation and a lot of crazy from her mom was as good an excuse as anything.

He was a stranger.

An incredibly attractive stranger. Close to her age. If he'd been nicer and unattached, he might have been someone she could see helping her pass the time in Home, but she'd also made a complete fool of herself in front of him. Twice. Not exactly the best way to start something, even if the guy did make her nerves tingle being in the same room. A new sensation for her—and one that was entirely too distracting.

"It's at the end of the month, right?" her mother asked.

What were they talking about? His birthday? He must be close to her mom for her to be aware of his birthday coming up.

"Uh-huh. I'm throwing him a little surprise party at The Walrus." Rochelle tapped her shoulder. "You should come and bring a date. Everyone will be there. I want it to be a huge blowout." Rochelle clapped her hands together. "Oh, I can make it a birthday and welcome home Queenie Jones party. Oh my gosh, it's going to be the biggest thing since Bobby Jo Henley married Ricky Martinez and ended their families' feud."

"Could you not call me Queenie—" Vicky started, but Rochelle turned on a drier, drowning out her request.

She thought about what Rochelle had said. Date? Vicky had seen no evidence there was a pool of eligible men to have a date with. Rochelle had never had a problem finding a date, even bringing a boy from out of town to their junior prom. Vicky always had.

No one wanted to date the mayor's daughter. Oh, pity-party of one. Why did she have to relive those kinds of memories? Growing up in Home hadn't been all bad, just not how she wanted to live as an adult. DC was more her style now. After cleaning the mask from her face and styling her hair with her back to the mirror, Vicky was anxious to see what she'd let Rochelle do to her. "Okay, here you go. I just love it. Don't you?" Rochelle turned her toward the mirror. Vicky held her breath as her reflection came into view.

She leaned closer and ran her hands through her locks. "I love it." She examined the color in the mirror, surprised and pleased at just how good it looked.

Rochelle patted her shoulder with a nod. "Told you."

With her hair blown out and smooth, the highlights really were amazing. Whatever Rochelle had learned in Denver worked. Vicky couldn't stop touching her hair. It was soft, smooth, and looked the best it had in months.

"How long has John been in town? Doesn't seem the Home type."

She clamped her mouth shut around the question. Why had that been the first thing to pop out of her mouth after some oohs, and ahs over her hair?

Rochelle laughed and shook her head. "Finally got lucky

with some fresh blood in Home. He's John Pearce, back now and running the hardware store. Old Jed died and left him the house and everything. Did you know him when y'all were little? I didn't even know Old Jed had a family."

What? Vicky scanned the blank expressions of the almost never silent women in the other chairs—nothing at that drop of news? *That* John. She spun around to face her mother. "You couldn't have said something earlier, Mom?"

"I assumed you wouldn't remember him. And anyway, you weren't exactly at your best last night. Or this morning."

"I'd never forget JP. It's just . . . he looks different than I would expect all grown-up."

John Pearce had been her best friend until fourth grade, always hanging around her house, shadowing her dad in the basement or her mom in the kitchen. His parents had divorced at Christmas of that year and he and his mother moved away two weeks later.

She'd cried for weeks, begging her mom to adopt him so he wouldn't have to move away. He'd been her only real friend, the brother she'd never had, and the best friend she'd never had since. Her closest friends knew her and her grown-up dreams and fears, but it wasn't the same as growing up together and knowing what each other had been like as kids.

Why would he say no when she asked if she knew him? Maybe he didn't remember her? But John had been a part of almost every happy memory she had of her elementary school years. He couldn't have forgotten that.

Hurt at the idea, Vicky slumped in her chair. Maybe he was messing with her and waiting to call her out on not recognizing him either time?

So, he'd returned, all grown-up and apparently attached to Rochelle. Well, fantastic. Here she was, back home with her mom and dad, no love life to speak of and no exciting job to brag about. She really needed to get back to DC. At least there she could be anonymously single and unhappy instead of feeling like everyone around was discussing her life in humiliating detail. She needed a change in subject.

"Is that your son?" Vicky asked, pointing to a picture of Rochelle and a small boy about three years old. Her mom had mentioned Rochelle having a baby but hadn't told her about them moving back to Home.

"Yeah, Jason." Her voice softened. "He's with his dad for now. Until I get this place up and running and fix up my house."

"He's adorable."

"He's a real character. He's going to love it here. My lawyer says I have a good chance of gaining full custody with my business doing well, and a supportive, healthy environment. I've been fighting the bastard since he left and took Jason with him, along with all our money, while I was here taking care of my mom.

"I'm sorry, Rochelle." She couldn't imagine living apart from her child. The wild-child Vicky had known had grown into a mom ready to settle down in the hometown they'd both claimed to never want to live in again. She and Rochelle had planned to be city-girls and have a life bigger than anything Home had to offer.

"Now, Mom's in remission and living close to her sister in Nevada, and I have the business and a nice little house I'm renting until I can buy. John helped me fix Jason's room up like a dream. He built a train track that runs along the wall and a fort bed. Looks like it belongs in a magazine. Jason's going to flip when he sees it. I just have to spend every last dime I've saved on a lawyer to file for divorce and custody. The new wedding plans for Home are going to help me do that."

One more life affected if her mom's plans didn't work out. Rochelle needed the business and her home for her son. What would she do if those plans didn't materialize? Did she even have a plan B? Was everyone relying on the weddings to such a crucial extent?

"Has Blake tried to buy this place?" Vicky asked Rochelle when her mom went into the back to use the restroom.

"Vicky, now's not a good time to talk about that mess. We're here to have a fun couple of hours," her gram admonished.

"They want this whole block," Rochelle answered in a rush. "We have to stick together. If they get the whole of downtown and all the outside land they want, Home is gone. Without us, the park, and the Carlisle land beyond, what would Home have?"

The worry in Rochelle's voice was real. Vicky bit her lip and regretted bringing up the subject. With a look from her grandmother, she dropped any further questions.

Her mother's cell phone rang as they were checking out. Busy smelling every new concoction Rochelle handed her to look at, she only caught a few words of the one-sided conversation.

"You tell that sheriff he better keep his ass onsite until I get there. I'm on my way."

"Come on, Queenie. You need to see what kind of mess Blake's making in this town.

* * *

Callan waited as the sheriff assessed the damage. The set of St. Paul's Cathedral that surrounded the pavilion-turned-chapel had almost been complete. What a waste. From sharpie art to real destruction was a big escalation. The teens will be teens narrative didn't fit this. The fence blocking the view of the construction also hid the damage until his guys had shown up to start the day's work. He kicked at a board, one of many that had been ripped from the wall and strewn about the lawn around the replica. The vandals had been more aggressive this time, setting them back a solid two week's worth of work before his crew could get to the finishing touches. They still had three more facades and a carriage to complete.

"I've got what I need, John." The sheriff stopped next to him and jotted a few more notes before pushing his notepad into his front shirt pocket. "Whoever did this didn't leave much evidence. Sure you didn't see anyone on your morning walk?"

"Wish I had. Didn't make it out here this morning."

"That'd be a first, I imagine." The sheriff shot a glance at him and paused as if weighing and then dismissing the idea that maybe he had something to do with the damage.

"Yeah, maybe." He couldn't blame the guy for thinking it. No one liked coincidences. If the sheriff knew about his routine, then others could too. A good reminder to vary his route.

The nightmares had been bad enough he'd wished he'd kept the sleeping pill prescription his doc had insisted on giving him. It had been several months since he'd had a night that bad. Instead, he'd spent the wee hours of the morning beating the hell out of his punching bag and the imaginary monsters destroying his ability to sleep. He'd passed out on his couch for a few hours and had barely made it in to open the store on time and get out to the work site at the Jones's early. And he'd still run in to Vicky.

If the sheriff, who didn't even live in town, knew his habits then it wasn't a stretch to think whoever had done the damage did as well. Either they got lucky, or it was someone close enough to be watching for him, just in case. Neither possibility was good.

"What are you going to do about all this, Sheriff?"

The sheriff flinched and mumbled a curse under his breath as the mayor charged toward them. "I'm gonna skin whoever called her," he muttered.

Callan held up his hands. "Wasn't me." He nodded over the sheriff's shoulder to the approaching women.

"Watch where you step, there might be some loose boards with nails in them," the sheriff called to the them as they neared.

Damn. Callan had been hoping to avoid her a little longer. After seeing her at Rochelle's, he'd planned to stay out of her way. A brief phone call to John the night before hadn't given him any new details he should know about Vicky. John had been too drugged up from his last surgery to be much help beyond hopeful she stuck around long enough to see him when he returned. He'd reminded Callan to be careful because she'd been smart and nosy as a kid and probably still was.

Callan's internet search had given him plenty as far as what she'd been recently up to. None of it made him want to sit and have a long chat. He'd read most of her articles and the gossip about her he could find. From that, he'd pegged her as an intelligent, insightful, and politically savvy journalist with bad taste in boyfriends. Not someone he wished to match lies with.

"Did anyone see who did this?" Mayor Jones demanded, stepping between the sheriff and Callan. Her face was flushed, and her mouth was set in a tight frown.

"No one's come forward."

That was his cue to get out of the way.

"I need to check on my crew. They've started the cleanup," Callan assured her. Avoiding Vicky's gaze, he ducked behind the building and began a checklist of work that needed to begin immediately. Their conversation carried over the sounds of his crew picking up the debris.

"Why wasn't I called right away?" Ms. Jones used her full-command voice that could carry over a crowd at the high school gymnasium or a contentious board meeting—signaling loud and clear she would not be calm about whatever was going on.

"We needed to conclude our review of the crime scene."

"This was Blake, Sheriff." Her accusation was met with a rumble of agreement from the other's hanging around. One he agreed with as well.

"You don't know that for sure, ma'am." Sheriff Collins's retort was to be expected. One month until retirement, his age had caught up with him. Stooped over and moving slowly, his frail stature and sun-ravaged skin made him look older than his years and less able to take care of business.

Callan made a mental note to contact Deputy Hayworth. Primed to take over as sheriff, Hayworth was someone Callan already had an understanding with regarding Blake. Everyone liked him and he was a shoo-in for the next election. Callan didn't care about elections. Hayworth understood the need for more security and what Blake might do if push came to shove. That was all that mattered.

They needed to get the cameras up and running as soon as they came in. He'd worked out a deal with several of the other business owners but didn't want to advertise it too much and scare off whoever was behind the vandalism. They needed to be caught in the act before their setbacks escalated.

From the roof of the chapel, he tracked Vicky and her mother's movements. Avoiding conversation was easier from up high, and he could assess the real damage without interruption.

The two of them were peppering the sheriff with questions—the man reminded him of a bobble-head, desperately nodding at whatever the two said. They finally broke away and the mayor headed back toward the parking area, but Vicky picked her way around the set. He ducked to stay out of her sight. What a coward move. He couldn't avoid her forever. Wouldn't avoid her. But he needed to talk to John first.

Judging by the way she drew the attention of his crew, she was after something. Not him since no one pointed his way. She wasn't supposed to be a problem. They'd assumed she would be back for her mother's wedding and that was it. She was weeks early and John wasn't ready to come home, and Callan still had too much work to do for his cover to be blown now. John assumed if anyone would question his return and figure out the truth it would be Vicky. Surely twenty years would have dimmed her memory of the kid she'd known. Callan didn't have any friends from childhood that would be able to pick him out of a crowd. Hell, he didn't have many friends from adulthood that would be able to do it either. He watched Vicky a moment longer. Was she going to leave soon?

What could she be talking with his crew about? Curiosity would not get him off the roof—not until she was gone. By then maybe he'd come up with a better strategy than hiding from a beautiful woman because she might be too interested in what he had to say. He'd have to engage and be John, but he was a soldier, not an actor. Hell, he wasn't even a soldier any longer. He was a guy who liked to build stuff doing a simple favor for the friend he owed his life to. Funny how something so simple turned so complicated so quickly.

4

*C*allan counted the cash register money for the fourth time. Visions of Vicky from his dreams the night before interrupted his concentration. At least his dreams had been pleasant for a few hours before morphing into the kind that woke him in a cold sweat. Not any more restful though. For reasons he chose not to think too deeply about, he felt an attraction to the woman. Maybe it was the way John had spoken of her with such genuine happiness at the idea of reconnecting with her or Callan's deep-dive into her life via the internet. He knew more about her than anyone else in Home, and he'd not had a real conversation with her yet.

The door to the hardware store opened and the click of heels on the cement floor stopped a few steps inside.

"We're closing, make it quick," he called without looking up; he wasn't going to count it a fifth time.

"Is that any way to greet a customer?" Vicky's smile was open and like a buzz to his system as she walked to the checkout counter.

"Most customers know I close early on Mondays," he replied with a shrug. "I'll make an exception this time, seeing as how you're new to the way things are around here."

"A lot sure has changed, but some things never will. This is Home, mostly like it's always been. What do you think of all the changes around here?"

And here we go. After being John for several months, he was out of practice on all the "remember when" conversations. Between his personality and the fact John had been away for almost twenty years, he'd convinced anyone who cared that he didn't remember much.

He'd spoken with John that morning about Vicky and after an hour of stories of them getting in trouble together as kids, he might know enough to bluff his way through a superficial reunion. A reunion that was about to happen whether he was ready or not. Vicky had the look of a woman who expected a conversation.

Hell. He cleared his throat, putting the cash in a bank deposit bag and met her gaze, trying to gauge her mood. Unreadable. Probably Difficult.

"You're right. Not much has changed as far as I can remember. I've heard you've been away a while too. Your parents miss you." He held his breath at his gamble.

Head cocked and lips pursed, she studied him a beat. "Which one put you up to lecturing me?"

He released it with another shrug. "I'm just saying, they won't be around forever. A little more face time isn't a bad thing."

She shifted from one boot to the other and glanced around the store. Going on the offensive during a conversation usually kept the deep personal questions at bay and gave him fewer opportunities to fuck up. Maintaining his cover with such a strategy might not help the real John transition into his future life in Home but it worked to Callan's advantage.

"So you dispense unwanted advice with your hardware, huh?" Her blue-eyed gaze swung back to him, a teasing grin lifting the corner of her lips.

"Comes with the territory, I guess." He spoke but wasn't sure where the conversation was going. She assessed him, soberly this time, as if she knew his secrets. Get your head in the game, soldier. Shit. A political reporter with an agenda could put a stop to everything he'd been working to accomplish.

"Why didn't you tell me who you were?" She stepped forward and leaned her elbows on the counter between them, hands loosely clasped under her chin. A casual and familiar act, he stopped himself before leaning forward and matching her stance. He caught a glimpse of honey skin flashing under the V-neck of her sweater. That was an altogether different kind of draw.

He straightened and backed up a step, crossing his arms in front of him. "You weren't in the mood for conversation, and it's been twenty years."

Sadness flashed across her features, and a blush crept up her cheeks. "I definitely wasn't at my best."

She dipped her head and tucked a strand of hair behind her ear before straightening. She'd recovered quickly and for a moment he questioned whether he'd seen what he thought he'd seen. Nah. He'd seen it. Hurt, definitely.

"I'm sorry about your dad." She stepped around the counter, placing a hand on his arm. Air whooshed around him, mingled with crisp citrusy perfume. Every nerve zeroed in on the warmth of her hand on his bicep.

He swallowed through the dryness in his throat and took another breath. Tension released from his lungs and his heart kicked a beat. She gave his arm another squeeze before releasing it, then turned toward the back of the store.

He hadn't pulled away. The realization stunned him for a moment. Sometimes he reacted poorly to unexpected physical contact. Other than a quick hug from Rochelle and Vicky using him as a human shield to hide from Mrs. Hanson, he hadn't had physical contact with another person in months. But with Vicky, he somehow didn't mind. It was as if he did have a history with her. The genuine compassion behind the sentiment reinforced what he'd expected. She was nice, dammit. John and his wife, Kaylie would be lucky to connect with her once the time was right. He couldn't screw that up for them.

"I like what you've done with the place," she said. "Didn't think I'd ever see you running it though. When you moved, it was like you and your mom fell off the face of the earth, never to be heard from again. No one would have guessed you'd be back in Home after all these years."

Back to the personal questions. She peeked at him over her shoulder before perusing the display of china patterns on the wall.

He really needed to get her off this reunion train and onto something else, but his mind still buzzed from her simple touch. He didn't even shake people's hands—habits like that tended to lead to an uninhibited slap on the shoulder or invasion of his personal space. He didn't think he'd react violently, that had been rare in the beginning, rarer still now, but better safe than sorry.

Yet she'd touched him twice.

And he hadn't even flinched.

His body remembered what body-to-body contact was like and begged for more. Vicky had managed to walk right through the war his mind and body were having. One missed the warmth and comfort, and the other reacted as if threatened.

But not with her.

He replayed the brief feel of soft curves pressed against his side, and the more innocent feel of her soft, warm palm on his arm. He shoved his fists in his pocket, refusing to follow her for the chance to catch another breath of perfume.

"You've got a nice selection here. China, crystal, knick-knacks of all sorts." She gestured to the wall of place settings and glass shelves filled with vases, trays, and stemware. "The banner is a nice touch. Real Romance at Home is an interesting motto to go with."

"The mayor thinks it's catchy." He shrugged. That part of the business wasn't in his wheelhouse. He watched her pick up various pieces before placing them back on the shelf. Wearing jeans tight enough to allow him to appreciate what they were covering and high-heeled boots giving her height an extra few inches, Vicky had walked straight out of his fantasies. He clamped his jaw and shot his focus to the ceiling when she bent over to look at a series of glass cat figurines on the middle shelf.

"Do you expect the same kind of business as the rest of the town?"

"If the town council delivers, the store will be ready."

"I take it you're on board with their plan to bring in tourists to revitalize Home." She stopped perusing the store and returned to him, a frown now firmly in place.

"It's a better plan than letting Blake take over everything." He met her gaze as her expression grew probing.

"What if they can't deliver the tourists in time?" She matched his stance with her arms crossed. "Will you sell then?" She was getting pissed about something, but he'd be damned if he knew what.

He held up his hands in mock surrender. "We'll have to see what happens. I'm not giving up what's mine if there's a chance otherwise." He never participated in an argument if he didn't know where the other side was headed and Vicky's thoughts on the town's business venture was a mystery wrapped in a dangerous cover. In time for what? To hold off bankruptcy or something else? How up to speed was she? Presumably, the mayor had told her everything. Whether she agreed with her mother's stance on the town's future and supported her plans was unclear. The answer could be important to his mission but now was not the time to discuss it.

"Do you need anything that's urgent? I'm ready to close."

He offered his best rendition of a friendly smile. The sensation felt odd, smiling at a strange woman while trying to come off as an old friend.

"No, Mom just wants to know how long the cleanup will take and when you and your crew will be back on track with the schedule you gave her. And she wants me to interview you about the building of the different sets." Vicky shrugged and pushed her hands into the pockets of her jeans. "If you have a hot date or something, I can come back tomorrow."

"Tomorrow would be better. No hot date. Something I have to do in Grand Junction."

"No need to explain yourself to me." Her words were friendly, but her demeanor had definitely changed. She'd gone from warm to cold when they'd discussed the town's plans and hadn't returned his smile.

Maybe she didn't agree with her mom's direction for the town. Was there a rift there? His instinct was to stay out of any family drama. He had enough of his own. But who would know the mayor better than her daughter? What if she knew something about plans the mayor hadn't told him? He needed all the intel, or he wouldn't be able to accomplish the mission.

Would she open up to her old friend about whatever was bothering her?

He'd been managing so far by doing the exact opposite. Not reminiscing. Not getting involved with gossip, or relationships, or conversations that started with "Do you remember when?" He wouldn't be able to avoid those with Vicky if he wanted her to confide in him.

"Would you like to have dinner tomorrow night?" He went out on a limb and ignored his instincts to stay out of it.

"You're asking me out on a date-date?" If he thought she'd been cold earlier, she went downright frigid at his question.

"Yes." He hesitated to answer because of the retreat signals his brain fired.

"I can't believe this." All humor left her face, and she shook her head at him. It was not a response he'd encountered before.

"Or coffee then?" He hedged, unsure where the anger he was sensing was coming from.

"So, one woman's not enough for you? You're not the same John I remember. I can't believe this."

Stunned, he watched her stomp out of the store and to her car and get in before he could answer the string of curses that lumped him in with lesser animals, dung of some sort and graves. Her grave? His grave? One woman? She was right about one thing. He was definitely not the John she remembered.

* * *

Vicky slammed the door leading from the garage into her mother's laundry room and dropped her purse onto a hook on the wall that held jackets and scarves. She took a deep breath and sat on the shoe bench for a moment of peace. If she ran in to her mother right then, she'd get asked a million questions and she might just cry. First Jeremy and now John. He wasn't Jeremy. They weren't dating. He was not cheating on her. She might have overreacted, but her anger at John was still making her want to curse. Did he think because she'd just gotten back that she wouldn't have noticed how Rochelle fawned all over him? He had her absolutely wrapped around his finger and he still had the nerve to ask Vicky out.

John was supposed to always be the sweet, quiet boy whom she'd confided all her secret wishes to as a kid. Why did she care anyway? She hadn't thought about John Pearce in years. Now that she had, though, she couldn't stop wondering about him and how he'd grown up. Had he missed her? Why hadn't he written to her after his move? She'd felt the connection and noticed the way his eyes had followed her every move. If he'd been single and free, she'd have said yes to a date and the attraction that begged to be explored. What should have been a happy reunion had turned sad and frustrating.

"You're in time for tea," Grams said as she tried to rush through the kitchen and up to her bedroom.

"Not in the mood." Vicky wanted the quiet solitude of her room.

"Oh, dear, what happened now?" her grandmother asked.

Vicky turned and paced back through the kitchen, stopping at the island where her grandmother was pulling assorted pastries from a box labeled DeVito's and placing them on a silver platter.

"I'll tell you what happened. John's what happened."

The John she'd known shouldn't have grown up to be a player or cheater.

He'd obviously changed. And it had been a long time. What did she really know about his life since moving away? Not much. Vicky popped a petit four in her mouth.

"Oh my god, that's good." She said around the vanilla and almond decadence.

"They're from our new baker. He's in charge of the

wedding cakes. Aren't they delicious!" Her grandmother gushed.

Vicky reached to grab another, but Grams smacked her hand away.

"Do not stuff another one of those in your mouth until you tell me what you're talking about with John."

"He asked me out. Can you believe it?" She grabbed another—chocolate this time—before her grandmother could stop her.

The chocolate glazed cake was suddenly too thick to swallow.

"Hey, pumpkin," Her dad breezed past and grabbed a tart before giving her a quick kiss on the cheek. "We lucked out with this guy. I'm taking a box of my favorites on a fishing trip next week. The guys will be fighting me for them." She had time to force the bite down and smiled.

"I can't wait to taste his cakes," she managed to answer.

"You'll love them." He grabbed a second tart and balanced it on the top of the first and waved. "I'll be in my shop if anyone needs me." They watched him balance his pastries and a cup of coffee in one hand and open the door to the back yard with the other with the ease of someone used to that routine.

"Now, back to John and him asking you out." Her grandmother leaned against the island, concern creasing her brows.

"Why would he do that?" Vicky blinked back the moisture burning in the corner of her eyes. She'd gone to see him expecting some kind of teasing about not remembering him, maybe some catching up on what he'd been doing with his life. Maybe see a glimpse of the boy she'd loved with all her ten-year-old heart. Instead, she'd let her emotions get the better of her. Again.

"Well, why not? He's very handsome. If I were thirty years younger, I'd go for him myself."

"Grams!"

"What? I would have been one hell of a cougar." Grams grinned with all the innocence an eighty-year-old woman could have.

"Dear God, does no one care about Rochelle around here? Don't you think she'd be a little upset if I went on a date with her boyfriend?"

Her grandmother's mouth puckered into a tight purse, wrinkling the age-defying smooth skin of her cheeks. "Queenie, dear, I hope you weren't too hard on him."

The petit fours dropped like a stone in her gut at her grandmother's look. She knew pity when she saw it. "Why?"

"Because that man isn't dating Rochelle. She might wish it, but they're only friends. In fact, John hasn't been seen with any woman since he's been back. Your mother's been trying to set him up for weeks with no success."

Vicky groaned and sat at one of the barstools. "Well, great."

"I'm sure he'll understand." Her grandmother patted her hand then carefully pushed it away from the tray of pastries.

"I hate having to apologize." That made two instances she owed John an apology for. Having to apologize meant she'd done something wrong. She hated being wrong.

"Apologize? What did you do?" Grams asked as she helped herself to one of the mini tarts.

"I may have used a few words you would have washed my mouth out with soap for." She groaned again and put her head in her hands. Her grandmother made sympathetic noises around a mouthful of chocolate heaven.

"Maybe I could send him a text?"

Her grandmother shook her head. "Oh, no, honey, this is one you'll have to do in person. Matters of the heart deserve the respect of honest conversation. Especially when we make fools of ourselves."

Her stomach twisted with humiliation, but she bolstered herself. "There's no heart involved, don't get your hopes up."

Grams wrapped her in a brief hug. Insecurity had been weighing her down for weeks and she'd overreacted after misreading a pretty straightforward conversation. Where had all her hard-won confidence gone?

She'd gone to see him wanting an explanation of why he'd pretended not to know her. Why'd she care if her child-hood best friend didn't remember her? That kind of thing shouldn't really hurt. It's not like they'd kept up over the years. Instead, she'd gotten off on the other wrong foot. Was this one big cosmic joke on her? A short visit home wasn't supposed to be so complicated.

And now she'd have to go face him again—for yet another apology.

But between her new job duties and the newest vandalism causing her mom so much worry, that would have to wait for another day. Maybe some of the embarrassment would wear off.

Her mother pushed through the doors into the kitchen. "Oh good, you're here. We need to talk about what you're going to do next and how it went at the *Home Daily*."

The last thing Vicky wanted to do was have one of those chats with her mom. She'd embarrassed herself and feeling defensive would certainly not help a conversation. She cleared her throat, looking at her. "Do next?"

Her mother sat at the kitchen table and poured herself a cup of tea from the tray Grams had placed on the table. "This latest incident is worse than before, and we have to do something about it, Queenie. We can't let this set us back too far or we'll never get out from under Blake's threats."

"How many other incidents have there been?" Vicky asked, relieved the question wasn't about her conversation with John.

Her mother puffed a quick sigh. "Two that caused actual damage that set the timetable back. Blake's damn minions are trying everything to ruin the weddings before they even start."

The vandalism and the sheriff's response were top of the list to investigate. But so was her mother. In her brief time there, she could tell her mother knew more than she'd let on, and all the workers she'd talked to said they'd been waiting for it to happen again.

"Why do you think it's Blake and not some kids screwing around? The damage wasn't extensive."

"Because they want us to think it's kids or some stupid stunt. We were almost finished with the construction. I know this town and one of our own wouldn't do this."

"I'm not necessarily disagreeing with you. I talked with John's crew—the ones that were cleaning up the mess—and the opinions were mixed. Most agreed that Blake had to be behind it but believing it and proving it are two different things."

"Exactly why someone needs to investigate Blake on a different level." She cut a glance her way and back to the cups and teapot. "We've got to find something that will make them back off or they'll win. If they're doing it here, they are doing it somewhere else or have already succeeded."

"I get it. I understand." Vicky shifted in her seat, facing her mom. "But you have to take a step back. What if they aren't behind the vandalism? What if they're only putting pressure on landowners to sell, but not doing anything outright illegal?" In other words, what if her mother was wrong?

"For once, can you not argue with me and do what I ask? Trust me when I say I know they're up to no good, and if they haven't done anything outright illegal yet, they will.

Trying to deflect the conversation with the "trust me" line wouldn't work. "What are you leaving out?"

She huffed and slammed a fork down onto one of the folded napkins Grams had placed at each seat. "They're on a timetable and they're going to be getting desperate soon."

Standing up to her mom had always been hard, but she threw her shoulders back and met her eyes. No more surprises. "How do you know?" Her question met silence.

"Back me up on this, Grams." She appealed to her grandmother seated across from her. "You understand, I have to have all the information, or I could get blindsided." She turned back to her mother.

"You should tell her everything you know, Judith. This is too important to let stubbornness take the lead." Grams using her mother's full name instead of her usual Jude or Judy dear was a clear sign of her opinion. Her mother let out an exasperated sigh.

"I haven't been sitting around wringing my hands, you know." She plopped a sugar cube into her cup. "I do have a friend or two who can find things out. I have it on good authority Blake's in a bidding war with an investment group, and if they can't prove they're clear to start construction by the end of the year, a large chunk of their investors will move on to another project."

"Was that so hard?" Seriously, why couldn't she have come out and said that in the first place? If she wanted it secret, Vicky would keep it secret. "Who else knows about this timeline?"

"Only me and a few others. We don't want Blake to find out what we know. If they think we're about to fold versus biding our time, they might keep more aggressive actions in check."

"Or they'll step up those actions to close the deal." Which made more sense to Vicky's way of thinking.

"That's what John believes too." Worry laced every one of her mother's words. "There has to be some proof somewhere."

"I'll see what I can find out, but as a reporter, I'm limited with what I can find out versus what investigation the sheriff can pursue. Until proof of illegal activity is found, there's no legal action we can take to push them back."

"I know you can find it if it's out there. Your job as official town blogger and publicist is the perfect cover. How did it go with Mr. Baker at the *Daily*? Did he get you settled to take over for Myra? You should get started right away. Maybe there're some contacts back at your old job you could call to help dig some dirt up on Blake's board or something."

"I left a message for my information guy, Neal, and expect he'll have something for me in a day or two." She left out that he'd said he'd do it if she promised to get back there as soon as possible. Her mom wouldn't appreciate it, but it was nice to know she still had a least one ally at the paper. Between Neal and her best friend, Laura, she had two people to talk to that weren't also friends with her ex. Neal was a master at digging through online data and always managed to find something for her to sink her teeth into, but this was a personal job and helping her was a risk.

"Good. Even if your investigation doesn't turn up something we can use right away, if we get the business going quickly then we can stay ahead of them and win the fight. That's where your job as publicist can help us the most."

"Right." Publicist might be getting a bit too creative with title placement.

"This is important to Home, Queenie. We need this to be important to you too."

"It is. I promise, okay?"

The weight of her mother's anxiety pushed at her. She was asking a lot from someone who hadn't planned on being around more than a couple of weeks. The mock drawings her mother had shown her were ambitious, optimistic plans. A royal park, complete with their version of St. Paul's Cathedral and Westminster Abbey. Her mother had been an Anglophile for as long as Vicky could remember—obsessed with the royals and dreaming of attending a royal wedding, it was no surprise she'd push for a royal themed wedding. Finding another couple interested in the same fantasy had been a surprise—at least to Vicky. But who knows? Maybe it was the place where Home could find its niche.

She'd dig up what she could on Blake and blog about the town businesses as much as she could in the time she was there. Her priority, though, had to be to find a way to work on a new story to pitch to her editor while doing it. If she didn't come up with something fresh soon, she'd be out of sight, out of mind.

Only day three of vacation and she had more work than she could handle.

5

*C*allan stopped at the front entrance to Grand Junction Veteran's Hospital and took a deep breath, trying to loosen the tight bands around his lungs. He blew it out hard, counting backward from ten, waiting for the tension from the two-hour drive to ease its hold on his shoulders.

The whoosh as the sliding doors opened sent a blast of heated stale air rushing out.

No one exited.

The loud clank of the doors hitting the rails on either side reverberated in his ears and kicked his pulse higher, morphing the metal-on-metal clash into an echo of a not-so-distant memory.

He shoved his hands in his pockets and moved toward the automatic doors as they were closing again. Stepping through, the answering clank echoed in the back of his skull.

Bypassing the lobby waiting areas, he avoided any passersby's direct gaze and took the familiar zigzag walk toward the door marked stairs.

Elevators were out of the question. Stairwells weren't much better but at least they weren't a moving, tight-walled trap.

He clenched his jaw against any mental protest and ran up the steps three at a time. Hitting floor four, he paused before opening the door marked with a large red number and stepped through.

He stood to the side of the stairwell exit, letting the door close quietly. The low voices of the nurses at their station filtered to him from the left. Cataloging his surroundings, he waited for the subconscious all clear.

Some habits were hard to break.

A few of the doors along each side of the transitional rehabilitation wing stood open. The quiet hum of evening television mixed with the unnatural sounds of hospital life sifted out.

An odd clicking brought his attention to the corridor on his right.

A buzz-cut, hollow-eyed kid on crutches passed without giving him much of a look. His right leg was half-gone and white bandages covered the remainder of his knee. *Click, click, shuff.* Callan nodded a quiet acknowledgment at the soldier's vacant stare.

He tried to time his visits for when the ward was empty of family members, most of whom were desperate to ease the process of putting their loved one back together.

Whether through luck or timing, the hallway cleared. The tension headache that had started at the city line eased a notch from jackhammer to sledgehammer strength. The envelope pressed to his side, under his jacket, felt heavy with the urgency to get it out of his hands.

Finding nothing out of place, he moved toward the familiar room.

The door was propped open enough for him to see the occupants going about their evening routine. The flat screen on the wall played ESPN highlight reels with no sound.

Kaylie sat in the only chair with her head bent over a book. In the hospital bed, John had his eyes closed, back propped up against a couple layers of pillows. The stumps where a missing half an arm and half a leg used to be created a strange shape under the blanket covering him. There were no prosthetics to make him look whole. Only a stark reminder of what he left behind in service of his country.

Callan should have waited but the paperwork needed to be delivered. The morning visits were better. This was their quiet time.

"John, Callan's here." Kaylie's soft voice broke the silence.

"I can come back if it's a bad time." Callan forced the words through constricted lungs. Their business could wait, at least until morning.

"Hey, Cal." John opened his eyes and cleared the gravel from his throat. Fatigue, etched deep in the hollows of his cheeks, marked the struggle his best friend was going through trying to live again.

Callan flicked a glance from John to his wife as he walked in. Kaylie shrugged and gave him a somber smile. Rough day.

Callan wasn't going to make it any better.

"I've got more paperwork from St. James. Blake upped their offer and Dewey wants in."

John sighed and his swollen lids fluttered closed, his face

pulled into a grimace as he shifted in the bed, slowly sitting up with Kaylie's help. "I can't believe Dewey sold out."

"I've stalled them for a little longer, but they're gaining ground." With Dewey and Carlisle land as a buffer, John hadn't been the only holdout not selling. Now, with Dewey caving and the Carlisles too old to put up much of a fight, the only true resistance left was John. Callan handed Kaylie the envelope. "They're offering a lot of money."

"You of all people know it's not about the money." Her tone, sharp and full of worry, rebuked him more than the words.

"Kay, he knows," John said. His quiet assurance or the flash of apology in her eyes weren't needed.

With her lips clamped into a tight line, she took the envelope from Callan, opening it and helping John hold the papers in one hand.

Callan paced the length of the room as they read, trying to give them their time to take in the offer and not think about the trouble Blake threatened. His skin itched under his flannel shirt. Stretching his shoulders, he locked his hands at the nape of his neck and focused on his mission.

John blew out a low whistle. "I could buy a nice arm and leg for that."

Callan stopped himself from marking his paces one more time. Showing his agitation wouldn't help the discussion. "You could."

"No deal." Steel underlined his words as Kaylie shoved the paperwork back into the envelope and tossed it on the table next to the bed. "We aren't giving up our only home." The finality clenched it for Callan. It was the answer he'd expected. It was time to take more direct actions to get Blake to back off.

"I'll get some coffee." Kaylie placed a light kiss on John's forehead. She scooted past Callan and out the door.

Callan was once again struck by how close they were. They'd only been married six months when he and John deployed the first time. Now, they were each other's best friends. Hell, they were the closest things Callan had to a real family. With all the responsibility that sentiment carried.

"What's the deal, Cal? What's got your panties in a twist?" The tiredness had been replaced with the probing directness that had made him top of their commander's list for quick advancement up the ranks.

"Besides the usual, you mean?" He tried to brush off John's questions, but he couldn't brush off the real concern eating at him. Blake was poised to step up the pressure for homeowners to sell out and they had enough power to cover heavy-handed action. They were big enough not to worry about someone getting hurt. Someone like John. Or Kaylie.

John pointed to the now empty corner chair. "Sit down before you fall on your ass and tell me what the hell's been going on."

"They're not going to go away. I'll keep the store running and stall them until you're ready to go home, but the town's not up for a real fight." Callan could only do so much on his own. "I've done everything the mayor and the town council have asked and no one suspects anything unusual. This wedding business has about bankrupted the town, but they're managing."

"And Mayor Jones really thinks this celebrity wedding is going to kick off some big business boom?"

"She does as far as I can tell."

"Then everything you're doing with the store and with running the construction of the sets is vital. I understand if you've had enough. I should be out of here soon. This should be my last surgery and then it is what it is as far as the docs are concerned." He slapped the bed lightly and gestured to his bandages.

"I'm not going anywhere until it's done. When you're ready, I'll bring in Mayor Jones and her husband as planned. They'll understand why we did what we did, and you and Kaylie can get on with your life in Home."

He didn't need the thanks he could see on his friend's face. He owed the man more than he could ever repay. Besides, being John was doing him a favor too. It was a win-win.

"And how's it going with Vicky?"

"She won't be a problem. I've got it covered." The lie was easy. The truth was more ambiguous. He didn't know if she'd be a problem or not.

"She was as stubborn as her mom back when we were kids. Sure you've got it covered?"

"The mayor has her busy and she's there on vacation. She's the least of my concerns."

"Really?"

Callan gave John a reassuring look. "You told me everything I need to know to handle Vicky."

"Glad that's settled." John shifted, straightening and leaning toward Callan. "We've got another problem to warn you about."

"What's up?"

"One of your father's people called Kaylie's cell phone yesterday asking to interview me about you. Something about wanting to do a piece about your service and if you'd consider running for office one day. Same kind of fluff shit they tried to pull while we were over there. She didn't tell him anything and made some excuse for me, but he asked several times when we'd seen you last."

Callan tensed and had to fight the urge to get out, fast. The last thing he could afford was to run into one of his father's hired hands. He'd been careful. Coming to Colorado was a risk. His father spent as much time here as he did in DC. He'd done nothing online as himself except cash out some of the trust fund that had been sitting untouched for years. He'd taken the cash from a bank in Denver to keep his whereabouts as muddy as possible. If his father had found him, he'd be the one called not Kaylie.

"They're searching blind if they've hit on Kaylie's cell number. Calling the family of my old unit won't get him far. Certainly not here to me. It's election time soon. He'll have no reason to search after." His father, the ambitious senator, made it a point of pride to never take no for an answer, and his son going off the grid instead of being used as a campaign tool was a challenge that wouldn't go unanswered. He'd been lucky to avoid detection as long as he had. Back to pacing, Callan ran a hand over the beard covering his chin and cheeks.

Hiding right under his father's nose and taking on the identity of his best friend were gambles Callan was willing to make. The senator's disadvantage was that he hadn't raised Callan. If you don't know your prey, it's exponentially harder to track. But he needed to take care, or he'd be forced to leave Home before the plans were complete. If Blake were to find out who he was, his hands would be tied even more. His father would be Blake's first call and the senator would turn whatever he could into a boon for his campaign—from a talking point or feel-good story to making Blake Corporation a potential financial donor. Pro-anyone with deep pockets, his father could easily be persuaded by Blake to back their side and by keeping Callan distracted, John and Kaylie would be the target of their escalated pressure. No. Everything needed to stay as it was for at least another month.

"Hey. You okay?" John's voice brought him back to reality.

"It's all good. We planned for this possibility," Callan answered quickly, not looking at his friend. John, the one in the hospital bed, shouldn't be asking if *he* was okay.

"What's got you climbing the walls? So far, everything's gone about as well as expected, even with your dad being your dad and Blake's employees snooping around. What aren't you telling me?"

Callan sighed and faced John. "The mayor is, well . . . the mayor, and she might have a chance with her plans, but she's stirring things up with trying to dig into Blake's past dealings. She didn't come out and tell me that's what she's doing, but it would be the obvious play given Vicky's background."

"She was always stubborn and eccentric." John agreed with a short laugh. "I never thought anything of it when I was little. Perhaps we should up our timeline and let her in on who you are earlier than planned?"

"I don't think it's time for that yet. Most of the town is

on board with the plans and think they can pull it off, but they're scared." The mayor had avoided the hard questions, basing much of her plan on hope and optimism. Callan preferred action. Hope wasn't something he'd bank on when fighting an enemy, but he'd do what he could with the time he had left as John. He'd already spent weeks building theme sets, stages and park areas with their limited resources and he'd keep doing it until they were done, or she called it off.

"Doc says four to six weeks of therapy if this last surgery goes well and I can go fight my own fight and you can go back to being you." The thought depressed him. What the hell would he do when he couldn't pretend it was his home they were after? Where would he go then?

"What else you worried about? I might be missing some parts, but I'm not blind. Yet."

"St. James had a new guy with him, I don't like him. He's a heavy hitter, not a salesman."

"I'm not giving up my land or my store. Not now that it's finally mine." John paused and took a shaky breath. "Kaylie's pregnant."

The words dropped like a dud missile between them.

"Pregnant?"

John's goofy grin told him it was good news. Relief thumped his chest, restarting his breathing.

The grin turned to laughter. "Confirmed today, jackass. They didn't blow off all my dangling parts and we'd been trying since before this last round of surgeries happened." The obvious happiness in his friend's expression pulled at him. He now had a baby to think of.

"Congrats." He lightly slapped John's shoulder. "I'll be sure to teach little John the appropriate appreciation of football. Since his dad will try to taint him with that rugby bullshit."

"You've been officially dubbed Uncle Cal. Next on Kaylie's to-do list is to find you a girl so there'll be an aunt in the picture too. Apparently, early pregnancy hormones are making my wife go a little overboard on the mothering."

Envy flared, niggling the part of him that used to think he'd have that kind of future. A wife and kids—a family—with him giving them what he'd never had. He buried those thoughts back in the vault they'd been hiding in.

That wasn't his future.

Not anymore.

"Thanks for the warning." He didn't want to hurt John or Kaylie's feelings but any attempt at matchmaking would be avoided or ignored. He had enough problems in his life, he wouldn't saddle a wife and children with them too. Not when he knew what it was like to grow up with a parent neighbors whispered about behind their hands. Sometimes not so secretly. His parents' divorce when he was little had devastated his mother. His father's treatment of him as a pawn to be used and then discarded when inconvenient only added to his mother's depression and erratic behavior. No, he wouldn't put a child through having a parent with emotional issues.

"The store means everything to us now." John's voice turned serious.

Callan nodded and retreated toward the door.

"I'll take care of it. Whatever it takes."

He slipped out of the room, pulling the door closed behind him. Kaylie sat in the lobby chairs reading her book. No way to avoid her as he headed to the stairs.

"I hear congratulations are in order." Nodding, she stood quickly and walked with him toward the stairwell door. A pretty blush darkened her cheeks. She was the perfect match for John. Quiet, but with a strength honed during those first weeks of John's return when he'd wanted nothing more than to be left alone. She wouldn't give up and she hadn't let John give up through the initial months of surgeries and rehab and adjusting to life at home just to do it all over again now, a year later, after complications and setbacks. She was a fighter. Home will be lucky to have them.

Her eyes, bright with unshed tears, locked on his. "Thank you for everything. You don't know how much knowing you're handling things in Home means to us. Even if the store fails. Even if the town folds. Having you there, fighting for the only thing we have, means everything to us."

"Please don't cry." Crying required attention, usually in the form of a hug or some kind of encouraging words. None of which he did well. He reached and gave her shoulder a quick pat. "I'll always be there for John. He's a brother to me. My only family."

She nodded and he could practically see her gathering her strength and pushing the worry aside.

"Are you getting any sleep?" she asked.

"Sure. The town's quiet. Not much nightlife to keep a guy awake."

"That's not what I mean and you know it."

"You've got enough to worry about. I'm fine." The hallway walls were closing in on him and not being able to look out a window made it worse. He'd been in John's room too long and now all he wanted to do was get outside. "I'll be back in a few days. Call me if my father contacts you again, day or night."

Callan double-timed it down the stairs. He needed to see the sky, the stars, and breathe fresh air with nothing and no one blocking his way. The memories of being trapped in a crashed and burning helicopter, unable to move from the weight of something hot and metallic pinning him down, had a way of fucking with his brain.

By the time he was back in his open sided Jeep and the lights of Grand Junction were behind him, the night air had washed some of the tension away. Ten miles further and he could take a deep breath without the stabbing pain of fear lacing through him, blurring his vision and his thoughts.

The docs had tried to explain why his PTSD manifested as claustrophobia and anxiety attacks—everyone had different triggers, they said. Eighteen months after his hospital release and discharge, tests and drugs and therapists had done what they could.

He'd learned how to deal the best way he could—get out, stay out, and keep moving.

John had followed him out of Afghanistan by a couple of days, closer to being in a coffin than not.

Callan should have been in John's place that day.

Because he wasn't, John had to deal with more than some faceless, invisible fear and a few scars. The town and that damn hardware store were where John could start a new life and a family. No casino resort and horse track would push his friend off his family's land and out of business if Callan had to fight his own father to do it.

6

"*T*his can't be right." Vicky muttered to herself as she pulled into the almost full gravel parking lot. A large sign at the top of the renovated gas station turned convenience store read DeVito's Bait and Tackle. Underneath was a smaller neon sign flashing Fresh Donuts and Coffee. Judging by the group of people waiting outside the door, either the bait was exceptional, or the donuts were.

In her cover as reporter for the paper and chronicling the town's new venture, the man behind the wedding cakes was high priority. Recognizing most of the dozen or so people in line, she returned several waves and good mornings. Rochelle waved her over.

"Is the line like this every morning?" Vicky asked as they shuffled forward with the group when three people exited at once.

"Oh, yeah. It's like nothing we've ever had in Home. Even Jo sells some of his cakes and pastries. Still makes her own pies, though." Rochelle shivered and pulled her coat closer. "The éclairs are worth the wait."

"Good to know. I'll have to try them. I'm here to interview Mr. DeVito."

Like nothing Home's ever had? That wasn't a very high bar. Home had never had a real bakery. Jo did her best, and her pies were always tasty, but cakes, donuts, and éclairs—were an entirely different level of baked goods mastery.

"No special treatment, Queenie, just because you're the mayor's daughter, you know," someone called from the end of the line.

Vicky smiled at the crowd and raised her notebook and pen. "Official paper business" she called to the crowd and entered the store. The mouthwatering aroma of hot glazed donuts filled the air making her stomach rumble with the reminder she hadn't eaten breakfast. Skipping it to dodge Grams and her mother in the kitchen only meant she wouldn't be able to avoid bingeing on whatever smelled so good.

Judging by the looks from the customers inside, line-cutters were not tolerated in or out. Vicky made her way to the bait and tackle side of the business and perused the shelves full of gear to wait for the crowd to diminish and make her own first impression. It was an interesting space. A half wall divided the store into two unequal halves.

The larger side had everything needed for a day of fishing in any of the area's popular fishing holes. The smaller side sold coffee and donuts and other assorted pastries and sweets. Large signs proclaimed both sides were open mornings only. Business must be good enough to keep such shortened hours.

"Hey, you must be Vicky from the paper. Mike DeVito," He waved her over to the opening that led behind the counter. "Have a seat. I'll be done here in a few." His accent was as thick as his waist and as loud as the Hawaiian shirt he wore under a crisp, bleached-white apron. He motioned for her to come around and sit next to him in one of two stools up against the wall while he rang up the last of the morning rush customers. When the line cleared, she bought a half dozen glazed from the last batch—still warm, and a latte.

A true, honest-to-god latte—pure heaven to her caffeine deprived system and as good as any she'd ever had. Maybe better since she'd had to start her days with her mother's expired instant powder until she got some grocery shopping done.

There were no tables or chairs inside the coffee shop, only a long bar and a few stools along the window side. Everything was made to go.

"So, you close early too?" Vicky asked as she set her purse on the floor before grabbing a donut from her stash. Was that a trend she was unaware of?

"I open at four a.m. and close at eleven a.m. sharp. If you haven't bought your donuts or your bait by then, you ain't serious about either."

"This is certainly not what I expected when my mother told me to talk to the town's best baker."

Vicky savored the last bit of the single, lightest, sweetest, most melt in her mouth glazed donut she was going to allow herself.

"I figured if I can't combine my two passions in life then I don't need to be running a business. It's what my wife would have wanted." Mike blinked rapidly, watery eyes disappearing into the folds of his soft round cheeks and heavy brows. His hair was dark and retreating quickly from his forehead. Not much older than midfifties, but every year showed on his face, contrasting with the energy bouncing through him. From ringing up customers, fixing espressos, to wiping down the counter, he worked with a flurry of movement.

"My Jeanie loved Colorado and she loved fishing as much as I do. I'm naming my wedding cake business after her. Jeanie's Joy Bakery. I've got the kitchen, now I need the orders."

Her heart melted at the clear love and devotion to his late wife that shone through his words. If his cakes were as good as everything else she'd tried, his contribution to the wedding business would be crucial to its success. A new sliver of hope began to form. Mr. DeVito was a professional that knew what he was doing and having him on board provided real value to what Home was offering. Ideas about how to emphasize him on the blog began to form as she ran through her questions.

"Can you tell me a little about what you expect business-wise with the town's wedding venture?"

"A town this size and the surrounding area, I'd say not more than one a month from the locals, but with the wedding business bringing in tourists, I can easily accommodate four to six a month if the mayor's plans work the way she says."

"You seem to do great business with what you've done." She motioned to the almost empty donut shelves in the case in front of them.

"I get by." He shrugged, "But wedding cakes . . . they're

something special, and I like doing them." Excitement lit his features as he handed over an album. "My portfolio."

A wedding cake wasn't something she'd ever spent time fantasizing about, but the layers and flowers and beads and details shown in glossy color were dream worthy.

"New Jersey is where you had your first bakery?"

"Yeah, I sold it to pay my wife's medical bills, and we came out west for the dry air and to give her some peace in her last months." He cleared his throat and wiped his face with a towel. "We stopped in Home and weren't able to leave. Jeanie always wanted to retire in a place like this. I said what the hell and took over the bait shop and added the donuts and coffee. What goes better in the early morning than fishing and coffee and who doesn't love a good pastry with their coffee?"

"I sampled your petit fours yesterday, they were wonderful."

Mike nodded his head and beamed, flashing a row of perfectly straight white teeth. "My mother's recipe, you won't find anything like it anywhere."

"Do you have a cake order for the first wedding yet?" If her mom wouldn't tell her who the couple was, she'd figure it out on her own. Starting with the cake design.

"Oh, yes. It's a modified version of Princess Diana's wedding cake." He pulled out another small binder from under the counter and turned it toward her. "Here's the sketch. My assistant has perfected the roses, and the chocolate pearl beads are on order. It's going to be magnificent."

"No groom's cake?" Maybe she'd get lucky with some initials or a sports team or something.

"Not this one. Only the four-tier cake. Your mom's is similar, but much smaller."

"Gorgeous." No clues about the couple, but it was beautiful.

"Did you get to speak with the bride? Any impressions of them?"

"I tried to guess what kind of celebrities they might be, but your mother wouldn't break. When she says anonymous, she means it." His face settled in a puzzled frown as he pulled a seat up next to her and sipped from his own cup of coffee.

"They sent me a few emails," he shrugged, "it's the way things are done now. They knew exactly what they wanted. I even sent them samples to taste in the mail."

"Do you still have their email?" Tracing an email address would give her more to work with. Frustration added to disappointment at the shake of his head.

"We did everything through the mayor. She's like the wedding coordinator. I never contacted them directly."

Vicky moved on to plan B. If he didn't know anything about the couple maybe he had some opinions about what's going on in town. "Have you heard about the trouble in town with vandalism?"

"Whoever is messing around with the sets, you mean? Yeah. I'm sure John and the mayor will take care of it."

"One last question. Has anyone tried to buy this property from you?"

He took another sip of his coffee and nodded. "I had one guy from Blake Corporation ask me what it'd take for me to sell a about a month ago, but I told him I wasn't interested. See him in here for donuts every now and then, but he's never asked again."

"Do you remember his name?"

"Sure do. St. James. Seemed nice enough, but he didn't look like someone who wanted to sell bait or serve coffee."

She took another glance around the shop. Inviting and warm with enough charm to make an impression, it was a gem among Home's service businesses. "Investors love turnkey businesses in high demand but I bet it wouldn't be the same without you."

"That's the plan."

She asked a few more questions before tucking away her notebook. "Thanks for everything." Wrapping up the interview, she had everything she needed for an article on the place but little else for her other assignments.

The name St. James had come up several times in her conversations around town. Obviously, Blake's go-to man for interacting with the people of Home. And the first one on her list of Blake people to talk to. As far as suspicious Home citizens, Mike certainly didn't seem like he had much stake in what the town did. The shop was far enough out of town, Blake probably didn't consider his land a priority. Up until then, she'd been concentrating on getting to know the newer people in town—assuming one of them, if any, might be more inclined to help make Blake's deal happen. Unfortunately, new-to-Home residents made up a short list.

As she left, Mike handed her a to go box with a half dozen of the delicious petit fours she'd gorged on the day before. "These are seriously addictive. I'll be dreaming about them when I get back to DC."

Her phone buzzed in her pocket as she crossed the

parking lot. She pulled it out, one-handed and thumbed it open.

"Hang on," she said as she juggled her notebook and purse and the box of goodies. She turned the car on and let the Bluetooth pick up the call.

"You still there, Neal?"

"Here, babe. Ready to come back yet?" She rolled her eyes at her friend's question. He knew as well as anyone that it hadn't been her decision to leave, the paper's board wanted her out of sight until the lawsuit was settled.

"You keeping your couch warm for me or has Mike permanently banned me as a roomie?" She'd surfed from Laura's couch to his couch after her breakup before she decided to come back to Home. His husband had been very understanding but their hospitality could only go so far.

"You know he loves you. Just more when you have your own place." Neal's laugh came through staticky over her mom's speakers.

"I get it. I love myself better when I have my own place too."

"In all seriousness, are you doing okay out there?"

"Things are different. But the same too. I don't know. My mom is hell-bent on this wedding business and her theories about Blake Corporation trying to buy out the town seem pretty legit. I haven't managed to speak to anyone that would confirm on their end. Have you found out anything about what I asked you?"

"What I've managed to dig up isn't much. They've applied for permits all over the area around your town. They want a casino, a horse track with betting and a resort. And for whatever reason they want it between Grand Junction and Telluride, right where Home sits. So, yeah, they have serious interest. You need to be careful. These permits have gone far for a company that doesn't actually own the land yet. Which means they have backing and clout. There's a lot of red tape and more than one company tied to these permit applications. It will take me a while to find out anything more. It's hard to tell who else is backing this scheme."

"That's what I was afraid of." Her gut twisted at the news. She assumed her mother was telling the truth, but she'd learned her lesson the hard way to trust but verify. From what Neal was saying, Blake expected to own enough of the land in and around Home for their project to be viable. And her mother and her promise to bring in tourists to prop up the businesses in Home is all that was standing in the way.

"We miss you. Stan misses you. He won't admit it, but he tried to get the board to give you another chance. You should call him."

"I don't want to put him in a position like that. He knows my side of the story. And frankly, we both know my punishment could have been worse."

"You were doing your job."

"Not well enough or I would have spotted that fake bull-shit being fed to me, and I wouldn't have rushed it to print. Fool me once . . . and you know the rest. I'm going to get back. Once I get somewhere with this Blake business, I'll focus on a story for Stan that the *Chronicle* can't turn away and I'll be back in town and you'll be sick of seeing my face again."

"Okay, promise. Cause when you do, you-know-who is going to get smacked down hard."

She stiffened at his words. "Oh, sorry. Didn't mean to bring her up. Forget I said anything."

"No, it's fine. Jeremy has a type, and I'll just have to get over it."

"You were too good for him."

"That's what I keep telling myself. Please tell me it's Stan that's going to kick her back down to covering restaurant week instead of my desk."

"Eh, she keeps pestering him so it might happen."

Vicky didn't want to think about her ex's new girlfriend taking over her job while she was on leave. He had a type all right. Young and dumb and starry eyed over his good looks and notoriety in the DC social circle. She'd been that person. Not anymore. She shook her head and focused on the road leading back to Home. Letting her anger push her into a worse mood wouldn't help anything. "Listen, I'm driving and need to run."

"No worries. I'll send what I've got and give your love to Mike."

She made kissing noises before cutting off the phone on the steering wheel. She pushed any thought of Jeremy and his cheating out of her mind. That was the past. She had bigger problems to deal with right in front of her.

A twinge of guilt needled at her for not heading straight to see John. She had her story and blog info for the day, and now she really didn't have an excuse. Her dad and his buddy had returned the rental she'd driven into town with and her mother had given her permission to use her SUV. It was a much nicer ride but that also meant she had to run errands like stop by Pearce Hardware and pick up some supplies her mother had ordered and invite John to dinner on their behalf. In person, her mother had insisted. She also still needed to apologize.

Main Street and Pearce Hardware came into view. Every one of the buildings she'd passed held a memory or two that fought to spring to the surface of her thoughts. Vicky pulled over to the edge of her lane. She pulled the seatbelt off her shoulder and leaned forward to see the side mirror and reversed to parallel park the large vehicle.

A loud crunch stopped her backward movement in an instant.

Her forehead hit the steering wheel with the force of the crash and pain exploded behind her eyes. Her vision dimmed and then flared back into focus.

Sucking in a breath, her heart dropped to the pit of her stomach before she could process what happened. Someone had hit her from behind while she was backing up. Or had she hit something? She pushed the gear into park and waited for her heart to stop racing. In her rearview mirror she could see a man getting out of a large truck now stopped behind her. She opened her door and stepped out on shaky legs.

"Are you okay?" the man asked. Taking off his sunglasses, the man stepped closer and squinted.

"Miss, are you okay?" Still and calm, he waited for her to answer. His expression full of genuine concern. Deep grooves bracketed his mouth and smaller ones etched around his ice blue eyes, softening the hard edges of his chiseled features.

"Um, yeah, I'm okay. A little surprised." Her temple throbbed from the hit.

"Makes two of us." He held out his hand. "Grayson St. James. You must be Vicky Alexander."

St. James. Some coincidence. "How do you know my name?" She shook his hand out of habit, still dazed and somewhat confused. His suit and sunglasses were too expensive looking for the street they were standing on. She didn't know what stunned her more—that he drove a huge dually truck or that he was so damn clean and handsome.

"It's my job to know who's who around here. The mayor's high-profile daughter is hard to miss." He was direct —probably knocked people off their guard—but so was she. Vicky returned a polite smile as the momentary brain fuzziness cleared.

"If you wanted to meet me, you didn't need to crash into me."

"I've used some questionable tactics in the past, but potentially injuring someone is generally frowned upon."

"Is it?" She let the challenge hang with no clarification.

His smile tightened under his sharp gaze. "Always."

"Glad to hear it."

"Vicky, are you all right?" John appeared from behind her.

As soon as he reached them, he grabbed her shoulders and turned her toward him and then ran his hands up and down her arms, patting her down. "What hurts?"

"John, what are you doing? I'm fine." She tried to shrug out of his grip, but he held her tightly, examining her forehead, before pulling her into the crook of his arm and ushering her toward the store entrance. She walked with him a few steps, unsure what had him upset. His grip tightened briefly, and she could feel the urgency in his movements.

"John, I'm okay. Let me go." She dug in her heels and pulled out of the circle of his arms.

"We should call the doc. You could have a concussion." He touched her forehead and she flinched. "You have a bruise forming there."

"I'm okay. It's a small bump. I was leaning too close to the steering wheel when Mr. St. James—"

"Grayson." Blake's representative had followed them to the doorway but stepped back when she'd stopped.

"When Grayson hit me from behind. Nothing serious."

John turned and stalked forward, hands fisted, blocking Grayson from her view. "What the hell were you doing, St. James. You could have seriously hurt someone."

"It was an accident, Pearce, and Ms. Alexander is fine. There isn't even that much damage. We can handle this." Grayson stepped around John to Vicky. "It was my fault, I didn't see you backing up in time to stop as I was pulling out of my spot. We can exchange insurance now or later. I'll pay for whatever repairs are needed." He pulled out his wallet and handed her a card with a smile that could draw anyone in.

She took the offering, glancing from the flirty stranger to a seething John, whose hands were clenched into fists.

"Are you sure you're fine?"

"I'm fine."

"Call me when you get an estimate." Grayson winked. "Perhaps we can talk more over dinner? Tonight?"

"Uh, maybe another time."

"Another time." Grayson's smile deepened for a moment before disappearing. He faced John. "Let me know if you change your mind, it's a good offer. You should take it."

John didn't move or indicate he'd heard what the man said. Grayson opened his mouth as if to speak but closed it with a click of his jaw and shrugged before leaving them.

Vicky put her hand on John's arm. "Hey, are you okay?" His gaze never wavered from over her head. "John?" She gave his arm a light shake. He pulled away abruptly.

"I'm fine, really." She tried to reassure him. He was taking the accident harder than she was.

After blinking a couple times, his attention returned to her briefly, his eyes burned with some deep emotion she couldn't identify. Someone honked in the street and he flinched, backing away and retreating inside the store. Another honk reminded her she needed to move her mother's car into the spot she'd been trying to get in to in the first place. She sighed and waved to the honker. "I'm coming."

* * *

Callan marched straight to the storeroom and to the first box marked heavy in his path. He pulled on gloves and lifted the box onto the second to the bottom shelf and let the ache in his shoulder center him in the space. He chose the storeroom over taking a jog out to the main road. He couldn't take the sound of cars driving past until the threat of a flashback subsided. The push and strain of muscles stretching and flexing with a load built for two helped take his mind off the freak-out he'd been on the verge of committing. He let the air out of his lungs in a quick shot and squat-lifted the heaviest of the weight.

He knew the instant Vicky stepped into the storeroom. Her perfume cut right through the dust, sweat, and grease to tickle the memory of her last visit to his store. John's store.

"Are you going to tell me what that was all about?"

He slid the box into its space with a grunt. "Not today." He needed to keep his body moving or she'd see the physical effects of the adrenaline spike coursing through his veins.

Moving to the next stack, he worked his hands under another box. He ignored her sigh and hefted it onto the shelf area he'd cleared for it. Inventory didn't need to be rearranged as often as he did it, but it had become a meditation exercise for him.

Another deep sigh from his not-so-silent observer, as if exasperation could only be shown through the audible breathy exhale instead of coming right out and saying what she must be thinking.

"Okay. I'm here to pick up the stuff my mom ordered."

"I'll have Tyler deliver it this afternoon." He flicked a glance her way but didn't pause what he was doing. "You should go home and put some ice on your head."

She didn't move to leave, and his gut tightened. Polite conversation was out of the question for him right then. He busied himself with pulling inventory from a box and stacking it in a roller cart for Tyler to shelve later. If he kept moving, maybe he could get through whatever she was waiting for.

Her laughter drew his attention. "Why is there a life-sized Prince Charles with penis glasses in your store? Is that some kind of fetish?"

He looked from her smiling face to the cardboard cutout he hadn't replaced yet and shrugged. "Never give a teenager a sharpie." He turned back to his lifting and maneuvering. His episodes were unpredictable. He needed to work until he knew for sure it was over.

"Well, I guess I'll talk to your back then. I'm sorry for jumping to the wrong conclusion about you and Rochelle and calling you names. And I'm sorry about barfing on your boots."

"I accept your apology, and I'd like to be alone. Go have a nice dinner with St. James."

Fucking smooth St. James. Coming on like he was some good ol' country gentleman when five minutes before he'd been laying out Blake's version of the disaster that would follow for John's store, his home, and the town if Blake Corporation didn't get his cooperation.

It's the only way to come out of this clean. The town's guaranteed to fail. Your property is worth more, right now, than it will be even a week from now. Wait and you'll miss your chance. Blake will win, he always does. The state wants this deal to go through. Home doesn't have a chance, but you do.

"If I do or don't, it's none of your concern. Anyway, my mother asked if you'd please come over for dinner tonight."

"Tell your mother I got her last work request, she doesn't need to ask me over for dinner to nail down more plans." Playing at being John and a dinner guest was not a good choice for him given the state he was in right then. He'd just stepped out of the store when he heard the crash, and it brought a rush of memories he hadn't had in a long time. Already angry at his confrontation with St. James, the unexpected sounds and his immediate concern for Vicky triggered a reaction he'd thought he'd had a lock on. Apparently, he wasn't as good as he'd been pretending to be.

He huffed before leaning his elbows on the shelf, his forearms shaky from the exertion and his fingers cramping from his too-tight grip. He tilted his face toward her when she didn't leave. Stubborn didn't begin to describe Vicky.

Arms crossed, back straight and head cocked at an angle, all that was missing was a tapping toe and she'd be the spitting image of her mother directing a city council meeting. She opened her mouth, but he held out a hand to silence any more protest. "Save it. Please."

Her gaze narrowed, boring through him with a steely glare. She whirled around but instead of stomping out as he expected, she stumbled and flung a hand out to catch herself on the doorway. Her other hand flew to her head accompanied by the hiss of a quick inhale. He was beside her in less than a second. Her lightly tanned skin had paled, and her eyes were now squeezed shut.

"Goddamn stubborn woman." He caught her around her waist when her knees buckled and helped her to a chair. She groaned and held her head in her hands, elbows on knees.

"You need to lie down, and you aren't driving home like this."

The weight of her in his arms felt better than it should have. She could have a concussion for Christ's sake and his thoughts are zeroing in on the feel of her against his chest and the soft scent of her perfume.

He helped her to the apartment over the store and set her on the sofa, careful not to jostle her too much. She sat up immediately but winced at the movement. "Thanks."

"You're going to have a little bump there for a while. It's already starting to color." The raised bruise showed at her temple hairline.

"Dammit." She brushed her fingers over the sore area,

testing the pain. "I think I'm fine. I just need to get the swelling down a little and eat some real food. I've only had a couple donuts and coffee, it's probably a blood sugar issue." She leaned her head on the back of the sofa and listened to him rummaging in the kitchen.

He handed her a bottle of water and a couple aspirin and laid an ice pack next to her.

"Don't have much here. I usually eat at Jo's. Have some of these." He handed her a canister of mixed nuts. "A little protein might help."

She shrugged slightly and popped the pills in her mouth and shook a handful of the nuts into her palm. He saw the moment she noticed her surroundings.

"Did you do all this yourself?"

Vicky's gaze swiveled around the loft apartment from her perch on the sofa as she finished the snack.

"I've had some time on my hands lately."

"Some time?" A short laugh had her clutching the ice pack to her forehead with a groan. "It's stunning."

"It suits me." Embarrassed, he wanted to change the topic. He'd done too much to the apartment above the store. Time on his hands had been an understatement. The loft fit him perfectly, from the furniture to the stained cement floors to the corner gym with a hanging bag and floor mats. He'd worked as if the space belonged to him. When he'd first arrived, he'd thought renting the place from John might be a possibility. The stairs led out to the alley, so he'd never be a bother to whomever was manning the store. But no longer. He didn't expect the townsfolk to be happy when they found out he'd been lying to them, and Vicky was churning with a curiosity that would soon demand satisfaction. Which could only lead to trouble, and he'd definitely need to leave Home then.

"The skylights are perfect. Did the Army teach you to love home improvement? You'd sneak over to my house instead of working with your dad in the store every chance you got."

"Some things change, I guess." He recovered from his musing enough to remember he was still hiding. He stood away from her at the wall of windows overlooking Main Street. She moved to stand next to him. Within reach. A few more inches and the length of her body could easily be tucked against his.

"I'm sorry. I didn't mean to bring up any painful memories. Just curious what you've been up to the last twenty years." She bumped him, shoulder to shoulder, playfully, before facing him.

He turned toward her, so close he could pull her to him and taste her lips in one easy move. She watched him from beneath hooded eyes. A blush brightened her pale cheeks, and her mouth opened slightly. His pulse skyrocketed. Any faster and his heart would explode from his ribcage, all due to what had to be an unconscious move. Maybe she felt it too? The idea was fodder for his overactive imagination. He broke eye contact.

"Finish your water, and I'll drive you home." He needed her out of his space before he gave in and did something really stupid, like kiss her.

After an agonizing ten minutes of more questions and half-truth answers, he put a "be right back" sign on his door and settled Vicky into the passenger seat of her mother's SUV.

Sweat beaded his forehead and his shoulder ached where tension fisted as he slid behind the steering wheel. He could do this. The short drive from his store to the mayor's house would take only a few minutes. He'd been driving more and more lately and had almost gotten over the more intense reactions to being in a vehicle. Muscle tension, accelerated heart rate, stomach cramps, flashbacks that made him forget where he was for seconds at a time—nothing anyone wanted to experience while also operating a metal cage at forty miles an hour. That was then. He'd gotten better. He only needed to drive her home, park, and then he'd be free. He'd walk off the spark of desire yet to be drowned out by the crunching sound of metal hitting metal that screamed through his mind on a loop and get his head clear again.

"Can we start over?" Vicky stopped him before he started the engine.

He looked at her offered hand and back to her face. "Start over? Why?"

"Hi, John. It's great to see you again. I can't believe you're back in Home." She kept her hand held toward him and her gaze on his face.

She offered him a chance to start over as John instead of pressuring him with questions about his reactions earlier. The tension inside him lessened a fraction.

"Vicky, It's been so long." Callan placed his hand in hers, palm to palm and let the electricity from the contact race through him. "Home hasn't changed a bit." He dropped the handshake and gripped the steering wheel.

"Good. Now get me home before my mother gets back so I can try and hide this from her. She'll nag me until I'm in Telluride at the nearest hospital getting an MRI if she sees me like this." Her smile was bright and sweet. "And she won't take no for an answer on dinner tonight either. Don't even try."

God, she was beautiful. And all wrong for him but what choice did he have? As far as everyone in Home was concerned, he was John, Vicky's childhood friend. He'd positioned himself to be an integral part of completing the town's plans to turn Home into a business venture. He couldn't turn back now.

"She's a force of nature, your mother. I wouldn't want to be on the receiving end of her nagging."

"Aren't you already?" She buckled her seat belt before pressing the ice pack she'd snagged to her forehead.

"We've done a lot of work together lately. No nagging, yet."

"She always liked you." Vicky laughed softly, catching him off guard. "It helps that you're cute when you get frustrated."

"Cute?" He would not look her way.

"You know you are. Always did have her wrapped around your finger."

"What about you? Did I always have you wrapped around my finger?"

"Maybe. Only because I knew I could kick your butt if I wanted to." He couldn't see her face hidden behind her hand, still holding the ice pack, but he heard the smile in her voice. Indulging in her flirting wasn't wrong, he told himself. For a moment, he felt almost normal. A pretty woman smiling at him, sending the right signals—nice and normal.

She sighed and leaned against the headrest. He couldn't

leave now nor could he ignore the mayor and what she might be hiding from the town about Blake or her daughter and the possibility she might find out what he'd been hiding. There was no harm in being nice. He stifled the voice that wondered what John would say. But John wasn't there. Callan was.

7

"What, no construction crew?" Vicky asked, looking around John at the empty driveway behind him.

"What no hello or thank you for coming?" He countered her teasing with his own. He must be in a better mood than he'd been earlier.

Damn. She'd thought he'd looked good in faded denim and a T-shirt, but he was downright devastating in a deep green button-down and camel blazer. Dark jeans hugged his form in all the right places. Vicky's heart hammered as a slow grin rolled across his lips, causing entirely too much excitement in parts that shouldn't be responding.

"Going to let me in?" He remained in the doorway, hands in the pockets of his jeans.

Vicky blinked as heat rushed to her face.

"Sorry, yes." She stepped back and ushered him through the doorway. "Mom was happy you accepted her invitation. She and Grams are going all out on dinner."

"You're not helping?" he asked.

"Are you kidding?" She snorted. "Me and cooking—not a good match. I'm supposed to be nice and entertain our guest until the food's ready."

Her stomach clenched at the heated look he sent her. She thought maybe she'd imagined their connection at his place earlier, but here it was again.

"Would you like a drink?" she asked, forcing herself to stop thinking about how good he looked and remember who he was and where they were. Not the right person and not the right time.

"As long as it's not one of your grandmother's appletinis. I've seen what those can do."

"Ha, ha. Don't remind me." She led him into the den where her parents kept a well-stocked bar.

"My mother always told me funny guests were the best kind to have around." His voice rolled over her skin, setting every nerve on alert.

"Hmm, my mother always told me the best guests knew when to leave," she retorted with sugar in her voice. His low chuckle made her grin.

"Children, please, behave." Vicky's mother dried her hands on her apron as she walked up to John and gave his hand a soft squeeze. "It's so nice of you to join us."

"Thank you for the invitation, ma'am."

Vicky busied herself making a couple drinks at the bar.

"How's your head? The bump is barely noticeable," he asked as her mother headed back to the kitchen.

Vicky sent him a scrunched-face look and rolled her eyes at him. Her mother stopped and turned back to them. "Did you hurt yourself?"

"It's nothing, Mom, it's fine. I'll tell you about it after dinner."

"You can tell me now," her mother insisted.

"I had a little fender bender earlier, and I bonked my head on the steering wheel. No real damage done and I'm fine. Right, John? Tell her I'm fine. I don't need a poultice or a tonic. Unless you count this one." She held up her glass and clinked the ice.

"Oh my god, you could have a concussion. You should be sitting down." Her mother turned to John, "How could you let her drive herself home after a car accident?" She emphasized car accident as if talking about an earthquake.

"Mother, for God's sake, please, it's okay. I'm fine and John drove me home and I've been resting all afternoon."

"Fine. But you'll sit and stay seated until dinner." Her mother waited, not moving until her request was followed. Fine.

Vicky slumped down onto the sofa and stifled the wince when the sudden move sent a sharp pain to the not-so-noticeable bump she'd spent thirty minutes carefully covering with makeup. It wasn't serious and any nagging she received about it would only keep her from her work. Her mother had many great qualities, but a touch of over-protectiveness combined with extreme sensitivity to any injury or illness brought out an equally extreme side of mothering.

"Nice going, getting me in trouble right off the bat," she whispered to John. Her mother may have gone back into the kitchen, but she'd be on high alert now. He should remember the Jones women went overboard on the taking care of boo-boos. When they were kids, if she hurt herself or if anyone had so much as a scratch while playing at her house, her mom or grandmother had a homemade remedy waiting to take care of it.

John sat on the other end of the sofa and turned toward her. "Sorry." He shrugged with another devastating smile. "She's worried."

"Like you were?" Vicky asked but instantly regretted when his open expression shuttered closed. Why couldn't she stop digging? A curse of the last decade of always looking for the story.

"I'm sorry if I scared you." His voice softened.

He seemed so sincere, Vicky felt even worse. Damn, he was being nice. Being around him was easier when he was moody or ignoring her. He was dangerously sexy when he looked at her with such sincerity. She could melt right down into a puddle of hot hormones.

"Whatever, you don't scare me." She took a sip of her gin and tonic.

John was silent next to her. His gaze slipped over her head and toward the living room window. The sunset was visible through the open curtains and slashed a ray of light across his features, highlighting the contrast between his light eyes and dark beard. "Good," he said.

She thought he was about to get up, but he surprised her and relaxed back into the soft leather of the sofa, seemingly at ease again. "I don't want you to be afraid of me." His answer traveled over her skin and sank deep with a weight and meaning behind that single syllable that made her belly flutter.

She cleared her throat and tried not to fidget under his gaze. It seemed to glide over her, kindling a fire inside her. Where had he learned to do that with his eyes? She couldn't get even a little bit romantically involved with John no matter how tempting. She wasn't looking for serious. John was . . . John. The boy she'd wished had been a real brother because he'd been perfect in her ten-year old eyes. He was sweet and funny and had loved her parents and grandmother like they were his own. He'd moved back to her—their—hometown. She hadn't. What was the use in starting something that couldn't go anywhere?

"So, back home after all those years in the army. The town is very proud of their local hero."

He shrugged. "I'm lucky I got out alive and mostly intact."

The finality of his statement screamed "I do not want to talk about this." She was on a roll hitting every sensitive subject with an accuracy a dart player would admire. Perhaps she should ask about his love life. Maybe he had some painful ex story she could get him to relive.

They sat in quiet for a few minutes, each sipping their drinks, lost in their own thoughts.

"Vicky," her mother called to her from the kitchen. "A call for you."

Who'd be calling her at her mom's house instead of her cell phone? She patted her hip, searching for whichever pocket held her cell. Had she missed a call from Stan? She wrinkled her nose and sighed, feeling self-conscious. The wrap dress she'd put on at the last minute didn't have pockets, so she'd left it in her room. "Sounds important." Her mother motioned to her office where the main landline phone was kept.

"Be right back," she said to John. Seconds later, she was speaking to Kristin McBride.

Smug delight rode the undercurrent of her temporary replacement's over-the-top sweet southern drawl. Instantly on alert, Vicky fought the urge to hang-up. "I'm on vacation."

If Kristin was that thrilled to talk to her—enough to have tracked her to her mom's house—the conversation was not about Stan wanting her to come back to DC right away.

"I'm calling for a comment on the hospitalization of Walter Parks. The *Chronicle* is running the story in the morning. Is there anything you'd like to say on your behalf?"

"What are you talking about?" Vicky's stomach dropped. Walter Parks? The man who'd fed her false information about Standridge Pharmaceuticals was old and wasn't in the best health. Why would his hospitalization need a comment?

"Oh. You haven't heard?" Kristin's breathless, annoying-as-hell voice perked up.

"Heard what?"

"Mr. Parks tried to kill himself this morning and his wife is blaming your exposé and ill treatment of his boss as the cause. Of course, the fallout from your article is hard to deny. I mean, if it weren't for you, he wouldn't have lost his job, and he's facing charges along with Standridge. Did you think about any of the hundreds of employees that counted on Standridge Pharmaceuticals for their jobs before you crucified the owner over campaign contributions?"

They were really going to let them blame her exposé? Her heart climbed to her throat. Oh, God. The *Chronicle* and her bosses were distancing themselves from her and Standridge's lawsuit even more.

"Vicky?" Kristin's eager prompting pissed her off.

She pulled herself together. "Is he okay?"

"Apparently. Any comment?"

Relieved, Vicky kept her voice firm and even. "My exposé was on the alleged unethical and illegal acts of the CEO and owner, Gustav Standridge, not his employees."

"Anything else?" She asked, testing Vicky's control.

"Does Stan know about this?"

"Who do you think gave me the lead? I'm giving you the chance to defend your piece."

"No comment."

"Is that all?"

"Goodnight."

She hung up before the bitch could ask her anything else. Releasing her stranglehold on the phone, she shook out her hands and tried to bury her anger and frustration.

She's trying to upset me.

It's working.

Her mother and grandmother were in the kitchen, their chatty voices filtering through the closed door of the office. John was in the living room. She couldn't leave, but the idea of small talk when all she could think about was the giant sucking sound of her life and career heading down the toilet, wasn't appealing. She needed a few minutes alone. She waited for her mother to leave the kitchen then tiptoed up the stairs to her room when her grandmother's back was turned. She snagged a crocheted pillow from her bed and squeezed it as hard as her shaking hands would let her. Her job was gone. Probably the reason Stan hadn't returned any of her calls. She thought about Mr. Parks. She'd talked to him several times during her investigation. She didn't mean for anyone to get so hurt by the scandal they would try to kill themselves over it.

Should she call Mrs. Parks and offer her sympathies, or would that make it worse? She hated not knowing what to do. She'd always had a clear path, knew right from wrong. She'd never dreamed that one day she wouldn't trust herself or her instincts.

She couldn't stop the tears. Frustration and embarrassment washed over her. This would not be the end. Being a journalist was the career she'd always wanted and spent her adult life working toward. Searching for the truth, keeping the public informed, striving to write articles that brought light to the darkness surrounding the wrong side of politics, her job had been important. And she'd been good at it. Better than Kristin could ever dream of being. There was no other plan for her. No other way to be, except to keep going forward. There were other magazines, papers, and online news sources she could look into. The *Chronicle* had been her family for years, and sometimes families had to breakup. She wouldn't accept that as inevitable. The bottom line was, she wouldn't just disappear. She could fight for her job at least as hard as Home was fighting to remain Home.

Swiping the moisture from her face, she checked her makeup in her dresser mirror before opening her bedroom door. For a moment, she'd forgotten about John, but there he was, in the hallway, his back to her.

"Uh, John?"

He turned from the closet door he stood in front of, lowering his hand from a knocking position. "Your mom sent me up to find you."

"In the closet? You practically lived here, I can't believe you forgot which door was mine."

He shrugged, moving toward her. "Dinner's ready. You okay?" Standing in front of him, away from prying family, she felt exposed. His gaze drilled into hers, compelling a response.

"I'm fine. Work stuff." Vicky scooted past him before he could ask more questions, but he followed on her heels.

"You don't look fine."

She stopped midstep and faced him. "Tell you what. I'll spill all my problems and secrets if you tell me what happened with you this afternoon."

His face tightened, a frown pulling at the corner of his mouth. Thought so. She raced down the last few steps. That was probably too harsh, but if she tried to talk about it then, she'd cry, and she was holding on by a thread. He'd just have to understand.

She wasn't ready to lay out her fears to anyone. What could talking about them do for her except make her cry again? For what? John had his own problems he didn't want to talk about either.

Dinner went on around her but all she could think about was her life imploding back in DC. Her mother discussed the upcoming wedding structures that still needed to be built and her father peppered John with questions about fishing while her grandmother, not-so-subtly, hinted he should ask Vicky to be his date for the weddings. She was happy not to be the center of their attention. Her mother shooed her and John out on to the back patio after dessert was served. Whatever kind of matchmaking she was doing, Vicky didn't have the strength—or maybe the will—to fight it. She welcomed the distraction.

She tucked her feet under her on the cushioned patio chair and pulled the blanket up to her shoulders, shivering under it. John immediately moved to throw another log into the outdoor fireplace. Her heart did a little flip at his thoughtfulness. She studied the shadow of features on his face as he leaned against a column. His hands were in his pockets, but no other concession to the cool weather was given. They were on her parent's patio, barely twenty feet from her family but felt completely alone. She couldn't help wondering how he wasn't getting as cold and how warm his skin would feel.

"You were quiet at dinner."

Vicky caught his gaze briefly before looking away. "I guess."

"That phone call upset you. Want to tell me about it?" His question was straightforward, as if he actually expected her to tell him. He would probably listen too.

"The last nail in the coffin of my former life."

"That's dramatic."

"It's a long story, but suffice it to say, I screwed up and I let my emotions cloud my judgment and I rushed to print a story that should have had more research, and that call was to let me know someone got hurt." Emotions like pride and conceit and single-mindedness allow a story to be written at any cost. She'd gotten knocked down hard—and it was time to re-evaluate how she'd strayed from where she'd started.

"Is it something you can fix?" he asked.

"It's too late for that. I ran with a story without properly vetting the source of the information. I screwed up and that fact doesn't change even though it turns out that most of what I wrote was true. Anyway, I can't do anything about it until I'm back in DC."

She didn't expect him to let it go, but he did. He nodded as if he understood it was too close, too much to talk about right then. Her ex would have pushed, assumed he could fix it and so would her mother if given the chance. It wasn't that she didn't want to speak of it ever, but right then, she needed space and time. John seemed to get it. They watched the fire in silence for a bit.

He blew out a breath and moved into the yard. Surprised at his quick withdrawal, she had to follow. She left the blanket and the fire and followed his path around the new gazebo and toward the far edge into the shadows.

When she caught up with him outside her father's workroom, he literally paced the back fence. The image of a caged cat came to mind. Not comforting like "here, kitty, kitty," but the kind that bit your arm off for trying to pet it. "Is it something I said?"

"Didn't mean to bail. I just needed to move." He answered, coming to a halt in front of her.

He faced her with such an intensely heated look before resuming his march, she almost turned back. She couldn't keep up with his mood swings. She wanted to know what was suddenly bothering him and she was too pissed at life to be subtle. But this was John. The guy who'd been the understanding friend a minute before. She should do the same. She had a thought.

"Hey, can I show you something?"

His eyebrow shot up.

She liked the quirk to his lips that followed. She brushed

off the innuendo. "Not something like that, come on." She grabbed loosely at his sleeve and pulled him toward the line of shrubs behind the garage turned man-cave.

His low laugh came from right behind her. It was dark in that part of the yard and the only light came from a small lamp her father had left on inside the garage. "Stay here a sec." She slid behind the back wall and dug out the treasure she'd found earlier.

"Remember this?"

He shook his head when she held out the rusted metal tackle box.

"It's our secret box." Still no response. "You helped me work a hole in the back of the garage to hide it in. I thought it was the greatest secret we ever had."

"Uh, sure." At his blank look, she felt stupid. Of course, he wouldn't remember such a thing. It was only the one place she felt she could actually hide something and keep it for herself alone.

"I found it out here earlier. I couldn't believe it's been hiding in there for almost twenty years."

"Cool."

Embarrassed to be excited over something that obviously didn't mean much to the man, she tucked the box under her arm. No need to keep it out there anymore. It wouldn't be holding any more secrets now. She'd thought since he was the one who'd helped her break out the boards and build the little cubby under the siding he'd be a little more interested.

"Come look at this." She opened the door to the studio and turned on the overhead light. "I kept a diary of that summer."

She'd written everything down the year she'd turned ten

but stopped when John left town. She'd forgotten about it until picking some of the roses climbing the back fence had brought back the memory. Maybe because John had been on her mind the whole afternoon.

"See if this rings a bell." She pulled the pink notebook with a heart shaped locket out of the box and opened it to the middle. "Pop let John solder part of a bracelet today, and he gave it to me. After lunch, he cut his hand on a chisel, and we took him to Doc to get stitched up. We had ice cream at Jo's for dinner."

Vicky grabbed his hand and turned his palm toward the light. The skin on his hand revealed no scar. "I can't believe it's gone. You needed several stitches that day. But you have a new one here." She turned his hand over and traced the ridge of a scar that ran along the top of his hand.

He pulled his hand away quickly. "Scars fade."

"You really don't remember?" One of the most important summers of her childhood. He'd practically lived at her house.

"It's been a long time, Vicky."

She snapped the lid open on the metal box and slid the diary inside. "You like woodworking, you don't remember much of all the time you spent here, so bad you didn't remember where my room was upstairs." She laughed, a deflated sound at the memories she'd cherished. "And now, you don't have the scar that was wicked looking for a ten-year-old." He crowded next to her, close enough she could reach out and run her fingers along a scar that ran across his jawline just visible through his beard. His hand's scar might have faded, but he'd added more than just the one recently. "Who are you and what have you done with my John?"

He froze at her attempted humor. Not just froze, looked downright uncomfortable and as guilty as anyone she'd ever caught in a lie. She hadn't meant it seriously, but his reaction set bells ringing in her reporter brain. She'd been on the receiving end of too many lies to let it go.

"Oh my god. You're not really John."

He stared, forcing a half-assed smile. "Are you always this suspicious?" He pushed away from her, striding out of the studio.

"You can't run away from me." She was one step behind him, when he abruptly stopped. "Prove to me you're John." He spun on his heel at her demand.

"You think I'm not really John? That's ridiculous."

"Show me some ID."

"I don't carry any." He shrugged and stuffed his hands in his jean's pockets. His face was set in an unreadable mask. "Who else would I be if I'm not John?"

His questions sounded reasonable. Was she being overly suspicious? Looking for a problem where none existed? No, he'd squirmed like a child sneaking candy—brief as it was. He's hiding something.

"A little bit of digging and I can find out anything about you I want. I've got resources you know."

"You should be more careful when you threaten a man while alone, in the dark." Uncertainty tingled up her spine, but she didn't give in.

"Now who's threatening?" She wasn't about to be intimidated. There was no heat behind that threat. Though his crack about it being dark and them being alone did register a bell or two in her head.

"If you're really John, then what's my full name?" She

blurted the question. The real John would know the answer without hesitation.

"Victoria Jones."

"Wrong."

"You're asking me to remember stuff from over twenty years ago. Sorry, I've had a lot of life since then."

"I don't buy it." She tilted her chin up and waited. What would he do now? Their gazes locked and she held her breath. "Are you working for Blake?"

He pushed away and stomped a few steps toward the house, cursing a colorful string of words. With a heavy sigh, he returned to his spot less than a foot from where she remained rooted.

"If I tell you who I am, I need your assurance you won't tell anyone else."

All kind of scenarios zinged through her mind at his confirmation. He's not John. Who was he? What was he doing in Home? He hadn't denied he worked for Blake. What kind of scam was he trying to run?

"Oh, no, I don't give assurances like that, period." She didn't make bargains with people she didn't know. Not anymore. "Where's the real John?"

"He's at the VA hospital in Grand Junction."

He'd answered without hesitation. Either he was a really good liar, or he was telling the truth.

"Is he okay?"

"He's okay. Rehabbing from injuries from our last deployment. He's a friend, and I owe him."

"Owe him, why?" More questions begged to be asked. What could he owe John that made him take on his identity? How had he fooled everyone in town?

"He asked me to come out here and take care of his store after his dad died."

"So you told everyone you were him? What's in it for you?" Braver now that he'd confessed, she pressed for more answers.

"That wasn't the plan at first, but it's working. Blake Corporation had been hounding the property owners around John's place and he'd received a few notices but no visits. John knew how much the town needed the hardware store and when everyone assumed I was him, I didn't correct them. He's got enough on his plate surviving. He doesn't need developers visiting him at the hospital or harassing him and his wife or thinking his place was easy pickings."

It was the most she'd heard not-John say since meeting him. So many emotions collided at his confession. Relief John wasn't dead. Sadness because he was badly hurt, and way too much interest about the guy who'd drop everything to help a friend.

"What happens when he's ready to come back to Home?"

"Everyone will either get over it or they won't."

"And your real name?"

"Callan."

"Callan what?"

"Just Callan." He answered, short and to the point.

He seemed to be telling the truth. Could she be sure? She barely trusted herself to know when she was hungry, much less trust her bullshit meter to give her a clue about this man's honesty. And he was hiding his full name. Would she if their roles were reversed? Maybe. She was giving him a lot of leeway for someone who'd just confessed to lying to her. But her instinct was to trust him.

"You'll keep my secret, won't you, Vicky?" He reached for her in the darkness and tucked a loose strand of hair behind her ear. The soft caress awakened an awareness she'd tried to stifle. The slash of moonlight across his features kept them shadowed, mysterious. They were as alone as they'd get, and her body slammed her with messages her brain couldn't track. His intensity made it hard to breathe. He wasn't John. He was someone new. Supposedly a friend. Maybe a really good friend.

"I—" She licked her dry lips and tried again. "I need to see John."

Callan took a step back. The spell broken. The desire she'd glimpsed disappeared.

"Of course."

"As soon as possible," she added.

"I'll talk to him in the morning and make arrangements."

"I have questions."

He crossed his arms over his chest and nodded. "I'm sure you do. I won't answer them. Not right now."

"One more for now. Does my mom know?"

He shook his head slowly. "Only you."

A breeze caressed her cheek, making her shiver in the cold. "Then we'd better get back before she wonders what we're doing out here." She headed back to the fireplace and her blanket with more questions than answers.

"Vicky?" She turned at her name. He hadn't budged from his spot. "You didn't answer my question."

"I'll keep your secret. Unless John says differently."

"Fair enough."

Except she didn't get the impression he played fair. Ever. Then again, she didn't always play fair either. For the first time since arriving, Vicky looked forward to waking up in Home the next day.

8

"*D*on't let him charm you. He's good at his job and has half the town believing he's not the devil." Vicky's mom set a plate of bran muffins on the kitchen table as she lectured and then slipped into the seat at the head of the table next to her.

"Grayson isn't a devil. He's a salesman."

"Same thing in my book." Her eyes flashed with conviction over the rim of her coffee mug. "Eat a muffin, it's a new recipe." Her mother reached over and dropped one next to the donut crumbs from leftovers from DeVito's. "Quinoa and teff flour and no refined sugar. Healthy for you."

Sounded horrible, actually. "I think I can handle a smooth talker." She glanced at her watch and jumped up. "Speaking of, I need to go!"

"But you haven't eaten—"

"No time. I'm meeting him at Jo's in ten." She left the fiber-filled ball on her plate. Why would anyone want a healthy muffin? If it didn't have blueberries or chocolate and loads of sugar, what was the point?

Eight minutes later, Vicky paced the sidewalk in front of Jo's. She'd set the meeting with Grayson the afternoon before. Before she'd found out about the real John. Now, all she wanted to do was see John and get some more questions answered by Callan. Confusion over her feelings had kept her up most of the night. She'd keep the charade going until she spoke with John directly. Face-to-face. Meeting with Grayson and being sold on his company's vision of Home was the last thing she wanted to spend her morning doing. Callan had promised to take her to John that afternoon. Being the person she was, she'd called the VA hospital in Grand Junction and confirmed John was currently a patient there. Callan had told her the truth, which meant her instinct to trust him was spot on. A revelation that skyrocketed her curiosity about what made him tick. Anticipation churned her stomach—thankfully, she'd declined the bolus of bran. It would probably have pushed her system in to some kind of shock. Might as well get it over with.

Walking into Jo's was like walking into her past. Only a few customers were up as early as Vicky had wanted to meet. The fewer people to see them together would hopefully mean a less gossip being spread.

"I wondered if you were going to come in or if I was going to have to eat a slice of Jo's pie all by myself."

His laugh was good-natured and open—the perfect practiced pitch to put the conversation at ease.

"Pie for breakfast? You should have said so sooner." She slid into the booth seat opposite him.

"Something wrong?" He nodded toward the door and his view of the sidewalk beyond. "Or should I be worried my company is so abhorrent you have to psych yourself up to talk?"

"Just giving you time to get comfortable," she quipped.

"Coffee, Queenie?" Jo stopped at her side, pouring her a cup before she had a chance to answer.

"Sure, thanks."

Jo turned to Grayson and topped his off as he held the cup toward her.

"I'd love another slice of your pecan pie. It's truly the best I've ever had."

A quick pleased smile crossed her face before the scowl returned. "I'll see if I have any more."

Vicky smiled. "You've figured out her weak spot."

"She's a tough one. Not the toughest in town, but I'm patient."

"I bet." She took a sip of coffee. "I'm not sure which one of us deserves the ugly stare of death from Mrs. Tuttle at the counter behind you, but I'd be worried if I were you."

He peeked over his shoulder and back to Vicky. "I'm not even going to try with that one. She scares me."

"Speak of the devil." Vicky took another quick sip as Mrs. Tuttle marched their way.

"I can't believe this. First your mother wants to ruin this town with her silly wedding business and now you're out with . . . him . . . The enemy!"

"Mrs. Tuttle, I assure you, I am no one's enemy," Grayson replied smoothly.

"We," Vicky pointed to Grayson and then herself, "are not out, out. And my mother's not trying to ruin the town."

"We'll see about that." The older woman's gaze flicked

from Grayson to Vicky, pinning her to her seat. "Tourists will ruin Home. Riff-raff and outsiders will be everywhere. My great grandfather was a founder of Home as was your mother's and they'll be rolling in their graves if she—or he—turns this place in to a circus."

Wide-eyed at the hostile outburst, Vicky watched Mrs. Tuttle storm out of the diner. Jo set two pieces of pecan pie between them. "Someone peed in her cornflakes this morning. I wouldn't get too worked up over it, Queenie. We know your momma's fighting for us." She sent a glare in Grayson's direction and huffed off again.

"Well, I guess we know how she feels about the situation." If Grayson was ruffled by the confrontation, he didn't show it. If anything, he seemed to enjoy the attention. Amusement lit his smile as he shrugged. "Everyone's got an opinion. It's my job to show people why our offer is what's best for the town.

"Okay, let's hear it."

"I think you'll be surprised at what we're offering here. Despite what your mother may think."

"I'm not my mother. I'd like to hear what you have to say."

"And ask your own questions?"

"Of course."

"Okay, let's speak frankly. Blake's most interested in the property around Home. The Carlisle, Dewey, and Pearce lands make up the majority of the real estate we're interested in. The old bed and breakfast would also be part of the deal. We might even re-open it as a luxury private villa."

"Then why are you pressuring some of the businesses in

town to sell? There aren't many, but what's here supports the whole town and everyone thinks you're going to buy them up and close them down." She scooped a forkful of pie. Delicious and with enough sugar to make up for the healthy muffin she'd almost had to eat.

"The land around town, it's mostly large homesteads and ranches, right?"

"Yeah. Not much to look at except wide-open space between here and the next big town that can accommodate tourists."

"And beyond all that space is a national preserve."

"The scenery is nice, but as far as Colorado goes, there's prettier." Their mountain view was quite a distance.

"Actually, part of what we want is the flat scenery. Once we've got the casino and resort built, the horse track, the family entertainment area with swimming pools, hot tubs, and a heated lazy river along with other outdoor amenities for everyone to enjoy, we won't need the mountains as a draw."

"Oh, I get it now." The full expanse of what they were planning hit her. "That's why you need to buy some of the town. You want to be closest to the federal land so nothing can come between you and it."

"The town, especially your main street, lies in the middle of the land we want. Land we're willing to put a substantial amount of money toward purchasing. What we've suggested moves only a few homesteads and businesses."

"A few is a lot when we're talking a population of a few hundred makes up an entire town."

"A heavily compensated population that's, let's face it,

one emergency away from bankruptcy," Grayson countered with practiced sincerity.

"With a huge resort full of tourists taking up their wide-open space and raising their taxes and putting a burden on their infrastructure."

"Our compensation is more than adequate for all those concerns."

"How far is Blake willing to go to make this deal happen?"

"I can tell you they've almost reached their limit on what they're willing to spend. But they're highly motivated."

"They? Don't you mean we?"

"I'm only a middle-man. My job is to make the deal, not get personally involved."

"Sabotaging the business the town's trying to set up could be considered a personal attack, no?"

He paused, mid-forkful of pie. "Sabotage?"

"There's been some trouble with the wedding sets being vandalized, causing delays and setbacks."

"I'm aware."

"Pretty convenient timing, I'd say."

"You believe I had something to do with it? Do you have any proof to back up your accusation?" He placed his fork carefully on the plate with a clink, and folded his hands on the table.

"Not yet, but you have to admit the timing works in your favor. One would naturally assume—"

"I can assure you, I'd never stoop to petty vandalism. Money speaks louder than threats, and Blake has authorized me to offer large sums of it."

He seemed genuinely insulted, but then again, he could be an excellent liar.

"Perhaps someone else Blake has sent out here doesn't have the same confidence in money you do. You haven't managed to get as many people to sign on the bottom line as you need. How long are you going to keep asking nicely?"

"Unless you have proof, I'd be careful spreading rumors about Blake in connection with any illegal activity." Grayson leaned forward, his humor gone with the turn in conversation. "They have a large legal department with the resources to pursue potential defamation cases, however small or insignificant."

"See, now I'd call that a threat." Vicky matched his attitude and leaned forward. She was not going to be intimidated.

"I take it as a no on the proof?"

Vicky paused before answering and took a sip of her coffee. Something was off about the way he asked for it. Did he expect her to have something? He seemed almost hopeful, which sparked an idea for a line of questioning if she could just get him to be a little less in control.

"It's only a matter of time before you and anyone else involved are caught. Once the wedding business brings in enough to shore up the town's resistance, Blake will have no choice but to give up."

"Listen to me carefully, any accusation of illegal or unethical practices is met with a severe legal response. Blake never gives up."

That's what they all said.

"We both know this isn't the first time your company has tried to buy out a town." Her voice raised, tempting him to take the bait. "You can say Blake doesn't threaten, harass, or use underhanded tactics to get what they want, but I don't buy it."

Movement in her periphery caught her attention. Callan stood a few feet away, arms crossed, frowning at her and Grayson. Where had he come from?

"Is he going to stand there and watch or should you invite him over?"

"What . . . Ignore him. We were discussing your use of underhanded tactics." She tried to keep him on topic. If she looked at Callan, she'd get distracted, and she'd almost had Grayson where she wanted him.

"No, we weren't." Grayson frowned and cocked his head toward Callan. "Can I help you, Pearce?"

"Is this asshole bothering you, Vicky?" Callan spit the charge at Grayson and stepped closer to the table.

"We're having a private conversation." Grayson answered, a snarky grin plastered to his face.

"Sounds more like an argument." Callan took one last step, reaching the table. Grayson stood to the challenge. Like a gauntlet, Grayson's words caused the reaction he'd no doubt wanted. Great. Now, she'd have to start over with him.

She didn't need a knight in shining armor. "It's fine . . . John. Grayson and I were about finished anyway."

Needling Callan, Grayson offered his most charming smile yet, directing it at Vicky "I'm always happy to discuss business with an informed and intelligent counterpart. I look forward to spending more time on the subject soon."

Callan stepped aside, letting Grayson leave.

Once he was gone, she glared at Callan. "I didn't need

you to come to my rescue." She sat back with a huff and finished off the last bite of her pie. Her anger at Grayson's willful denial of Blake's activities added fuel to her irritation at Callan's bodyguard like attitude. Grayson wasn't a threat to her personally and Callan was as much of a stranger. "I needed to ask him a few more questions."

"Everyone could hear what you were saying. He's not lying about Blake pursuing defamation claims."

She looked around Jo's. A few more tables had filled up since she'd sat down and, of course, every freaking eye was on them. Okay, maybe she'd pick a more private place for a conversation next time.

"Coffee, John?" Jo called from her usual spot behind the counter.

"To go, thanks." His attention split from her long enough to catch a breath. She'd warmed up to digging into Blake's background with Grayson and had to shift gears to Callan, who disturbed her on a different level. The transition jarred her senses.

"I thought we were meeting at noon?" She asked when he returned his gaze to her.

"I'm only here for some coffee but if you're ready, we can go now."

"You aren't needed at the store?"

"Tyler's covering. I'm free all day."

That news made her earlier irritation at his interruption disappear. "I just need to grab a few things from home. Meet back here in twenty?"

Callan agreed and she left the diner feeling a mixture of excitement and nervousness now that she was going to see the real John from her childhood and spend two hours alone in a car with a virtual stranger. A handsome, mysterious stranger that made her too curious for her own good.

* * *

Callan paced outside the door to John's room and checked his watch one more time. Vicky had asked for him to wait and let her see John alone. Okay. He'd done that. What the hell could they be talking about for a half hour? He swiped at the beads of sweat forming along his forehead. He took a deep breath, willing his heartbeat to slow. Everything was fine. His secret was safe with John. The feeling of needing to punch the wall or take a six-mile run eased as his breathing practice calmed the rush of anxiety.

He raised one hand, ready to knock when the door opened, and Kaylie stepped out.

"You can go in now." She smiled and grasped his forearm in a quick squeeze before dropping her hands. "Thank you." He hadn't flinched at the contact. Preoccupied or getting better, it didn't matter. Kaylie's eyes widened a second before her smile followed.

"What's that for?"

"For bringing her here. He's had a couple of bad days, and she's made him laugh. She's a good one. For you too, I think."

"Don't look at me like that, Kay. She's the mayor's daughter and a reporter for Christ's sake. You know what that could mean for me."

More laughter bubbled out from inside John's room.

"I'm grabbing some coffee to give you all some space. Go

on. She won't bite." She winked and left him to man-up and get the explanations ready.

Vicky turned when he entered, and her smile faltered a bit. But not before she nearly took his breath away. She didn't seem the least bit uncomfortable, sitting in the small hospital room, looking at bandages where flesh and bone used to be. John was laughing, more animated than Callan had seen him in months. Kaylie was right. She was good for John, and Callan would pay whatever price she wanted to see his friend happy.

Vicky fidgeted with the strap of her purse and refused to meet his eye. There was something in the room making her uncomfortable. Him.

"Don't worry, Cal, I assured Vicky you weren't some kind of deranged serial killer."

"Thanks for that." He tried to catch her eye again. He didn't like seeing her stiffen when he entered the room. The ride to Grand Junction had been tense. He couldn't help it. He hated driving, and it took all his concentration. That's why he always drove alone, until this time. He'd put the doors back on, but the open roof and windows made conversation difficult, which would normally suit him, but with Vicky it had felt strange.

"Vicky's been filling me in on the town gossip. I knew she'd be the hardest one to fool, and I was right."

"Why don't you let me tell a few people you're here?" Vicky spoke up for the first time since Callan had entered. "My mom and dad, at least. If there's anything you need, we're here. They'd be hurt to know you didn't trust them with the truth. Why does this have to be a secret?"

The warmth in her voice directed at his best friend

shouldn't have bothered Callan. They'd known each other when they were kids and, apparently, their bond remained. Callan buried the part of him wishing some of that warmth was directed at him.

"It's better this way, trust me." John's face reddened, and his gaze flicked from Vicky to Callan and back. "At least until I'm stronger and out of this place. With Kaylie pregnant, it's better that Callan is handling all the work your mom has been giving him and the store. As me, he fit in naturally. If he'd been a stranger, things would have been different. You know that."

She looked like she wanted to argue but stopped herself. Home was a small town like most others. Strangers didn't get the welcome that a local would. Even one who had been away for decades.

"I get it. When you're ready, my mom would be a help explaining the deception if you get her on board before you come back.

"That's the plan. My doctor says I might need one more surgery if this one doesn't take, then a few weeks of rehab. It will work out. We weren't sure Home was where we wanted to live, but from what Callan says, we think it'll be a good fit. I have to admit I don't remember much of anything that didn't interest a ten-year-old kid. Except your mom—she sounds like she's exactly the same."

"That's for sure." Vicky let the change of subject stand. "Besides, Callan's doing an excellent job as you. But I know everyone will be happy to have the real John Pearce home, with a family too."

"I need a little more time before I can get there and handle Blake's intimidation tactics on my own terms."

"I'll keep your secret. But you can't keep me away. I get to come and visit, okay?"

"Kaylie would skin me alive if I did something to keep you away. She's never met anyone from my childhood."

The affection between the old friends was palpable. They hadn't seen each other in almost twenty years, but he and Vicky acted like no time had passed.

Callan knew John would never look twice at another woman. Kaylie was it for him. But he wasn't John, and Vicky wasn't any woman. When she'd thought he was John, he'd felt the attraction they shared. Was what he'd felt coming from her based on past friendship? Would knowing he wasn't John change how she acted around him?

She's not looking for what I have to offer.

What if he could offer her what she was looking for? He knew better than to be thinking in what-ifs. What if his one strand of sanity finally snapped and he walked into the mountains and never came back? No. What-ifs were not worth thinking about. Never going to happen. She was a political reporter and belonged in DC. He'd promised himself and his old man he'd never set foot in that city. A promise that suited him and one he planned to keep. He couldn't have it both ways. Vicky was either off-limits or he needed to get close to her to make sure there wasn't anything the mayor was hiding about what's happening with Home. What he might personally want didn't factor into this situation. He needed to remember that the next time he waited for one of her smiles to be aimed at him.

The heat in the room started to get to him and the urge to move made his legs restless. He'd been inside the hospital longer than ever before, and all for a single visit. Vicky sat next to John's bed, showing him pictures on her phone and didn't look like she was ready to leave, but he needed to get out. He paced to the window, hoping a clear view would help. Deep breaths and visualization had run their course. His hands were clammy when Kaylie handed him a cup of coffee from the cafeteria. He clamped his jaw shut, willing his hands to grip the cup lightly.

"I'll be back next Monday." All attention shifted to him at the blurted statement. "You can ride with me if you want."

"Maybe, but I'll have to check the weather first. Not sure I could handle the wind-mobile if it's not sunny."

"I told you to bring a hat and a scarf." One thing he could not do was close himself up in a vehicle for a long drive with or without Vicky in the passenger seat.

"It's time for my PT anyway," John said, holding in a laugh. "You can take your squabble back to Home. I'll see you both next week."

Callan scowled at John's obvious amusement.

Kaylie walked them out after a round of goodbyes and gifted Vicky with one of her hugs. "Thanks for coming. It really cheered him up."

"I'll come Monday, but I can visit another day too. Maybe this weekend? Would you like to go to lunch?"

"Oh my god, yes. That would be great. Can't wait to hear more about John as a kid."

Callan practically dragged Vicky out of there. He needed out. A-fucking-SAP. No more chitchat. No more closed off rooms. He hit the door to the stairs and didn't stop until he'd reached the bottom step. Vicky's heels slapped the cool cement of the steps behind him.

"In a hurry?" She wasn't out of breath, but she sure sounded annoyed.

Welcome to the club.

"I have a lot of work to do back in Home."

Liar. He gritted his teeth at the flimsy excuse. He would not beg her to hurry. Barely holding it together, he headed straight out of the hospital and to his truck.

9

Thirty minutes out of town and Vicky could see Callan physically relax. It changed the energy between them in the open-air Jeep. She shivered and crossed her arms tighter to her chest.

"Here, you can use this if you're cold." Callan reached behind her seat with his free hand and dropped a light blanket into Vicky's lap.

"Thanks. I think it got colder while we were there." Pulling her hair back, she secured it into a ponytail with the one grungy hair band she'd found at the bottom of her purse on the drive to the hospital. Tucking the shorter strands behind her ears was the best she'd be able to do to protect her face from the constant whipping. She opened the blanket and draped it over her legs. "I'm fine now."

Callan eyed her over the rim of his sunglasses. "You sure?"

"Positive." Sunglasses helped, the blanket helped, but a roof and a closed window would help more. *Next time, I'm driving myself.*

The quiet gave her free rein to let her thoughts flow about the man next to her. She'd studied his grip on the steering wheel as he'd maneuvered through the traffic and out of town. Face tilted and her body angled toward him kept the majority of the breeze from slamming her head-on. It was also the best view of his profile. Jaw clenched, knuckles white and back straight—there was no way he was comfortable. She checked the speed, a few miles over the limit and steady. As soon as the road opened up and the traffic fell away, he'd relaxed. Bit by bit. He never said a word and Vicky wasn't going to try to start a conversation when his concentration was elsewhere. But looking at him was interesting. The scars under his chin hadn't been that noticeable before, but now, with time to scrutinize him, she could see his close beard hid some that trailed into his collar. How far did they go?

"You're staring."

She was surprised those were the first words he chose after almost an hour of being alone with her. "Sorry."

He shrugged and finally glanced her way before returning his gaze to the road. "Why aren't you asking me any questions?"

"You seemed to want quiet. I was trying to accommodate." Vicky shifted the blanket over her shoulder. It really was quite warm and comfortable now that she'd gotten used to it.

He glanced her way again, his gaze staying on her for a moment. What did he see? Damn sunglasses, she wanted to see his eyes. His set jaw and tight mouth didn't give her enough clues to what he was thinking. Learning to read body language had helped her career, but Callan was still a mystery.

"I like Kaylie." She offered. Safe subject.

He grunted and nodded in the affirmative.

"When did you meet them?" She could play twenty-questions all day. Maybe he'd actually answer some this time.

"Now you're going to ask questions?"

"Hey, you started talking. And it's a pretty simple one, don't you think?" She wasn't trying to get his life story. Yet. Mundane small talk was the easy stuff.

He grunted. Was that a yes grunt or a no grunt?

"Hungry?"

She knew exactly what he was asking, but she answered innocently with, "You met them in Hungary?"

"No, are you hungry?"

She bit her lip to hold back the giggle at his frown. "Always. Except there's nothing between here and Home." Teasing Callan might be a fun way to pass the time and maybe keeping the conversation light would allow him to relax a little more.

"I've got it covered."

She hadn't noticed the dirt road cut off from the highway until he slowed and turned. As far as she could see, the road led nowhere. Southwest Colorado might not be considered the prettiest part of the state for some, but within its plains there were pockets of gorgeous undeveloped areas. Soon, the dirt road gave way to a patch of flattened grass and a trail that led into a copse of trees. He pulled off to the side and parked. "A small stream runs through those trees."

With that little announcement, her stoic driver hopped

out of the truck, leaving her to decide whether or not the small stream was worth the risk of hiking alone with a virtual stranger, even if he was John's friend. She didn't really know John anymore either. Whatever Callan was hiding, though, she felt like she could trust him. Maybe it was the way John told her he was a good guy, or the way Callan handled her mother. Oh, who was she kidding? The one objection she'd had for trying to keep her libido in check had been satisfied. Nothing stood between her and her desire to get closer to the prickly bad-boy new to town. And if she were reading it right, the way he looked at her showed a mutual appreciation she'd like to explore.

Vicky waited a beat before opening her door and stepping out. Trying to smooth her hair with the aid of the side mirror didn't help. Could wind permanently damage hair? She'd have to talk to Rochelle about that.

Walking around the back of the vehicle, she spied Callan pulling a small soft-sided cooler over his shoulder. Stance wide, hands in his pockets, he waited for her. Sex appeal, unintended she was sure, oozed from his posture and rooted her to her spot. He hid more under those sunglasses than anyone had been able to hide from her in years. And had he planned a picnic with her? The guy was prepared.

"Okay, I'll bite. What have you got in the cooler?" He could have anything from beef jerky and beer to wine and cheese to who the hell knew. He'd surprised her a number of times that day. More perceptive than she'd given him credit for, he did save her some embarrassment with Grayson. An all-out argument would have been fuel for the town gossip and not help her maintain her cover. And the way he protected John and Kaylie—her heart ached at the struggle they were going through. She hadn't figured him out, yet. He was a thrilling discovery which sparked more questions.

"Do you ever not ask questions?" He slowed for her to catch up to him at the head of the trail.

"Do you ever answer them?" What could he have against those beautiful things called words?

A smile flashed, quick but real. Outdoors must agree with him. "Come on, if you dare."

The little taunt was all she needed to get moving. Pride had always been her worst flaw, and she rarely backed away from a challenge.

A few feet within the tree line, the trail widened. The temperature dropped in the shade, but the movement kept her warm.

"I recognize this place now. My dad brought me out here for a fishing lesson when I was really little." She looked around the meadow and could see the trail slope ahead. Hearing the water before seeing it brought back a hazy memory. "I didn't really like fishing as much as I liked throwing rocks and trying to climb the trees. A couple locals were out here that day and they all tried to get me to be quiet, even bribed me with cookies. I couldn't do it. Dad didn't bring me again until I was much older."

"Fishing is taken seriously here."

"That's for sure. We went to more public places until I could learn to keep my every thought to myself and not chatter the whole time." Finding a flat, dry place to sit, she laid out one of the blankets Callan had given her to carry. Sunlight dappled through the canopy, the dry rustle of leaves from the light breeze carried enough noise to blend with the slow running water.

"Think you can keep quiet with me?" He stood close for the tantalizing question. She could feel the heat from him and smell the clean, fresh scent of his soap. She shivered, a small thrill of excitement at the unknown raced through her. She turned quickly, nearly colliding with his solid frame. Her foot slipped on the rocky path under her. One moment she was admiring the view and the next she'd flung her hands out to try to catch hold of anything to stop her from falling on her behind.

Instead of hitting the ground, she'd ended up snuggled close to warm man and muscle. Her heart and breath stuttered before banging back into rhythm, but as soon as she steadied, he let her go and stepped back. Not the pulling-her-into-his-arms-for-a-kiss image that had flashed through her mind at the too-brief contact.

Embarrassed at her clumsiness, Vicky dropped to her knees on the blanket and faced the water. A breeze cooled her heated skin, and she pushed her sunglasses to the top of her head, adjusting to the sunlight shining on the water while keeping her eyes off the enigmatic man at her side.

* * *

Callan watched Vicky pull at a patch of grass beside her, picking through the blades. He didn't want to make her nervous. He'd packed the damn picnic as a way to give him time to convince her to keep his and John's identities and whereabouts secret and to go along with the plans. He'd assumed she'd require some bargaining, maybe a little quid pro quo, but she'd already told John she would. Could she be trusted? What if she found out the rest? He should be staying away from her, not letting her draw him closer. He'd let the excuse of needing to know if the mayor was hiding anything keep him from using his own damn sense and here he was with a hard-on for a walking, talking, potential disaster in the making.

He didn't have to bring her to one of his favorite quiet spots. He'd made that decision on his own. Her perfume changed the scent of the place. Her presence changed his feeling about the place too. Now, he would never be able to sit quietly and practice meditating without the image of Vicky, lounging on a blanket, skin warm from the sun, eyes sparkling, looking relaxed and sexy as hell invading every one of his senses.

Moving to the blanket beside her, he knelt and opened the cooler. "Sandwich?" he asked.

"Sure. What do you have?" She smiled over her shoulder at him, and his gut tightened. Natural beauty came to mind. Little makeup, hair back, soft sweater over jeans, a woman had never looked so good to him.

"Ham and cheese or chicken salad from Jo's."

"Oh, I love her chicken salad. Is it the kind with the nuts and grapes?"

Her smile widened at his nod. With nothing to cover his arousal, he placed the cooler between them and sat on his towel. He pulled out a sandwich and a bottle of water and handed them over to her. The sooner they ate, the sooner they could be back on the road to Home.

"Thanks. This is nice. Do you come out here a lot?" She turned back to the stream. Good. Her direct focus was unsettling.

"I do." He took a bite of his own sandwich. "I like it here, and it's a good place to take a break on the drive from seeing John."

"You don't like driving much, huh."

Apparently, Vicky couldn't eat without conversation because she shifted and faced him, legs crossed in front of her, sandwich in her lap, expectation written all over her face.

"That obvious?"

She raised an eyebrow and uncapped her bottle of water.

"I have a little problem with enclosed spaces. Vehicles are a challenge. So, I had mine changed to accommodate, and I drive as little as possible."

She eyed him while taking a swallow of water. He braced for the next why-question.

"Driving's over-rated. People should walk more."

With that, she dug back into her lunch, and they ate in silence. Not the heavy kind that usually built when he met someone new and couldn't avoid the expectation of conversation. Interesting that the reporter in her wasn't always in control.

After a few minutes, her gaze caught his. "Can I ask you a question? I want your honest answer."

And here it comes. "Go ahead."

"Do you really think the town can save itself from bankruptcy with this wedding scheme?"

That wasn't the question he was expecting. His ego in check, he thought about how to answer her truthfully.

"I think it's their only chance, but it's a slim one."

She blinked, eyes wide before nodding and sweeping her gaze to her lap. About the town, he could be brutally honest. Someone needed to be.

"Do you think it can actually work?"

"I'm not a business or wedding expert. I'm trying to run the hardware store and build wedding sets. But from what the mayor has presented to the city council, there's a market worth tapping into. It's a question of how fast things can get going and how long people already hurting can hold on."

She faced the water with a sigh, "Yeah, I guess."

Finished, he tossed the wrapper to his sandwich in the bag and pulled out another baggie.

"Are those Jo's oatmeal cookies?" She balled up her trash and rose to her knees, sitting back on her heels, she held out her hand. "Trade you." He replaced the trash with a couple of cookies.

"Why don't you think it will work?" he asked. Maybe she knew something he didn't. Or maybe he wanted to hear her talk.

Vicky shrugged "I guess, I don't really know. I hope it does. For my mom's sake, and John's and the others who want to live in Home." She pulled her lower lip between her teeth and tucked her hair behind her ear. "Sometimes my mom's schemes backfire."

"She was the only one to stand up and come up with a possible solution. At least it's something. A reason to fight."

"Do you think Blake will really have to forfeit if their investors go a different direction before the deals are done?"

"That's what your mother says, according to her source."

"Do you know who her source is?"

"Nope." She hadn't confided that any more than she'd told him who the celebrities they were all planning a wedding for were. "She knows how to keep a secret."

"Don't I know it. It sounds plausible though, right, when she explains it. But the way Grayson spoke this morning, he made it sound like Blake never gives up on something it wants. I'm not sure just holding out until their investors give up is an option." She was expressing many of his same concerns. At least in that, they could agree.

The longer he sat next to her, the more he could imagine pulling her into his lap and kissing the lips that had been haunting his dreams. Pushing to his feet, he strode the few yards to the water's edge. The quiet solitude usually calmed him. Vicky had started an itch in him. An itch to feel something besides the constant need for space. An itch to feel someone else's skin under his fingertips, her lips under his, her body against his. Bad fucking idea.

He felt her fingers brush his shoulder. He whipped around, tense and ready to flee at the light touch before his brain registered the action, showing him just how far he still had to go.

She pulled her hand back at his sudden movements, insecurity clouding her features. "Sorry, didn't mean to—"

"We should head back." He sidestepped around her and grabbed his blanket and the bag in one sweep as he passed their picnic spot.

He cursed himself the whole walk to his truck. He'd seen the flash of uncertainty on her face. Way to scare someone, O'Shea.

If he'd thought the drive to Grand Junction was tense, the ride back was worse. He endured probing glances as if he were going to explode, or worse was something delicate to be handled with care. The kicked up speed, and the dropping temps of the late afternoon, dampened any opportunity for talking. Exactly the way he wanted it. Why did he feel like he needed to apologize?

10

*V*icky crossed the street toward the Stitch and Sew where Lily, the owner, waited for her interview to begin. She took a deep breath of the morning air and lifted her face to the sun. It had finally warmed up from the cold snap they'd had, and the golden rays made the landscaping around the park she'd walked past practically sparkle. She peaked in the window of the hardware store and caught a glimpse of Callan talking with a customer. She slowed, but he never looked her way. That was pathetic. She could just go in. He was occupied and she had an interview to get to, but she'd stop in and ask him to lunch when she was done. She hadn't been able to stop thinking about him since their trip to Grand Junction, and her curiosity was killing her.

Vicky opened the curtained door to the fabric shop and stepped in.

"Just a moment." Lily, the store owner, stood behind a large table pinning a pattern to bright yellow fabric.

"No problem," Vicky answered, taking in the store's

details. She hadn't been in since it had changed owners. The lightest scent of jasmine and vanilla filled the air. Rows of bolts of fabric lined one wall and shelves of colored yarn flanked another. Three small circular racks of clothing filled the middle of one side of the large space. The other held a large three-sided mirror and a platform with racks of wedding dresses next to it. Two brocade armchairs and a small sofa surrounded a coffee table and delineated the two areas of the store. The calmness of the space clashed with the confident energy of the woman who stepped around the table to greet her.

"Welcome to the Stitch and Sew, it's nice to meet you in person. Your mom has told me so much about you."

"Thank you. And the same." Vicky motioned to the dominating mirror and dresses. "My mom is thrilled with the dress you've made her. I'm excited to feature you on the blog. Are you ready to get started?"

"I'm a little nervous." Lily fidgeted with folding material and rearranging some of the quilting circle's works on display. She couldn't be more than thirty-five. Petite and fit, a wine-colored turtleneck sweater over a flowing multi patterned skirt and wide belt showed off toned arms and torso. Her cropped hair and deep-bronze skin contrasted strikingly with hazel eyes.

"Please don't be, Ms. Dorset. I want to get a feel for what you provide for the potential bride to be and her wedding party or guests. Just tell me about you, the store, and your designs."

"Okay. First, call me Lil. Ms. Dorset makes me think of my mother."

"Got it," Vicky said. She pointed to a large quilt hanging

from a wooden rail high on the wall. "The color and pattern are incredibly intricate. Did you make it?"

"Oh, no. That's my family quilt. My great grandmother started it and passed it to my grandmother who added several rows of squares before passing it to my mother."

"It's beautiful."

"Thank you. My mom added rows and taught me how to quilt and then passed it to me when I left home."

The priceless family heirloom was the one piece in the entire store that looked old-fashioned. Everything else was contemporary to Vicky's eye. Not the quaint country feel some places had. Lil's gaze followed Vicky's as she perused the space.

"Tell me about the fabrics you stock and what you see as your specialty for theme weddings."

"Let me show you."

Vicky sat in the seating area while Lil disappeared into the dressing area and then came rushing back with a handful of costume samples.

"We've been working on these new patterns for additional themes. Of course, the royal designs are all finished, and your mother's wedding party costumes have been made. With measurements, we can have the celebrity wedding costumes made in a very short time."

She replaced the samples with another set for Vicky to admire and returned again with several dresses in her arms. The techniques the sewing circle ladies had been working on were beautiful and professional looking. The lacework and beadwork rivaled anything she'd seen in high-end bridal shops.

"This is *the* dress." Lil held one up to show off her creation.

The replica Princess Diana wedding dress was an incredible sight. They'd chosen not to try to make the big poufy million-mile-train one, but a simpler version, which was stunning.

"Wow. I have to get a photo of it. Anyone who sees it will want you to design a dress for them. I'm sure of it."

Vicky reached for her camera to snap a few photos, but Lil shook her head and quickly hung the dress on a hook on the wall. "I don't really want to be in any photos."

She looked so uncomfortable as she sat next to her; Vicky didn't push.

"What brought you to Home?"

"I got tired of the hustle and bustle of the city." The pain that flashed didn't match the flippant answer. "I was a costume designer in New York and didn't think I'd find that kind of work again once I left. Thanks to your mother, I'm back to doing what I love."

"What if the town's plans don't bring in the business that's expected?" She had to ask. What did Home need with a costume designer if the theme wedding plans didn't bring in business like they all hoped?

Lil stared at her, thoughtful for a moment.

"When I left the city, I didn't know where I was going to go. Then I came out west and wandered through Home and never left. This place, it's not just a town. It's special. I have faith everything will work out."

No one wanted to talk about a contingency plan. Neither Mike nor Rochelle had one. Lil didn't seem to think she needed one either. It sent another charge of urgency through Vicky.

Lil patted her hand, stood, and motioned to a small rack of garments along a wall.

"These are some of my favorite modern dresses, but we can accommodate most requests."

"They're gorgeous." Lil's craftsmanship was extraordinary.

Lil showed her patterns for period dresses from the renaissance to the sixties and everything in between. From costumes to straight wedding attire, you name it she had a pattern for it or knew where to get it.

"I think this would look lovely on you." Lil unzipped a black garment bag she'd hung on a display hook on the back wall. "It's similar to one I saw in an old wedding magazine from the fifties. I updated the fitting a bit and changed the sleeves to elbow gloves."

"Oh, it's beautiful."

"You should try it on." She gently shook out a cream-colored, silk, straight wedding dress. The strapless, sweetheart neckline and crystal and pearl detailed bodice were amazing.

"I don't know." The dress was simple and stunning. If Vicky could have picked a wedding dress to try on, this would definitely have made the list.

"Come on, I want to see it on someone instead of my dress form. It should be perfect for your frame."

"I don't think so. I'd hate to rip a seam or something." She shook her head and stepped back from the dress, almost afraid to touch it.

"What kind of seamstress would I be if I couldn't fix

that? Anyway, if there's one thing I learned early on in my career, it was how to assess someone's size with my own eyes —everyone lies and sometimes measuring takes too much time. This dress is perfect for your figure. I'll go put it in the dressing room for you."

Vicky took a tentative step forward. There was certainly no harm in it. No one else had arrived yet and it would give her a deeper feel for Lil's talent and probably make the woman less nervous. Five minutes later, Vicky held her breath as Lil buttoned the row of tiny pearls up the back of the dress. "Oh, wow." She turned to see her back in the dressing room mirrors.

"Maybe I should save this one for you?" Lil raised an eyebrow at Vicky's snort.

"I love it, but it's wishful thinking. I'm not heading to the altar anytime soon. Someone else will be a lucky girl to wear this."

"Come with me."

Vicky followed Lil to the big mirrors in front. The natural light brought up the highlights in her hair and the beadwork on the dress. She was speechless.

"Beautiful. Smile." Lil aimed a camera and clicked away. "Nothing will sell this dress better than seeing it on someone."

"Oh my, Queenie! It's perfect." Her mother and Grams stood in the doorway of the shop.

"I think this might be the most beautiful dress I've ever tried on." She couldn't help it. She had to gush. She'd never felt prettier.

"A tall, strong, dark-haired man would look stunning in a black tux next to you too."

Vicky rolled her eyes. "Subtle, Mom."

The women oohed and aahed over her for another minute before she reluctantly headed back to the fitting room to change and await the rest of her mother's wedding party. The loving care these businesses put into every detail was special and personal. Her chest ached with a fierce pride in her hometown. She'd be honored to have such a wedding. She'd just pulled her sweater over her head when she heard her mother shriek. She rushed out at another screech.

"What's going on. What's wrong?" She couldn't identify an immediate threat. What had her mother so upset she was pacing around the sofa, furious. Her grams and Lil stood back, looking at a phone. They held it out to her at her approach.

"I cannot believe I trusted your father with a photographer recommendation. I knew it was a mistake."

"Oh, is this the proof for the business brochure?" Vicky asked, taking the phone and glancing at the photos.

"Oh. Oh, no." Her stomach sank at the images. Was this person even a professional photographer?

"They simply won't do. We can't put those in brochures. I wouldn't even put those in a family photo album."

"And they took so damn long. We have to get a brochure out as soon as possible. We'll have to find another photographer. One who can work fast. And more models. Why did I let your dad plan something as important as this? I knew it was a mistake to let him use one of his fishing buddies."

"I've got to have at least one good photo for the first round of brochures. I just need one or two at most." Her mother got that calculating look in her eye.

"Just a couple. That's all we need. It's a perfect day for some photos in the park."

"A little sunny, but not bad," Lil agreed.

They looked at her. "I do some nature photography on the side. It helps my creative process."

"Okay. Vicky, you're going to put that dress back on, and we're going to get some photos in the park. Lil would you please help us get some useful photos until another formal shoot can be scheduled?" She shooed Vicky toward the dressing room.

"Wait, I don't want to be in the brochure."

"Now's not the time to be stubborn. The dress fits perfectly, and you look stunning." Her grandmother spoke up while her mother made a call. "We just need to find you a groom."

She heard her mother talking to someone about getting the carriage out there before she could object again.

"A groom? Who?"

A shadow broke the rays of the sun streaming through the store window. Callan was walking by. The other three women looked at her and back at Callan about to pass out of view. Her mother rushed to the door. "John! Could you step in here a moment?"

That was so not a good idea, but those photos were really terrible. She'd keep her mouth shut and see how this played out. Would he agree to be her pretend groom for some photos? Doubt it.

Callan stepped in and froze at the doorway, finding four sets of eyes on him.

"Can I help you all with something?" he asked.

"We need your help desperately," her grandmother said.

"Yes, we're in a bind. You're our only hope."

"You're about a forty-four long?" Lil asked.

Thoroughly ambushed, he pivoted from one woman to the next, not knowing which to respond to first. Vicky decided to come to his rescue. "We need you to put on a tux and let Lil take a few photos of us for a brochure. The photos we have are unusable. It would just be a couple." She smiled, trying to soften the request. He immediately stiffened and shook his head.

"Sorry, I can't help you with that." He tried to leave, but her mother stepped in front of him blocking his path.

"I know I ask you for a lot. And you have always met every request—gone above and beyond, but this is important. I have to get some brochures out as soon as possible. The printers are waiting on the photographs. I just need a couple.

"I understand but get someone else to do it."

"But you're here, and you would fit next to Vicky in her dress perfectly."

His gaze bounced from her mother's pleading to her.

"It would only take an hour, maybe. Please."

"Where are these brochures going to go?"

"Just in some local shops here and surrounding areas. Just until we can have another set of professional photos with models done."

"I don't like the idea of being part of advertising."

"What if we don't use your face. We just want your body," her mother said. Vicky bit back a snort at the look he gave her mother at that. "We could probably make it where you're turned away from the camera or something like that.

Right, Lil? Something artistic while maintaining John's privacy?"

"Definitely. Like this." She pointed to some of the dress-maker advertisements in a stack of bridal magazines on the coffee table where the bride eclipsed the groom.

"But in the carriage. And maybe one or two with a costume around the finished part of the cathedral?" Grams added, getting into the excitement of the moment.

"I don't know."

"Good. That's a yes."

Vicky couldn't hold in the laugh at the shock on Callan's face. Every objection was being shot down. Outnumbered, he was ushered in and standing on the platform for Lil to measure within minutes. Callan sure was cute when he was shy. He wanted to be a model even less than she did. Vicky smiled and gave him a thumbs-up at his pleading look. She wouldn't have to corner him for a conversation after all. They'd be pretend married by lunchtime.

* * *

What the hell had he allowed himself to get into?

"Come on, at least try to smile," Vicky coaxed.

"Come over here to the carriage. That's right. John why don't you hold Vicky's hand while she's stepping up into the carriage? Yes, that's good. Smile at each other." The mayor and Lil gave directions, overlapping each other in their enthusiasm for the project.

"We're trying to sell romance here, remember?" Vicky teased. He caught the humor in her voice but didn't feel it himself. He'd rather be dropped back into the middle of a fire fight getting his ass handed to him than pretend to be the ecstatic groom enjoying wedded bliss with his princess bride.

He grasped Vicky around the waist and hoisted her up onto the top step of the carriage. Wide-eyed she looked down at him, a grin tilting the edge of her pink lips.

He held her there a minute, and her breathless surprise pulled to him. He stepped one foot onto the bottom rung of the small three step ladder which moved him a few inches closer.

Cheers and claps interrupted the train of his thoughts, which had been running toward pushing her further into the carriage and taking the reins and driving the horses to anywhere but there.

Vicky laughed and stepped back, out of his hands. "I think you have some fans." He followed her up into the carriage.

"Good, now, sit closer. Half toward each other," Lil called. They moved around each other and tried to figure out what the amateur photographer wanted.

"Vicky, lean in, and John, put your arm around the back and move closer." Ms. Jones demanded from her side of the spectacle. Their impromptu photo shoot was drawing a crowd. The mayor had immediately had the carriage and horses brought over, and by the time he and Vicky were dressed in their wedding attire, a smattering of people stood around discussing what the fuss was all about. An hour later and there was a sizable crowd cheering on every move and making their own suggestions. It was an absolute nightmare, save for the vision sitting next to him.

The horses whinnied and Tom, the horse wrangler

turned driver, quieted them in a soothing tone. "They want to go for a walk now that I've got them all hooked up," he explained.

"Not yet, Tom, we need a few more shots. Can you get out of the way?" The mayor turned her attention back to the models. "John, why don't you get up there on the driver's bench, and, Vicky, you stay in your seat. Lean back, yes, look up like you're running away for a romantic honeymoon."

Callan moved to the front and took the reins from Tom. Tom hopped down and the horses shifted and whinnied. "Whoa," Vicky said behind him with a short laugh. The team shifted again but held still. "You got this, John?"

A hint of nervousness tinged her question. "It's fine. Just stay seated."

He liked the outdoors fine and had spent plenty of time roughing it, learning to like rocks and dirt as his mattress and pillows, but horses were a whole different realm. His father being a senator from Colorado meant the one summer he'd spent with him as a kid he had to take riding lessons, and that was about as much horse-knowhow he had.

Tom spoke slowly and quietly, "Don't you worry now, John. As long as you talk to them real nice and keep a steady hand on the reins, they'll listen for sure. These angels have been through it all, they aren't likely to do much but want to walk you around and get a snack. Pretty much have to drop a firework in their face to spook 'em now."

"Thanks, Mr. Tom. They're beautiful." Vicky smiled at the man who jumped down, leaving them to manage on their own. For the first five minutes, the horses did exactly as he expected.

The suit itched around the collar, and he started pulling at it. "We're almost done. You're doing great." Vicky sounded half like a mom and half like a cheerleader.

"Just hold them steady. That's great." Lil snapped some photos from the side and then climbed on to a ladder one of the spectators had brought her.

"Now, let's move to just under that tree over there. Can you do that John?" He managed to drive the team over toward where Lil had pointed, with Tom running alongside, just keeping up.

"Okay, now do something fun. Tom, can you keep the horses steady and stay out of the shot?"

Tom grumbled under his breath but agreed, smiling at Lil. "Sure thing." He looked up at Callan and winked. "It's best to just agree. I see you got that memo early. It will serve you well."

"Okay, now, John, how about you and Vicky in the driver's seat, and, Vicky, you on John's lap? Let the dress drape over and . . . here, hold these and lean back and laugh." She handed over a bouquet of flowers another person from the crowd had given her.

"Now, remember, you're the princess marrying her prince." Her face reddened at the directions.

Vicky held the flowers in one hand and moved the other toward him for help sitting on his lap.

"You don't have to sit on my lap if you don't want to," he said. They didn't need to put on a show for everyone watching. It was awkward enough just being on display.

"You sure you're okay with it?" she asked. The tentative question rubbed him the wrong way.

"I'm fine. The sooner we get this over with the better."

He pulled on the collar of his suit and brushed the hair off his forehead. She reached over and adjusted his tie.

"You look very handsome." She smiled, and her cool fingers were a light caress where they touched his neck. His response stuck in his throat. She might think he looked handsome, but she was downright stunning.

"Maybe you could take the shawl off for just a photo or two while snuggled on John's lap?" Lil asked.

Vicky rolled her eyes. She unbuttoned the fluffy silky shawl that was draped around her bare shoulders. She shivered and turned her back to him. He moved back and put his hands on her waist, guiding her in the tight space to sit cross ways on his lap.

"Try not to look so—" Lil started.

"Just smile dammit." Mayor Jones yelled to them both. He couldn't help but focus on Vicky's laughter.

"That's great. Wonderful." Lil gave a few more directions, and Vicky leaned back in his arms. He could almost forget reality and enjoy the moment. Her carefree reaction to the ridiculous spectacle they'd become was contagious.

"Perfect," Lil announced.

The crowd began to clap and cheer.

"You did a good thing today. Thanks for being a good sport."

His arms around her waist, her face toward his, he could have pulled her into a kiss. Instead, she leaned down and gave him a hug, squeezing a moment before leaning back and tossing the bouquet toward the crowd. Another round of cheers went up.

A loud screech from above them cut through as the crowd began to disperse. Tom was chatting with Lil a few feet away. A hiss sounded, and out of the corner of Callan's eye, he saw a gray shape fall from the tree onto the middle horse. The horses had been still but whatever dropped onto the back of the middle one must have made an impression because it whinnied. Then the others joined, and they began to stomp. A kitten, he now recognized it, was straddling the horse, four sets of claws digging into the blanket covering it's back. Another screeched meow and it tried to move but then flattened against the back of the horse again with a pitiful cry.

"Oh, no, the poor kitty is scared." Vicky made soft cooing noises to the cat. "It's okay. You're going to be okay." Becoming agitated, the horses shifted again. The more the horse moved, the more the feline seemed to flatten and dig in. "It will be trampled under there if it falls."

"Tom," she called to the owner. He didn't look up, intent on his conversation with Lil. "Do something." She turned to Callan. What was he supposed to do?

"We can't just leave him there." Her voice pitched higher. Callan stood, leaning toward the front of the carriage. As soon as his weight shifted the horses moved again.

Vicky sat down hard on the seat, and he hit his knee on the front board that boxed in the driver. "Son of a bitch." He straightened and then tried to stretch to see if he could coax the stubborn animal to him, but it wouldn't move. "Don't do it." The kitten stood, hissed, and jumped from one horse back to the other and then to the trunk of the tree and ran up it. The horses moved just enough to rock the carriage. Callan started to pitch forward. Vicky grabbed him about the waist and pulled at the same time, he reared back, trying to stop any fall and, instead, landed back on the seat with an oof. She burst out laughing, hugging him. Pressed against him, he could feel her body shaking with laughter.

"You two need to be still. That's enough playing now," Tom called to them as he grabbed the mouth bit of the horse closest to him, and the team immediately settled down again. He helped Vicky out of the carriage. The damn kitten up in the tree took that moment to issue the most pitiful cry from over their heads.

"Oh, no, the sweet baby is stuck. Look at it."

"That thing isn't any more stuck up there than it was on the horse a minute ago."

He looked into Vicky's pleading eyes. "We can't just leave it out here. It's getting cold at night. What if it's lost."

Callan looked around for some backup. Tom was leading the horses and carriage away, Lil and the mayor had their heads bent over the camera, and the crowd was leaving now that the show was over. He looked from the cat up in the tree to Vicky again. "What do you expect me to do?"

"I don't know. Don't you have some training for tree rescue or something. Come on. Maybe just climb up there and get it. I'm sure it would be very grateful."

He assessed the tree. "Just climb up there? In a suit?" She nodded and smiled, eyes wide and pleading. All over a damn kitten that probably had a full belly and a warm place to sleep. He tested the strength of the first branch he could reach and sighed. It might hold him. It was about three below the one the cat now clung to. The others he wasn't so sure about. At least it was the biggest oldest tree in the park. He shrugged off the suit coat and undid the tie, handing both to Vicky. If he was going to fall out of a tree, he was going to at least be comfortable.

He hauled himself up onto the first branch and crouched. His prey watched as he got closer, climbing onto one branch up and then the next. He crouched and scooted as far out as he could without going further onto the branch that swayed under his weight. "Come on you, let's get out of here." He took another step out and was within inches of the kitten, who watched him with a wide-eyed stare. His fingers touched the tip of a paw and tried to grab a hold. The furball meowed and then stood, swirled around, and flicked its tail in Callan's face before scampering back toward the trunk and climbing from one branch to the next further down, now below Callan. "Little bastard." He cursed under his breath. For every branch Callan lowered himself onto, the cat jumped further down.

"That's it. You're making him climb down. Come here, baby."

On the last branch, it jumped down and circled Vicky's feet, rubbing against the dress around her ankles. Callan jumped to the ground and managed to grab it by the scruff before it ran away. It meowed in his face. "You and I are going to have a talk about that little display."

His answer was a meow. "Don't be mad. Poor baby was just scared." Vicky cooed to the little beast and scratched its head while Callan held it in his arms and did a quick check for injuries. "*She's* fine, by the way."

By then Vicky's mom and Lil had noticed what was going on. "You aren't bringing that home. You know your dad is deathly allergic."

They looked at Lil. "Oh, no, I can't be bringing pet hair

into the costume room. If I made a bride or groom have an allergy attack on their wedding day, I'd never forgive myself."

Vicky looked at Callan, and he saw the question on her face. "Uh-uh. No way."

"Just until we can find her a good home and make sure she's not lost or sick or anything."

The cat must have figured out it had a sucker on the line because it chose that moment to meow and bury its little head in the crook of Callan's arm.

"Okay, but just until we find a place for her to belong."

Vicky's smiled and leaned closer, "Thank you."

The way she said it made it sound like she was thanking him for rescuing a busload of children or something. He hadn't even done anything. The damn cat had managed to lead him up the tree and down without ever needing any actual help. But he wasn't going to argue; the look on Vicky's face was enough for him to keep his mouth shut.

"These photos are going to be perfect for the brochure." The mayor's proclamation brought him back to reality.

"And where are these brochures going to go?" he asked again.

"The printed ones will be local and a few shops in Telluride and Grand Junction, and, hopefully, we got at least one or two good shots for the website for now, until another shoot can be scheduled." His gut clenched at the thought. He didn't recognize the civilian he saw in the mirror every morning; odds are his father wouldn't recognize his profile and beard if he was standing right in front of him. But Telluride was a little too close for comfort. He'd have to trust this wasn't the biggest mistake he could have made. Callan had made the choice to return to

Colorado and help John. He'd have to live with the consequences.

"If we're done here, I'm heading back to change. I've got work to do." He had to move. Playtime was over. He nodded to the mayor and Lil and headed toward the fabric store where he'd leave the suit and change back into his work clothes. Vicky was hot on his heals.

"Hey, you okay?"

"Yeah, just got to get back to the job at hand."

"You really don't want your face shown on those photos, huh?"

"It's complicated." He wasn't sure how to answer the questions she was sure to start asking, so, he sped up, but she kept pace with him.

"Well, whatever the issue is, thank you for doing it anyway. It won't take long for another photo shoot to be scheduled and for our time as models to end." He appreciated her light tone. He didn't want to bring her down with his change in mood. "What are you going to name her?" She changed the topic.

"You don't want to know the first name that came to mind."

"I bet."

"Probably just cat for now. I'll let whoever keeps her name her."

Once back at the Stitch and Sew she held Cat while he changed and then gave it back so she could. The furry beast seemed to be pleased with the situation, purring and sleeping on her lap. She awoke the minute Callan took her back.

"I guess I'll see you later," Vicky said, now back in her street clothes.

"Sure, later," he agreed and watched her walk out of the store. Still as beautiful dressed casually. She was approachable and warm. The kind of woman he could see relaxing on the couch for a movie or snuggled up reading in front of the fireplace. He couldn't be sure he'd be able to take care of a self-sufficient kitten much less have any kind of relationship with someone like Vicky. He needed to make sure any thoughts like that stayed deeply buried.

11

The delightful dream of strong hands running down her back, kneading tight muscles into warm pools of deliciousness had just turned good when an annoying knocking dissolved the fantasy. She was too sleepy to jump right up and see what the hell all the commotion was about. Vicky pushed her hair out of her eyes and yawned. Hushed voices grew louder. When she couldn't ignore it any longer, she stomped down the stairs, pulling an old sweatshirt over her tank top. Her mom and Callan were in the foyer.

"What's going on Mom? Cal—" She broke off and regrouped. "Can I . . . help you with something . . . John?"

"There's been another incident at the chapel."

Suddenly self-conscious at standing in front of Callan in her pj's, Vicky ran a hand over her hair. She'd gone to bed with her hair wet, and the curls were rioting from the neglect. Awesome.

"How bad is the damage this time?" her mother asked.

"Someone tore the doors off and set fire to them. Cut

the fencing in a different area to get in. Took some pieces of the facades. My guy that was watching the place got a little roughed up."

"Oh, no."

"He'll be fine, more of a bruised ego than anything else. He got there late and spooked whomever was doing it. Got a little banged up when he tried to stop the person from leaving." He answered, turning toward her, and sweeping his gaze over her from head to toe before returning to her mother.

"Dammit. We were almost done. Whoever keeps sabotaging us is getting bolder. Blake has someone on the inside working against us and we have to find out who it is."

"This does seem to be an escalation." Vicky yanked the hem of her sweatshirt down over the waist of her hot pink yoga pants she used for sleeping since the bleach spots and worn patches weren't fit for any asana, much less hers. Home alone sleepwear. Or when Jeremy had worked late on a story and hadn't come home. Okay, now that she was awake enough to think about her ex, she needed coffee. Callan's voice stopped her motion toward the kitchen.

"That's not all. They sprayed the grass with some kind of chemical. Someone got creative with the drawings."

"If they were going for the teenage vandal vibe they missed the mark. Did your guy recognize who was there?" If Home was larger she might believe it was teenagers. Of the few in town, there wasn't one that would be able to keep such a thing a secret for long.

"He saw one guy in a mask."

She continued into the kitchen, she needed a jolt of caffeine. Her mother and Callan followed on her heels. This news was very disturbing, but she wasn't sure what it meant in the grand scheme of what Blake wanted.

"Vicky, you need to find out who it was," her mother demanded.

"I can't exactly barge into Blake headquarters and make demands. We know Grayson St. James is stonewalling any further investigation as much as he can. Other than that, I'm looking close to home."

Coffee. Coffee. Coffee. Maybe the chant would drown out the conversation she wasn't awake enough to have.

"You need to get more aggressive. Grayson's not just a pretty face for Blake, but if he likes you maybe you could get more out of him."

"Mom, I'm a journalist, not a cop, and I'm not setting up a sting with myself as bait. Let the sheriff handle the vandalism and now possible assault investigation."

"She's right, Mayor," Callan interjected as they crowded into the kitchen. "This is something the sheriff should look into."

"Listen to him, Mom." She knew the discussion wasn't over. Her mother making plans usually meant everyone should fortify themselves for the inevitable.

"Queenie," her mother began. Vicky held up her hand.

"Uh-uh. Wait. Let me get a cup of coffee."

"Do not—"

"Zip." She held a finger up to her lips in a shushing motion.

"Queenie Jones, that is quite enough childishness."

"I'm ignoring you. Whatever you say you'll have to repeat after I have a cup of coffee in my hand." She prepped the coffee maker to start its heavenly drip.

"Ladies, may I speak?" Callan stood with his back against the island, watching them.

"Of course, John," her mother purred.

Vicky rolled her eyes and leaned on the counter, silently begging Mr. Coffee to work faster. She had to hand it to Callan, there was no amusement in his voice at her antics. It was early, dammit, a nice dream had been interrupted and she'd greeted the man who'd starred in her hot fantasies in the most unflattering pair of pajamas she owned. She could act a little pissy if she wanted to.

"I'll ask around, see if I can get any information about Blake we don't already have. Vicky doesn't need to get any more involved."

What was that supposed to mean? She'd been doing what her mom asked. She'd been interviewing people and writing the damn blog and investigating Blake's public dealings over the last ten years. She had stacks of notes from people in town and had been slogging through file after file on Blake, information she'd managed to gather by calling in every favor Neal owed her. She wasn't going to argue; she didn't need to justify what she'd been doing. Instead, she pulled the carafe from the coffee maker and placed her cup under the drip.

"I've informed the sheriff," Callan continued over the hiss of coffee hitting the hot burner that the exchange produced. "No harm in asking around about any local getting antsy about Blake's offers."

"We already know who's not supporting the plan. They voted no," Vicky retorted.

"Some may have changed their minds, some may have been offered more money." Her mother crossed her arms, tapping the toe of her slipper on the ceramic tile. "I didn't want to believe anyone from Home would do harm, but now, I'm not sure."

Vicky took a good look at her mother. She looked truly worried for the first time since Vicky had arrived. Her mother had been angry at what she thought was Blake interfering in the town's plans, but she'd kept the same kind of stubborn confidence that, in the end, Home would win.

"Then it's settled. You and Queenie work together to find out who the hell is behind these recent events." Her mother's tone offered no discussion. The mayor had spoken, and her will would be done.

"Seriously, Mom, I've got it covered, and I don't need John to help me."

Her mother raised an eyebrow at her. "I thought you were ignoring me."

Vicky pressed her lips together and poured two more cups of coffee. Handing one to Callan, she sighed, glancing from him to her mother and back. "You don't really need to help." Sexy and intriguing as he might be, she was better off investigating on her own, with her own resources . . . and fewer distractions.

"No, you need him. It's become more dangerous," her mother protested. "I don't trust these people."

The phone rang as they sipped their coffee in a silent standoff. Her mother left the room to answer it in the office, leaving Vicky and Callan to declare a truce.

"I can take care of myself." She'd faced threats from people who had the power to ruin her and hadn't backed down. She wasn't going to be afraid in her own hometown.

"I'm sure you can." His tone suggested he agreed, but

who the hell knew? Damn inscrutable, non-emotional response again. This man kept his thoughts as closed as a whistleblower on their way to work.

"You're not going to let me handle this alone, are you?" She eyed his stance. Arms crossed, feet slightly apart, shoulders tense. Could he look more stubborn?

"Nope." He unfolded enough to snake one arm out and reach for the mug he'd placed on the counter. His gaze locked with hers. Her breath caught as his lips touch the rim. Why did he have to be so deliciously attractive on every freaking level? She turned away, disgusted with herself. Lusting after a complete stranger. Well, not complete. They were friends by mutual association. Like that was a real thing. She blew a breath into her own mug, hard enough to almost spill some over the side.

"Careful, you don't want to burn yourself." Yep, definite amusement this time, a smile in his words and a hint of shine in his eyes.

"I can take care of myself, and I work better alone." She needed this conversation back on track before she did something she'd regret, like kissing him to feel his coffee-warmed lips on hers.

"Your mother's worried, and it's smart to prepare for the worst."

"Don't forget, I grew up here. I've known the people of this town my whole life."

"You know people are the same everywhere, the good and the bad."

She didn't like the idea someone might want to hurt her or her family. Maybe having Callan as backup wasn't a bad idea. As long as his help was on her terms.

"Fine. We'll start at The Walrus. Tomorrow, tonight rather, is karaoke night and almost everyone over twenty-one and under ninety shows up."

His gaze slipped from hers. If she hadn't been staring straight at him she would have missed the slight paling of his face.

She frowned at his clenched jaw and took another sip of her coffee. "Not a fan of karaoke? I can go myself."

"It's fine. I'll see you there." He turned and left the kitchen without saying goodbye.

"Where's John?" her mother asked, returning from her office.

"He left. Who was on the phone?"

"The sheriff. They didn't find anything else at the scene except some beer cans and cigarette butts out where you kids used to build bonfires."

"Holler's Hill? Kids still go there?"

"Most everyone pretends they don't know, but it's as safe a place as any for them get away from town. There's nothing conclusive to tell us if it was some kid's idea of a prank. And now we have more to clean up during the town workday tomorrow."

It was a place to start. "Between karaoke tonight and the workday tomorrow, we should be able to rule out any suspects in town. I'll try to reach Grayson for another chat." Vicky glanced at the clock on the wall. "But not for another three hours. Damn, Mom. I'm going back to bed." And ponder what made big bad Callan scared of a little karaoke. Or maybe she would just think about his hands.

· · ·

A few more hours of sleep never came, and after spending the day helping her dad clean out part of his garage, she was more than ready for a night out. She'd left Home before she'd been able to become a regular at the only bar in town. Back then, the owner hadn't had much in the way of management skills. Or housekeeping skills. The place had been a dump. Sly, the new owner, was different. He'd really cleaned up the place and the improved craft beer selection didn't hurt either.

Every unattached woman within twenty miles of Home had become a regular. Catching a glimpse of Sly's muscular, over-six-foot frame, she could see why. It sure wasn't the quality of the voices displayed that evening. Where the women went, the men followed, and most everyone seemed to be enjoying themselves. She'd finally settled at the bar after making the rounds of small talk with everyone she knew, which made up ninety percent of the patrons. She'd had lots of conversation about the town's plans but little to show for it regarding her Blake investigation. Whether behind the venture or against it, none had been afraid to express their opinion. And no one in there rose to the level of suspect for the vandalism so far.

"Another round?" Sly asked from his station behind the bar.

"Sure, why not." She'd nursed the last one until the final sip had been warm.

"Not going to sing anything for us tonight?" He took her empty mug and poured another draft beer, settling the cold beverage and dry coaster in front of her.

"I think you want your customers to hang around, not run out with their ears bleeding."

His quiet laugh could be heard in the break between beats before his expression smoothed to a pleasant handsomeness. Here was another man as hard to read as Callan except something about Sly was more approachable. Not that he had ever shown any interest in wanting to be approached, and she'd only met him a couple years earlier. He'd become a fixture in town almost immediately upon buying The Walrus, and the town treated him as if he'd always been there. She wondered briefly if he could possibly be on Blake's side, but his reasons for supporting the mayor seemed legitimate. He claimed to like Home the way it was, and for him, that sounded right.

She checked the time on her phone. Damn Callan. He had another few minutes to either respond to her text or get his ass to the bar. If he didn't show by the end of this round, she was out of there. Not like she needed him, but if he said he'd show, he should show. She tried to ignore the disappointment. This wasn't a date. This was a job for her mother. And she definitely didn't care that she'd walked all the way there in a short-ass skirt and shoes that were not made for a cold Colorado night unless there was someone actually looking. No use drowning her self-pity when she should be finishing up what she was there to do. DC was calling—she couldn't afford to forget her life was on hold.

"Here comes another one." Jessie, the waitress who'd taken Sly's spot behind the bar, raised her voice to be heard over the latest round of Dolly and Kenny's "Islands in the Stream" being belted out by the school principal and his wife of forty years. Neither looked—or sounded—anything like their idols, but sure tried. Him, with the silver beard, and her with the blonde wig. At least they knew all the words.

She spied the man heading toward her in the mirror behind the bar. He was one of five men who'd huddled around a pool table in the corner of the spacious bar and the third to approach her and the empty seat beside her. Damn Callan for standing her up. She'd sipped her way through at least three Shanias—going old-school was popular. Then there was Pink, surprisingly better coming from Karen, the pharmacy clerk. She had decent pitch but after a pitcher of margaritas too many, the lyrics were a problem. Then Preacher Cooper hogged the stage with three Willie songs in a row. He sung each in the same pinched monotone he spoke his sermons in. With each sip of her beer, Vicky added up the points—Callan was not winning.

She recognized the latest taker as Randy, the older brother of one of her former classmates. He was also the one who'd creeped out all his little sister's friends by hitting on them when he was in college and they were still in high school. Balding, but trying to hide it with too long hair and wearing enough cologne to make an impression, the man boldly eyed her from chest to knees and back before leaning against the barstool next to her.

"Hey, Queenie, me and the boys got a little bet going. I say your mom's going to sell out as soon as she gets the big wedding she wants. Jimmy over there says she'll stick around and take whatever money Blake gives her so she can rule over the little bit of Home that'll be left when all the rest of us have been squeezed out. Which way is the mayor planning to screw us?"

He'd leaned closer to be heard but yelled the accusation-laced question loud enough for the guys to high five each other in a show of pack like stupidity.

"Sorry. My mom has higher standards than to screw someone like you."

He swayed closer before straightening and using the bar to balance "That's how the Jones family usually does it, isn't it? Take what they can get and run." He went on as if he hadn't heard her response. "Or maybe I should give up hauling freight and use my truck for hauling flower bouquets?"

"Leave her alone, Randy. No one wants you at their wedding anyway. Keep driving cross-country. Your wife will thank you."

Randy's narrowed gaze held Vicky's for a heartbeat before swinging in the direction of the speaker. A shiver raced over her skin. This winner might look like another drunk, but he couldn't hide the true hostility she saw in his eyes. Vicky didn't recognize the woman's voice, but she was thankful the man's attention had shifted.

"Gary," he yelled loud enough for everyone within sight to turn their way, "tell your girl to mind her business, this conversation is between Vicky and me."

She didn't need to put up with this. It was too late for conversation, and she was tired. Randy was the last straw. By the time his focus had swung back to her, she'd grabbed her purse and was ready to push her way out of the crowd. Her exit was blocked by another wall of flannel and beer breath. Her stool and the bar at her back, Randy to her left and new dude in the way, she was stuck.

"Tell me that again."

Gary must not have agreed with Randy yelling about his girlfriend. He pushed his way between Vicky and the offending son of a bitch. She saw her window and scooted back on to her seat to move around the men.

Sly had disappeared from sight. She glanced around for help. The crowd edged away but no one stepped forward to defuse the situation.

Where the hell had Sly gone? These two looked like they were ready to do some damage. Jessie pulled a baseball bat from behind the bar. Her hands shook and she didn't look much like she'd have what it took to scare the fight outdoors.

"I don't know where Sly went."

"I'll take care of this, you find Sly." She reached for the bat, and Jessie handed it over with a relieved nod. "I'm sure he's just in the back."

Turning back to the male standoff, she scooted around the men facing off.

Fine. Vicky walked over to the karaoke setup and unplugged the main amp powering all the speakers. The instant the sound died, she expected everyone to look her way. Only about half the customers did. The other half had their attention on the two idiots and the band of merry men who looked to be making bets on the outcome of whatever testosterone fueled duel they were about to witness.

She held the bat over her head. "Gentlemen." She had to call out again, a little louder when no one looked her way. Perhaps unplugging the mic had been a mistake.

"Hey!" She yelled, raising her voice as loud as she could. "You all know me. And you all know who my mother is. I will not hesitate to use this bat on this precious karaoke machine if there is one punch thrown inside this bar. Am I making myself clear?" She shook the bat over her head.

There were a few murmurs but by then the majority of the crowd was looking her way. She held the bat over the karaoke machine with both hands, daring anyone to try to take it from her. Karen from the pharmacy stormed over to one of the men behind Gary and pulled his arm.

"Come on, Steve. You know she's crazy enough to do it, and I don't want to wait for a new one before I sing again."

Once one left, the others behind Gary shuffled away. She wasn't sure if it was her threat or that Sly was heading their way, but it didn't matter.

Vicky walked over to him, and Sly took the bat with a nod. "Thanks for not busting anything up."

The karaoke machine was intact, but her evening was officially busted.

"See you another time. I've had enough fun for the night."

Callan paced a few more steps from his perch across the street from The Walrus. He was acting like a fucking stalker. What the hell was he doing? He'd been watching the bar for the last two hours. He'd clocked everyone coming and going. No one he didn't recognize had entered. He'd been there when Vicky had arrived but had remained across the street. He couldn't make himself go to her. He'd watched her, dangerously sexy in a tight miniskirt and a soft looking sweater that perfectly enhanced everything underneath to a T. With an imagination born from abstinence, he had a crystal-clear picture of every curve in his head. She was a present he couldn't have, candy he couldn't taste.

He should have explained or made an excuse not to meet her there. He'd walked off the anxiety that had built as he debated just going home. Snippets of conversations among couples or groups filtered to him before a blast of music would rush out as they opened the doors. He'd only flinched the first few times until his body and mind got on the same page and expected the quiet night sounds to be interrupted with blasts of laughter, voices, and music. He could live with the progress he'd made.

Could he go inside for a limited chunk of time? Yes. He'd been there before.

But it had all the negatives he tried to avoid—crowds, loud music, the expectation of having a relaxing time. Relaxed wasn't in his wheelhouse right then, but it might be in John's one day. The bar was the last place he wanted to spend any significant time as John. He'd already been shown incredible generosity from the people of Home that should have gone to John, he didn't want to taint the bar with the lie they were living. Even if it was necessary.

Maybe it was for the best. Vicky could handle asking around about Blake. Hell, she was one of them. He was the outsider. If anyone could get people to talk it would be her. She didn't really need him.

The excuse sounded good in his head but didn't do a damn thing to dampen the sharp desire she'd fired in him. He was royally screwed. Fuck it. He had to go in.

He reached the double doors as both flew open and a small crowd of people streamed out.

"Randy always has to ruin a fun night."

"It was all Queenie's fault. Why'd she have to keep bringing up her mom and the weddings?"

It was the mention of Queenie that made his pulse jump. The expected blast of music and sound didn't filter out. Adrenaline kicked in. What if Vicky was in trouble?

Two steps inside, he spied Vicky tossing a baseball bat to Sly in front of the bar. What the hell? The dance floor and stage to the right was half-filled with people standing around staring at Vicky. What had he missed?

He reached her in a few strides.

"Good to see you in here, John." Sly greeted him with a nod. "Want a beer?"

Vicky spun around and glared at him.

"Now you show up?"

"Are you okay?" He eyed her from hair to boots before meeting her fierce gaze.

"Me? You're concerned about me?" Crossed arms and raised eyebrows emphasized the sarcasm of her words but they didn't reassure him that she was unhurt.

"What happened?"

"Nothing I couldn't handle." She sidestepped him and shrugged away his hand on her shoulder.

He hadn't meant to come off as overprotective. He was supposed to apologize and get the hell out of there. He had to take a moment before following Vicky as she stomped toward the door.

"Looks like she's not that into you, John."

He'd only met the guy who spoke once. Randy something. Asshole category but harmless. Or was he?

"Shut it, Randy, and don't come back if you can't keep from starting a fight every time you're in here." Sly's cold order from behind the bar got the man to move.

Callan wanted to punch the pasty bastard for his smirk,

but instead he stared him down. He might feel better after a little tussle, but he wasn't sure he'd be able to control himself and the much-needed adrenaline release. The man shrugged and sauntered back to a group around the pool table.

"See you another time." Callan called to Sly and left in the direction Vicky had. He owed her an apology. The best one he could come up with before catching up with her anyway. He'd worry about his terrible lack of awareness another time.

He rounded the corner of the building to the back parking lot, expecting to find Vicky at her car. He scrubbed a hand over his face. She'd only had a couple of minutes head start. Turning a full circle, he didn't see her anywhere. Goddamn it. He did the only thing he could do, he started walking to her house. She couldn't have gone far. His eyelids had felt heavy while stalking the bar, reminding him of his lack of sleep. Now outside in the dark, hunting for Vicky energized him and all tiredness fled.

"Following me?" Her voice broke the silence of the sleepy town at night and carried all the way to him.

When he'd spotted her a few blocks ahead of him, he stopped himself from jogging to catch up. It took several blocks to get within earshot, yet she'd spoken to him without even turning around.

"It's not safe to be walking around at almost midnight. Alone."

"You do it." Her voice quieted for her retort but held plenty of sting.

"We still don't know who's sabotaging the wedding sets, and we don't know how far they're willing to go to get the town to give up. It wouldn't hurt for you to take a few more precautions."

She stopped midstride and turned to him, hands firmly on hips over a wide stance. "I didn't expect to be walking home alone. Since you seem to prefer to walk instead of drive, I stupidly assumed you could walk me home. That's what you do isn't it? Walk around all night?"

He didn't stop until he was close, almost chest to chest. "I'm here and walking you home, so half your night is going as planned. I'm sorry I didn't get there earlier."

"If you didn't intend to go tonight, why'd you agree to it in the first place?" She looked up at him, her chin lifted defiantly. The moonlight turned the blue of her eyes to liquid silver, drawing him in.

How did he explain? "I did intend to go." He hesitated but had to push through. She deserved some truth. "I have a hard time in crowds and with loud music. You've probably guessed that." She nodded but kept quiet.

"I've been a few times, but—"

"If it's too much, it's too much. You don't have to explain.

"I really did intend to go in earlier. It wasn't until I got there, that I hesitated."

"But you could have called or texted. I would have understood."

Damn, he didn't want to see pity in her eyes. "It's more than just my fucked-up brain. I can work around that. The Walrus is the only bar in town. John deserves to have at least one place to go that isn't somewhere I've spent a lot of time in as him."

He watched as she seemed to evaluate his excuse. One

step and he could be the one nibbling the glossy pink pout of a bottom lip instead of her. He ached with the need to touch her. Her mouth opened slightly before molding into a straight line. He'd caught the flash of arousal in her eyes before it disappeared. He should let her take the first step, but patience was not one of his virtues.

"Apology accepted. This time." She turned back toward the direction of her mother's house. Frustration gnawed at his reserve. How could she turn it off instantly?

"Any suspects?" Maybe a change in subject would do them both some good. She'd thought about him walking her home—the possibilities that brought up were worth some thought of his own.

"No one there tonight."

"You sure?" She'd been right about the turnout for karaoke. At least a third of the town's population had filtered in for a song or two. He'd avoided the area around the bar on karaoke nights because of it. Perhaps that had been the wrong move.

"There was enough booze and beer going around. If anyone in there knew anything about the vandalism, I'd have heard about it." She shrugged and pulled her coat closer around her. "Everyone was happy to talk about their opinion of the town's makeover. And what they thought of my blog. Seems I have to work on getting the ambiance of Home right."

"They'll come around. Your style of writing is different than what they're used to from the *Home Daily*."

"I guess that's true. They'll find someone better suited once I'm back in DC."

He matched steps with her around another corner and

onto her street. He didn't want to think about DC. Either her returning or his own connections to the place. That was a surefire way to ruin his mood. He focused on Vicky instead. They were as alone as they'd been in his car, but outside he was clear-headed, and the only tension was from his own body begging him to get closer. He couldn't help noticing her lips every time he looked at her face. Full and soft, they pulled to him along with the way she scrunched her nose when she smiled or laughed. Every emotion played across her features, drawing his attention to each detail.

"That leaves who for the next step?" He kept his opinion to himself and tried to keep the conversation on the task the mayor had given them. Those other thoughts would have to take a back seat for now.

"It's got to be someone from the developer's office. I can't think of anyone in town who would deliberately destroy another person's work, even if they didn't agree with it. Everyone knows the sacrifice that went into what the town has done thus far. Maybe it's kids, but that's a lot of work for a prank, and where the hell would they have hidden anything they stole? Not too many places around here without someone noticing."

"Sly and I are putting cameras up around the sets and businesses as soon as we can. That should have been done first thing."

"So was it coincidence or planned. How well do you know your guy that was late?" Vicky asked.

He had to admit, it was convenient. "I vouch for my guys, but I don't believe in coincidences. Whoever it was either lives here and is playing spy for Blake on the side or Blake's not involved at all."

"Perhaps Dewey? He tried to get you . . . John . . . to sell."

"Or he's a convenient target to keep us from looking any deeper." It was something Callan had been contemplating. How far would Blake go to keep suspicion off them if the town had more trouble than it could handle. How many innocent people would be caught in the crossfire?

Vicky frowned and bit her bottom lip. "I can't see Mr. Dewey doing something like that. He might want to sell his land, and he might be pissed you're holding it up, but if that were the case, he would be better served destroying the store or John's house or something. Especially since you've been spending a lot of time out there, so I hear, anyway."

"It suits me." The unasked question hung in the air. He refused to take the bait. He'd used the same excuse often enough it was almost the truth. He didn't sleep comfortably at John's house, but he'd been renovating it. Only sleeping a few hours a night had its advantages.

They stopped at the walkway leading to the front steps.

"Goodnight, Callan. Tomorrow, don't skip out on the workday. Everyone who wasn't at karaoke tonight should be there."

"I'll show up, I promise."

He didn't want the night to end. He wanted to talk to her more. Outside. Under the stars. Where he could breathe. "One question before you go. Why does everyone call you Queenie?"

"John didn't tell you?"

He shook his head. He hadn't thought to ask.

She stared at him a moment. "Well, you know my mom's kind of obsessed with the royals?"

"Figured, given the sets we're building."

"My full name is Victoria Alexandra Mary Elizabeth Jones."

"Okay." She eyed him for a moment, as if waiting for him to get the joke. "And?"

"The names of the last four Queens of England."

Understanding dawned and a smile tugged the corner of his lips.

"Vicky Alexander is your pen name?" His smile widened.

"Don't laugh. It's not funny. As soon as everyone found out at school in third grade, I got the nickname Queenie and it stuck. Even after being away for years, I will always be Queenie Jones, crazy Mayor Jones's daughter."

"You're Vicky Alexander to me. I didn't know Queenie."

Vicky's smile widened and his heart jumped. His mind seized as she leaned closer still and placed a kiss at the corner of his mouth. Her breath was warm and her perfume sweet, all he had to do was move slightly to kiss her fully. She glanced up at him, almost shyly. The tightening in his chest eased a fraction. She hadn't questioned why he didn't go into places with people around. She hadn't questioned why he walked everywhere and almost never drove. Her acceptance and openness stoked his desire to be near her.

Her breasts brushed his arm as she moved in front of him and placed her hand on his chest, leaning a fraction closer with agonizing slowness. His gut tightened in an involuntary clench. He stood as still as a sniper with a target sighted. He didn't breathe, didn't make a noise as blood rushed in his ears. His focus was on her gaze locked to his, her mouth less than an inch from his.

The heat of her hand on his chest burned through the material until warmth radiated to all parts of him. With more hunger than he could control, he closed the minute distance between them and captured her lips in a kiss.

Her welcoming sigh didn't help him regain control. Focusing on the taste of her, he let everything else go. She gripped his shirt, and he shifted, sealing her mouth to his. Cool fingers slipped into his hair. Arms locked around her waist, he gathered her close and fitted her to him as he deepened the kiss. It felt better than anything he'd fantasized. Her mouth opened under his and their tongues collided. Sliding his palms down her lower back, he cupped her curves.

Dangerously close to losing control, they separated slowly. Seeing her breath come out in quick puffs between soft, swollen lips was an invitation he'd take on the devil himself to accept, but he couldn't. Not outside, not in front of her parents' house. He waited as her focus cleared, and she eased her grip on the back of his neck, sliding her hands down to flatten her palms against his chest.

"If you aren't going to kiss me again, you should probably let go of my ass."

He unlocked his arms from around her and she took an unsteady step back.

"Nothing to say?" She'd matched his stance, but her expression was unreadable. Her earlier openness was gone, replaced with a watchful expectancy.

Stunned at the intense heat one kiss generated, he didn't know what to say.

"I'm not apologizing if that's what you're asking."

"Hell no, you better not." A spark of irritation flashed across her face before settling into a smirk.

"Good because I wasn't going to. You liked it."

"You liked it more." She turned toward the walkway to her front door, grinning at him over her shoulder. "Good night, Callan."

For a brief moment, he forgot about everything and grinned with genuine amusement. As soon as the door closed behind her, reality set back in. He couldn't take things any further. He wasn't prepared to. With anyone.

Taking the long route home, he walked until the taste of her faded. The feel of her against him wouldn't leave his mind. She'd fit perfectly and every curve had been an invitation to explore.

He walked for over an hour before his desire cooled enough that maybe a cold shower and some invoices would clear his head enough to sleep.

One thing he was sure of—by the time his head hit the pillow—some things might be worth the pain.

"Well, well, an artist too, huh?"

Callan turned at Vicky's greeting. Her open smile made his gut clench, it had been too damn long since he'd felt anything close to attraction, and he found himself wanting more time with her and less time alone. She'd become some kind of fantasy, and the more he told himself not to go any further than the kiss they'd shared, the more he wanted her.

"I'm a man of many talents." He returned her smile. She faltered a step but didn't stop until she was standing next to where he sat.

"Did you paint all the details on this whole thing? It's amazing." Hand in a wide salute, she shaded her eyes from the sun and studied the facade that had been placed around the building.

"Most of it. Ms. Green, the art teacher at the school, helped too. It's good to have something to copy from." He held up a sketch and photo of the real thing. "It's not as amazing as you think. We had a company print a giant poster of the outlines and we go in and paint over it to give depth and color."

"Still, it's beautiful. The stained glass looks real."

"Some of it is. We placed a few real windows where picture windows had been and added identical stained glass. When the sun shines in, it will look even more realistic."

He'd enjoyed painstakingly painting the outside of the movie-set pieces as if they were as important as the inside. More than the heavier work of remodeling the permanent buildings. Vicky's appreciation was evident, and pride swelled at her interest. Here was something he could be open and honest about. The wall between them was thinnest when they were outside, with no one around.

"What's on your mind?" He put down his brush and paints and stood. He wasn't one to question good luck. She smiled at him again and rational thought flew out the stained glass window.

"I'm thinking the hill is right over there."

The hill? She cocked her head, a flirty smile on her pink, shiny lips.

"An excellent observation, Ms. Alexander." He glanced over her shoulder and back to her. Heat rushed through his system. "I've heard of its interesting reputation. Are you suggesting a visit?"

She glanced back toward the clump of trees hiding the not-so-secret make out place and raised an eyebrow at him. He didn't need another hint. The pretty pink blush staining her cheeks was all the encouragement he needed. Tugging her hand into his, he pulled her close for the short walk.

He felt like a teenager, sneaking off to the woods. He hadn't felt actual excitement like this in a long time.

He backed her up against the first tree they came to, unable to wait for another taste of her sweet lips. Cupping her cheeks, he tilted her head and sealed his mouth to hers and explored every delicious corner, taking his time, until she melted against him.

She moaned and rocked her hips, stoking the heat that burned between them. Her eyes fluttered closed, and he let himself get lost in the feel of her against him, her mouth under his, her fingers kneading his shoulders.

"I see we weren't the only ones thinking along these lines, Camille," a man's voice said.

Vicky pulled back from Callan's kiss hard and smacked the back of her head against the tree. "Ow!"

Callan was slower in his reaction, pulling his hand from under her shirt, palm still tingling from caressing the hard tip of her nipple through her bra. Entangled like horny teenagers, he hadn't heard anything but the rush of his blood and Vicky's sweet sighs until the voice interrupted them. His brain shifted back in gear when she smacked him on the shoulder. He let go of her leg at his waist and steadied her before turning his back to let her straighten her clothes.

Her grandmother and an older man strolled a few yards away. "Oh my god, Grams. What are you doing out here?"

"Well, hello, Queenie dear. And John. Pleasant day isn't it?"

"Yes, ma'am." He returned her wave as the older couple walked right past them.

"There's a crowd making its way here. You might want to keep that in mind before you continue," Grams tossed over her shoulder.

Callan laughed. "Thanks for the heads-up."

Vicky kicked at his calf with the toe of her boot.

"Want to take this indoors?" He might have been able to let her go in the face of her grandmother, but he was far from finished. He didn't even flinch at the idea of dragging her to his apartment and keeping her inside and away from the eyes of everyone in town for the rest of the day.

Vicky's voice brought him back to reality. "Did Mr. Purdy call my grams Camille? And thinking along what lines?"

"I'd say your feisty Grams has a boyfriend." Callan leaned toward her, resting his hand on the trunk next to her head and slid his lips over hers in a sensuous tug-of-war, lightly sucking on her bottom lip before releasing. "I guess the Hill isn't a secret make out place anymore. Maybe we should pick somewhere more private next time."

Vicky shifted the hem of her shirt back in place and pushed her fingers through her hair. "We should talk about that."

He could see the regret building from her stance. Here it comes. What had he thought would happen? Did he think she'd jump at the chance to fall into his bed? She was the first woman he'd met that made him want to get out of his head, but that didn't mean she felt the same.

"I want to sleep with you." She fidgeted with the sleeve of her blouse, shifting from one foot to the other, her gaze swept to the ground before meeting his again. "And I think you want to sleep with me."

"Just sleep?" Warring messages hit him at once. Hell yes, he wanted to sleep with her. Straightforward was his usual preference, but this was something else. This was hiding.

"You know what I mean. I want to have sex with you."

Her gaze slipped away from his to peek over her shoulder, as if expecting another surprise visit from nosy people.

She shifted again and crossed her arms over her chest. She wanted sex—nothing else. Was it easy for her to shut it off and keep herself separate? He'd been doing it for over a year, and it was a struggle every day.

"Just sex, no strings. Is that what you're trying to say?"

She was telling him she wanted exactly what he wanted —yet anger surged at her casualness, as if she were scheduling a hair appointment.

"Exactly. I mean, I'm not planning on being around long. And, well, I'm sure you—"

She paused, her eyebrows drew together as she studied him a moment. She took a deep breath and continued. "You and I are not looking for more, right? So, we could maybe agree on some ground rules."

He swallowed the attack of pride or whatever the hell it was that made him want to argue with her about what he may or may not be planning, knowing she was right, however disappointed he might be. A no-strings thing, while it lasted, was all he should want.

He pulled her to him. She didn't resist and he took the opening for a slow, deep kiss until she was clutching at his shoulders and making a sexy hum at the back of her throat. She stepped away slowly, and he didn't want to let her go but it wasn't the place or the time to continue what he wanted to do. "Can we talk about this more over dinner? Tomorrow, my place?"

He'd be wherever she wanted, whenever she wanted. He'd almost screwed up the best thing that had happened to him in years.

"That sounds good. I need to get back to the work or I'll never hear the end of it." She gave him a quick kiss to the cheek. "Looking forward to tomorrow." She whispered before walking away.

He spent the rest of the workday with one eye on the actual work and another on Vicky as she moved from one group or project to the next. She was never far from his sight or his thoughts. She wanted one thing from him. One thing he was more than willing to give.

* * *

Callan woke from his nightmare with a jolt and sat up, his legs entangled in sweat-soaked sheets. He scrubbed a hand over his face and closed his eyes against the memories that had played out in the fractured and distorted dream. What had started as a pleasant fantasy of Vicky by a stream, on a soft blanket, her sun warmed skin under his hands, had warped. It turned violent and devastating, drowning his subconscious in images of burning metal and searing heat. Too restless to sleep anymore, he got up. Four a.m. wasn't too early for a workout. Maybe a round with his boxing bag would clear his head. The thudding rhythm of his fists slamming against the one-hundred-pound heavy-bag drowned out the sound of metal scraping metal that continued to ring in his ears.

"Fuck. This. Shit." Callan punctuated his last three swings before dropping his guard. Stripping the tape from his fingers, he paced the apartment, waiting for his heart rate to drop and the exhaustion-born trembling of his hands to ease. His knuckles would be swollen and sore, but the exercise helped.

"Hey, John." A heavy-handed knock accompanied the call and the already cracked open door pushed wider. "Sorry to drop by so early but I needed to speak with you privately." Sly's voice echoed into the apartment.

"Is there a problem?" Callan slowed his pacing and faced the bar owner.

"No problem. The cameras came in and I'm setting a few up before anyone opens this morning." Sly leaned against the doorframe, not in or out, waiting on Callan's invitation.

"Come on in." He motioned to the bar stools at the counter. Pulling a bottle of water from the fridge he offered one to Sly.

"No thanks, got any coffee?"

"Out of luck on that one." Callan shrugged and guzzled the last of his water.

Sly looked around the apartment and back to Callan. "You alone?"

"What do you think?"

"Just checking. I've heard some rumors."

"What's on your mind." Callan didn't care what rumors the bar owner had heard, he wasn't in the mood for town gossip.

"I talked to Deputy Hayworth for any updates."

"Let me guess, no information on the vandalism." Callan leaned against the counter and crossed his arms.

"You'd be right."

"Hayworth isn't giving up though and the sheriff gladly handed him the investigation. He's on board with suspecting Blake. He's also agreed to help guard the sets. Between us, him, one of the other deputies and your crew, we should have enough bodies to keep someone stationed until we can figure out a better plan."

"Good. I'll talk to the mayor and see if she can offer any kind of payment for the volunteers."

"Maybe you can get her to tell you more about what Blake's planning. She's got to know more than she's saying. She probably knows who in Home would be the likeliest to be our vandal. She just doesn't want to admit it."

"Maybe." Callan stayed noncommittal on what the mayor may or may not know. He'd been thinking the same.

"Anyway, it's the cameras I stopped by to talk to you about." Sly slid a pocket knife out of his jeans and slit open the tape on the box he'd brought and pushed it toward Callan. "These are yours and an extra set for Mr. Singleton's storefront and one for the end of the alley on his side. I can help you set them up—maybe tomorrow morning, early. The fewer people who know they're there, the better. I've got the park, my bar and the rest of my side of the block almost covered."

Callan eyed the sleek, compact cameras and components.

"Going to tell me how you got these at such a discount?" Wherever Sly had gotten the equipment, it wasn't from any regular catalogs. This was state-of-the-art beyond basic business security systems.

"Perks of my old job looking for bad guys. Don't worry about it. This one's on me."

Sly was fairly new in town himself, a few years he'd said. Even so, he was someone Callan had come to trust as an ally for John. He didn't push. Didn't overstep. Acted as comfortable behind the bar as he probably was in front of it having a beer and watching a game. But Sly had a hard look. The kind that told Callan he was searching for or running from something big. Either way, it wasn't his business. What they had in common was an investment in the future of Home. Neither wanted to sell out or see Blake move in. Simple and straightforward reasoning.

"Whatever happens next will hopefully be caught on video. The Main Street feed will come to my central system, but each business will have direct access to their own feed as well as viewing it remotely. Some systems will overlap to cover neighboring businesses, but not fully. We need a few more sets to get all the angles on the main businesses and the park access areas."

"It's the waiting that's a problem."

Sly agreed with a shrug. Callan popped four ibuprofen and rolled his head from side to side. His workout had helped ease some of his anxiety and knowing the cameras were going up was a huge security concern taken care of, but that didn't dispel the constant undercurrent of worry.

"So, Vicky. She's back in town. The mayor has her working some angle." Sly didn't usually circle a topic if he had something to say.

"And?"

"And . . . maybe she'll tell you."

Callan eyed Sly as he leaned against the counter, his smirk saying more than his words.

"Hey, info travels fast around here. I'm the only bartender in town. Means I hear the most gossip. Tongues are wagging about you and her spending some time together."

"I've known her since I was a kid. We're old friends."
The lie felt heavy and stiff.

Sly nodded, "Uh-huh. Okay. Whatever you say."

His guest rose and headed to the door. "I'll stop by in
the morning to put these up."

"I'll be here."

"You're up early, Mom." Vicky walked into the kitchen and kissed her mother on the cheek. "Coffee on already? Bless you."

Her mother didn't respond from her chair, where she sat angled to look out the window.

"Mom?"

"Huh." She turned slowly. "Oh, yes, coffee. I don't think I've had enough this morning yet." She gave a short laugh and shrugged off Vicky's concern. "We'll be leaving for Gram's doctor's appointment in Grand Junction in about an hour, can you be ready by then?"

"Sure. Are you okay?"

"Of course, I'm fine. I have a lot on my mind."

"Do you want to talk about it?"

Coffee in hand, Vicky sat at the kitchen table. Her mother's expression changed from far away to sharp and present. Whatever she'd been thinking was locked up and the mayor was back in control.

"How are things with John?" Her mom countered.

"John?" She choked on a sip of her coffee, sucking it down the wrong pipe.

"Please don't get distracted. You and John are supposed to find out who's behind the vandalism. Any leads?"

"Not yet. Not real one's anyway."

"Oh, come on, you two have to have done more than kiss in our driveway the other night."

"You saw?" How had her mother not have brought it up before now? She really was preoccupied.

"I happened to be up, not the point. What about yesterday? You had all day with most of the town in one place. Feel like letting me in on what you and John have been doing if you haven't found a lead yet?"

"I've been digging through public records on Blake's dealings for the last ten years, and so far, nothing has jumped out. A few lawsuits are pending, and the complaints run the gamut from pay-scale disputes to upper management fraud. Again, nothing too out of the ordinary for such a big business. They have several subsidiary companies out of Denver that concentrate on resort investing, like what they're trying here, and infrastructure contracts." She took another sip of her coffee. She'd not found one thing proving anything illegal she could take to the authorities or even anything to take to Grayson for leverage.

"Well, keep looking. There has to be something."

"I told you my colleague Neal from the *Chronicle* has been helping me sift through their dealings. I'm not sure we're going to get far going that route. I think we should try to get at Grayson. Some things he said the other day had me thinking."

"He's a wolf, Queenie, don't you get sucked in by his charm."

"No, it's almost like he was hoping I had some proof that Blake was behind the vandalism. I can't imagine why though. Even if we proved it, what would the harm be to a company that big?"

"They're behind it, but you're right. That won't move the needle on making them back off or getting help from law enforcement."

"What about your source inside of Blake Corporation. Anything new there?"

"Nothing." Her mother sighed and clasped her hands together on the table. "A friend from high school was a temp for a few months but is done now. Maybe you could get Grayson to tell you what's going on with the investors? If he's got some problem with his employer, he could turn into a mole for us."

"That's a long shot." Vicky pulled the ponytail holder from her hair and ran her fingers through the waves. Just as frustrated as her mother at the lack of anything to pursue. "The blog traffic is picking up though. That's good news."

"And the brochures will help when we get those in a few days. I've got permission to leave them in my favorite art and gift boutique in Telluride. The owner is a friend, and she says she gets a lot of traffic from the famous crowd that likes to visit. It wouldn't hurt to have more than one celebrity decide to make Home their wedding destination." As if invigorated by the positive thought, her mother stood and pushed her chair to the table. "Getting those photos up on the website needs to be your number one priority today while I'm in the appointments with your grandmother."

"You know it's a pain in the ass that I have to go to a whole other town to get better bandwidth for uploading photos."

"I know. What can I say? That too will improve one day."

Her mom dropped a kiss on her forehead. "Now, I'm going to get dressed. There's some biscuits staying warm in the oven."

Biscuits? Since when did ultra-health nut Mayor Jones bake biscuits?

She spied the DeVito's bait bag in the trash. "Oh yeah."

Snagging a couple to go with her coffee, she headed upstairs to get dressed.

An hour later, Vicky settled her briefcase and laptop next to her in the back seat of her mother's SUV. The ride to Grand Junction would take a couple hours and she could finish the update on the sets and get the weeks business highlight written up. Everything was ready to publish as soon as she had the proper Wi-Fi speed. It would be helpful to know who the celebrity couple who'd already booked was so she could focus the blog a little bit more on the reason behind what they were doing. Even if she didn't come out and say who was getting married, she could target it without being obvious. Maybe have some of her media contacts that do celebrity gossip pick up some hints.

There was only one person who knew the identity of the secret couple, and she was buttoned up tighter than a nun in church.

A little snooping was in order, which would have to wait until after their girls-only day trip and her dinner with Callan. Butterflies flapped delicious little flutters when she thought about finally being alone with Callan. No distractions.

Would he cook for her or pick something up? Nerves made it difficult to concentrate. She hadn't been on a date with someone new in a long time and Callan was . . . intense. Her attraction to him was off the charts compared to what she'd experienced before. The fantasy of one-on-one time with him was distracting, not to mention the anticipation that was probably going to kill her. Was she ready? She only had to remember the feel of his body against hers and the way he kissed. Yes. She was ready.

The drive was more pleasant than expected. Her mother and Grams were able to catch her up on some of the gossip she'd missed. They had some excellent suggestions for changes to her articles. If there was anything these women could do it was highlighting the positive and hiding the negative. By the time they'd reached the city limits, she was ready to upload and impressed with the results. If they managed to get Blake to back off and gain some experience in the wedding venue department, Home could make their business something really special.

"I'll be at the Starbucks up the road. Call me when you're done." They parked outside Gram's doctor's office and Vicky took the keys from her mother.

"It shouldn't take too long, then we can have a little shopping time. There's the best little boutique in downtown. Maybe an early lunch before we go?"

"Sounds great."

Vicky moved into the driver's seat and waited for her mother and grandmother to head into the clinic. She'd have time for a nice visit with Kaylie and John before picking the women up.

Arriving at the hospital early, she settled into the coffee shop in the lobby for a latte and some work. Blogs uploaded with time to spare, she spent a few minutes watching the bustling crowd of patients, families, and employees.

Coffee shops, whether in a hospital or on the corner, used to be one of her favorite places to write and work through a story. The constant movement helped her keep pace with the thrill of a scoop and the tedious work that went in to checking facts. The reading, the phone calls, the researching—all the details she'd prided herself on including in her articles. All gone and out of reach for now. She might have investigated and reported on illegal or unethical behavior, but that rarely meant active or dangerous fieldwork. As shy as she'd been as a kid, often hiding behind a book, she still hid, but behind a computer and phone.

Hiding wouldn't work any longer. She'd need something big for Stan or another magazine to give her a chance. Her mother's genuine worry and the real, but unprovable threats from Blake had gotten to her. She wouldn't leave Home until something was resolved. Then there was Callan. She didn't know what to think about him. The depth of their wild attraction was better left unexplored. Keep it simple. There was no need to complicate something that neither of them was prepared to follow through on. He was lying to a whole town about his identity, and she'd be gone with the first opportunity that came her way.

Hot mocha burned a line down her throat from taking too big of a swallow. She'd make a plan, keep her cool, and work. She had two, maybe three more weeks in Home. By then, someone else would be in the spotlight, then she could move on quietly, get a place to stay, and put her reputation back together. One big scoop and she'd be forgiven.

It's not the news you made, it's the news you make that counts.

A few other customers stood in line. Some bought lunch items, some coffee. Several in hospital scrubs or typical Coloradoan student wear. One man was short, his face hidden by the rack of snack offerings in her way, but she could hear him loud and clear. The suit pants, long coat, and expensive shoes were not your typical hospital dress code. She tried to picture Callan buying a pair of those loafers and snorted, almost sucking coffee up her nose.

Loud-talker wasn't paying attention to his surroundings and reached for his coffee in his rush. He cut off a man in scrubs as he turned with his tray of drinks topped with mounds of whipped cream. The collision was comical. Scrubs guy managed to save his tray of goodies, but Loud-talker fumbled his cell and his coffee tipped, dripping down the front of his shirt and pants. Scrubs guy had at least a foot of height on him. He shrugged as an apology and walked away.

She caught a clear view of Loud-talker's face while he grabbed handfuls of napkins to soak up some of the stain. She stared. Something about him was familiar. From where? She definitely recognized him. He passed her and she caught a bit of his conversation.

". . . Senator Fletcher can't be there. He's delayed for at least another week. Yes. The hearing's been postponed until next month."

Senator Fletcher? That's where she knew him from! His

rude aide, something Lewis. He'd interrupted her conversation with the senator at a fundraiser and then refused to schedule her any time with him for an interview.

"Mr. Lewis?" Vicky stood and called to him when he pulled the phone from his ear, catching his attention with a wave and a smile.

"Yes?" He pushed his phone into his pocket and met her gaze.

"Hi. I'm Vicky Alexander. We met at a *DC Chronicle* fundraiser a few months ago."

He rocked back on his heels before steadying and balled the coffee-soaked napkins in his fists.

"I thought you weren't working for them any longer. How did you know where to find me?"

Why was he hostile? "I . . . I'm visiting family."

He paused for a split second before dipping his chin. "I have to go."

"But—"

And then he was gone. Not very politician-like. Maybe he was worried about a patient? Anxiety can turn a low-grade jerk into an even bigger ass. Her radar was buzzing. He'd recognized her, so why the brush off? And why would she have been looking for him?

She had a few minutes before Kaylie and John expected her. Enough time to get Mr. Lewis to talk to her. Whatever had him suspicious was more interesting than wedding search terms and uploading photos of Dot and Dom's skin refresher.

A stumbled upon opportunity? Maybe. She wouldn't know if she didn't follow him. Snooping was her business.

She caught sight of him in the lobby as he headed out

the front doors. She followed his route but lost him in the parking lot. He'd disappeared fast. Maybe a car was waiting for him? Well, damn. There had to be a reason behind his behavior. If she was reading more into it, she'd find out in a few. A quick text to a few contacts back in DC about any gossip involving Fletcher or his aide might prove to be something interesting. Grand Junction was a long way from Washington. Giving up for lack of another direction, she headed to the elevators and John's floor.

"Hey. Knock, knock," Vicky called before walking through the open door to John's room.

"Hey to you. Callan with you?" John sat up in the bed, pulling the covers over the freshly wrapped knee.

"Not this time. I'm in town with my mom and Grams. They're running some errands. Kaylie said it was okay to stop by."

"She'll be right back. Thanks for calling and talking to her. She's been missing her friends from back home."

"My pleasure. She has lots of questions about Home, your dad's house, and the store. I think she'll love it there."

"How are the town's plans coming? We've been keeping tabs on the blog."

"Good to know. Just need a few thousand more people keeping tabs on it, or I'll never get to leave again."

"That wouldn't be so bad. Maybe Callan will stick around too."

The thought didn't seem bad on the surface. John's the only person she could ask for some insight into Callan. Awkward or not, she had to try.

"Has he always been so complicated?"

"Complicated? Yes. But there's no one I'd trust more to

have my back. He's a good guy." John paused, his probing gaze seemed to look right into her soul. "He needs to find someone who won't let him push away."

How was she supposed to process that? He wasn't pushing away. If anything, they were going to get much closer.

"If there's one thing I've learned the last few months, it's sometimes, everything would feel easier if I didn't have any one else relying on me. Then those days when I want to give in, I wouldn't have the guilt. If I didn't have Kaylie to fight for, pushing me to get better, I don't know where I'd be. Callan needs someone to push him to fight the darkness." She didn't like to think about her friend fighting just to be there with his wife. Adding in the possibility he might lose it all on the gamble her mom and the town were making was harder still.

"The prick finally left—" Kaylie stopped when she saw Vicky sitting in her chair. "Oh, hi!" She set a tray of food on the bedside table and gave her a warm hug.

Vicky swallowed the lump in her throat and tried to clear the tears pricking the corner of her eyes. She returned the smile and hug, Kaylie's warmth lifted her mood instantly.

"The prick? Everything okay?"

"Huh? Oh, nothing. Just one of the staff. It's nothing." Kaylie shook her head and smiled. "Tell us something good from Home."

"Status quo as far as things go." Vicky answered, not wanting to go into detail about her own worries. Her problems were nothing compared to what they'd endured—she needed to remember that more often.

"I'm glad you came." Kaylie eyed her before sitting next to John on the bed. "Are you okay?"

"Very okay. John's giving me some good advice." Vicky pulled out a small package from her purse. "This is for baby Pearce."

Kaylie opened the small wrapped gift.

"Oh, it's adorable." She held up the red and black striped onesie with Daddy's Girl embroidered on the front over a row of ladybugs. "Kelsey Grace Pearce will love it."

"What a beautiful name." She made a mental note to have a few more things made with those initials. Baby clothes shopping had given her a weird kind of pleasure.

"Named after Kaylie's mom." John smiled at his wife. and the love in his gaze was enviable.

Vicky hadn't spent much time worrying about her ticking clock before but walking into the baby store and being surrounded by all the adorableness had brought her lack of a real relationship into sharp focus. A family of her own had always been a "one day" kind of assumption easily put off for the next big career break. What was it about baby clothes or pregnant friends that made her think about starting her own family? She kind of needed a few things first. Like a father for the children. A home. A job. Seeing the love radiate from Kaylie for John and for the baby she carried, brought attention to the big whopping area of her life currently full of disappointment, which then made her feel pathetic and ungrateful.

After visiting and promising to come back when she had more time, and a few more hugs, Vicky left them to their day.

A senator's aide acting suspicious this far from The

Capitol definitely pricked her curiosity. If she uncovered something new and newsworthy, Stan might go to bat for her one more time, or she'd have something to go to another paper with. A quick internet search didn't reveal much. Maybe she'd found a scoop waiting to be had?

A new plan formed as she drove to wait for her mom and grandmother. Her professional career options were limited, but at least she had a possibility where a week prior she'd been out of ideas.

She dialed a number and waited for it to be picked up through the car's Bluetooth.

"This is the only time I'm picking up. There better be a good reason you're using my investigator."

His terse greeting threw her off. "What if I brought something good. Would they give me another chance?" She didn't need to beat around the bush with Stan. He knew exactly what she was asking.

"Depends."

"On?" She sat on her hands in the car, her heart racing. After he'd given Kristen of all people the follow-up piece she didn't know if he'd talk to her at all.

"On timing, on the subject, on what else is cycling that might make what you did look like nothing more than an amateur mistake." Her heart sank at her editors quick run-down of what she was up against.

"Should I worry about any more articles linking me to the fall out of any Standridge employees?" She was still humiliated that they'd highlighted her reporting in the article in the first place.

"No, that was enough to give them cover. You've been beaten up over it, and now they want it swept away. I'm giving you two minutes. What've you got?" At least that was one good thing.

She quickly highlighted the possibilities she saw with Senator Fletcher. She held a breath when she was done. Colorado was his home state. His aide being here didn't really mean anything. Yet.

"I assume Neal is going to take some time to work on this for you too?" Stan asked.

"Just a cursory glance at what's on the senator's agenda." She assured him, letting the breath out slowly.

"I'll say okay to this but only because your Standridge guy didn't die and only because you turned out to be mostly right. If you ever do that again, the paper will never allow you to write for them. You understand?"

"I got it. I'm on thin ice."

"More than thin. The board is talking settling with Standridge. That means you cost them money. It doesn't matter that the controversy also sold papers. You're in the red. Thinner than thin, with a crack coming your way."

"I promise. Only sure things this time."

He hung up with a grunt which was more than she usually got. She had one chance to make good. If there was nothing going on with the senator, she wasn't sure where she'd go after that, but this was the chance she needed to get her professional life back on track.

Her personal life had certainly picked up. A fling it might be, but Callan wasn't some boy-toy she'd flippantly thought she'd find to get over Jeremy. He overwhelmed her when they kissed. He made her as nervous as a teen on a first date but also challenged her to stand up for what she wanted. She'd come out and told him she wanted to have a no-strings fling as if that was perfectly normal. When she was with Callan, she didn't worry about what anyone thought of her or who her mother was or what she had to prove. With him, she could be Vicky with no heavy expectations from either one of them mucking up a good thing rather than Queenie.

He was a distraction for sure. A good one.

Callan glanced at the old clock hanging over the hardware store's door as if looking at it would make the time tick by faster. He'd spent most of the morning on paperwork and then rearranging the back stock in the storage room. After a small morning rush of customers needing supplies to finish their projects, he'd had no one but a graffitied Prince Charles to keep him company. Tyler would arrive soon and then he could get outside and finish painting Westminster Abbey. He'd have to stay busy to keep his mind off the date he'd planned for the evening and the disturbing phone call from John.

His father had actually sent someone to talk to them in person which was a new tactic. He'd have to stay out of Grand Junction for a while and probably Telluride, where his father liked to spend time. His years in the military and wanting nothing to do with his father's public life was reason enough to stay off any social media, and his issues with being around people made it easy to stay out of any photos. Even if his father stooped to hiring a private investigator, they wouldn't find much but an old address. They could stake that place out for as long as the checks cashed and never find him. He needed to not get caught in person at the hospital and then deal with whatever happened once John was back in Home.

He had much better things to think about. Like Vicky and some one-on-one time with her. If he thought about it anymore, he wouldn't get anything done the rest of the day. As it was, he'd spent half the night planning it, dreaming about it, and all-around obsessing like a fucking idiot. If he didn't get his head on straight, he'd look like a desperate freak ready to jump her the moment she made it through the door. Desperate or not, little else made it past the buzz the night's potential events caused.

They'd shared a couple of incredible kisses and she'd come right out and told him she wanted to have sex. Every inch of him agreed with that desire. It was the best damn idea anyone had shared with him in a long time. He'd enjoy what they had, while it lasted. What more could he do?

The door closing pulled his attention away from his fantasy and back to reality. He'd been standing with his back to the open door; the realization sent a chill down his spine. He was really screwed if he was letting himself be that vulnerable.

"You're late—" Turning, he expected to see Tyler, but the man standing in front of the now closed door was twenty years older and twice the size. The man who'd been with St. James and Dewey a few weeks prior. "What are you doing here? Barnes, isn't it?"

"Glad you remember me." The quiet southern drawl did nothing to detract from the man's show at intimidation.

The man looked around the store before stepping away from the door at his back and toward Callan. He'd wondered when the first real warning would arrive and was surprised they'd sent someone alone.

Callan assessed his options as the man took another few steps into the store. Definitely carrying on his ankle. Probably under his coat too. He outweighed Callan by twenty, maybe thirty pounds, but a lot of that was turning to flab around his middle. He'd start with the nose—red and blue veins spider-webbed over the skin. Big, but not fit. If the subtle limp was from an old injury, his knee would be vulnerable. Callan let the man take the lead on how their interaction would go as he catalogued his options. "Alone this time?"

"St. James has other work to do. I thought you and I could chat."

The man neared the register counter. He walked as if his size didn't slow him down, calm and with purpose. This guy wasn't playing around. If St. James was the charmer, this was the enforcer. "About damn time you showed up. I was beginning to think Blake had forgotten about me."

"Your town is an important piece of Blake's newest venture. Make no mistake, it's not crucial they buy you out. There are other ways to make it happen. Blake will get the land, they will build, and Home can either go along and everyone get a piece of the pie or Home can resist and go under."

"I haven't seen an offer I can't refuse. Yet. If Blake is serious, they need to show it." He was buying time. Whatever it took to stop these guys.

"This is the last offer. It's your choice, take it or . . ." The man shifted and picked up a glass and silver picture frame from the shelf and studied it a moment, as if testing the weight. "Suffer the consequences." He set it back with a clink that echoed through the store. He moved down the row, checking out the crystal and porcelain items, occasionally picking one up before placing it back in its spot, hard enough to make a noise, but not break.

"You know, I never understood why people buy this kind of crap when they get married."

"Tradition." Callan didn't shift his gaze from the man.

A quick smirk raised the man's cheeks, squinting his eyes before settling back into a bland expression. He nodded and shoved his hands into his pockets before stepping in front of the counter, eye to eye with Callan.

"The town's going under. Blake's building a casino. When we get the land, Home will be cut off. There will be nothing here but Blake as far as the eye can see. Sell to us now, the rest will follow, and everyone walks away with a check."

"Why aren't you talking to the mayor?"

"We don't need her. With you, Dewey, and the Carlisle's, we have the town surrounded. Once that happens, the fight's over. The mayor and the few businesses that want to keep things the way they are can't stop progress if Blake owns everything around miserable little Main Street.

He pulled an envelope from inside his coat and placed it on the counter between them. "Take a good look at this. It's the last one you'll see."

Callan's jaw ached from clamping it shut. Arms crossed, he stood his ground. His visitor pivoted on his heels and walked slowly toward the exit. "Think carefully about your decision and the consequences of your actions."

Breathe. The satisfaction of breaking something or

punching the stranger in the face wasn't going to help John but would satisfy the primal urge beating at Callan to respond to the threats and intimidation tactics.

He followed the man's path out the door and onto the street. Tyler would be there any minute if a customer happened to stop in. He spotted Barnes, a little more than a block ahead, strolling along the sidewalk. Anyone watching would think the man was a tourist enjoying some window-shopping. Callan followed from a safe distance but ducked into the barbershop when the man slowed in front of Rochelle's salon.

"You here to let me shave that beard from your face?" Mr. Singleton rasped the question as he sidled up behind him at the window.

"Not on your life." He answered without turning from his view of the man in front of Rochelle's.

The old man laughed and shuffled to the doorway, looking out the glass, trying to match his line of sight. "If you aren't here for a shave or a trim, you must be hiding from that girl of yours. She's one hotheaded little lady."

"My girl?"

"Queenie. She'll give you a run for your money if you let her. My advice—marry her quick before she gets the notion to go back to the city."

"Uh, thanks. I'll keep it in mind." Callan shot a glance to the barber then back to the street. Their not-so-secret affair hadn't even happened yet, and people were putting them together. That was one part of the small-town life he'd heard about but never experienced until then.

Barnes had moved on to the alleyway next to Split Ends. Ducking out of the barbershop after a hurried goodbye,

Callan crossed the street. Nothing good happened in an alley. One ran the length of Main street behind most of the businesses with intermittent breakthroughs between buildings. He stopped at one of the entrances and peeked around the corner. He could hear Barnes's voice raised in conversation. He followed the sound to where the main alley intersected his route and stopped to listen.

"I told you to stay out of it." Callan recognized that voice. Grayson St. James was arguing with Barnes. Interesting. He pressed against the wall, out of sight, and listened.

"I'm just doing my job." Barnes's snarly response made Callan want to punch him and he wasn't a part of the conversation.

"You're being reckless."

"And you're being soft. This nothing town should have folded weeks ago and the bosses know it."

"I'm handling it. Stay in your lane."

"Or what?"

"Do you really want me to answer that? You're on your last lifeline. Go rogue again and you're out."

"Fuck off, Gray, you don't have that kind of power anymore. I've heard some rumors too. Maybe you should be the one warned off going rogue," Barnes shot back. Callan didn't need to know exactly what they were talking about to know these two didn't like each other.

"Do you want to find out?" The conversation quieted as Barnes and Grayson separated. Callan crouched behind a dumpster until they'd gone.

Callan liked Grayson's gumption. He sounded serious. A rift between these two might be something they could exploit. But that didn't explain why Barnes was in Home. He could still be working with a local in town.

He'd check the block again just to be sure. If Barnes wasn't there to meet Grayson, he might be there to talk to someone else. Callan checked in at the hardware store to make sure Tyler was covering and then headed out again. He needed the walk anyway, if for no other reason than to work off the remainder of the adrenaline and satisfy himself that he'd done everything he could. He wasn't more than five minutes behind the man's stroll through town. If he had any luck at all, he could narrow down his field of suspects to whomever was out and about that morning as a possible contact for Barnes.

He retraced his steps down the alley and stopped at the newspaper office's open back door. Peering inside, he scanned the room, finding it full of shelves, rolls of printer paper, and two overflowing desks.

"Hey, John. What can the *Home Daily* do for you today?" Mr. Baker, the newspaper's owner was the only one inside.

"Is Vicky around?" He didn't know anyone else connected with the paper and couldn't think of a reason to be there.

"Not today. She does most of her work out in the field. How do you like her articles? Great, huh? I tell you, I've had more circulation since she started writing for me than I've had in the last decade. Well, except for election years. You know how it goes, once the vote is decided, people forget there's other news to read. Now, everything's online. Carl was just in here working on a website for the paper. A website for a newspaper doesn't seem right to me. But who am I to stand in the way of progress?"

Nodding was all Callan needed to do to keep up his end of the conversation.

If he'd been talking with Barnes in the alley, Callan would have heard it. Mr. Baker's voice carried throughout the office and projected over the machine sounds coming from the back room where the printers were running.

"Carl been working for you long?"

"Off and on for a few months now. He's kind of our tech whiz-kid, helping with the businesses around town, fixing up their Wi-Fi, building websites, and such. Now that I have Vicky here too, the *Home Daily* has made the leap into the twenty-first century. Hope it's not too late."

"You expect to see Carl again today?"

"Oh, no. He was only here to check on something to do with storage."

He added Carl to his list of potential locals on Blake's side. His access as the town's IT guy would be a win and would give them an advantage. Not as big of a surprise as the argument between Barnes and St. James. He'd have to think about that. There had to be a way to leverage that to Home's advantage. Having no other avenues to explore and the store covered, his mind went straight back to Vicky.

He had no control where she was concerned. Months and months of no attachments, especially romantic ones, keeping his life as simple as it could be given the lie he was living, and he'd willingly screwed it all up. He knew—the first time she'd touched him—he was in trouble. He sure as hell didn't care to get out of that trouble. No, he'd been digging himself deeper with no regrets.

The craving to be close to her, feel her skin, kiss her without interruption, was electrifying and terrifying. He was a man of control and discipline and he'd lost it all. But he wasn't the only one. Her reaction to him was addictive. He couldn't help but smile—a sensation that was becoming less foreign. Hopefully, there'd be no interruptions that night. They'd finally see how well they fit. For as long as it lasted.

14

*V*icky was still running the possibilities for snooping on the senator through her head when she walked up the steps leading to the loft over the hardware store. They were newly sanded and refinished, and there was no doubt Callan had done it all himself. Obviously, he was a man of skill and talent and had time on his hands. Hands that had played a huge part in her dreams every night since she'd arrived.

The door was propped open, and she could hear blues music playing from inside.

"Hello," she called before stepping in. Whatever Callan had prepared for dinner smelled good enough to make her stomach rumble. "Callan?"

She moved farther into the low-lit apartment. A long bar separated the kitchen and eating area from the living space, and a large sliding door opened to a bedroom. Callan stepped out from behind the sliding door, a button up shirt loose around jeans. Black shirt over dark denim was a dangerous combination. He'd trimmed his beard, showing more of his strong jaw. She didn't think about the food anymore, a hunger of another type took over.

A smile tilted his lips, and his gaze rooted her to her spot. He moved with a deliberate grace that had her mesmerized. Standing in front of her, his eyes never left her face. Watching him was almost too much for her system to take. The air around them crackled with intensity. They'd been holding back from the sparks between them too long.

"Hungry?"

"Hell, yes."

His sudden burst of laughter caught her off guard. "Good answer."

The light touch of his fingers as he brushed the hair at her collar sent shivers down her arms, the caress magnified by the warmth of his skin.

She tossed her coat and purse onto the large sectional sofa. If she stared at him any longer, her panties would go up in flames.

He stepped behind her and brushed her loose hair aside and placed a soft kiss at her neck and caressed the length of her arms to the tips of her fingers. The need to lean into him was irresistible, making the contact her body begged for. He didn't disappoint.

"You're beautiful." He captured her hands in his. Tugging her palms to his lips, he kissed each one before turning her to face him.

Fluid and trancelike, she linked her fingers through the soft coolness of his hair, pulling him toward her.

"So are you." Her words ended with a sigh as his mouth closed on hers. The freedom to touch heightened the fever of need and anticipation. She wanted to feel all of him, skin-to-skin. Hard packed muscle flexed as he explored the sensitive skin along her neck. A shiver raced over her when he hit her favorite spot. "Like that?" He flicked the tip of his tongue along the dip of her collarbone.

"Yes."

His lips found hers for another scorching kiss. In no rush, he explored her mouth, ending in soft nibbles, enticing a smile. This was a man who knew how to take his time.

Every nerve in her body tingled with anticipation. He stilled, and his breath shuddered.

"Too fast?" Vicky froze at the thought as she asked the question. She'd jumped into the whole fling thing headfirst without much thought to Callan's feelings. Other than she knew he desired her.

"Never." He gently cradled her face in his hands. "I want to take my time and make every second count."

Heat pooled in her belly at his words.

He gripped the hem of her dress and slowly drew it higher, legs to hips, teasing the skin of her thigh with his fingertips.

The flouncy sheath dress and kick-off sandals had been the perfect choice. She stepped back and pulled it over her head. Eyes hooded, he watched her with an unreadable expression. She stilled and waited for him to make the next move, unsure of herself. Thank God she'd slipped on the matching panties and bra she wore when she wanted to feel sexy.

Every muscle tensed as his light touch traced a path down her arms to her torso, brushing the lacy edge of the demi-cups with his thumb. Gripping her waist, he guided her to the sofa. Each time she reached for him, he took control. Lost in another kiss, she gripped his shoulders to keep from falling over when the seat of the sofa pressed into the back of her knees. His lips never left her skin as he palmed her breast, teasing the tight nipple through the satin. All she could do was hold on.

The sensations built, one after the other. Lips, tongue, skin. Overwhelmed, she let herself go with the moment. He gently nudged her down onto the cushions, never breaking contact while he knelt beside her. He gripped her wrists above her head and flicked his tongue across a nipple before moving lower.

Callan trailed kisses to the lacy edge of her panties and then back to her breasts. His swirling tongue tortured first one then the other, the feel of coolness through the thin fabric heightened already sensitive nerves. He cupped her between her legs. She couldn't hold back the moan. She was on the verge of an orgasm, and she wasn't even naked.

Letting go of her hands, Callan gripped the back of her knee and pushed up as the other fell to the side. She closed her eyes, unable to stop the writhing of her hips at the feel of his mouth on her thigh, teasing the sensitive skin and moving slowly higher. He pulled at the edge of her panties, exposing her completely.

She pushed at him with her hips. One swipe of the roughened pad of his thumb over her clit and her body shook, then he suckled the hard bundle of nerves, and she exploded. She cried out in release.

She'd never just let it happen like that. With Callan she felt free. Free to be herself and enjoy their mutual pleasure. He moved over her and the weight of him between her legs heightened her excitement. Unable to keep from touching him, she tugged at the buttons of his shirt, desperate to get the soft twill to disappear. If she could wish someone naked, now would be the time.

Saving her from further distress, he separated from her long enough to allow her to unbutton his shirt and pull it off his arms before dazzling her with another deep kiss. The rough texture of his jeans was an erotic torture as her hips bucked, begging for more attention. Shirt gone, but pants and T-shirt still in the way, she pulled at the waistband of his jeans.

"Persistent." His chuckle turned to a groan when she palmed his erection through the fabric and squeezed lightly.

Leaning away, he pulled off his T-shirt, allowing her free access to touch. The scars registered briefly, but the expanse of tightly muscled chest sprinkled with dark hair that tapered low along the hard ridges of his abdomen snagged her attention. She was busy unbuttoning his jeans and teasing the hard bulge under the zipper as she lowered it when he caught her hand and pulled her gaze to his. Her heart clenched at the anxiety she saw as he watched her look at him for the first time. Spurred on by a desperate urgency, need built low in her belly.

Muscles and man, a body carrying the cost of war, were bared to her and all she wanted was to give him the pleasure he'd given her. She traced a light caress over burn marks that marred once tattooed skin. Cupping his cheek, she pulled his head toward her. "You're not done yet."

She ground her lips against his. One hand pushed down the waist of his jeans and briefs, circling the hard length of him in her palm. He groaned against her mouth before crushing her to him and rolling her on top of him. Together they discarded the little clothing left between them. He grabbed the foil packets he'd stashed in his pockets.

"Always prepared. Thank God." Vicky took the condom out of his hand and ripped it open. Hands locked behind his head, he gave her full access. She rolled the sheath down the length of him and smiled at his stifled curse. Positioned over him, knees on either side of his thighs, she could take it as slow as she wanted.

He cupped her breasts and rolled a hard dusky peak between his thumb and forefinger, eliciting a gasp. She arched her back, pressing closer. He pinched harder on one and drew the other into his mouth. Nails raked his chest in exquisite torture. He was about to burst. She scooted forward and rose up. He helped guide her over his erection. "Vicky. Fuck!" He wasn't going to last if she kept the pace slow.

She clenched around him and moved, up and then down again. Harder this time. He gripped her hips and kept her steady and pushed up, meeting her every move with a thrust of his own. Faster until her panting moans increased, ending with the quick catch of her breath and the most beautiful orgasm he'd ever witnessed. He lost control and soon followed her over the edge.

She collapsed over him, her body trembling as they shared languid kisses and murmurs of satisfaction.

"Wow." The word was whispered against his skin. He tucked her onto his chest, not wanting her to leave his lap, and pulled a blanket over them. "Yeah. Wow."

"Can we do that again?" Her mouth spread into a smile against his neck.

"Anytime you want."

She circled the scars on his chest with her fingers. He clasped his hand over hers, stilling her inspection.

She rested her head on her hand and peeked up at him.

"What happened?"

He hadn't talked about it in so long. For a second, the words wouldn't come. He wanted to tell her. Wanted her to understand what she could and couldn't expect from him. "When my unit was deployed the last time, I was pulled out of patrol for a special assignment, and John was sent in my place. They were under heavy attack almost immediately. The convoy John was in was hit. He was barely alive when they got to him."

"That's why you say he saved your life? You didn't come out unscathed."

"Our helicopter came under fire. A lucky shot and something ignited. I was trapped, going in and out of consciousness. I remember the hot burning metal on my shoulder and not being able to move my legs. The rest is mostly a blur."

"And now you don't like being inside or driving."

She didn't come out and say PTSD, but he saw the understanding in her eyes. "I handle it better now than when I first got back. Docs told me it might lessen with time. It's not so bad out here."

Her focus on him held none of the pity he'd seen in others. A smile and an acceptance of his explanation was all that was needed, and she'd given it. They stayed intertwined on the couch while their bodies cooled.

"I like what you've done with the apartment. It fits you." She kissed a light trail across his chest and hugged her body closer to his. "Wait, where's Cat?"

"Tyler took her. Apparently, he couldn't resist her charms."

She grinned at him. "Too bad. She was perfect for you." The weight of her lying on him was perfection. She centered him. No incessant need to move to lessen the imaginary burning of skin or pinned legs. No flashbacks to the ear-splitting scream of metal exploding, followed by a sudden chaotic silence where nothing registered but the pain and then blackness.

"How about you show me your bedroom."

He didn't need to be asked twice. Her laugh as he pulled her up to stand was the light he needed more of and didn't want to let go.

Waking, naked and with Vicky nestled in the crook of his arm, her head resting on his chest, he felt relaxed for the first time in months. Instead of waking up with the need to move, to get out, he stilled and listened to Vicky's soft breathing. Judging by the blackness through the skylight over his bed, it wasn't close to morning yet. He debated waking her again. She was incredible. He could get used to this. The thought made him uncomfortable enough he eased out of his side of the bed and padded barefoot into the kitchen. Instead of opening every door and window, he poured himself a glass of water and tried not to think about the deep trouble he was in. Sometime between thinking how easy no strings would be and the reality of what he actually felt, she'd chipped a hole in the wall around his heart, and expectations didn't sound so bad. Guilt pricked his conscience. Expectations came with consequences. It wouldn't be fair for him to try to change the terms of their arrangement without being fully honest. Something he wasn't sure he was prepared to do. Vicky stirred as he gently nudged her and met his gaze before sitting up. He motioned to the bottle of water he'd snagged from the fridge and sat on the bedside table. "I can heat up some dinner when you're ready."

"Thanks. Maybe later." She yawned and moved to lean against the headboard, wincing at the stretch. Looking embarrassed, she half laughed. "Not used to so much driving . . . followed by last night."

"Grand Junction is a long way to go for Wi-Fi."

"Yeah, Mom and Grams had some errands and we had a little wedding shopping to do." She took a sip of the water. "I had an interesting time, though."

He listened in stunned silence as she told him about her run-in with Senator Fletcher's aide and her snooping. She thought she was about to discover some scheme that could put her career back on track. In his gut, he knew her getting involved with his father would only lead to disaster.

"If I can track down his latest whereabouts, I might find out the reason Lewis was at the hospital.

"What if it's personal not political?"

She shrugged. "Maybe it is. But I sure would like to know what Fletcher's hiding from and the reason he's canceled two confirmation meetings. I might be able to use that to get my editor to give me another chance."

"You'd use him to get your job back?"

"I report the news and a senator mysteriously rescheduling confirmation hearings is potentially news."

"Doesn't sound like much of a lead to go on."

"Sure, but not looking could help him hide something that would make him unfit to re-elect. He's in the middle of a pretty close race. Either way, it's news and it could get me back in my job. If I don't check into it, someone else will. Guaranteed. Nothing is private anymore."

"What about the work you're doing in Home?"

"Don't get me wrong. I love Home and the people here. Childhood memories aside, I don't live in Home any longer. My job isn't in Home. I'm only here to help for the short-term."

"That anxious to leave?"

"I didn't mean it that way. This might not pan out to be anything real. I'm just following a hunch. You didn't see how weird Lewis acted when I spoke to him."

She let the sheet slide off her as she crawled to the edge of the bed. "I'm sorry I brought it up. I'm not here to argue the merits of my chosen career path." If she'd wanted him to stop arguing with her it was an effective way to get his mind onto a different track. "I'm here for you."

"That makes me the luckiest man in the world." He pulled her to him for another round of lovemaking.

Later, the soft sounds of her sleeping next to him invaded his thoughts. Vicky belonged in DC not Home and he wouldn't be stupid enough to get any ideas otherwise. What she didn't know wouldn't hurt her. Eventually, if she searched hard enough, she'd find his connection to Fletcher. What she did with his father wasn't his problem. As long as she left him out of it, or he was gone from Home before she needed to make that decision. He knew his keeping away from his father wasn't part of a political scandal. The man had a way of running roughshod over Callan's life and it was always his friends that got hurt more than he did. He'd learned the hard way that self-preservation meant keeping himself separate from his father's political and personal life. With what Home is going through, Senator Fletcher getting involved would be a disaster.

Callan buried his conscience. He would enjoy his time with Vicky however long it lasted.

15

*V*icky snuck into her parent's house and up to her room, missing every person who might happen to be awake at that ungodly hour. After their lovemaking, which she could classify as the best sex of her life, and she was sure Callan hadn't been disappointed, he'd turned restless. He'd paced around and opened the windows but couldn't relax. Something had changed after their conversation. It wasn't really an argument, but something had crept in to change the mood.

Talking about leaving Home and going back to DC wasn't supposed to hurt. She wasn't supposed to think anything other than she couldn't wait to get back to her life, but saying it out loud, to Callan, while naked and in his bed hadn't felt right.

Dammit.

They had to go and mess up a perfectly good plan. He couldn't move to DC to explore what they had. There was no reason to even think about anything more than a temporary arrangement. They had an agreement, and she'd have to deal with it. An affair. Nothing serious.

She was supposed to be finding out who was sabotaging the wedding sets and who the mysterious celebrities were to actually market effectively, not agonizing over a guy. Worrying about Callan's reaction to their lovemaking would have to wait. A nap and shower were first on her to-do list for the day.

The house was empty when she headed back downstairs. Taking the opportunity, she looked around her mother's office for any information on the secret couple. She'd been so busy outside her mother's home and had not had a moment alone inside, this was the first time she'd had to snoop in peace. Vicky drew the line at trying to get into the locked office files, but not in perusing through the stacks of wedding plan information on her mother's desk and had taken over the dining room table. There had to be a clue hidden in there somewhere. It might take some time, but she'd find it.

If only her mother had told her. But no, that would have been too easy. She wouldn't understand why Vicky needed to know. The greater good of Home was all that mattered. If the mayor had promised anonymity, she'd never budge an inch. Vicky wouldn't out the couple either but hinting and letting a few influential entertainment bloggers figure it out —at a safe time—wouldn't break any promises. A big enough couple could bring in tons of business. She squashed the kernel of guilt forming in the back of her mind. She wasn't doing anything wrong.

After sifting through six different books jam-packed with articles, pictures, and samples she was weddinged out and it wasn't even the tip of the iceberg as far as files went. They were serious about putting on weddings. Every conceivable invention to make the day perfect had been catalogued. Detailed plans on which sets to build, which supplies to have on hand, which suppliers had the best deals and the best reputations. Pages and pages of reports on trends, markets, and venue options Vicky had never heard of.

She'd known her mother was a planner at heart and one of the toughest businesswomen she'd ever met, but this went beyond expectations. This was serious business. She didn't have any more clue who the couple was, but she did have a better sense of how much work the town had put in.

Hours later, Vicky passed her mother in the foyer as she was returning.

"Hi, sweetie. Have a nice date?"

"I did. I'm grabbing some lunch at Jo's. Want to come?"

"No, thanks, why don't you meet John? He usually eats there on Fridays. But don't mention his surprise tomorrow."

"Surprise?"

"His birthday party, remember? Everyone's going to be there."

Vicky had forgotten Rochelle had planned it. With so much going on, she hadn't heard it mentioned again.

"Uh, Mom. I don't think that's a good idea. He doesn't spend much time at The Walrus." If he didn't want to participate in karaoke, he wouldn't want to be part of a birthday party either.

"Nonsense. It's the perfect spot. We can't surprise him somewhere he's always around, and the whole thing's planned."

"He really doesn't like being there. You have to have

noticed how he avoids crowds." She tried to get through her mother's stubbornness.

"Sometimes, where you need to be isn't always where you want to be." Her mother's gaze locked on her. "Now run along, I need to finish up some work."

No debate would change her mother's mind once she had it made up. She left her to her work and headed into town. Maybe if Vicky warned him beforehand, he'd be more prepared for their surprise. It wasn't just another night at the bar they were talking about. It was a special party for John.

Callan had opened up about his scars and the nightmare he'd been living with. If the town knew, they might be more sensitive to him not wanting to have a party at the bar. It wasn't her place to share his life story, and it wasn't her place to tell the town they were going out of their way to celebrate someone's birthday who wasn't actually there. Even so, she'd try to get him to go.

The cool rush of barbecue scented air hit her as she walked into Jo's.

"Oh, good, you're here. I've got a revised menu I want you to put on the blog," Jo called to her from behind the counter.

Vicky sat, aware of Jo's scrutiny, and tried not to seem like she was looking around for any sign of Callan.

"John's not here," Maggie whispered as she brushed past on her way to a table of four in the front corner.

"I wasn't . . ."

Maggie threw her a raised eyebrow over her shoulder at the pathetic attempt at denial. "Whatever."

"I was thinking of having a 'name this dish' contest. What do you think?" Jo asked as she slipped a piece of paper in front of Vicky. "Here's a list of new signature sandwiches I'm adding to the lunch menu."

"Looks like these all have names." The list of six offerings had names in bold, printed over a description. "Uh, Sex on the Beach? I think that's already taken."

Jo rolled her eyes and her scarlet-painted lips flattened. "Mitch's stupid name for his creation. Roasted turkey with Havarti and a jalapeño aioli."

"It's brilliant." Mitch's voice carried from his station behind the pass-through into the kitchen. "You're roasted, then toasted and it's all going smooth, but you finish with a little something that bites back. Like sand where it don't belong."

"That one's definitely getting renamed," Jo whispered.

"I told Jo she wouldn't be sour if she'd try it sometime." His grin turned to laughter when Jo threw a dishtowel at him.

"I'll have you know, I have tried it, probably before you were even born. Thank you very much."

"I mean the sandwich, Jo."

Jo's growl at his laughter didn't hold much heat. She looked like she enjoyed the teasing as much as Mitch seemed to enjoy dishing it out.

"I see you two are getting along well."

"He's an ass, and way too young to be as good as he is in the kitchen. But I guess I'll keep him around."

"Are you two . . ." Vicky motioned from Mitch, who'd returned to his spot behind the grill, to Jo.

"Are you kidding? Honey, I'd break him in a week. Besides, I think he's carrying a torch for someone else. Kind of like someone else I know."

Vicky frowned. "I'm not carrying a torch."

"Oh, you weren't looking for John when you came in here?"

"I'm here for lunch. John and I are . . . old friends."

"Uh-huh. Home does that, you know."

"Does what?" The older woman was speaking in some kind of code and looking at her like she should know what was being implied. This was the kind of conversation that made Vicky squirm. Insider language about Home she'd never felt a part of.

"Brings old friends together. You ever wonder why people who have visited here never seem to leave? It's because Home has what they're looking for. Maybe it's an old love. Maybe it's a safe place to live. Maybe it's a family they never had. You're here now, and I'd bet my secret ranch dip recipe you'll stay. John too."

"I wouldn't bet anything that valuable. I'm headed back to my life as soon as my parents' wedding is done."

Jo gave her a wink. "Then you better get this menu on your blog. I don't want to miss my chance. While you're here, try this pie." She slid a plate with a slab of cherry pie in front of Vicky. Taking a big forkful, she swallowed the lump that had formed in her throat. She would leave. What else could she do? Home wasn't the place for her. She wasn't some passerby who happened to like it there and decided to stay. She'd grown up there. Her mother was the mayor. No one could claim as deep ties to the town as Vicky, but no one seemed to understand why she'd left and why she wanted to leave again. She took another bite and shoved the plate away.

"Thanks for the pie, Jo. It's a keeper." She left some

money on the counter and hurried out before anyone else could stop her to chat. She'd lost her appetite for lunch and just wanted to get away and think for a bit.

The comfort of seeing familiar faces and being surrounded by memories made it hard to focus on her future. Add to it her confused feelings about Callan and she was turning into an emotional mess.

Focus, dammit. Remember your priorities.

She crossed the street toward Rochelle's. If she wasn't going to spend time over a nice lunch, she might as well try to do something nice.

"Hey, Queenie, glad you're here. I could use some help." Rochelle shoved a box into her hands and picked up another from the counter. Balancing it on her hip, she turned the closed sign toward the door and locked it. "Follow me, I need a hand getting these party decorations to my car. Can you come tomorrow to help set up? Sly's letting us in early. I've got balloons, streamers, and a sign. Also, Mike's made a huge cake. Everyone's pitching in."

"Yeah, that's what I wanted to talk to you about. I, um, don't think having a party at the bar is a good idea. John doesn't seem to like hanging out there."

"What? It'll be fun," Rochelle said over her shoulder while Vicky followed her.

Would it? "He's not really much of a partier."

Rochelle dropped her box into the open trunk and turned, hands on hips. "You might have hooked up with him, but I think I know him pretty well too, and I'm sure he'll be happily surprised."

"I don't know." She didn't miss the jab, but Rochelle was right. What did she really know about Callan? Besides what he looked like naked. Gorgeous, exciting, deliciously naked. She thought she understood why he felt he needed to avoid the bar on busy nights for John's sake but what about a party that was specifically for him? She wasn't sure how he'd react. Not for certain. Not without asking him.

"Since we're on the subject of you hooking up with John." Rochelle grabbed the box Vicky'd been holding and dropped it next to the first. "What do you think you're doing with him anyway?"

We were not on any such subject. "That's none of your or anyone else's business."

"It is when you make a scene in public like at the workday. It is when everyone knows the great Queenie Jones isn't planning to stay around Home. Do you think John will follow you to DC or wherever it is you plan to move to next?"

"What's between John and me is our business." She knew she sounded bitchy, but she wasn't prepared to answer questions about how she and Callan spent time together. It was too new, too complicated. Add the guilt of knowing he's keeping his real self from the people that care about him and she could see why he'd been stand-offish as "John."

"You always said you were too good for this place." Rochelle slammed the trunk closed and faced Vicky.

"If I recall, you left Home the same time I did and didn't plan to come back either."

"Too good to live here but not too good to hook up with one of the only single men in town."

Only single man? That smacked of plain old jealousy.

"Since when is that a crime? Or are you just mad a guy

likes me more than you? After all these years, we still have to compete like this?"

Vicky had always been second to Rochelle whenever they'd liked the same boy in high school. But this wasn't high school, and Callan wasn't some boy she didn't expect to see past graduation. Maybe there were a few similarities. She hadn't expected to want to see him for long. Unfortunately, their one night hadn't scratched any kind of itch and had only made her want more. More time with him. More conversation. More sex. More everything.

Rochelle's lower lip trembled, and she blinked. "Don't hurt him, Queenie. He's special and important here."

The anger was punched right out of her at Rochelle's quiet pleading. What kind of power did she think Vicky had over the man?

"I don't want to hurt him." As if she could without hurting herself in the process. She was already avoiding thinking about the day she'd have to walk away.

"Oh my god, you're really into him." Rochelle sniffed, rubbing her nose with the back of one hand.

"It's unexpected." The heat from her earlier accusation was gone, Vicky decided to be honest. There were enough lies going around. "Does everyone know?" Stupid question. Of course, everyone knew.

Rochelle snorted and nodded. "Uh . . . yeah."

Figures. Small-town-gossip line was strong and wide. She wouldn't deny it. There was no reason to. Their little secret fling wasn't so secret.

Rochelle leaned against the car and rubbed her eyes with her fingertips. "I'm all over the place. Sorry, my anger isn't directed at you. I just want one thing to go right."

"For the record, when he first asked me out I called him a two-timing asshole and told him where he could stick his dinner invitation."

Rochelle's eyes widened. "You did not."

"I did. I thought he was with you. Grams told me you were just friends. I should have said something to you, but I stupidly thought we could keep it under wraps for a couple of weeks."

"You should know better. But I'm glad to know you had my back." She flashed a wry smile and cocked her head to the side. "He's been different since you got here. In a good way. This party is for him and you. Maybe he doesn't want to be acknowledged for all the hard work he's done, but we need to show him we appreciate him. You make sure he's there."

16

*D*riving out to John's family home brought back a wave of memories. The old farmhouse was surrounded by acres of flat land that hadn't been worked in years. The mountains in the distance were just visible behind the cloudy sky. The barn had seen better days, but the house —wow. She slowed to a stop. This was the place, but Vicky didn't remember the house ever looking this good. Callan had been busy here too.

Stepping out of the car onto the packed gravel driveway, she could imagine John and Kaylie raising their family there. Plenty of room to run and play, plant a garden, and enjoy life. Not a bad childhood or life if you were looking to settle down.

The closer she walked to the house, the more the details stood out. Fresh paint glistened along the screened-in porch running the entire length of the front. The small brick steps leading up to the screen door had been replaced with wide stone steps bracketed by a double rail. A wheelchair ramp had been added to the side.

Paint fumes permeated the air, along with the old smoke smell of wood burned in a fireplace.

"Callan? It's Vicky." She didn't want to knock in case the paint was still wet, so she carefully opened the door and walked in. "Callan?" she called again.

Wow didn't cut it. The inside was nothing like she remembered. The updates layered over the memories that flooded as she took in the space. Awed at the details, she turned a half circle in the extra wide foyer. He'd thought of everything. A large living room and dining area on the left led into an open kitchen. Emotion she couldn't identify caught her breath and weighed heavily on her chest. Joy or pride or gratitude at what her friend would come home to— whatever it was, she couldn't pinpoint. Callan had worked tirelessly for something so special that seeing it physically hurt.

A small bundle burned in the fireplace and the smell of coffee percolated from the kitchen. Callan had to be around there somewhere.

The interior had been freshly painted, its scent sharp. The old wallpaper had been replaced with a light color palette that made the place seem bigger and brighter. The kitchen was small but perfectly put together. The ugly laminate bar that had blocked the cooking area from the eating area was gone and a built-in breakfast nook ran along one wall with a farm table and four chairs on the sides. The space was cozy and accessible to John, even in a wheelchair.

Callan stood at the open back door, his silhouette outlined through the screen. "What are you doing here?"

She jerked back at the harshness in his voice. Her

defenses shot up. "Looking for you. Tyler said you'd be out here."

"Is there a problem in town?" The screen slammed behind him, punching the tension between them.

"No. Everyone's fine." She smiled through sudden insecurity. Was he mad she'd barged in on him while he was working? Had she crossed a boundary of some kind? "Is it okay?"

He walked toward her. "Yeah, sorry. Just surprised to see anyone in here."

"Did you do all this yourself?" The butcher-block counter was cool as she ran her hand along its smooth line and tried to change the subject. "It's amazing."

"I had some help from my crew on the exterior." He seemed almost embarrassed at her inspection, but she couldn't hide her amazement at the transformation of the space from what she remembered. "I told them I was fixing a couple things and got a little carried away. But I like it and it keeps me busy."

"John and Kaylie will love it." She swallowed the sudden catch in her throat and blinked away the tears that formed. Now wasn't the time to cry in front of him. "It's perfect."

Vicky passed through the kitchen and back into the entryway. A hall led to the other side of the house. A doorway had been boarded up. "Wasn't this the den?"

"It was. I'm closing it up to make a nursery right next to the master bedroom. The other bedroom is downstairs." He seemed to relax, talking about the renovations. The tension between them eased. She followed him through the small main floor of the home as he described the updates. "I'm sketching out an extension for the west side. Another bedroom and bathroom. My crew can handle it once they've moved in."

The pride and passion he had for the remodeling of a house that wasn't even his astonished her. The care and amount of work had to have taken months of intense dedication. And he'd done it for a friend. She knew guilt was a bitch of a taskmaster, but this was more than payback. This showed true loyalty and love.

"I'm working on the basement now. The stairs needed refurbishing, but he should be able to get up and down them without too much trouble once he's used to his new prosthetic."

He'd said John was like a brother—clearly, he meant it. What would it be like to be loved that selflessly? This man of few words had done something to show what he felt. What he considered important. A place to call home. But where was his place to call home? If John was like a brother, wouldn't he want to stay and be part of the group who considered John family? "You've completely updated this place in what, two months?" She tried not to pry with too many questions, but her curiosity had become a physical need she couldn't keep contained.

He shrugged. "It's the least I could do."

"I know it's not my business, but how are you doing all this for him? For the town? The store can't be making enough profit to afford this renovation."

He bristled. "You came all the way out here to talk about this? Why now?"

"Are you paying for all this yourself?" The question was crass, she knew it, but she had no filter left. How could he afford all this? Another thought filtered in to jumble her up some more. The town's new park and wedding buildings—Home had been nearly bankrupt but somehow had the money to try to pull off an elaborate plan. The town couldn't do it all on credit. What kind of collateral did it have besides the land it was trying to keep out of Blake's hands? That meant someone else had to be eating some of the cost. "Have you been bankrolling the town too?"

"Are you kidding? Throw money away on a gamble?" His gaze slid from hers to the window, then he clamped his jaw shut.

"Somehow, a lot has been done through the hardware store you run." She placed a hand on his chest. He didn't move from his stance, hands pushed into his pockets, legs locked in place.

His gaze caught hers. "You're not going to let this go, are you?"

Let it go? How could she? Did her mom know? She doubted it. Doubted John knew either. Callan claimed to be helping his friend, but he'd been giving more than anyone could ever ask. Time, money, and hard work—he deserved recognition for all he'd done but didn't ask for any. "I don't care about your finances." She ran her hand up his arm to his shoulder, his arms opened to the invitation and settled around her waist. She linked her fingers behind his neck and pressed a light kiss to his cheek. "But I do care if you are pouring personal money into my mom's scheme. There's no guarantee it will work. The town could fold tomorrow."

Would he be that dedicated to the woman he loved? Yes. Vicky knew he would—that much was clear. She'd be a lucky woman if she could reach him through the wall he'd built out of guilt and whatever it was that made him capable of doing all he'd done. All the while, planning to leave it behind when finished. She brushed another kiss across his lips, lingering until his arms tightened around her waist and pressed her to him.

"Trust me when I tell you I'm not being reckless." The corner of his mouth hitched up in a half-smile.

"Okay, I'll drop it. What you're doing here. . ." she motioned to the room around them, "for your friend—my friend—is about the most wonderful thing I've ever seen."

He opened his mouth to speak, and she placed a finger over his lips. "I don't know what you're hiding from, and I'm not going to ask again. I'm here if you need someone to talk to. But right now, I want you to kiss me and be happy to see me."

That he could do. Kissing her eased the tension eating at him. Working in the basement had been harder than he'd thought it would be. He'd saved it for one of the last projects, knowing the closed off space would be tight. He could only work in short bursts before having to get outside. The more he completed and could see the end, the better he felt. He was getting used to being there alone, in the quiet with nothing to disturb him except the sounds of the night and the knocks and groans of an old house growing young again. It had become comforting. Not like the isolation he'd sought when he first got out of the hospital, but the contentment of a safe place where his nightmares didn't inhibit his life.

Now, here was Vicky, throwing his comfort out the window and making him sway off course again. Making him want things he wasn't sure he could keep. Pressing her body to his, all thoughts zeroed in on her until all he cared about was kissing her. With a sigh, her arms tightened around his neck, and her mouth opened in an invitation that buzzed through every nerve in his body, until one desire blocked all others. Her. Naked. Now.

His shirt was off, and he carried her to the rug in front of the fireplace before another coherent thought formed in his brain.

"My purse." He felt the words purr against his neck more than heard them. "Condoms."

He retrieved her bag and was back before the pleasurable tingle of her lips on his skin had faded. A flurry of hands, buttons, zippers, and mouths followed until they were naked and restless on the floor.

She met him move for move. Caress for caress, never hesitating, never taking more than she gave. He told himself not to rush this, but he was quickly losing all control around her.

All blood fled from his brain when she caressed his chest, sliding over the rough skin of his shoulder. In the daylight, there were no shadows or dim light to hide the extent of the damage. Her gaze held his as she straddled him, slowly sliding along the length of his shaft. A gorgeous triumphant grin lit her face at his strangled groan.

"Too much to handle?"

He gripped her hips, holding her steady as he rose up and pulled her to his mouth, kissing her until she squirmed and moaned his name. "Sweetheart," he nuzzled her neck and palmed her breast, kneading the hardened peak. "I'm always up for a challenge."

"We'll see." A light nip at his shoulder caused a frenzy of heat to shoot through his system. She wanted to play, he'd play. He let her push him to his back, enjoying the minx-like mischief in her eyes. Holding his gaze, she teased her way down his chest and abs. He held his breath, every kiss, or scrape of teeth or flick of tongue sent electric heat humming along his skin. She slowed the closer she got to his cock. Her gaze never left his as she lowered, running her tongue along the length of him.

He clamped his teeth around any words.

He would not break. Hands fisted at his sides, he relished the erotic torture that was her mouth.

"I like seeing you squirm." Her carefree laugh lightened his soul. He'd gladly give in to anything to hear it.

Two could play this game.

In a quick move, he shifted her up and rolled her underneath him. "Now it's my turn," he slipped on the condom then cupped one hand behind her knee, and settled between her thighs.

The tip of him brushed her swollen entry, her hips bucked and her back arched. He wanted to spend all night worshipping every inch of her body. Pleasuring her in every way he could think of. She gripped his shoulders, her restless movements begging for release. He stroked a thumb over the sensitive bud at her wet core and entered her in one long, slow slide. She clenched around him and his breath caught in his chest.

"Damn, you feel good."

"Don't make me wait." She rocked her hips, urging him on. The bite of her nails at his shoulders drove him to move faster. To feel more, take more. Around him, time stopped.

Their surroundings disappeared until all he saw was Vicky. All he heard was the sexy, desperate gasps at each thrust. In that moment, his world was perfect. *She* was perfect.

Sweat slicked his body, and he squeezed his eyes shut, willing himself to remember every detail of the way they felt entangled and buried in each other's desire. He pulled out, a breath away from breaking contact. He needed her. Needed this.

Her moan was his undoing. He moved in and out, faster until she clenched around him once more and yelled his name. His muscles shook, trembling with his own powerful release.

Collapsed on the rug, the heat from the low-burning fire and a small blanket from the sofa kept them warm as they floated. Vicky curled into his side, one leg draped over his, they lay together in easy quiet with nothing but the sounds of their breathing in the intimate space.

Vicky had been open and honest. Guilt tugged at his conscience. He watched her doze on his shoulder. The setting sun sent rays of gold and crimson through the open curtains, highlighting the contours of her face and shimmering blonde of her hair.

He shouldn't feel guilty about enjoying the moment. He should take it for what it was, a nice fling with a beautiful woman. It had been her idea in the first place. Didn't stop him from feeling like a douche bag weasel for keeping his true identity from her. Did he really think she would use him to get to his father?

He was uncomfortable with the answer that came to mind, nevertheless, he couldn't take the chance. Self-preservation was on the line if he did. Not to mention he wasn't done helping John and until he was, nothing was going to get in his way.

He caressed the smooth skin of her back, remembering the little catch she made in the back of her throat when he traced small circles along her spine. Now she opened her eyes slowly, and practically purred at his touch. "Mmm . . . I'd say you won that round." She placed a string of light kisses along his chest. "I want a rematch."

"Any time, beautiful." Her easy smile tightened, and he saw the questions in her gaze. She sat up and pulled the blanket over her shoulders and looked around the living room.

"Are you staying out here a couple days?"

"I was planning on it. I have more work downstairs. Tyler's managing the shop. Want to stay with me?"

"What about tomorrow?"

Her question pulled him back to reality. "They're still having the party?"

"You know about it?"

Of course, he knew. Everyone knew. "It's hard to keep something like that a secret."

"Everyone will be really disappointed if you don't show up."

"Not my problem." He sat up and grabbed his boxers and jeans from a pile of scattered clothing.

"It's a little surprise party." She pulled her T-shirt over her head and yanked it down over her chest. "Okay, not that little, but Rochelle has put a lot of work into planning it."

"Don't care." He shoved his legs into his jeans and pulled them to his waist.

Not bothering to button up, he walked to the kitchen.

He didn't want to hear about how much the surprise party would mean to the others.

"You're not going to show up at all?" Her voice was muffled as she dressed but he caught enough. That was a view from the kitchen he didn't mind looking at.

"Sly asked me to stop by and help fix some loose boards on the stage tomorrow evening. I didn't say yes or no."

"The town really cares about you."

How could he explain that it wasn't only the crowd he was avoiding? "The town cares about John. It's his birthday, not mine."

"It's also a thank you party and a welcome home party for me. That takes some of the pressure off. Come back to town with me. Come to The Walrus with me tomorrow night."

"No." He could only pretend for so long. Lying in the face of the genuine respect and love many had showered him with was too much to ask.

"That's it? No?"

He paced in front of the fire. The restlessness from earlier was back. "That's it. No." He didn't want to disappoint Vicky, but she didn't understand what she was asking. "I've got to go split some firewood."

"I should be heading back," she said. "Are you sure I can't give you a ride?" She threw the question out there. Maybe ensuring she'd have to ride back to John's house later would entice him to leave with her.

"I'll see you when I'm back in town. There's a lot I need to get done still." He turned his back on her disappointment. She didn't have to understand his reasons. They were his demons, and his alone.

17

"I didn't warn him. He already knew and wasn't planning on coming." Vicky shifted in her seat to face her grandmother and relaxed the forced smile she'd plastered on to face the crowds. Her cheeks already ached, and she'd only been there an hour.

"They don't believe you, dear. You went out to his place yesterday, and he didn't come back to town today. Even if you didn't tell him about the party, you did something to make him avoid coming in today."

"Seriously, Grams. How is this my fault? I told you all this wasn't a good idea."

Vicky sat in the corner of The Walrus with a handmade "Welcome Home, Queenie" sign over her head. The table on the other side with the "Happy Birthday, John" sign was empty. The more she intercepted every glare thrown her way from the partygoers, the angrier she became with Rochelle and her mom for not listening to her. And at Callan. She knew it would be a struggle for him. But he'd been in there before, and she'd hoped he'd do it again. Even if he'd just shown up for a few minutes, he'd see how much they'd tried to make it a welcoming place for him.

Ignoring the stares and whispers, she'd guided the party planners to place a table close to the propped open side door for him. They'd moved the other tables away so there wouldn't be any crowding. Jo had set up a wonderful barbecue buffet and two enormous cakes were positioned on a table in front of the bar. Mike and his assistant had worked to impress. The jukebox was on, but the speakers were turned down. The town, with a little coaxing from her, had done their best to give John a party he might have been able to relax and have fun at. All without knowing anything about why he was the way he was or that he wasn't actually John.

She fired off another desperate text.

Vicky: You're missing something special. They think I warned you. I swear if you don't show up, they might not let me come back. Ever.

He probably wouldn't get the stupid texts out at John's house, what with the spotty cell coverage. Damn, stubborn man. Just when she thought she'd broken through, he closed right back up.

Why did she even care? But she did, more than she wanted to. John's words came back to her. He needs to be in Home. He needs to be where he's appreciated.

She slumped at her table with her chin in her hands. Few people talked to her when her Grams left her for a dance around the floor. She'd had several warm "welcome homes", but for the most part, the crowd ignored her. Small groups huddled around the bar where Sly poured beers and around the food table Jo had set up in the opposite corner.

Couples danced to the soft country music playing. Overall, it was not a party atmosphere, and the blame had been laid squarely upon her shoulders.

Didn't Callan see John's to-do was as much birthday party as a way for the town to let him know they were glad he was back? Callan should have understood. Vicky's part in the festivities were more of an afterthought—a nice gesture. Few people besides her mother expected her to stay around town for long. Even so, they'd put forth more work and care than the quick meet up for a drink she'd received from Neal and a couple of coworkers as a bon voyage from the job she'd given years of her life to.

The party had been going on for over an hour, and the bar was finally full, but everyone kept a distance from John's table. When the people of Home decided to do something, they did it all the way. *John* would have the whole night to show as far as the partygoers were concerned.

"I'd say everyone's as mad at you as they are at my mom these days for all her protesting and complaining." Carl Tuttle pulled a chair up next to Vicky.

"Yeah. Some things everyone can agree on." Crap. "Uh, sorry."

"Don't be." He shrugged and sent her a wry grin. "I know my mom's reputation, and I've tried to tell her she's not doing herself any favors, but listening isn't her strong suit."

"She's pretty passionate about Home though," Vicky offered.

"She doesn't like change. Trust me, she almost moved in with me when I moved to Denver for my freshman year at college."

She snorted at the sarcasm. "I know how that goes." Vicky took a sip of the beer growing warm in front of her. "Mine thought I'd be dead in less than a week when I moved to DC."

"How about a dance? If we can't beat them, might as well have some fun." He motioned to the dance floor.

"I'm not sure that's a good idea."

"It's a party, right? I'm here to have some fun. Isn't that what people do at parties?"

Vicky hesitated.

"I know what you're thinking. It's all over your face." He held a hand out to her. "I'm a hell of a lot of fun, let's show our mothers we know how to enjoy ourselves."

She couldn't help laughing. He was charming, in a young and cocky kind of way. "Why not?"

He whooped and pulled her into his arms for a two-step around the dance floor. She was out of breath after the third song in a row.

Slumping into her chair, Vicky swiped the perspiration from her forehead and blew her bangs out of her eyes. "You have a lot of energy."

He wiggled his eyebrows at her statement.

"You're incorrigible."

"But fun. Always fun. I'll refresh your beer."

"Are you old enough to buy?" A grin stretched her mouth at his feigned insult.

"Turned twenty-one last month. It's all good."

He was a fun kid. It had been a long time since someone had whirled and twirled her around the dance floor. Letting go had felt good.

"Here you go." He set a bottle and mug in front of her. "With a fresh frosty glass no less."

"Thanks."

"Listen, I know you and John have something going, but if I were him, I wouldn't have let the prettiest girl in town go to a boring party by herself."

"You sure you're only twenty-one?"

"Age doesn't matter when we're both adults."

She laughed then. Not meaning to laugh in his face at his sincerity. He didn't seem to take offense. Could nothing faze this kid?

"I bet you had a blast at college. Clearly confidence is not an issue with you."

"As far as computer geeks go, I didn't do too bad."

"Why are you here? And not there?"

"Graduated early, and haven't figured out where I want to go next." He shrugged and took a long swallow of his own mug. "As of a month ago, I thought I'd be helping my parents move. But now it looks like that's on hold."

"Hopefully, it won't come to that. The town's worked really hard."

"Yeah, hopefully. Would hate to sell out and move away from all this." He gestured around the bar, a wry smile twisting his lips.

She'd been young and sure once too. Sure, she needed to leave Home. Sure, she needed to get out from under the mayor's shadow. Sure, she would take on the world and make it her own.

She had—for a while.

All that wasn't as important as it once had been. The taking on the world part, anyway. She didn't want to leave so much as she wanted to get back her old life. The passion she'd once had. The assuredness she'd been creating her own future. Such melancholy thoughts didn't belong at a party.

"I'm heading home. Maybe the mood will pick up with me gone."

His grin faltered. "Speaking of parents. I better go see why my dad keeps waving at me. I think I'm making him nervous." He leaned toward her. "Sure I can't convince you to leave here with me? We could go for a walk, maybe coffee at your place?"

"Sorry to crush your fragile ego, but I'm good."

"I'm heartbroken." He stood and pushed the chair to the table. "Seriously, if John doesn't start treating you better I might have to have words with the man."

"What kind of words?"

The smile disappeared from Carl's face and Vicky almost spit out the sip she'd taken. She'd been entertained by Carl's flirting and hadn't noticed Callan come in. The rest of the bar noticed—and had grown quiet.

Everyone looked frozen, as if moving would spook him and he'd flee. Rochelle broke the spell with a high-pitched squeal and yelled, "Surprise," and the tension left the room as if no one had been contemplating banishing her a few minutes before.

"Uh, happy birthday, John. Glad you could make it." Carl glanced from Callan to Vicky and back.

"What kind of words?" Callan repeated.

To Carl's credit, he shifted his feet but stood his ground. "The kind that say Vicky's not a woman to be left alone at a party. She deserves someone who can show her a good time."

Callan's expression didn't change at the challenge in

Carl's words. He had only a few inches height on the kid, but he had to outweigh him in muscle by at least thirty pounds.

The bravado in Carl's stance diminished the longer he stared, but he didn't leave.

"Hey Carl, thanks for the dance. Could you give John and me a minute? I need to talk to him."

* * *

He looked like he wanted to argue with Vicky's request. That took some serious backbone, more than some of those men he'd seen hitting on her the last time he stepped into The Walrus. Maybe he'd underestimated Carl and the damage he could do to the town if he was in Blake's pocket.

Vicky placed a hand on Carl's arm. "Really, thanks for the company, but I need to talk to John."

"Sure thing." He turned his back to Callan. "Anytime you want to have some real fun, call me."

Was he kidding? Vicky was eating it up. Her soft smile at the smug kid was ridiculous. She couldn't be falling for that kind of fake charm, could she?

"Oh, stop scowling. Carl's been a perfect gentleman."

"He's still in diapers."

"He's perfectly legal." She laughed and hugged his arm, slipping her hand into his. "But he's not you."

Vicky brushed his cheek with a kiss. "I'm so happy you came. There's a line of people waiting for you." She nodded her head toward the other side of the bar where his Happy Birthday banner hung.

"Do I really have to go sit under the sign?"

"Yep. Have a piece of cake. Smile." She brushed his lips with the pad of her thumb. "This is their way of saying thank you."

"What's your way of saying thank you?" His gaze locked on her, taking in every detail. Did she know every thought showed on her face? She might fool the people who didn't know her or didn't pay attention. Not him. The spark of desire in her eyes ignited his own.

"Hmm, maybe you'll get a chance to find out later." The sultry deepening of her voice sizzled along his skin. Being near her turned him on and quieted the voices in his head warning him not to touch. Not to get too close. To walk away before he hurt someone.

"Keep looking at me that way and the gossip mill will be working over time." Vicky shooed him toward his table. "Go on."

The back of his neck itched as he crossed the room. Every eye in the place seemed to weigh on him. He could practically hear the group exhalation when he accepted a beer from Rochelle.

He stood by the open back door—he would not sit like some kind of exhibit—as partygoers came up to him, one or two at a time to wish him happy birthday. He was aware of Vicky's whereabouts the entire evening. Even over the music and conversation around him, he zeroed in on her laughter or searched her out in the crowd to see her smile. Her presence was a balm to his anxiety.

"Glad you came. Didn't think we'd see you when Vicky arrived on her own." Sly turned a chair around and straddled it, two bottles gripped in one hand.

"Thanks." Callan took one of the offered beers and matched his seat choice. "Had a lot of work at the house."

"Things have been quiet, lately. Haven't seen Barnes in town again." Between swigs, Sly filled him in on the last few days' surveillance. "No sighting is not a good sign."

"Have you seen St. James around recently?" He wasn't surprised Barnes hadn't shown his face since giving him an ultimatum. But St. James had become a regular, visiting Home several times a week. If he'd backed off, then something was up.

Sly shook his head. "You think they're about to strike?"

His thoughts had been running in that direction. He'd had as direct a threat as Barnes would probably give them before acting. So far, he'd assumed the threat was meant for him and John's place, but any of the bordering properties as well as the businesses holding steady in town could be targets.

"We're as prepared as we can be without making our concerns public. That argument between St. James and Barnes has me concerned. If Barnes is going rogue, he could be more dangerous if it's been St. James holding him back. Or it could be the other way around."

Sly drained the last of his beer and tossed the bottle into a recycle bin by the open door. He leaned closer. "They don't have much time left if the mayor's timeline is correct. Perhaps we can speed things up."

"I've been thinking about the cameras we finally have around the sets. Since they've been there, no one's messed with them. What would happen if the word got out they weren't working? Maybe our little spy will come back out of the woodwork?"

"Roger that. I'm more suited to doing something stupid than sitting around waiting." Sly said.

"Make a fuss about taking one down. Let a few of my crew know and see how far the word spreads. With the mayor's wedding in two weeks, we need the sets secure. Maybe we can snare Barnes and St. James in the same net as their Home ally."

"I'll take care of it tomorrow and be in touch." Sly stood and righted his chair toward Callan's table. "I think she's ready to forgive you for making her wait."

Callan caught Sly's line of sight to see Vicky walking toward him. Her smile drew him in, and he didn't want to think about Blake or the town or vandalism or threats. He wanted her.

"How are you holding up?" She took over Sly's chair, pushing it close to his side and resting a hand lightly on his forearm on the table. A clear signal to the crowd watching of their closeness. A few weeks before he'd have moved away from her touch without a second thought, now his body all but craved any bit of physical affection she could give. "You made a lot of people happy by showing up. Thank you."

"I guess you were right. I still don't think I should be celebrating John's birthday. He's going to be here soon, and this just adds more explanations and apologies that will be needed."

"If there's one thing I know about Home, we forgive and move on. Besides, you're doing this for the town, not for yourself."

He wanted to accept her assurance, but his mom had been on the wrong side of a bad reputation, and he'd found out at an early age that people could get ugly. It was one thing to lie to the town for John's benefit. It was another to accept so much hospitality as John. It was a fine line, but an important one.

"You and Sly were having a good conversation. What did I miss?"

"Nothing important. He's got the cameras set up at the sets now. Shouldn't have any more vandalism problems."

Her smile took his breath away. The weight of her hand on his arm and the comfort of her body close to his filled him with warmth, replacing the cold anxiety he'd felt most of the day. What would life be like with her close all the time? A dangerous wish.

"I think you've served your time as the birthday boy. Cake's gone, food's gone." She twisted as if looking around the room before her gaze swung back to his. "It's safe to leave. If you're ready."

"What about you? Are you ready to leave?"

She stretched in her seat, in an exaggerated move that pushed her breasts up, outlining their form against the clingy fabric of her top. "Are you going to walk me home?"

"Anything you want." His brain stopped functioning as she touched his denim-covered thigh under the table.

She leaned against his arm, resting her chin on his shoulder and spoke softly into his ear. "Maybe you should walk me to your place instead."

"Yes, ma'am."

She surprised him again, when instead of leaving separately, she grasped his hand and stood. Walking out of the bar, hand in hand, was a clear message. They made their way through the crowd, saying goodbye and thank you. With Vicky at his side, he didn't flinch at the rough claps on his shoulder and slurred goodbyes in the middle of the crowd. What did that mean for him when he'd have to let her go? And what about when the entire town found out he wasn't John?

What the hell are you thinking? You can't stay in Home once the real John moves back. It will be easier for the town to accept John if Callan wasn't there to remind everyone of their lie. Knowing John and Kaylie, the people that mattered would get over it. And with the mayor's help, the town would come around. They might need to be reminded that Blake was the bigger threat and without their deception, Blake might have been able to take advantage of John's situation.

"Don't go all broody and quiet on me now. You made it through the party without scaring anyone away. What's got you scowling now? The moon? Are you going to turn into a big scary werewolf? Is that your dark secret?"

She teased, but the dark secret part? That hit a little too close to home for him.

"You better watch out. You might be Little Red Riding Hood."

"Catch me if you can." She jogged a few steps forward, out of his reach, turning to walk backward.

Two long strides and she was in his arms, grinding her body into his. Her lips were soft under his, and her mouth opened for him to deepen the kiss. Damn she was perfect. They managed to get in the door of his apartment before undressing.

"Have I thanked you yet?" She spoke between laughing, kissing, and tugging at his clothes.

"I don't think you have."

She paused, arched an eyebrow at him and pursed her lips into a thoughtful expression. "Would you like me to show you?"

"Hell yes."

The remnants of the wall he'd built to protect himself, crumbled. She'd somehow managed to push her way into his soul. His thoughts were as full of Vicky as they were of the town or John, or even on how to avoid his father. She was as much a part of his life at that moment as anything he'd ever held important. Since returning from war, finding love hadn't been in the cards. Not the ones he'd been playing.

It looked like the deck had been reshuffled.

18

$\mathcal{C}$allan parked his truck in front of John's house. Nothing seemed out of place. No other cars on the road, coming or going. He read the text from Kaylie again. Damn his father. He'd called personally this time. That must mean he suspects Callan is back in Colorado. He knew it was a risk, coming back to his father's home state. He was hiding right under the man's nose. He punched the steering wheel, letting out some of his impatience. The darkness surrounded him, and he quieted. He could call him. That might shut him up, but it would also give him reason to believe his pressure on Callan's teammates was working.

He tossed his phone onto the passenger seat and got out. "Fuck that man," his voice echoed in the wide-open space. He was close to done. The mayor would be getting married soon, and the celebrities would be bringing their chaos to Home just in time for John and Kaylie to move back and Callan to disappear. Then there was Vicky. He couldn't warn her about having any dealings with the senator without it being personal. How could he tell her that the man didn't care who he ruined as long as he got what he wanted.

That was personal experience talking. He'd wanted a son only after he was running for his second term and he'd married his second wife. He'd harassed Callan's mother day and night and convinced her to send him to Colorado to stay. Callan had to endure being dragged from one picnic and stump speech to the next. Once the election was over and his father was in DC more than Colorado, Callan's new stepmom didn't want to be stuck with a ten-year-old and his father agreed to send him back to his mother. By the time he'd made it to Wisconsin where his mother had moved, the damage had been done. The fighting with his father had taken a deep toll. She was never the same.

The bastard had tried it again at Callan's graduation from high school. He'd thank his dad for one thing—if he hadn't shown up to graduation pushing an acceptance to his alma mater, Callan might not have joined the Army. Unfortunately, being deployed across the world hadn't kept the man from interfering, and once again, someone Callan cared about had paid the price. That would not happen again.

After a careful perimeter inspection, Callan was assured nothing had been disturbed. He relaxed and tried to forget about his father and focus on the here and now.

He'd spent most of the day with Vicky. After a late morning in bed, she'd kept him company while he finished painting the cathedral and replacing the doors. Without her by his side, the quiet solitude of the night didn't hold the comfort it once had. She couldn't spend all her time with him, and he didn't want to leave John's home empty for too long at a time.

The only light he'd use inside was the fireplace and a small lamp in the living room where he slept. In his first weeks in Home, he'd installed new security lighting outside: along the porch in the front and the back, at the detached single car garage, and the barn. All were on, illuminating the perimeter of everything of value on the property. Mainly, the house.

Nothing had been tampered with. If Blake had John's home on a list of potential targets, they hadn't made a move yet. He slipped into the shadow of the porch as a Jeep pulled into the gravel drive.

Sly sat in the driver's seat, but whoever was in the passenger side was obscured by the dark until he stepped out.

Callan opened the screen door as a stone-faced Sly pushed Carl up to the porch steps.

"Thought you could use some company," Sly said by way of hello.

"Not usually."

"This time you do. We've recorded some interesting footage. Carl here is going to explain some of it." The larger man grabbed Carl's collar and pulled him toward the doorway. "Isn't that right, Carl?"

"Yeah. Right," the kid mumbled.

Callan motioned them through the foyer and into the living room. "Don't mess with anything."

Sly not-so-gently pushed Carl into a chair. "Stay here." He and Callan conferenced in the doorway, voices lowered.

"I've got some footage of Carl and that asshole Barnes. Watch him," he told Callan.

That's all it took. While Sly grabbed what he needed from his Jeep, Callan stood guard in front of Carl.

"A mole for Blake, huh? Hope it was worth it," Callan said. His suspicion had been right. Carl could go around town unnoticed, and his mother was already against the wedding business. "Tell me what they have planned."

The kid stared up at him, wide-eyed. "It's not like that. Not what you think."

"Seems pretty simple from my point of view. What did they offer you to vandalize the sets?"

"That wasn't me." He tried to stand, but Callan pushed him back with an easy shove.

Carl seemed to shrink into his chair. "Okay, some of that was me, but I was just trying to delay the wedding. No real harm done. The plans are still on and you haven't sold out. Vicky's still here and making progress with the publicity."

Sly opened his laptop and set it on the coffee table in front of Carl. "Now, you're going to tell us about Barnes and what he's planning next."

He clicked some keys and brought up a video. "This is from yesterday, around midnight when the party was over."

Callan watched the video. The picture was remarkably clear for security footage of the bar's parking lot.

"There's our friend here, heading toward his truck."

Carl stiffened in his seat. "Isn't that illegal?"

"Actually, it's not. Now, shut the fuck up until I ask you a question or I'll show you what is illegal."

Callan smirked at Sly's act. Carl bought every bit of it. He had no doubt Sly could get as rough as needed, but this wasn't one of those times. Carl had been caught at something and was ready to talk.

"Here's where it gets interesting."

Callan watched as Barnes walked up behind Carl and pushed him into the door of his truck. Interesting.

"Someone's getting kind of rough. Want to tell us why?" Callan searched Carl's face and could see a reddened patch of skin under the hair hanging at his temple.

Callan sat on the edge of the coffee table in front of Carl. "Listen, we don't want to hurt you. We want to know what Blake's up to." The kid's eyes tracked Sly's every move. Someone's scared him.

"Did you talk to Carl's parents, Sly?"

Carl's face turned pallid. "Not my mom. Please. She'd kill me."

"Then tell us what you know."

"Okay." Carl scrubbed a hand over his face and sighed. "Okay. Look, it's not what you think."

"Of course not."

The kid straightened at Sly's sarcasm, a mulish expression tightening his features.

"My mom was ready to sell to Blake, she doesn't like the mayor's plans. Then my dad decided the town's plan was the way to go and wouldn't sign the paperwork. She was really mad. They could have moved and helped me pay for graduate school with the money Blake was offering."

"You decided to play saboteur because mommy and daddy wouldn't pay for college?"

"Not at first. Blake's representative stopped by a few times and my mom told him what the town was up to. As much as she knew anyway. One thing led to another and I got this message on my cell phone from the rep asking if I wanted a consulting job with them."

"The rep being St. James?"

"Um, yeah. At first and then it changed to this guy Barnes. I thought the job was tech related, but when I met with Barnes, all he wanted to talk about was how the job was when they got the town. Not before. If I wanted the job, I needed to do my part in helping them close the deal with the casino."

"Why's this guy not happy with you?"

"Cause he wanted me to do some things that could get me arrested, for real. I'm not stupid. He wouldn't put my job offer in writing. No way was I going to set myself up to take the fall for them and not get a job too."

"What did they ask you to do?"

"I stole some parts for the sets. Okay, I admit that. I drew the line at messing with people's homes or the stores. I wasn't going to hack into any more of the city's servers either. He liked having someone in town on their side. When I told him no more, Mr. Barnes, the douche who punched me, wanted to change my mind."

"I don't suppose you have any of this recorded in writing or phone messages or anything."

"No, they're totally clean. Just because I wouldn't do it doesn't mean they don't have a line of people waiting to do their dirty work. They thought offering me a dream job and my parents more money for their land would be enough."

"So walk away."

"They've got me over a barrel and my parents too if I don't give him what he wants. If I go to jail for this, they'll never live it down. He says he can make it look like my mom was involved too and I bet most of the people in town would believe it. You have to help me. I can't go to the police. I have no proof of anything and if I confess to that little bit of vandalism or about the hacking, I go down and they get away with everything."

"Tell me everything you know about Barnes and St. James."

"I only dealt with that Grayson guy in the very beginning. He left me alone after my dad refused the deal. Everything else was Barnes. I got the feeling Barnes doesn't like him."

Finally, they had something to work with. Carl remembered a surprisingly large amount of detail. He was a smart, if misguided, kid. He might be a decent adult one day. They finally had enough information to set up Barnes. Carl would be the perfect proxy to relay the unfortunate problem with the cameras overseeing the sets to Barnes, and Sly and Callan would be ready.

* * *

"Sure you can leave your girl for a night?" Sly asked, eyes never leaving the binoculars trained on the wedding sets in the distance. Callan ignored the question. He and Vicky were no one's business.

"Any movement?" Callan asked.

"Nothing since the sun's gone down." Sly handed him a pair of night-vision binoculars and stretched his shoulders. "Let's get closer. Even with a few streetlamps turned off, there's too much light here." He rolled onto his back and stood in one swift move.

"Who knows if they'll even take the chance tonight or

wait and see. We're going off the word of a scared kid with mommy issues."

Callan squatted next to where Sly had been perched behind the small wall along the roof line of the hardware store. "We don't know, but I'm willing to risk one night's sleep over the odds." It's not like he ever got much sleep anyway.

"Do you miss this shit?" Sly motioned to his pack. "Cause I don't."

"At least no one's shooting at us. You're the one with all the cool toys." Callan didn't know Sly's exact background, but he was pretty sure there were some alphabet letters after his name at one point in time. Glad to have him on the town's side.

"Habits, man. I'm an idiot with old habits too hard to break. And no one's shooting at us, yet. I don't hold out any hope this standoff between Home and Blake will end peacefully. You shouldn't either." He saluted and disappeared down the alley-side fire escape.

Callan waited, taking in the dark sky with clouds covering the white moon. They'd picked a hell of a night to try to catch Barnes in the act. Especially with only an assumption that what Carl said could be trusted. With his friend's dire predictions ringing through his thoughts, he surveyed the town on his shadowed route around to the east side of the park where he'd lie in wait. Ten p.m. on a normal weeknight—nothing special happening in town. He'd dodged the view of the few vehicles driving past. The stores were all closed. Even The Walrus would be closing in a couple hours. Then, anyone out and about would be suspect.

Midnight rolled around and the temperature dropped fifteen degrees as a cold front moved in. His muscles ached from lack of movement. The cloud cover deepened until the darkness shrouded his hiding place in an inky veil, impenetrable to the naked eye.

"You asleep over there?" Sly's voice jarred him from his quiet contemplation. He tapped the earpiece he'd forgotten he had on.

"See anything?"

"I've got movement. From Main Street. Someone sneaking in, keeping to the trees. Not sure where the hell he's going."

"Hold for now."

Callan scanned the area. Beyond the sets, along a line of oaks was a shadow that didn't belong. Gotcha. He got a good look at the man's face before he ducked into the darkness.

"St. Fucking James. I knew it."

"He's on the move. Heading for the sets."

St. James jogged from his hiding place to the chapel where Callan lost track of him.

"Move in from your side and I'll flank from here," Sly said into his ear.

He made it to the chapel and waved to Sly coming from the opposite edge. Callan moved around toward the doors.

"Out for a midnight jog?" St. James whipped around to face Callan.

"Fuck, Pearce. Where'd you come from?"

"Same place I did," Sly responded from behind them.

Callan grabbed Grayson by his shirtfront and pushed him against the wall. "I knew you were no good."

"Hey, watch the shirt. My tailor would be appalled at your treatment of his work."

"Maybe your dentist would appreciate this." He raised his fist, but St. James twisted, knocked his arm away, and blocked his oncoming punch. The man had skills.

"It's not what you think. Really." St. James held up his hand. "I'm not here to fight you either. Not my job."

Sly pointed. "Uh-huh. What's in your pocket?" Sly, watching from the side hadn't moved to intervene, only pointed.

St. James pulled out a hammer and a flashlight and shrugged. "It was all I had in my truck."

All the proof Callan needed to justify punching the asshole at least once before they called Deputy Hayworth.

"Seriously, guys." St. James threw up his hands, fending off Callan's advancement with a hammer and flashlight. "I'm here for the same reason you are. Trying to catch Barnes in the act."

Callan scoffed. "Yeah, right."

"I followed him here this evening," St. James said. "I lost him once we were in town."

"He's probably doing what your company hired him to do. Same as you," Callan challenged.

"But he's not." St. James lowered his voice to just above a whisper.

"I'm not saying Blake is above hiring out that kind of . . . assistance. But Barnes is off-script. Blake thinks they have everything they need to force their way as long as Barnes doesn't do anything stupid."

"Why should I believe you?"

"You don't have to." St. James lowered his hands and slid the hammer and flashlight back into his pocket.

"You're following him around for the sake of what, "Goodwill to Home? What would you do if you'd found him here instead of us?" Sly sounded as disgusted as Callan felt.

"Me? Just managing my future investment. I'm strictly a watch and report kind of guy."

"Your future investment?" Callan prodded. Had that been a slip or intentional.

"My employer's future investment." St. James corrected and held Callan's gaze.

Callan shook his head. "You said you lost Barnes. Where?"

"I could explain every move I've made over the last few hours, but that would keep us here. Exposed and not able to catch Barnes in the act of whatever he's up to if we haven't spooked him already."

He'd never trust St. James, but on the off chance he was telling them the truth about Barnes, they wouldn't stop him by standing out in the open.

Shoving Grayson inside the chapel ahead of him was pure spite. Smiling inwardly at the man's grunt when he landed against a pew. The need to inflict his own kind of harm pushed at him from a deep dark place he'd kept locked up tight.

Sly whistled from a far window, drawing his attention from the fight in his mind.

"I think I see some movement."

Callan and St. James rushed over to the window. Callan tracked the dark blur with his binoculars—Barnes, getting into his car parked in one of the alleyways darkened by the lack of streetlamp light and within view of where Callan had been stationed earlier that evening.

"Son of a bitch." They'd spooked him. Callan spun to face St. James. "I'm still not convinced you aren't here to help him."

"Too bad, Pearce. You'll have to fucking deal. Now, I've got to start all over again tracking him. Good job, fellas. Nice work catching the wrong bad guy."

"Not so fast. I want some information."

"That's not my business model."

"Your mouth is starting to piss me off." Sly put a hand on Callan's chest stopping him from moving closer to him.

Blake's front man let out a sigh. "Okay, look. I'm going to level with you. The powers that be are of two minds on how to move forward concerning Home.

"A power struggle going on with the board and the investors?

"You do have someone inside. I wondered." St. James said.

"Anyway, what Barnes is doing is not sanctioned but someone internal is directing it. You don't have to trust me. My bosses don't want a guy like Barnes messing up what they think is a sure thing here. I don't know why they changed their minds, but they did. They think they have the political pull to get the casino built no matter what the town does. As far as Barnes is concerned, I've been given the job of reigning him in or getting rid of him."

He laughed, bouncing his gaze from Sly to Callan. "Not like that. As in, handing him his papers and making it clear he's not needed in case he resists the idea."

"Why were you trying to catch him here then?" Callan asked.

"Because catching him in the act would help me get him back in line. It's simple and effective."

Callan wasn't sure he believed everything Grayson had said, but if true, it did hold some interesting possibilities. If there was internal strife at Blake headquarters then the project they had planned for Home could get shelved if it proved too problematic. They parted ways outside the chapel. No one expected Barnes or anyone else that might be working with him to try to get to the sets that night, and the cameras would be back up and running the next. They had a description and, hopefully, some photos of the car Barnes was driving, thanks to the cameras that they'd left on along Main Street. He left the park with more questions than answers but little he could actually do about it. They needed a break.

19

"Hey, Mom. You're up early." Vicky flopped onto the sofa, restless with a need to get her day started. She was out of interviews and no leads had surfaced to follow up on the senator. She was waiting on Neal to send her some more files. On the Home side, she had a nice drive to Telluride to deliver brochures to look forward to. Maybe she could get Callan to go with her.

"The website looks great, Queenie." Her mother sat in her favorite living room chair in front of a window overlooking the garden. "You've done an excellent job of highlighting everyone and all we have to offer." Her mother's compliment didn't match the tone of her voice.

"What's been going on with you lately? You haven't once lectured me, given me advice, tried to manage my aura, or get me to meditate. I think you're losing your touch."

Her mom didn't take the bait. "Blake has most of the outside landowners on their side now. Only John stands between them and the town."

"Yeah, but your big day is just around the corner, and we

only have a month until the big celebrity reveal. Now that almost all the plans are complete, can you tell me who it is? Have you been in contact with them recently?"

Her mom covered her face with her hands and started sobbing. "It's gone. It's all gone."

"What's gone?" Panic shot through Vicky. Her mother never cried. "What are you talking about?"

"There's no couple. They're gone. They backed out. We have no big wedding to plan anymore."

"Mom," Vicky said slowly. "The whole town is banking on this big splash in the news. Is there a contingency plan? Some kind of deposit at least?"

"Of course." Her mother sniffed into a tissue. "But the deposit won't even cover a fraction of the expense the town has put into it."

Part of Vicky wanted to scream and cry at the same time. "You have to tell everyone and stop the work."

"I can't. Don't you see? If we stop, the casino will win. They'll start selling their businesses and the town will be dismantled and put back together as some kind of quaint amusement park for tourists."

"You don't have a choice, Mom," she said, but in her mind, a ticker tape looped. Rochelle's fighting for her son. John and Kaylie. Callan's work on their house. Lil expanding her business. Mr. DeVito working so hard to honor his late wife. This wasn't some quick scheme that fell through—this was people's lives her mother had been playing with. "They deserve to know the truth."

Her mother grabbed her hands, squeezing tightly. Desperation gleamed in her unshed tears. "You have to promise me you won't breathe a word of this to anyone. I'll come up with a way to fix this. I'm not done yet."

Judy is ever the optimist. "Sometimes when things fall apart they can't be fixed, they have to be dealt with."

"I need your help, Queenie. We can fix this. Doesn't your friend Laura have some contacts in Hollywood? Her mom's some kind of director or producer or something, right?"

"I think. But what are you going to do? Call up a celebrity couple and ask if they'd like to rush a secret, themed wedding in nowhere, Colorado? That's not the way to make this right."

"You and the truth. Sometimes the truth hurts more than helps. In this instance, the truth would take away all the hope and crush the people here. No, we have to fix this."

"Just let me think. How long ago did they back out?"

"Last week."

Vicky's mouth fell open. "Last week?"

"The wedding was going to be spectacular. Have you seen the dress? It's the most beautiful one ever. I thought I'd found a kindred spirit. Someone who shared my dream. Someone who wanted to be the most beautiful princess bride the world had ever known."

The woman was delusional.

"You have to help me come up with a new plan, Queenie. I've gotten several inquiries about what we offer. If I can get several weddings booked, we might be okay. Another celebrity couple would be better and would bring in the kind of business we need to really keep Blake off our backs for good. The company's timeline for their investors will be up soon. We just have to keep going until then."

"Also worrying news."

"Yes, but we've held off this long. A little longer is all we need." Her mother's insistence on keeping up the appearance that everything was fine went beyond normal optimism. This was desperation and denial at its finest.

Vicky's phone buzzed in her pocket. Numbed by the magnitude of the secret her mother expected her to keep, she ignored the call. Suddenly a nice latte and a blog were preferable to keeping up another lie to the entire town. "I need to think." She grabbed her keys and purse from the table. "I'm going for a drive and deliver those brochures. While I'm gone, try to come up with an alternate plan besides a dream."

Sitting in her car, she waited for the shock to wear off a little before trying to drive. What were they going to do?

Vicky pulled her phone from her pocket at its third buzzing ring. Two missed calls from an unknown number and a message from an old coworker about a potential opening at a magazine. That was promising. Just as things were falling apart here. Of course. Timing was everything.

Her phone buzzed once more. The unknown number again. She answered with a curt, "If this is a sales—"

"Ms. Alexander. Nice of you to answer my call."

Vicky didn't recognize the man's voice. The deep tone was laced with a smugness that irked her already frazzled nerves.

"Who is this?"

"A friend. Do you want to save your town and keep Blake off your back?"

She wasn't in the mood to play around with mysterious

callers. "What do you know about Blake? Either tell me who you are or I'm hanging up."

"I have the evidence you need to stop Blake."

"What evidence?" Whoever this was, he sounded too confident in whatever scheme he'd cooked up. "Who are you and why should I believe you?"

"Do you want to make Blake back off or not?" She pulled the phone away from her ear at his outburst. Her questions had touched a nerve. She waited a beat before speaking.

"How do I know this isn't some kind of prank?" Reaching for her purse with her free hand, she rummaged for a pen and notepad.

"I know you've been investigating Blake and digging up past complaints against the company. I also know why you won't get anywhere with that line of research and what else they've got planned to break your little town."

"You're going to hand me evidence out of the kindness of your heart?"

"I have my own reasons for screwing Blake. We can discuss it when we meet. In case you've forgotten how this is done—come alone."

He rattled off the location for a wilderness trail between Home and Telluride and demanded to meet her at two that afternoon and hung up. Vicky stared at her phone, her thoughts whirling. She knew how this kind of thing was done. She also knew better than to go alone. However, the possible reward was worth the risk.

Telluride was just over an hour to the south. And the trail closer still. It was only ten in the morning. She could scope out the meeting place, set up some safeguards. She'd have to bring along someone to help. She knew who she could rely on, but would he do exactly as she asked?

There was only one way to find out.

She parked in front of the hardware store. Tyler was behind the counter helping a customer, which meant Callan was still in his apartment. She walked through the alley, up the steps and knocked.

The door was opened almost immediately. "You got here fast." Callan said with a smile, pulling her to him for a kiss.

"I was headed out when I texted you," she said.

He leaned back at her words, his gaze on her face. "Something wrong?"

"I need to ask you a favor."

They walked in and he shut the door behind them. "What do you need?"

She squeezed her hands around the straps of her bag, suddenly unsure of what to say.

"I received a call a few minutes ago, and I set up a meeting with someone and I want you to come with me."

"Okay."

"Before you say anything, I want you to remember I know what I'm doing and I've done far more dangerous things on my own."

"I don't like the sound of this."

She had trouble meeting his gaze and hesitated. "A man called me claiming to have info that could incriminate Blake Corporation for illegal activity." Her chin tipped up, and she stood straight-backed, ready for any challenge he gave her. He blew out a breath and crossed his arms at his chest.

"Who was it? What kind of evidence?"

"He didn't give me a name, and he wouldn't say over the

phone. Only in person. He gave me a place and a time to meet outside Telluride in a few hours."

"Not going to happen." Callan laid down the directive as if he had the authority to tell her what she could or couldn't do. She knew it was out of concern, but that didn't stop her pride from bristling.

"I'm going, and I'm asking you to come along as backup." She raised a hand at his protest. "Yes or no?"

"What did he want in return for this info?" he asked instead of answering her question. She bit back her impatience. She needed him.

"He didn't say. I expect a demand for money. He might think I can get my mom to use some of the town's coffers to pay him off." She marched toward the kitchen counter to give them some space. Discussing this while standing at the apartment door made her feel unwelcome.

"Listen. I'm doing this with or without you. I was headed to Telluride to run the brochures to a couple of stores, and then I'm going to the meeting place early to check it out. You can stay here or come with, but I need to go now."

"I'll go. You'll stay here." He threw the ultimatum out like it was a done deal.

"You think I'll agree to that? He called *me*. He wants to talk to *me*."

"You're smart. You know it's better if I go."

"No. I'm smart enough not to actually go alone. This isn't some anonymous restaurant he wants to meet me at. I'm not meeting a stranger in the woods without backup. Backup—not you going in my place."

"I don't like it. This guy could be a psycho or it's a setup by Blake."

"Either way, I'm still going." She leaned forward and reached for his hand, twining her fingers with his. "It's a chance to find out if there is someone outside of Home who has an ax to grind with Blake and potentially gain real evidence. If I don't show, he might get scared off and we'll lose the chance."

"Better than a lot of other scenarios I can think of." He took her hand and tightened his hold.

She couldn't meet his gaze. How would she feel if the situation were reversed? She wouldn't want to watch him walk into danger unprepared.

"I brought some stuff with me that might make you feel a little more secure." She tapped her bag with her free hand. "I never go anywhere without my mini-recorder and I keep my phone on as a backup. I also have a hidden camera. With you watching my back, I'd be prepared for anything."

The stubborn line of his frown eased a fraction. "I need two guarantees."

"We'll see."

"I must always have you in sight. I will not leave you alone, don't even ask me."

"Okay. You can stay in the car. How about that?"

He didn't agree or disagree. Definitely going to be stubborn about this.

"Second, if anything . . . and I mean anything . . . feels off, if I see anything odd you'll leave immediately, no questions asked."

"I'm not sure how I feel about your overprotective side. I'm not an idiot, and I don't need a parent or babysitter. This isn't the first time I've done this sort of thing. I have my own condition—you stay back and trust me, or I reschedule without you when he calls to find out why I'm a no show."

His mouth drew down in a straight line. "I guess I don't have a choice, then."

*a*t least she'd agreed to take his vehicle. He'd thrown a few supplies in a bag and they headed to Telluride. If she didn't recognize the voice it had to be Barnes. She'd know if the caller had been St. James or even Carl. His gut churned at the thought of Vicky walking into a setup by Barnes. His mind could conjure up all kinds of scenarios for what he was likely trying to accomplish by luring her out of town. He sent a text to Sly to let him know where he was going, and that things might be about to come to a head, but he wouldn't know until they met with the caller. He looked over at Vicky in the passenger seat. A blanket covering her legs, her hair back, and sunglasses on her face. Damn. He didn't like this. He should have insisted he go in her place. Not that she'd ever agree. At least she'd asked him to go along. The trust she had in him made his need to protect her even greater.

"Don't look so glum. This might be a good thing." She turned and tucked a leg underneath her and smiled at him.

"I'm not optimistic." He wouldn't assume Barnes—if it *was* Barnes—had any motive that wasn't self-serving."

"I know. Let's just get the errands over with first."

She gave him directions to the art boutique the mayor wanted the brochures to be placed in. She guided him to park right in the middle of the town, surrounded by quaint shops and galleries. "There's the boutique." She pointed to one with a large mountain landscape painting in the window. "My mom and the owner went to high school together. She says that a lot of the more famous tourists vacationing here visit her shop. We're hoping to snag a celebrity for a wedding."

"Another celebrity?" He asked. "Wouldn't more than one bring the paparazzi they supposedly want to avoid?"

"Uh, yeah." Vicky hopped out and grabbed the box of brochures. "But it would also bring in all the publicity Home would ever need." She shut the door with a bump of her hip.

"I'll stay out here. Maybe walk the block." He said, pulling a baseball cap onto his head.

"Be right back." She waved, and he watched her cross the street. It was a little past noon, and the sun had brought out the tourists. It wasn't quite peak ski season but that didn't stop the crowds from enjoying the small town. He needed to move. Sitting in the car was out of the question, but Telluride was not a good place for him; his father frequented the small town. He could be there, and it would be just his luck to run in to him after managing to stay out of his sight for most of the last year. He checked his watch and glanced back at the store that Vicky had just walked into. He headed in the opposite direction to make a quick tour around the block.

Seeing no one he recognized, he circled back to the gallery. He saw her through the window talking with another woman behind a counter. He'd meant to snag one of the brochures since his photo was in them but had forgotten in the midst of his concern for what the rest of the day held. Just as he was about to return to his Jeep, he spotted a tall blonde woman walking toward him.

"Well, shit." He ducked his head and turned toward the window as she approached. She held a phone to her ear and looked as distracted as usual. He watched her reflection in the glass until she passed him. Once out of her line of sight he hustled across the street and into his Jeep. His father's long-time girlfriend probably wouldn't have recognized him, but he didn't want to take the chance. Whatever she was doing in Telluride meant his father was probably close. He never should have agreed to come.

Vicky wasn't far behind him. "We need to go," he said as soon as she opened the door and slipped into the seat.

"Is something wrong?"

"No. I just need to get out of the middle of town."

"Don't want that woman to see you here with me?"

Oh, Christ, did she see something? "Woman?"

"I don't want any lies. Tell me the truth. I saw the way you watched her and hid your face. Who is she? An ex? Wife? Girlfriend? What?" She looked at him, beseeching. She wasn't angry. It was more . . . hurt.

"I don't have a girlfriend or wife or lover on the side. There's only you." Some of the tension left her shoulders.

"Well?" she asked as he shut his door and started the engine.

"Well what? I don't know what you're asking." Did she want him to declare her the only one for him? It was true. He'd realized it the first time they'd made love but didn't admit it. Not even to himself. He wasn't capable of just a fling—he'd opened up to her in a way he hadn't before, and she got it.

"Who was the woman you were hiding from?"

He rubbed his hand over the back of his neck and tried like hell to think of something to get her off this line of questioning. "The crowds are getting to me, that's all."

She eyed him from her side of the cab in stony silence as he drove. He couldn't tell if she'd bought it or not. His gut twisted at the lie.

Dammit. He took a deep breath and concentrated on the directions she'd given him to the meeting site.

His truck was as cold as the air flowing in from the open roof.

As soon as they turned into the clearing that held the trailhead she was expected to follow, Vicky finally shifted from her stiff position and faced him.

"Look, I don't want to argue. But I don't want to be lied to either. Can you just tell me the truth?"

His stomach dropped and a hollow pounding in his chest stole his breath. No lie would come, but what would she think of the truth?

He strangled the steering wheel. "Okay, you're right. I have been hiding something."

Disappointment crossed her features, and she lowered her eyes to her lap. He pulled over to the side of the road and cranked up the heater. His excuses sounded hollow and weak now, but he needed to explain.

"Senator Fletcher is my father, and the woman I saw is his girlfriend." There was no other way than to just say it. No hedging or excuses.

Her gaze flew to his, eyes wide. "What?"

He glanced from her to the view of mountains all around. Usually, a sight worth taking time to appreciate. Maybe he'd be able to once all the truth was out.

"I'm the reason Lewis, the weaselly little bastard, was in Grand Junction. He was looking for me and trying to get information from John and Kaylie about where I might be. His campaign team has been trying to get me to be part of his reelection. Nothing looks as good as a son injured in war but fighting on, standing at his side. Total bullshit."

"Why didn't you tell me before?"

Her voice sounded remarkably calm. He peeked at her and his chest tightened. He couldn't read her. She'd get it soon. Would she walk away? He wouldn't blame her.

"I didn't want you to use me to get to him. I know now you wouldn't, but at the time, when you first mentioned my father, I didn't want to talk about him. I stay out of his political career and I plan to keep it that way."

She studied him a moment. "You didn't trust me not to respect your choice? Sleeping with me was okay, but trusting me not to use you without giving me a chance was too much of a stretch for you?"

He flinched when she said it so casually.

"You wouldn't have asked me what I thought? Or what I might be able to find out?"

She flushed, and guilt burned in his gut for laying that

on her. Of course, she would have asked about him. But maybe he'd been wrong not to trust that she would've respected his decision not to be involved. She was the only one keeping his and John's secret. Why'd he think his identity would have been too tempting for her to keep to herself? Because she was desperate to win back her job in DC? Too stubborn to allow himself to believe in them, he'd defaulted to self-protection over trust.

"You don't have to worry." She took in a deep breath and let it out slowly. "I won't ask you about him, but I'm not dropping the story. He's canceled some hearings, which have rumors flying about why he's gone missing a few times. His staff has been scrambling with excuses that don't ring true. He's been coming and going to Colorado more often than usual."

He snapped his jaw shut before he said anything more. If he didn't want to talk about it, he didn't get to ask about it either. He didn't blame her for continuing her story. His father was a public figure and one he'd known firsthand was swayed by money and power more than ethics. If anyone needed to be kept under watch, it was him, but Callan wanted nothing to do with it.

"I'm sorry," he said, bringing her attention to his face. "I didn't mean for you to find out this way. I need you to understand something. My father can't know I'm in Home or he'll show up and ruin what the town has going on in order to make it about him or a benefit to him in some way. It's what he does."

"Okay." She turned to the window. Even a foot away felt like miles. How he wished he knew the right words to make this better. Put them back where they'd been one day before.

The wall he'd built to keep himself from growing too attached had cracked and true feelings had snuck through. He couldn't pretend to only be interested in the light affair she said she wanted. But now, he had no choice.

"He showed up at the hospital the day I got back to the states." If they couldn't go back to how it was between them, she had to understand why his father couldn't be involved. "I was a mess. There wasn't enough morphine to stop the pain. I had to be sedated to be still enough to heal. He visited, and at first, I thought maybe there was something there. His concern seemed genuine." He'd been a fool.

"He was in my room several times as I drifted in and out of consciousness. Then, as I started to be awake more often, his visits tapered off to phone calls and then it was calls from his aide checking in. Then it was calls from his aide and representatives of the higher brass for interviews even though I'd refused to be a part of his political life. It didn't matter what I wanted."

Let's talk about a job when you're out of the hospital. Your father needs you. The campaign could really use you, and you owe it to him to be a part of it.

"As soon as I could, I dropped off the grid. I came out here to see John, and when his father died, well you know the rest."

Her gaze clashed with his. He could read the sympathy shining in her wide eyes. Motherfucker. He could kick himself for the catch he heard in his own voice. Dammit. He sure as hell didn't want her pity.

* * *

Vicky stared out of the window watching as the sun swept into another beautiful sunset.

Could she blame Callan for the way he'd felt? No.

Was she pissed he didn't trust her enough to tell her earlier? Yes.

Did she understand? Yes. After all, she'd been telling him all along she wasn't staying, and she'd told him about running into Mr. Lewis and how she planned to pursue the story and use it to get the *Chronicle* to give her a second chance.

She'd met people like Senator Fletcher before. From the way he'd been described, coupled with her own experience, the man was a self-serving career politician. He wasn't the first and wouldn't be the last.

She wasn't going to stop looking into what he was up to. She and Neal had dug up some interesting facts about him lately, and despite whatever Callan might think, Vicky had no plans to connect his father to anything related to Home.

She sighed and got out of the truck and waited as Callan followed her around to where she leaned against the bumper. "I promise I won't tell him I know you or where you are. Not that I'll be speaking to him anytime soon. I'm gathering data and will contact his aide for a response to my findings. He won't find out anything about you from me, I don't use the people I . . ."

"Sleep with?" he offered, his mouth pulled up in one corner.

She'd almost said love. Too much, too soon. She wasn't really sure what she felt about Callan right then, but she knew it was something more than the fling they'd started with.

"Yes. And . . ." Her throat seized, the words backing up. "Friends."

He scrubbed a hand over his face. She stifled an urge to soothe the hurt she'd seen.

"Were you ever going to tell me?"

He blew out a breath and gripped the tailgate with both hands. "I've wanted to tell you, but I wasn't sure when or how. It's not something I've ever talked about. Only John and Kaylie know. When you brought him up, I couldn't say anything. The town still had a long way to go, and I knew if he even thought I might be there, he'd show up or one of his people would and everything I've done to help John would be in jeopardy."

"Did you think I wouldn't find out?"

"I knew it was just a matter of time. It's not a secret, though it's not widely known. We're not a part of each other's lives and haven't been since I was a kid and he remarried a second time. That marriage didn't last for long either."

"I believe you, but I don't understand why you think one man could ruin everything you've done."

"All his life he's been out for number one. Himself and his power trip of a career. He divorced my mother when I was little and left to pursue a more respectable woman for the wife of an up-and-coming politician. My mother never forgave him for taking away the life she wanted. High society dinner parties, DC wives club, the whole works."

"I visited him the first few summer's after they split, but soon the visits got shorter and shorter and tapered off completely. One summer he needed me, but only for the campaign trail. He fought my mother and almost destroyed her to get me to live with him. As soon as he had what he wanted, I was sent back to my mom. She was never the same after that. He came to my high school graduation just to try to convince me to go to his university. I joined the Army the next day."

"Perhaps it's different this time?"

"Just before my accident, I told you I'd been pulled out for a special assignment. It turned out to be some bullshit representation thing with some reporter wanting a special interest story about a politician's active-duty son. John was sent on patrol in my place. They were under heavy attack almost immediately and when I requested to be sent to help, I was given the order to escort the journalist to his next post. If I'd been there, John would be okay."

"Your father put pressure on them to give the reporter access to you?"

"I didn't put it together as something my father had orchestrated until his aide mentioned it during one of his calls."

"You could have died, and I know John doesn't blame you for not being there because of something you had no control over."

"Perhaps, but I'll always know. If I'd been there, John wouldn't have lost so much. He had six days left on his tour." He paced a few steps away, out of her reach. She wanted to wrap her arms around him, but she was also hurt he'd been able to hide something like this from her so easily. She'd gone and jumped into something that was supposed to be light and fun and gotten too attached and vulnerable.

Faced with the raw pain that had fed his guilt all these months, her heart ached for him. Yes, she understood better why he'd want to keep his father far away and even why he'd go to such extremes to pay back a friend he felt he'd wronged so terribly.

"John loves you like a brother. And not just because of what you're doing for him. You could have a new life in Home."

"If Home exists in another few months, maybe." Crap. He came back to the problem that loomed over all of them.

She grasped his hand in hers, "We'll figure it out." He pulled her close and she let him envelop her in a hug. She squeezed her arms around his waist and breathed in the warm, clean scent of him before stepping back.

"Let's get this over with. Our mystery guest is supposed to be here in less than an hour."

* * *

Callan scanned the area and tried to focus on the tasks at hand. Secure the meet site. Keep Vicky safe. Gather information. The location was remote with an accessible area between the trail head and the road. They'd parked close to the trees with no other cars in sight.

The tension that had built lessened as they worked their plan. Vicky seemed to be taking everything he'd confessed in stride. Relief that she would keep him out of any discussion with the senator warred with concern over what his father might be up to and how it might hurt Vicky. A twig snapped to his left, startling him. *Get your head back in the game.*

"This is where he said to meet."

Not exactly the kind of place he'd expect Barnes to have picked for a clandestine meeting. There was only one way in and out unless he hiked in from the trail. The trees obscured the path after only a few feet. The mountains created a striking view in the distance.

"Stay here." Callan kept his eye on the horizon. His skin prickled. They were open and vulnerable. Whoever wanted to meet had half a dozen places to hide and watch them. His instincts screamed at him to take cover or better yet, get back in his truck and get out.

He slipped into the trees and brush flanking the empty parking area and checked the first hundred feet of the trail and the surrounding cover. Nothing moved that wasn't supposed to live there. Vicky sat in his truck with the window down, huddled in her coat. She hid her nervousness well.

"Anything?" she asked when he returned.

"If he's out there already, he's well hidden." He swiveled his gaze from the footpath to the road and back.

She got out of the truck and walked a quick circle, hands on her hips. She checked her watch. "He should be here soon. Time for you to get out of view."

"I'm not leaving you alone." Stand in the trees and hide? What would be the point?

"Just go on. I'm fine." She shoved lightly at his chest. "Far enough that if he's not actually watching us, he might not see you right away."

Callan left Vicky in the clearing. Every step he took with his back to her fought against his need to protect. He was supposed to avoid stressful situations. Checking over his shoulder every few steps, he assured himself Vicky was fine.

He took one step inside the tree line and stopped. He

wouldn't hide any further in. Vicky waved her hands at him. "Go," she mouthed.

He shook his head and held his stance. She stomped her foot and frowned.

Their silent argument was interrupted by a black SUV pulling into the parking area and flashing its lights.

He recognized Barnes the minute he stepped out of the truck. Callan stepped out of the tree line, in clear sight of Vicky and Barnes.

The man sauntered toward Vicky.

"I told you to come alone. You didn't have to bring your guard dog." His voice carried across the clearing.

"I live in the real world. I don't trust that you mean me no harm."

Callan smirked at Vicky's fierce reply.

Barnes stopped a few feet from her, their bodies angled toward Callan, but he couldn't hear what he said.

Barnes eyed him as he approached.

"Pearce. I guess you're here to protect your sweet little piece from big bad me."

"Fuck you, Barnes. Heard you were looking for a new job."

The man stilled, his features stone-cold. Whatever he wanted from Vicky, Callan didn't care. Barnes was dangerous.

"Grayson's been telling stories. A man like me, is never unemployed for long."

Vicky remained silent at Callan's side, but he felt the weight of her stare.

"What is it you want out of this meeting?" Vicky interjected her question into the icy confrontation.

"I suppose we can negotiate if you keep him on leash."

Callan tensed, itching to hurt the asshole.

"We're here to talk. Right?"

"Depends on how much you want to know what Blake is up to."

"You said you have credible evidence of illegal activities in Home. Their harassment. Their directive to buy out the town's businesses just to close them and force the citizens of Home out of their town."

Barnes rocked back on his heels and whistled, his black stare never leaving Vicky's. "I could be persuaded to find that exact kind of information."

"For the right price?" Vicky demanded.

"Of course. I have expenses, and my time in your little backward piece of shit town has cost me more than I'm willing to let go." Barnes shrugged, a tight grin lifting the corners of his mouth.

"How much?"

"Fifty grand. Up-front."

Vicky's surprised gasp elicited a laugh from Barnes. "That's a bargain basement price."

"Forget it. This guy doesn't know anything." Callan stepped in front of Vicky, eye to eye with Barnes, "Get lost and forget her number."

Vicky pushed up next to his side, elbowing him for trying to shield her.

"You know I can't pay you fifty thousand dollars. There has to be something else you want. Maybe you have your own reasons for seeing Blake fail."

Another vehicle sped into the parking lot, blocking

Barnes's truck. He and Vicky both jumped at the noise. Barnes turned, took one look at the truck, and cursed.

"St. James too? I'm disappointed in you, Ms. Alexander. I thought this was something a reporter of your caliber would understand." Barnes pulled Vicky in front of him before Callan could react. Panic flared. If he made the wrong move, Vicky could be hurt before he got to them.

Blocked from his escape by Callan on one side and Grayson next to his truck, Barnes pulled Vicky with him as he backed up a few steps and then pushed her, hurtling her toward Callan, who caught her, holding her close. "You're okay."

Barnes ran toward the trailhead and disappeared into the trees.

A split second of distraction by St. James and Barnes had had his hands on Vicky. He'd failed to keep her safe.

She pulled out of Callan's arms and straightened. "Why's Grayson here?" Vicky asked.

"Callan?"

Words wouldn't come. His hands were fisted tightly, his knuckles were white circles protruding from reddened skin.

He was ready to pound fucking Grayson into the ground. If Grayson hadn't distracted him, he'd have had his hands around Barnes's neck.

"You can hit me after you hear me out," Grayson called to him, hands out as he hurried toward them.

"He's not going to hit you." Vicky had managed to place herself between them and even with his fist half raised, she didn't budge.

"I don't know what you two are doing out here, but if it

involves Barnes, it wasn't going to end how you hoped it would," Grayson said.

"That doesn't explain why you're here." Vicky sounded as angry as he was feeling.

"I've had a tracker on his car, trying to find out how he was staying close enough to know what was going on in Home. His last signal came from here about an hour ago and he's been here before a few times." Grayson held his phone in his hand and looked around the empty area in front of the trailhead. "When the signal stopped here several times, I drove here to see what it was."

"Stupid move." Callan advanced toward St. James.

Vicky placed a hand on his chest before he could say more.

"What's going on, Grayson?" She gave him a shut-up look and he clamped his jaw closed with a loud click.

"For now, a warning. I'm out of Blake as of today, but you should know, there are some hard feelings about the latest obstruction to the company's plans and the fact not as many have signed on as they'd hoped. Barnes is not taking his forced hiatus lightly, and Blake Corp. wants to distance themselves from him. This might slow them down, but don't underestimate how much they want the land and Home. They'll send another one like him, eventually. Well, maybe one with more finesse, but with the same mission. They aren't the top developers in the state without having a lot of muscle."

"Can you help me prove it?" Vicky aimed her plea at St. James.

"I've been sidelined on this one but if it were me, I'd keep an eye on your place." He pointed to Callan and ignored Vicky's question. "It's at the top of the list of prob-lems to be taken care of. If they have Pearce land, the rest will fold."

"Dammit. Get in the truck, Vicky," Callan demanded. He looked at the trail Barnes had disappeared down and back to Vicky, already moving to the passenger door.

"He has to come back to his truck eventually. I'll wait. You go," Grayson said. "It's not worth trying to track him up the trail. Whatever he wanted with Vicky, he knows he can't get it now."

* * *

Callan eased the truck into drive but soon was testing the limits of his speedometer. "I'm dropping you at your car." After listening to Vicky's pleas for him to be careful, they rode in silence. An hour later, he stopped at her car. She opened her door and then turned to him.

"You shouldn't go out there alone. What if someone's waiting for you?"

"I can handle whatever Blake throws at me."

"I'm calling the sheriff to meet you out there." She wouldn't get out of the truck until he looked at her. "Promise me you'll be careful."

"Tell Hayworth I'll be waiting."

As soon as she was in her car, he took off for John's. If anything had happened, he'd never forgive himself. He'd forgotten his priority and his mission, and someone might have gotten hurt.

---

*T*wo days.

She's had no word from Callan since he went out to John's. Vicky reached for her phone but stopped before pulling it from her purse. She wouldn't send him another text. She'd alerted the sheriff the moment Callan had dropped her off and had raced home to find her mother. No one seemed as concerned as Vicky thought they should be. Deputy Hayworth at least had headed out to John's and put the rest of the department on alert, but without any proof and without anything actually happening, his hands were tied. Callan had assured her nothing had been disturbed at John's, but he'd stay out there to make sure no one saw it sitting unattended.

Then radio silence.

With nothing but time, her mom had dragged her into the chaos of last-minute wedding preparations. So much so, she craved a few moments of quiet to think. Pacing the length of her bedroom wasn't helping. A couple days of not seeing him shouldn't have affected her—keeping her mind off him was impossible.

Forget this. I have to get out and do something.

The voices of her parents in the kitchen floated up the stairs to her open bedroom door. The lovebirds were going over wedding vows. They didn't need her bad mood bringing them down. Vicky grabbed her coat and walked into the cusp-of-fall coolness. The sky, awash with purple and pink from the setting sun, highlighted her path into town. Time away from her parents and their soon-to-be-wedded euphoria would be a good thing. Soon her mother would have to confess about the celebrity non-wedding. Her own wedding wouldn't bring much revenue to Home's businesses. What would Callan and the rest of the town do then?

She couldn't simply let him handle it like everyone else did. He'd built more than half the sets. Stupid, ridiculous sets that were going to turn out to be a big waste of time, money, and energy.

None of the wedding business would have been possible without him. He'd assumed the identity of John and the burden the town had put on him with no thought other than to help.

She'd alternated between being angry and hurt. If she were honest with herself, her hurt mixed with a little guilt because she would have pressed him to tell her something about the senator.

She ignored the voice in the back of her head telling her to have faith. She was mad, yes. She felt guilty and responsible, yes. But she wasn't so mad she didn't want to see him anymore.

Their deal about a no-strings fling had ended.

Because there were strings, dammit. Lots of them.

She passed the hardware store entrance and had to stop herself from walking up the steps and knocking on his door to see if he was there instead of out at John's. She could have driven out there herself, but she'd stubbornly hoped for an invitation.

The temperature had dropped, and she huddled in her coat. The town was empty and quiet. It wasn't late but the sun had set and it was getting dark early. She'd gotten used to this walking thing.

The Walrus had a small crowd given the few cars in the lot, but that wasn't what she was in the mood for. The lights were still on at Split Ends. Peeking through the glass, she expected to see Rochelle inside.

Instead, she saw broken mirrors, bottles knocked over, and the cash register open. Her heart pounded. Rochelle. She pushed on the door and the bells jangled like normal. Opening the door brought with it the smell of ammonia, and other unidentifiable chemicals. Someone had spilled hair dye and bleach all over the furniture. Every surface was damaged in some way.

"Rochelle." Vicky called out. No one answered. She pulled her phone out of her pocket to call the sheriff. Stepping around the bottles and puddles, she picked her way to the back while dialing but the call was dropped.

"Rochelle?" Silence. Fearing the worst, she pushed through the curtains and into the back room and office. No one was there. Thank God.

She rushed back out on to the sidewalk. No one was around that she could see. She dialed the sheriff's emergency number, but the call was dropped again. Stepping further out, halfway into the street by then, she dialed again the second more bars popped up on her phone.

"Hello. This is Vicky Jones. I want to report a break-in at Split Ends."

A noise from her left caught her attention. A dark shape sped toward her. Oh, shit. She jumped out of the way as the car almost hit her. Tripping on the curb, she landed hard on her side, and her hands and knees scraped the walkway. Her phone tumbled out of her hand. She lay there a moment, catching her breath.

What the hell just happened?

Shaking and in pain, she sat up and felt around for her phone. Oh, thank God. The case had done its job. She finally reached the sheriff's office, help would be there soon. She'd keep any passersby out of the way until help arrived.

* * *

"What were you thinking going in there alone?" Callan paced in front of her as she sat on the curb.

"I was thinking my friend might need some help."

Vicky looked around at the spectacle Split Ends had become. The street had been blocked off, the sheriff and his deputy were there, emergency lights blazing. Thankfully, they'd turned off their sirens. But not before anyone within earshot had come out to see what was going on. She'd been sitting next to her mother, Grams, and Rochelle when Callan had come over to give her the same lecture her mother had.

He looked pissed. She couldn't help that. The sharp sting of guilt for not taking precautions pricked her conscience.

He paced and ran his hand through his hair and over his beard. He seemed to be getting more and more agitated as the commotion grew.

"Excuse me," she said to her mother. "John and I need to talk."

She led him out of the crowd, grabbing two to go coffees from Jo's. No one wanted to miss out and everyone wanted to discuss what had happened and Jo wasn't one to miss out on an opportunity for business so had set up a table outside. Was it the same vandals sabotaging the wedding sets? Was it Rochelle's asshole ex? She caught the tail end of one discussion as they walked toward the park, "It's Queenie's blog, I tell you. Publicity brings people in, and our town isn't ready for strangers." She bit back a reply and focused on Callan instead.

"You should stay with Rochelle."

"Jo's feeding Jason pie and ice cream, and Mom, Dad, and Grams are with Rochelle. She has more help than she needs right now." She reached out and grabbed his arm, pulling him to a stop. "I'm worried about you."

Sirens and blue lights flashed at the end of Main Street as another sheriff's deputy, or maybe a state police officer, approached quickly.

"I need to get away from here and back to John's." He tossed the still full coffee into a trash can and marched away from her.

Torn between finding out what was going on and racing after Callan, Vicky stood in the middle of the park and tried to decide which way she should go. Rochelle was surrounded by people to take care of whatever she needed help with. Callan was alone, and he didn't look like that was a good place for him to be.

Topping the small rise that denoted Hollers Hill, she found him sitting with his back to a tree. She could barely make out his shadow, and only because of the contrast his white T-shirt made against the dark night.

"Callan?" she called, grateful no one else was around. She didn't think calling him John then was the best thing to do. What she'd read about PTSD wasn't that informative, but if he's had some sort of episode, calling him another man's name probably wouldn't be helpful.

"I'm here." His voice rose out of the darkness.

"Hi." She sat cross legged next to him. She wasn't sure what to say.

"You really shouldn't have followed me."

He looked as tense as before, but he rested his head against the tree with his eyes squinted closed. His fists were on his knees. He looked like he was in pain. She placed a hand over his. "You can talk to me."

"I don't want to hurt you."

Her heart squeezed at the bitterness she heard.

"You won't."

He laughed, a brittle, coarse sound that held no humor. "You don't know that."

"I might not know all your secrets, but I know you wouldn't hurt me."

His fist slowly uncurled, and she linked her fingers with his, palm to palm. The moonlight glinted off the deep blue black of his hair. The lights from town were aglow through the trees, but somehow, they felt a million miles away.

She didn't say anything else. Nothing more was needed except to sit with him until his grip loosened.

Surrounded by night, cocooned in the shadows, his gaze locked with hers. She leaned closer and traced the scar along his jaw, running her hand over his beard along the way.

"It's soft. Have you always had a beard?" The question popped out without much thought. She didn't want to talk about what had happened yet.

His smile was small, but she caught the flash of white teeth in the dark.

"I grew it to cover the scar, it was easier." He humored her with an answer.

He brushed a lock of hair behind her ear, fingering its softness before lightly gripping the back of her skull and pulling her the few inches closer. She hesitated a fraction before giving in. What the hell? She wanted him. The truth of what she'd said earlier hit her. She trusted him, even though he'd lied to her. Right then, that was all she needed to make it okay.

His kiss started out light, his hand holding her softly. Leaning into him she opened her lips, the tip of her tongue exploring, pressing for more. He groaned and tightened his hold in her hair. His other arm snaked around her waist and pulled her into his lap, mouth slanted over hers. She locked her fingers behind his head and held on. They didn't separate until the cold air finally seeped through the layers of warmth around them.

"You're freezing," Callan whispered.

"I'm good," she insisted and pulled his head back down to hers. Even that couldn't stop her teeth from chattering.

"Okay. It's freakin' cold. Take me home. We can deal with this tomorrow."

"Sly will show the sheriff whatever footage they have from the cameras and whoever did this will be caught. If it's Blake, we'll know soon enough."

They walked over the hill toward Main Street hand in hand.

Their love making that evening was explosive and so perfect it made her ache for more. They fell asleep side by side but woke, and she could sense the restlessness in him. He told her she could stay, but she thought maybe he needed a break from her or maybe just a break from people in general. "I'll see you tomorrow." A long, lingering kiss swept any questions aside.

Once home, she had as much trouble getting to sleep as Callan had staying that way.

Vicky set her book aside and squeezed the bridge of her nose between her thumb and forefinger. The headache that had started wasn't letting up and she was too unfocused to read and too anxious to sleep. Pushing her feet into her slippers, she shuffled downstairs. Since she wasn't getting any sleep, she could at least get some work done. The light in her mother's office glowed through her glass paneled doors. *That woman, I swear. Resting is like a four-letter word to her. Maybe getting married in a couple of days was keeping her awake too?* Vicky knocked lightly while opening the office door.

"What are you doing up?" Vicky asked.

"Working. I thought you were a heavier sleeper."

Vicky plopped down into one of the plush chairs across

from her mother's desk. "I couldn't sleep either. I feel so bad for Rochelle."

"Wine?" Her mother pulled a bottle and a glass out from behind her desk. "I was going to have a glass but you caught me."

"Mom. It's after midnight."

"What? It's good for my heart and after everything, I needed to relax. With the video feed from the stores showing that Barnes guy sneaking around Split Ends, we might have leverage against Blake. I'm sure their lawyers will be able to weasel him out of any real charges but maybe we can use their distraction to gain some momentum on our weddings." She let out a long sigh and took another sip of her wine.

"In that case . . ." Vicky left to grab a glass from the bar. It had been a hell of a day.

Settling back into her chair, she sipped her wine in silence for a few minutes. She used to feel out of place in her mother's office. A space that had been off-limits as a kid. Now she saw it reflected her mother's personality to perfection. A comfortable place with a calming effect she admired.

"You know Dad and Grams aren't going to leave you alone tomorrow. They're going to force a day of leisure on you if it's the last thing they do."

"Don't tell them about this." Her mother raised her glass.

Vicky snorted, "Just add it to my list of secrets."

"We're almost there, Queenie. I responded to several emails requesting information about the weddings we could provide. The assistant for the bride we had scheduled gave our brochure to a few people. Word of mouth is all we have left to help us find another high-profile wedding. We've done all the advertisement we can afford. Blake has backed off while they clean up the Barnes mess. They won't just go away, but their pause is our gain."

"What if we don't get enough time? What will you do then?"

Her mother shook her head. "I don't want to think about it yet. One of these has to pan out. This one's local referred by my friend at the gallery in Telluride." She passed a piece of paper to Vicky. "Can you meet with them tomorrow. I can't do it myself and I don't want to put it off. Everything is ready and slowly building momentum for the small businesses. It's all coming together, one big wedding would set everything in motion."

"I hope we get one soon." That sounded weak even to her ears.

"Are you finally going to tell me what's really bothering you?" Setting her wine glass on the table, she used her serious mother voice and speared her with *the* look. The one that could see through any lie she might have tried to make up as a kid.

"What do you mean?" She wasn't a kid any longer.

"Oh come on. I'm your mother. I know when something's bothering my one and only child. Is it you and John?"

"No." Taking another sip, she tried to get her thoughts under control. "Yes. I don't know." One minute she was mad, the next she couldn't wait to see him again and the next she was on the verge of tears at the idea of not seeing him again.

"Are you falling in love with him?"

The direct question was like a smack to the head. "I . . .

maybe." Saying it out loud would make it real and something she'd have to confront. Easier to keep it to herself for a little while until his feelings were clearer.

"There's no maybe. You either are or you aren't, and if you don't know, you probably are."

"I'm close on a story that my editor is willing to give me a second chance with." She didn't mention the senator or the fact that she really only had pieces of a story without any real context.

"I see."

"It's what I've been looking for."

"I'm happy for you, sweetheart. Though I do wish you'd give Home's offer some serious thought. You've done a fantastic job with the promotions, and we need a public relations manager. How does Callan feel about it?"

How would Callan feel about it?

Her mother raised an eyebrow at her lack of response. "Haven't you told him?"

Vicky shook her head. Wait. "Callan?"

"Would you rather me keep calling him John?"

Vicky stared. "How long have you known?"

"Since about the second time I talked to him."

The matter-of-fact answer threw her a moment. Was she serious? How many more secrets were there for her to discover?

"I've kept track of the real John Pearce since he moved away. His dad asked me to help him arrange to leave the store and property to him when he found out he was terminal. I found out John had been badly injured and had returned to Grand Junction just before Jed died. When Callan took over the store and had Dewey and Mr.

Singleton calling him John, I didn't say anything until I looked into who he was. I know John's been at the VA hospital while this Callan has been working his ass off for us here."

"Do you know who he *really* is." Vicky asked.

"I know his name and that he's from John's old unit in the Army and what I could find online which wasn't much. I know he's been helping this town and remodeling John's home. I figured if I asked him for enough help, he'd get tired of it and confess he wasn't the real John, but he took all the requests and moved forward like it was expected. I couldn't figure out what was in it for him or if he was scamming us in some way. I decided to let the charade continue until John was no longer at the hospital. As far as who he really is —for anyone that loyal, I didn't dig further, nor do I care. Except when my only daughter is in love with him."

"Wow. I don't know what to say. He doesn't know you know?"

Her mother shook her head. "Not that I'm aware. And don't change the subject."

She puffed out a breath and slumped in her chair. "Why can't it be simple and straightforward?"

"Love is always complicated. Don't be too hard on him. If you want it bad enough, you can work it out. Look at me and your father—we've been together forever and are finally getting married. I'm having the dream wedding I never thought was possible. If it's meant to be, you can make it happen."

Vicky contemplated her mother's advice as she drained her glass. If it's meant to be, it will be. She wasn't so sure.

22

*Y*awning from her night of no sleep and too much wine with her mother, Vicky stepped into Jo's for something to eat before her drive to Telluride. The day's special was curried chicken salad and spiced tomato soup. Vicky eyed the other diners at Jo's. They were so close to making something of the town's crazy dream. So close she wanted to cry. They could beat the odds. They could make it if they had a little more time.

Maggie stopped at her table, sliding the plate with the thick sandwich and steaming soup to her as she leaned against the wall in her booth.

"What's the matter honey?"

"Nothing." Vicky smiled and tried to project happiness and confidence. "Just a lot of details to work out."

"Well, you better get your beauty rest, the wedding tomorrow is going to be a real shindig.

She left her to her thoughts.

A minute later, Rochelle came in, head wrapped in a sweatband, hair pulled back in a ponytail, and wearing a baggy sweatshirt over leggings. She smiled at Vicky and waved as she picked up her to go bag. Instead of heading back out the door, she stopped by her table.

"Hey, would you tell John when you see him how much I appreciate everything he's done. The store's almost back to new, and as soon as I have my stock delivered it will be. He's worked all night and his crew too. And tell your momma not to worry, I'll be ready for her bridal hair and makeup tomorrow as planned. See you in the morning."

She ate her lunch in blessed silence. No one else bothered her. Her appointment wasn't until the afternoon, and even with the drive, she didn't need to leave for another hour at least.

Please let this couple actually be serious about a wedding. The bride seemed to be, from the correspondence she'd had with her mother. She hadn't balked at the sizable down payment required. Between the plans for her parent's big day and everyone in town assuming their time would come soon, everywhere she went held a sense of expectancy.

Urgent, gut-wrenching, expectancy. She felt the weight of much of it as if she were responsible for delivering the grand prize.

Stomach fluttering the whole drive, she'd gone over the sales pitch a dozen times. Vicky maneuvered her mother's SUV up the mountain drive to the secluded cabin at the end of the steep paved circle. Cabin was an understatement. The two-story mountain home was straight out of last month's Colorado Homes magazine. At least they hadn't cut down too many trees to make a large yard. The landscaping was as natural as could be with a monstrosity of a house in the middle of it.

An older woman in what could be a uniform opened the door. Black pants and crisp white shirt, brand new looking and starched to the point they didn't crease when the wearer moved. "Hi, I'm here to see Ms. Sturgaard."

She was led to the den and asked to wait. The spacious room could have easily fit her last apartment inside it. The exposed beams and massive fireplace reminded her of the lodge her folks had taken her to when she was little. Beautiful details had been added to make this new home look old. She could smell the leather of the sofa mingled with the scent of pine and smoke. The den opened to a large sunroom off the back where the views were spectacular.

She could see Callan in such a room, enjoying a clear view through floor to ceiling windows in almost every direction.

She nibbled her lower lip. She could see Callan everywhere, which was a problem. She didn't know anymore where she began and he ended, everything got jumbled into "they."

A throat cleared behind her and whipped her out of her complicated musings.

"You must be Ms. Jones. I'm Sasha Sturgaard. Thank you for coming all this way to talk with us."

Vicky couldn't respond right away. This was the woman she'd seen Callan trying to hide from their last time in Telluride.

"Please sit. I want to see everything you brought. Would you like coffee or tea?"

"Tea would be great. Thank you."

She motioned for Vicky to sit on the sofa overlooking a wall of windows with another gorgeous view of the mountains around them. Not sure what else to do, she unpacked her briefcase and laid out all the town's brochures and a few samples on the table in front of them. She was teeming with questions but how could she ask without tipping Sasha off about Callan?

"Now, Ms. Jones. As I told your mother, I'm interested in your royal wedding facilities. My fiancé is more interested in the privacy. This isn't a first wedding for either of us, and I want it to be fun. You know, my first two were too serious. I hated them."

She cleared her throat. "Will your fiancé be joining us?" Her mind raced with what kind of excuse she could come up with if he recognized her. *Should she even say anything? She couldn't pass up the chance could she?*

"Oh, yes, he'll be here shortly. No more planning a wedding on my own. Not this time." Her laugh tinkled through the lofty ceilings, and Vicky found herself smiling back at the vivacious woman.

Around tea and conversation, she showed her the samples and photos of the wedding site. The stages and replicas that had been built as well as the wedding party costumes available.

"I'm already having my own dress made. Similar to the one you have here. Your mother's, correct?"

"Yes, she's getting married this weekend. If you want a close-up view of the sets, please think about coming for a visit soon. Of course, she's not going all out with her wedding. Yours would truly be one of a kind and the first of its kind. We have a decorated carriage for the horse drawn ride through the park. The options are open as to how you want your special day to be."

She clapped her hands in front of her. "I love it. How fun. The whole town participates?"

"Yes, it would be like your own mini London, or Scarborough Faire, if you prefer." This was going easier than she'd expected. "Are you planning on having a lot of guests?"

"No. Only a few dozen close friends and family. Like I said, this is a third wedding for both of us and my fiancé would like to keep it simple and low profile. When I read about Home and their theme weddings, I had to know more."

"Wonderful. Well, we have several private homes that have been turned into honeymoon suites for couples and their wedding parties to stay in for the preparations."

"Started without me?" A deep, stern voice interrupted their conversation.

"Oh, everything is perfect. It will be much more fun."

Vicky turned to the man walking into the room behind her. Braced for him to possibly recognize her, she plastered a serene smile on her face.

Sasha jumped up from the sofa and bounced her way to him for a big hug and a kiss before grabbing his hand and leading him to Vicky for an introduction.

"Ms. Jones, this is my fiancé, Graham Fletcher."

"It's nice to meet you, Senator Fletcher." She took his hand in a smooth shake. "Though I have to confess, we've met before, briefly, at a fundraiser in Washington."

She couldn't have cooled down the room any faster.

"What are you doing here?" he demanded.

"I really am only here for the wedding business in Home."

He turned to Sasha, "Honey, would you excuse Ms. Jones and I?" He turned to Vicky, "Follow me, please."

Sasha stared after them.

"What are you really doing here?" he asked the minute the study doors were closed behind her.

"I didn't know it was you and your fiancée asking for information about Home. I'm not here under false pretenses." She took a deep breath. She'd never have another chance to get him alone in a room. Now that he knew she wasn't simply a representative of Home's wedding business, he'd probably never talk to her again. An opportunity like this wouldn't come along again, so she went for it.

"What about you? Isn't there a committee hearing you should be working on scheduling?"

"So you're one of those reporters. Tell me why I shouldn't have security escort you out of here?"

"Your fiancée obviously wants what Home has to offer. And, frankly, Home needs the business and that's why I came. As a reporter, I have no agenda except the truth. Do you mind if I ask you a few questions?"

He sighed heavily. A tiredness she hadn't noticed when he was with Sasha settled over him as he sat behind his desk.

"Let's get this over with. Off the record."

Vicky dried her damp palms on her skirt and sat in the chair opposite him. She wasn't exactly prepared for a formal interview. "Off the record. Why have you missed the last two scheduled hearings and why have you been lying to your staff about your whereabouts?"

He raked a hand through his hair. That's familiar.

"Have you ever been in love, Ms. Jones?"

"Uh, actually it's Alexander. Vicky Alexander. My mother's last name is Jones. To answer your question, I think I'm in love now. Why?"

"Because love makes you do stupid things. Things like giving in to your fiancée's dream of a ridiculous theme wedding." He sighed heavily and shifted in his seat. "I'm getting old. What do I care? She wants a fun wedding. No problem. I've had several that didn't turn out well, maybe it's time to change the way the marriage starts. But that's not what you want to know." He leaned back in his chair and speared her with his gaze. "It's Sasha's son, Julian."

"Her son?" She prodded, waiting for more.

"Sasha was one of the highest paid actresses in Sweden in her younger years. She's still a star to me. But Julian . . . he has some problems. He's been here in Telluride for the last several months trying to get better. They have some exclusive facilities here for substance abuse. He's only twenty. Too young to give up on. When she needed me, I came. Rescheduling the first hearing to be here was an easy decision. The second one wasn't much harder."

"Then why the secrecy? There's no real scandal here."

"I let personal matters interfere with my work as a representative of my state. My opponent will have a field day with the optics, and I'm already behind in the polls. If I could get my son on board with my campaign things might turn around."

She bit her cheek at the mention of his son. He was within a few feet of a brochure full of photos of him. He had to have looked at them and not recognized Callan. Lil hadn't done that good of a job of keeping Callan's face out of them as she'd promised.

"Isn't your son interested in politics?" she asked. She wanted to ask all kinds of questions about Callan, but that wasn't part of her story on the senator.

"I'm still working on convincing him to become part of my legacy."

She nodded, waiting to see if he'd continue. When he didn't, she decided to get back to the main subject.

"I understand that personal challenges can get used in politics and delaying hearings for personal reasons is newsworthy in some circles but that's not the kind of thing I'd feel good writing up given your reasons. I don't think it will sell too many papers, but I can see how it would give your opponent a good commercial."

The reality of politics was that anything personal could be blown out of proportion and ruin a career. She knew firsthand how a career could be derailed overnight. There wasn't anything here she would feel good writing about. Nothing particularly sordid aside from his lying about his whereabouts. She ignored the part of her that was relieved.

"You're not pursuing the story?" His intense gaze never left her face. She understood where his authoritative power came from and where Callan got some of his too.

"You really should make a statement. Maybe get ahead of this." She wasn't a political strategist, but that seemed like the sensible thing to do.

"I'll think about it," he said, dismissing her advice.

"I have to report what is known, but there's nothing worth pursuing more unless I find out you're lying. I do, however, want to help you and Sasha work out a wonderful wedding."

He'd sat forward when she said lying but relaxed back in his chair at her mention of the wedding. He didn't answer right away. Was he trying to make her squirm?

"Sasha will be thrilled, of course. I want it low profile and quick. Everyone will know soon enough, I might as well tell you. She's pregnant."

"Oh, my. Well, congratulations."

"A surprise for both of us. I have a second chance, and I don't want to blow it this time."

Vicky managed to get through the meeting with the happy couple and even had a tentative date set for the wedding at Thanksgiving. As she drove back to Home, she thought over how she'd tell Callan.

She skirted Main Street and the construction crew finishing the sets for the weekend. They'd pulled out all the stops to get everything back in shape before her parents' wedding. Pride for her hometown swelled as tears of frustration burned, needing release.

Her parents would be happy to know she'd secured an actual client with real money for a down payment. Thinking about the weddings transitioned into worry over Blake Corporation. They claimed they hadn't paid anyone to vandalize the sets or hurt any of the businesses and that Mr. Barnes was not acting on any orders from his bosses at the company. She worried about John's house way out on the outskirts of town. She worried about the businesses too. If they kept going for another month, they might have something more substantial to market.

Advertisement offers were trickling in, and her blog was

going strong. Her mother's instincts had been right on. People seemed genuinely interested in theme weddings. Her mood plummeted thinking about what she was going to do about the so-called celebrity wedding they'd promised.

A thought started in the back of her mind. She'd been too distracted by who they were, she hadn't thought beyond her questions for the senator and selling Home to Sasha. She pulled over and googled Sasha Sturgaard. She should have done that the moment her mother asked her to take the meeting.

Home wanted a celebrity wedding, and they were going to get one. Except the couple wanted a quiet and low-profile event. Not to mention Callan wouldn't be pleased to know she was working to get his father more media attention in Home. Low profile or not, their wedding might fulfill her mom's promise to the town if they stretched it a bit.

Her mom met her at the front door when she arrived back at her parent's house. "How'd it go with the couple in Telluride? Why didn't you call me?"

"Sorry, Mom, it's complicated."

Her mother eyed her suspiciously "Complicated?"

"They're interested in the venue and want to come up and visit the sets and the town soon. They're also looking for a quick date, and to keep things low-key.

"That doesn't sound complicated. That sounds perfect. Except for the low-key part."

That was positive news at least. She'd lost her senator story.

If she told Callan about meeting his father and his soon to be stepmom, would he leave Home? She couldn't think about it; the thought of him disappearing from her life hurt too much. Almost as much as the thought of her walking away.

"Queenie, you're missing the fun." Her grams called to her from the dining table where the Jones women had roped her father and a few friends into helping make corsages and boutonnieres with Janine, the florist. The beautiful orchids were simple yet stunning. Looking into the smiling, laughing group, she pushed her worries aside. This was home. This was family, and this was where she was needed. Home was where she wanted to be. Would Home be the same without Callan?

"You're pinning the wrong ribbons, dear. Here, this is for the groomsmen," her grams handed her a deep purple ribbon. The purple matched the cummerbund her father and groomsmen were going to wear. This is for the ushers," she handed her a cream-colored ribbon that matched the color of her mother's wedding dress.

"I got it, now. Thanks." She slipped her arm over her grandmother's shoulders and gave her a quick squeeze.

"What's the matter, honey?"

"Nothing at all. I guess all this is getting to me. I can't believe Mom and Dad are finally getting married after all these years." She nodded over to her mother, who was head-to-head with her father, showing him how to pin a boutonniere. "They seem really happy."

"Your father's been after your mother to marry him for years. She's been saying she didn't need a wedding for so long, she couldn't back down until the town's plans for weddings became the perfect excuse. Too much pride in my daughter. And perhaps in my granddaughter?"

"Perhaps. I can't really do much about that now."

"It's never too late to change your mind."

Maybe she was right. Maybe she was letting pride get in the way of her happiness.

"You can think about it over bouquets. We have twenty more to go." Her grandmother handed her a basket of flowers, ribbon, and pins.

Why did she want to go back to DC? She wouldn't miss the cost of living. She didn't miss her ex-boyfriend. Yes, she missed her job, but not the paper. If she didn't miss those, what did she miss? It was the idea that she'd had to prove she could make it on her own, far away from her family and that she was successful.

But was she happy?

23

*A*fter an hour of photos, it was finally time to get to the park. Wishing she'd snagged more than one breakfast taco from the breakfast buffet Jo had set up for the wedding party, Vicky sucked in her stomach and waited for the hunger pang to go away.

She'd been so busy with last-minute details and spending time with her mother, and Callan had been working day and night to make John's place perfect, that she hadn't seen much of him since she'd seen his father. She still wasn't sure how to bring it up to him without causing him to disappear.

"You're late, and your hair needs a little lift." Rochelle pulled her to the side of one of the stations set up with a tent and chairs for the wedding party to await the carriage taking her parents on a ride through the park.

"Have you seen John?" Vicky asked. She'd texted him three times with no response. Any more, and she'd look as desperate as she felt.

"Once, over where the carriage is housed. Earlier today. Everyone's been trying to find him for one reason or another. Now, don't move." She worked on one of the pins in Vicky's hair.

"Ouch!"

"Well, your hair is picky, and it's humid today. Sorry, I'm a little nervous. So many of the photos will be in the brochure, and it's my hairstyling that will be listed. Rochelle pulled at a few hairs coming out of her updo and sprayed enough hairspray that there wasn't a single breath of oxygen in her vicinity.

Grams stuck her head in the tent. "Vicky, there's someone here looking for you."

Vicky pulled out of Rochelle's hold and followed her grandmother. She froze in her tracks when she spied Senator Fletcher and Sasha talking with Grayson close to the park entrance. The ex-Blake employee had been hanging around town the last couple of days and had wrangled an invitation to the wedding.

Vicky quickly looked around but didn't see any sign of Callan. Putting fire back in her steps, she rushed to the small group as fast as her heels would carry her.

"Senator Fletcher, Ms. Sturgaard, it's a pleasure to see you again. I'm sorry we're about to start my parent's wedding or I'd be happy to show you around Home."

She tried not to rush her words. What she really wanted to do was shoo them back into their SUV and out of town before Callan saw them.

"We apologize for barging in. We knew your first wedding was today, and we had to get a glimpse. Sasha's been talking nonstop about this place since speaking with you. I did a little digging and like what I've seen."

She flushed, not sure what to say and not sure entirely what he meant by doing some digging.

Grayson smiled. "Ms. Alexander has been doing an excellent job of marketing the town's business venture. I'm looking into some investment opportunities here myself. With Vicky and a mayor like Ms. Jones, you won't be sorry to give this place your business."

Vicky snapped her jaw shut at Grayson's glowing remarks.

"We're happy we met Ms. Alexander when we did. If you don't mind, would you excuse us a for moment?"

Grayson nodded and he and Sasha walked to a bench nestled under a tree and sat while the senator turned his full gaze on Vicky. Her stomach dropped at his change in demeanor. He was eyeing her like he was about to drop a bomb on her carefully laid plans.

"My fiancée changed her mind about waiting to come see the town. She wants the wedding here as soon as possible. Can you deliver?"

Vicky was nodding before he was finished. "Of course. Whenever you want it, we can make it happen."

"There's something else I want from you. It's not about the wedding, and it's not about Sasha."

"What?"

"I want you to help me find my son. My campaign is going to be in the midst of a public relations nightmare as soon as my opponent finds out what I've been up to. The hearing I've postponed is next week, and then I'll be in the fight of my career. Find Callan and I'll give you an exclusive. One interview to put it all out there before someone else does."

"I don't know what to say." Vicky tried to hide her shock at what he was asking. "I'm not sure I can help you."

"Exclusive access," he repeated. "It should help you get your paper to give you another chance, if you're interested."

"You did do some checking into my background?"

"That's not all. Seems Home could use an ally against Blake Corporation. In return, help me find my son. You'll be glad you did."

"If Callan doesn't want to be found, I can't help you. I'm not a private investigator." He narrowed his eyes and studied her. Dammit, that sounded way too familiar. She tried not to squirm under his intense gaze. She was sure he could tell she was lying. In no way could she come out and say she'd been sleeping with his son.

"Think it over. The offer stands until tomorrow. I can't wait any longer."

She nodded and he offered his hand for a shake and then walked back to Sasha and Grayson. Once the senator was sitting with his fiancée Grayson walked over to Vicky.

"I hope your mother doesn't mind she has two wedding crashers."

"She'll be thrilled. They seem pretty set on having their wedding here. What better PR than attending one and seeing how it's handled." She tried to hide her rising panic.

"Why don't you sound thrilled?" he asked.

"It doesn't matter. I need to get going." She checked her watch. "Crap, the wedding party is to line up in ten minutes. The carriage will be here in fifteen."

She rushed through the entrance to the park and to the waiting set of women in matching purple.

Craning her neck over the wedding party and onlookers lining the carriage path, she didn't see Callan anywhere.

She leaned over to whisper to Rochelle, not wanting anyone to overhear. "Have you seen John go in?"

"No. I thought he was with you."

Vicky bit her lip, worrying he'd stumble onto his father by accident or see him in the middle of the ceremony. Would it be a quiet argument, or would they get loud and angry? Too late, she was ushered into the chapel for the wedding.

Callan watched the crowd enter the replica of the chapel. Leaning against the wall of the pavilion furthest from the festivities, he waited. His legs refused to move, anger coursed through him, jumbling his thoughts. He'd spied Vicky rushing toward the entrance of the park and had called out to her, but she hadn't heard him. Then the last thing he expected to see happened, she ran straight to his father, Sasha, and St. James. He'd been in the shadow of one of the thick oak trees dotted around the park. They spoke for several minutes and then his father took Vicky aside. They shook hands. There was no way he could have found him. No way he could have gotten to Home if someone hadn't tipped him off.

"Aren't you going in?" Someone clapped him on the back, and he whirled around, hands fisted.

"Whoa, sorry. Didn't mean to startle you." Grayson took a step back.

"Didn't know you knew Senator Fletcher." Was he in on

it too? Did St. James know who he was? Or did Vicky bring him in, which would explain his sudden jump from working for Blake to being intensely interested in Home's businesses.

"I know all kinds of people."

"What's his business with Vicky?"

"Isn't she your girlfriend? Why don't you ask her?"

"Cause I'm asking you." He snarled, ready to punch the fake-innocent look off the bastard's face.

"Some kind of article Vicky's writing about him, and his fiancée is interested in the wedding plans the town has going on. Listen, if she's not your girlfriend anymore, let me know, huh?"

He stepped toward Grayson, but the man didn't move. Didn't even flinch. "Thought so."

"Go to hell."

He fumed while the cocky man walked toward the chapel and closed the door behind him. The last of the attendees.

His father wanted a wedding in Home? Not likely. Article on him for a job? Yeah. She promised she wouldn't reveal she knew him. If true, how did the man get to Home? It's not like him to come to the reporter. If Vicky needed to talk to him, she could have done it over the phone or flown to see him in Washington. No. The only reason he would be in Home was for Callan. She had to have told his father where he was. In return for what? Didn't matter.

Anger warred with the gut-wrenching proof the woman he loved had betrayed him. The only thing he'd ever asked was to be left out of it, and she couldn't honor that one request.

24

*V*icky watched her mother walk down the aisle with her grandmother at her side. Her father had never looked more handsome in his gray three-piece suit. The ceremony was simple, and the setting couldn't have been more perfect.

After the service, Vicky stood with the rest of the wedding party for more photos and greetings and congratulations from everyone who'd attended.

"Wait until you see what we have planned for the reception," her mother told Sasha, who'd approached them as soon as the guests had left the chapel. Vicky gnawed on her lip, searching for Callan, but trying not to look like she was panicking. The senator had disappeared with Grayson, presumably to look at the other buildings, and she'd been stuck with Sasha and her mother. *Please don't let them accidentally run into Callan.*

"Ms. Sturgaard, if you don't mind, I'll escort you to the pavilion area where the reception tents are set up." Vicky interrupted her mother's newest spiel about the town. She needed out of there and she needed to find Callan. He wasn't at the reception area and he wasn't answering his phone.

Ushered to the front where a large table was set up for the bride and groom and the wedding party, she couldn't look for Callan any longer. She sat, and someone pushed a flute of champagne in her hand. Toast after toast, she sipped and tried to keep from worrying about where he might have gone and why. Maybe he'd seen his dad and was avoiding him?

Her mother stood and raised her glass of champagne.

"I want to thank you all for coming. For all the work that has gone in to building this new future for Home. Yes, this is my wedding. And it's perfect. But it's also an important day for Home. The feeling I have now, this special, one-of-a-kind bride feeling is what we have to offer anyone who wants to get married here. Our love and care is what sets us apart from other places. Anyway, thank you all for everything." She paused, words thick with emotion, and took a sip of her champagne.

A round of applause brought tears to Vicky's eyes. This was a unique place and her mother's wedding had been exceptional for all the right reasons.

When the dancing started, her mother pulled her aside. "I haven't seen Callan. Is everything okay? I was hoping he'd use this opportunity to bring John and Kaylie so they could have been here to reveal the truth while everyone was gathered together."

"Callan?"

342

The senator and Sasha stood behind her. Fury blazed from the senator's gaze straight to her. The town could be expected to accept someone pulling one over on them for a good cause—especially with her mother behind helping the real John transition into his place. But she didn't expect the same from the man who had wanted to hire her to find his estranged son.

"I want an explanation, Ms. Alexander." Red-faced and stiff, the senator cornered her before she could sneak away.

"It wasn't my place. He asked me to keep his identity a secret." She held her ground when the older man pushed into her space.

"Not your place? He's my son. What the hell is he doing here? I demand to know where he is."

"No." She matched his stance. "I told you if he didn't want to be found, he wouldn't be. Look around, Senator. He's gone. All this wouldn't have been possible without him and he missed it. Probably because he saw you. He didn't want you coming in here and messing up everything he'd worked incredibly hard for."

"Don't forget who I am. You're missing out on a paycheck, not to mention that one phone call from me that would get your job at the *Chronicle* back."

"You can stuff your phone call and your paycheck." She poked a finger at his chest.

"None of that matters when your son hates you and would rather leave a place full of people who love him to keep us safe from you." She regretted it instantly. His flushed cheeks paled, and he took a step back. Tears clogged her throat and flooded her eyes. Too embarrassed at her rant, she fled as quickly as her heels would allow. Rushing into the bathroom at Split Ends, she hid until she stopped crying. Emotional outbursts were not her style. She groaned and grabbed another handful of tissue. At her parents' wedding of all places.

Callan wouldn't really leave without telling her goodbye, would he?

She knocked on the door to the apartment over Pearce Hardware, half expecting no one to be home. "Callan?"

As she was about to turn away, he opened the door.

"Missed you at the wedding and the reception." She managed to sound normal over the lump in her throat and panicked racing of her pulse.

He grunted and moved away from the door.

She followed him to the kitchen, where he leaned against the counter, arms crossed and face deadpan.

"I assume you know what's going on."

"Whatever he promised you. Take it and run. He's liable to renege."

"I didn't know your dad would show up in Home."

He shrugged. "I saw you and Grayson talking with him. I asked you for one thing—to keep me out of it."

"His fiancée seriously wants a wedding here."

"And Blake backing off Home? A coincidence too? Or did my father have something to do with that? You wanted your story on him. I hope he gives you what you need."

"How do you know about the interview?"

"Isn't that what you and Grayson were discussing? My father's a rich, powerful man. He can make things happen and he can make problems, such as Blake, go away if the incentive is there for him to do it. Just a warning, don't trust him to hold up his end." His hard expression and the bitterness of his words stung.

"I didn't make a deal with your father." She moved to face him, forcing him to look her in the eye. The warmth that had been there was gone. "I'm only interviewing him about his political career and he's here because he wants to get married." This conversation was out of her control. What he was accusing her of was the thing he specifically asked her not to do. Even to get rid of Blake's threat to Home—she wouldn't have done it.

"Look. It's fine. What we had, it wasn't serious. A fling with no strings. You got out of it what you needed. As did I. It's time I go."

"Go? You're leaving? Just like that?" After everything, he was willing to believe she'd betray his trust.

"John's back in a few days. The store's his."

"Nothing here for you to stay for?" Pain sliced through her heart, tightening her chest. She wouldn't cry. Or beg him to stay. Whatever his answer.

"It's just another town. Enjoy DC. I hope you get what you're looking for."

The room buzzed around her. She wanted to tell him she was thinking of accepting the job in Home. She didn't need to move. He could stay in Home with her and be a part of the town—the family—that wanted and needed him.

She'd pushed to get close and thought he'd been with her when their no strings attached fling turned into more. Shame smacked at the rawness of her emotions. Deep down, he wanted to be separate more than he wanted her.

Instead of telling him she loved him, she walked out of the apartment.

He'd made up his mind. His anger was greater than what love he might have started to feel for her. Tears blurred her vision as she raced down the stairs and back to her mother's home as fast as she could go.

He was leaving her. No looking back. She wouldn't beg him to stay. Even knowing what it was like to be in a relationship where the love wasn't real, she'd done it again. If he wanted to go, she'd let him.

No matter how much she told herself it was the right thing to do, she couldn't get her heart to understand it. She wanted to run after him.

Without thinking about it, she packed a suitcase. Everyone in Home was celebrating and all she wanted to do was be left alone.

Pulling her case behind her, she paused long enough to write a note for her parents and leave it on the kitchen table.

She'd called the one person who wouldn't have an opinion on whether she stayed in Home or not to give her a ride to the airport. A sleek black Mercedes pulled into the driveway where she waited. She couldn't even stay in the house—too anxious to get away.

"Should I be flattered you called me to be your knight in shining armor?" Grayson stepped out of the car and opened the trunk for her.

"If you're going to be nosy and ask a lot of questions, I'll borrow my mom's car and pay the parking at the airport." She rolled her case toward him.

"Not nosy." He held his hands up and smiled. "How should I explain your disappearance to John?"

"He won't be around either. You don't have to worry about him."

"You sure I can't convince you to have dinner with me instead? I've been told I have strong wide shoulders to cry on." He shrugged and tapped his shoulder with his palm. "I'm a good listener."

Underneath the flirting, she sensed sincerity in his offer. "Thanks, but I really just want to get back to my real life. Home doesn't need me anymore."

"With a senator on your side, Blake will have a tougher time harassing the businesses into selling when they decide to start up again." He opened the door for her. If she got in, there was no turning back. She looked around. Not sure what she was waiting for. Callan had been clear. They were over. He wasn't staying. Her parents were happily married, and she had nothing to offer the wedding business that couldn't be done by someone else. So why did she feel like she was giving up on a future that never was? Tears burned the corners of her eyes. Apparently, she wasn't cried out after all.

"Whatever stupid thing John has done to make you cry, he deserves the worst possible punishment."

A car headed toward them. Her heart skipped at the insane thought that maybe it was Callan coming to see her. Instead of slowing down on the curve toward her parent's house, it sped up.

"Who's that?"

Grayson turned, his eyes narrowed on the oncoming car. He tensed and cursed.

"Get in the car." He practically shoved her into her seat and slammed the door. Grayson ran around the front and had made it to his door when the squeal of breaks marked the new car's arrival.

The T-bone collision pushed the Mercedes off the driveway and into the brick mailbox. Thrown to the side, she hit the passenger window and pain exploded in her temple as air bags deployed around her. Her world went black.

25

"Too little too late," Callan said when his father walked into the hardware store carrying two cups of coffee.

"We need to talk, and if you won't come to me, I'll come to you."

"We have nothing to talk about. I'm heading out of town tonight."

"You will listen to what I have to say, dammit."

Callan bristled at the command in his father's voice. It was the same tone he'd always used on his mother and him when he wanted his way.

"I don't have to do a thing for you. Ever." He managed to keep his temper in check but just by a thread.

"I know. I'm not asking for anything. I want you to know a few things." He placed the coffee on the counter.

"Do we have to do this now?" Callan had been pacing around the hardware store for the last hour. After his conversation with Vicky, he didn't want to be anywhere that reminded him of her. John's apartment above the store.

John's home. The wedding where he'd have to face endless conversations.

"I . . . I loved your mother, but I didn't know how to be a husband or a father."

Callan stiffened. "That's an excuse?" His father never talked about Callan's mother except in a passing, polite kind of way. Where was this going?

"Yes. But it's the only reason I've got. I wasn't there for you or her."

"Now you're feeling guilty?"

The older man sighed and ran his hand over his face. "Look, I wanted you to be a part of my life. If you would have just been more open to sharing in my campaigning, you'd see."

"I'm not cut out for politics, we both know it. Cut the bullshit." His words were harsh, but this was not the conversation he'd expected. "I was a convenient asset when you needed it. Don't pretend I was anything more. And don't you dare say you loved my mother. You drove her into such a deep depression, she never recovered."

"That's all I wanted to say. I'm sorry. I hope one day we can be friends."

His father sounded almost defeated. His shoulders slumped and for the first time, he looked his age.

"Whatever bargain you made with Vicky, hold up your end. She and Home deserve a shot."

A confused look crossed his father's face. Instantly a weight dropped in Callan's gut.

"We have no bargain. I do believe that woman would rather roast me over a spit than deal with me again. Something she has in common with you."

"She told you where to find me in exchange for a story and your help with Blake."

"Hope you weren't too hard on her, Cal. She wouldn't answer my questions about you even after the mayor let slip you were here. In fact, she gave me quite a dressing down about my poor fatherly abilities. I wouldn't have known you were here except Sasha wanted to see if a royal wedding could be staged. Since we were close, we drove out here."

"You weren't looking for me?"

"Of course I was. I'd hoped to find you in Colorado through your friends. I knew you'd finally taken some of the money from your trust. After that many years, it had to have been for something important. When my aide talked with John and some of the other members of your unit, they all had a different story to tell. John was the best bet we had, and the only one you'd ever mentioned. My investigator lost your trail in Grand Junction."

Vicky's protests rang through his head. He hadn't let her explain. He'd assumed she was on her way out and had made it all too easy for her.

He left his father and the store unattended. He was done talking to him and just wanted to get to Vicky.

The need to see her rode hard on his shoulders as he drove to her house.

He saw the steam billowing up from a crashed car before he could register the cause. He threw the truck into park and ran the last yards to the wreckage littering her parent's front yard.

His heart beat wildly against his ribs and his blood pounded through his veins, momentarily blurring his vision.

The driver door had been crushed and the car had been pushed onto the rubble that had once been the mailbox.

"Vicky!"

Callan rushed inside the house and checked every room.

Had anyone been in the car? Had they gone to the hospital? Everyone who would have known anything was at the damn wedding reception. Think, Dammit.

First, whose car was it? St. James's. He'd been driving the shiny, new machine that afternoon. Whoever had hit the car hadn't stayed around.

He almost fell to his knees when he spied the blood on the window. That's where Vicky would have been if she'd been in the car. He'd fucking kill whoever did this. He forced open the trunk. Vicky's suitcase was inside. He found a cell phone in the grass on the driver's side. He pushed it into his pocket and searched the rest of the car.

He could hear his own panting over the drumming of his pulse. He almost dropped his phone twice as he dialed her number. Come on, pick up. Be okay.

No answer. He dialed again.

The line clicked as the call was answered.

"Vicky? Thank God. Are you okay?" The words rushed out in a tumble.

"She will be. If you do exactly as I say."

His world froze and dimmed. Barnes's voice flowed from Vicky's phone.

"Where's Vicky?"

"I have her and if you want her, you need to do something for me."

Callan gripped the phone, listening to the madman's instructions.

"You hurt her and you're dead."

"I'm sure I don't have to tell you how easily this could go wrong. If you want her, bring me the money I've asked for and she's all yours." The call ended and silence greeted his yell.

Sweat dripped from his temple, tickling a path down his cheeks. His knees buckled and he sat heavily on the grass. This was his fault. He should never have let her go. If he hadn't been acting like a self-centered piece of shit, she'd be with him right then instead of at the mercy of a lunatic. And where the hell was St. James?

Get it together, O'Shea. Maintain control.

He wouldn't let Vicky down. Not again.

If St. James had been with her, he might be hurt too. Or he's in on it with Barnes. Either way. He'd get the money and he'd get Vicky.

Focused on driving, he ticked off a list of what he had to do. The large stash of cash in the apartment was a start. For once, his paranoia about using his bank and credit cards had paid off. With what he had stashed and the cash in the store's safe, he had the fifty grand Barnes had demanded.

The engine was too loud in his ears, the air, stifling. He stumbled into the apartment and to the safe in the bedroom.

By the time he'd shoved the cash into a bag, he had his breathing under control.

He held his cell in one hand and the duffel full of money in the other. Come on, Barnes, call already.

The loud knock at the door made him flinch and he almost dropped the bag.

"It's Sly," the man announced before pushing the unlatched door open a few inches. "You in here?"

Callan must have moved, because Sly opened the door the rest of the way, but didn't step in.

"Hey. I didn't see you at the ceremony . . . Are you okay?"

"I'm busy." He needed to take some cash from the safe downstairs and the fewer witnesses the better.

"Whoa. Don't think so. You look like you're about to fall over. And why the hell do you have a shit-ton of cash falling out of your bag?"

Sly stepped in and lightly kicked the door closed behind him. He held his hands up in front of him, a neutral expression on his face. "Whatever you're doing, let me help you."

"Give me a fucking break. I'm not having a crisis or reality break." He cursed at Sly's placating demeanor and gentle tone. He considered his options. He didn't trust Barnes would hold up his end of the deal and involving the authorities was liable to turn the whole thing in to one big Charlie foxtrot. A mental image of Vicky with a head wound, pale and unconscious passed through his mind as rage burned a trail along the same path. A clear, purifying anger pushed aside the panic—locked it away where it could no longer interrupt his mission.

"Barnes has Vicky. And maybe St. James. I think she's injured. He wants money. You're going to help me get her back and nail the bastard. Got it?"

Sly stilled at Callan's concise rush of details, his expression changing from open to stone-cold and as deadly calm as anyone he'd ever seen in combat.

"Okay. Tell me everything. I need all the details."

He'd picked the right ally.

"Help me with a little larceny first."

Sly peppered him with questions about every detail of his phone call with Barnes and the scene at the mayor's home.

"Give me your phone."

Callan handed him the cell. Sly thumbed to the last call and punched in a number on his own cell. He went through a series of connections before getting to one he seemed satisfied with. "I need a trace on this number." He rattled off Vicky's cell number and waited. Callan paced as the minutes ticked by.

"Thanks." He ended the call and handed the cell back. "We can share life stories over a beer later." Sly must have seen the way Callan looked at him. Callan nodded. He was just happy to have some professional help.

"Her cell's turned off but as of half an hour ago, it hadn't passed out of the local cell tower's range. If he wants a meet with you. He's not going far."

"Barnes isn't a local but he's been hanging around enough to get the lay of the land. He'd have to have her somewhere close and somewhere he'd know he wouldn't be disturbed."

"What about St. James? You think he's with Barnes on this?"

Callan scrubbed a hand through his beard. "No. There'd be no reason to leave his car crashed at the house." St. James isn't dumb and that would have been a dumb move. He didn't want to say desperate. Because desperate men were unpredictable.

"Roger, then let's assume St. James is a hostage too.

What would Barnes want with him? Maybe if we figure that out, we'd have something to go on besides waiting for him to call you back."

Barnes hadn't given Callan a time frame. Just said he'd be in touch. Had this whole scheme even been planned out? He'd been the one to call Vicky and Barnes answered. Not the other way around.

Sirens wailed in the background. Out the apartment window, Callan saw Hayworth's Jeep, lights flashing, speed down Main Street. Someone must have discovered the crashed car on the mayor's lawn.

Callan's cell buzzed. "It's him."

Sly snapped his attention to Callan as he answered.

"I want to speak with Vicky," Callan said.

"Not until I know you've got my money."

"I don't exactly keep that kind of cash lying around. It'll take me a little time to gather it all. It wouldn't help you for me to get arrested."

"I'll give you until midnight. You've got connections. Make it happen. I don't care how. You're going to drop it where I say and then you'll receive directions. Give me a reason to leave town without the money and you'll be on your own finding your prize."

"I won't. Let's get this over with."

Callan listened to the directions, repeating them for clarification.

"Your girlfriend's being real cooperative. Even with the blood on her face, I can see why you find her attractive."

Barnes ended the call before Callan could respond.

"Details. Exact words."

Callan relayed the conversation in its entirety to Sly.

"Did you hear anything in the background? Sirens?"

If he'd heard sirens that would mean Vicky was being held close to where the deputy had been headed. No such luck.

"No sirens. Wait. I found a cell phone that wasn't Vicky's. I think it might be Grayson's. He was using some kind of app to follow Barnes's SUV a few days ago."

He'd forgotten he'd shoved the smashed cell into his pocket. He handed it to Sly. "Think you can get anything off of it?"

Sly studied the mangled electronic. "If it's got any juice, I can find something. But I need my equipment."

Callan followed Sly to The Walrus and the apartment above it, avoiding any people on the street. He'd seen command centers with less sophisticated equipment. "A simple bar owner, huh?"

"I'm layered. What can I say?" He rolled a chair to his desk and began working on the phone. "Please stop breathing over my shoulder." Callan stepped back from watching him work. He didn't know what the hell the guy was doing anyway and willing him to do it faster wasn't going to get them anywhere.

"Armory in the back closet. Help yourself to whatever you feel comfortable with."

Now that was more like it. Callan hadn't carried a gun since returning home. Today, he'd make an exception. Barnes had removed himself from being an innocent bystander.

He opened the closet double door and slid the jackets to one side.

"Push on the back panel."

357

What should have been old paneling on the back of the closet gave slightly and clicked open on one side. Within was a key-pad locked safe.

"Code."

Sly relayed a series of numbers. His cache was well stocked. Nothing too extreme—everything someone would need for either personal safety or local hunting. Callan grabbed two handguns and a rifle for Sly. If they needed more, they'd underestimated Barnes's training and abilities and were screwed. Sly could cover him at the money drop on the chance Barnes tried something.

The directions were to an old field outside town no longer being farmed. He'd be wide-open and vulnerable. He didn't care about the money. Money could be replaced. Vicky was his priority.

"Okay. Looks like you were right. He had a tracer on Barnes's SUV, but it's not active."

"Dammit."

"According to the GPS log, he'd spent a lot of time somewhere close to where Barnes is sending you. The only buildings out there are the old bed and breakfast. A good place to stash a couple of hostages.

"We've got two hours." They needed a plan. Barnes can't be in two places at once. Every minute wasted was a minute Vicky wasn't receiving medical attention.

"We'll check the B&B first."

Outside of the bar, they headed to Sly's truck.

His father rushed toward them from the parking lot. "Callan. Thank God I found you. Something's happened. The mayor's been looking for you and Vicky."

Callan stiffened at his father's hand on his shoulder, and he shoved the older man away.

His father's gaze pinged from Callan to Sly and back. "What's going on?"

"Nothing that concerns you."

"Mrs. Jones is worried sick about her daughter and you. Don't nothing me. There's a wrecked car on her lawn. That's a big concern."

"We've got it under control." Callan tossed the duffel in the back of Sly's truck.

"Where's Vicky? And why are you armed?" His father stood in front of him, back stiff, challenge radiating from his stern demeanor. "Do you need the sheriff?"

"Better tell him or he's going to be in our way."

Callan didn't need Sly's advice on how to handle his father.

"Tell me," his father demanded.

They'd never get out of town this way. "We don't have time for this. Just get in," Sly said, making the decision for him.

His father pushed his way into the back seat of the truck before Callan could stop him.

"Just what the hell are you two doing?"

"You might as well tell him. We need a third person anyway and he's the best we've got on such short notice."

Callan relayed the plan as Sly drove to the outskirts of the bed and breakfast property.

He needed someone to stake out the house and someone to watch his back at the money drop. A minimum of three people worth of need.

"You stay with Sly." Sly pulled over long enough for Callan to jump out and grab the bag of money.

"I'll go with you."

There was no time to argue. Their best chance to get Barnes was to ambush him at the B&B before he left for the drop site, but if they missed, someone would have to have the drop site covered too. If his father insisted on coming along, he'd have to go with it.

"I can have the FBI here with one phone call. You don't need to do this by yourself."

"No time. Vicky could be seriously injured, and we think we know where he's keeping her. I'm not waiting on the feds."

"You really love her, I see."

Yes, he really loved her. He'd been an idiot to think he could live without her. She'd been the best thing to ever happen to him, and he'd pushed her away. Why? Because someone like her could never love someone like him. Except she did. He saw it. Knew it, deep down. She'd been his, and he'd turned his back. He breathed through the pain slicing away at his insides and focused on the mission: find Vicky.

His only priority was her safety.

26

*V*icky pried open one eyelid just a slit against the throbbing pulse in her head. What happened? Stinging tingles lanced up her ankles and wrists as she tried to move. Her heart thudded against her ribs, and a sob tore from her chest as she pulled and twisted against her bindings until the room swam and blackness clouded her vision. Her hair fell over her face, sticking to her cheeks in itchy clumps.

She forced both eyes open and waited for her sight to focus. Where was she? Duct tape circled her wrists and forearms, keeping her arms bound together in front of her. Similar ties held her feet together. Flashes of memory put the pieces in place. She'd been in the car when Barnes had rammed it with his truck.

"Hello?" Her voice croaked, no power behind the call.

Her mouth was dry and coated with the taste of stale vomit. She'd thrown up on him. That she remembered. He'd carried her down some stairs.

She tried to wiggle around to see the other side of the room, but her vision tilted at the jerky movements, sending waves of nausea along with a thrumming pain at her temple. She squeezed her eyes shut against the onslaught and concentrated on deep breaths. If she passed out again, she might not wake up. She'd had enough first aid knowledge to know she probably had a concussion. She counted the seconds to keep herself awake. Slowly, she pushed herself up against the wall to a semi-seated position.

The dim room showed few details. "I know this place." Speaking aloud to the empty silence soothed her. She'd played in this basement dozens of times as a kid when the Carlisle's granddaughter would come to spend the summers with them.

The bed and breakfast's basement had the best hide-and-seek spots on the whole property. As huge as the main house and divided into three large rooms and several storage areas, they'd had plenty of old furniture and junk to rummage around in. Knowing where she was didn't give her any clue why she was there. What could Barnes get out of kidnapping her?

She opened her mouth to call out again but snapped it closed at the creak of footsteps along the floorboards above her. Was it better if Barnes thought she was still unconscious? Too many questions flooded her brain. What had happened to Grayson? Where was Callan?

Cold air seeped in from outside and hung in the damp air, permeating her clothes and clinging to her skin. Clamping her teeth around the shivers, she concentrated on pulling at her bonds. Bits and pieces of information on first aid, shock, and self-defense jumbled together in a cascade of panicked thoughts. Slowly letting out a deep breath, she focused on one action. Her hands. She needed her hands free.

She yanked and pulled and twisted until her muscles ached and her skin under the tape was raw. He must have used an entire roll, the sadistic asshole. Once loosened enough to bring the bindings close to use her teeth, she gnawed at the tape until pieces ripped away. She couldn't tell the passing of time—what seemed like minutes might have been longer.

The footsteps were back, heavy and solid along the kitchen floor above her. The linoleum floor echoed the thuds, but the other parts of the main house were carpeted and had better wood floors underneath insulating the basement from the sounds above. The movements spurred her on.

The footsteps continued first away and then closer, then she heard creaks and squeaks of the stairs. Oh, shit. He's coming down. She froze, gripped by fear, sobs clogging her throat, pressing to be released.

Barnes's voice floated through the wall from the next room. "Don't die on me yet, St. James. I'm not done with you."

Grayson was in the next room. Oh, God. Was he hurt? She needed to get help. Was her mother looking for her?

The tape around her ankles proved to be a strong deterrent for cold-stiffened fingers.

A loud pop and hiss and the single bare bulb in the room flickered then went out. Complete darkness engulfed her. She flinched at the string of curses from Barnes. She heard a door slam followed by shuffling noises from overhead. Then loud clicks, one after the other. The breaker box must be close. The place had been closed for years and had been old and in need of repair before then. What if the lights didn't come back on? She'd never find her way out in the dark. If only she'd kept her keys in her pocket. The little flashlight on her key ring her mother had insisted might save her life one day actually might have. She snorted at the ridiculous thought. Dead because she didn't follow her mother's advice.

Which way was the door?

She fought against the rising pain in her head and tried to remember the exact layout of the basement and her favorite hiding places. Maybe she could get Grayson and hide until help came.

Her cell ringtone echoed from above. Then it stopped. Barnes had answered it, but she couldn't make out his words. Then silence.

The lights hadn't come back on, but neither had his footsteps indicated he'd come back downstairs. Had he left? Whatever the case, the few extra minutes allowed her to get free. Crawling on hands and knees, keeping the wall or solid piles of boxes and furniture to her right, she felt her way to the door in the small room. She wasted no time using the same technique as if blind in a maze. She knew Grayson was in the room to the left of hers, so she kept the wall to her left in the near complete dark until she felt the wall give way to a larger open area.

"Grayson?" She raised her voice just above a whisper. A moan and hint of movement came from the right. On her hands and knees again, with arms outstretched, she shuffled along the floor until she found him. He was tied to a chair, and she felt her way up the back to his head and pulled the gag from his mouth.

His ragged breath proved he was at least still alive, but not conscious enough to talk to her. She pulled at the rest of his bindings. Less than what she'd had. Thanks, God. The tape holding him around his chest and to the chair came loose, easily. He slumped forward and onto her before tumbling onto the floor with a groan. She pushed at the dead weight of him on top of her.

"Come on. Wake up. I can't carry you out of here." At least he had keys in his pocket. The jagged edges felt like needles to her raw fingers when she pushed at his hips to roll him the rest of the way onto his back. Was it too much to hope he'd have a flashlight on his key fob?

Thrusting a hand into his pocket she pulled out what she could find. Keys attached to a standard car fob. A pocketknife. She collected the keys and knife—useless now, but maybe handy later.

His hand clasped over her forearm and twisted her arm away from him, searing the already raw flesh. She cried out, and he let go immediately.

"Vicky?" He slurred her name.

"Grayson. You need to wake up. We need to get out of here. "

"I can't see."

"The lights are out. I don't know where Barnes is. We need to go. Now."

She pulled at him, the need to run sending adrenaline spiking through her system. He could walk back down any second.

"Wait." His voice was weak. What if he couldn't stand?

"Please. Can you walk? We can at least get to the other side of the basement, maybe find a weapon or a way out."

"I . . . keys. Wait."

He gripped her arm again but this time, she helped him sit up. His hiss and groan at the movement told her he was hurt in some way.

"I have your keys. Now let's go."

"Give them to me."

She handed them to him. "Okay. Now come on." She stood, all the while keeping ahold of his hand. A light flashed in the dark, so bright it hurt. It took a moment for her to realize he did have a small flashlight on his key fob.

The beam didn't penetrate far into the darkness, but it helped them to get out of the room and to the other side of the basement. The problem was nothing looked the way it had when she was a child. Grayson leaned heavily against her, his injuries made walking difficult. Another groan from her partner and his full weight bared down on her, pushing her over as they both tumbled to the floor, again.

"This isn't going to work." They been moving a couple of minutes and hadn't found the stairs she'd hoped were up ahead.

Pulling Grayson into a corner, hopefully out of sight of the main room on the finished side of the basement, she left him. Once she found a way out, she'd come back for him or they'd both be caught.

* * *

Callan watched as Barnes took a shotgun from his trunk before getting in the driver's seat. He'd put in the call to tell him he'd gathered the money and was on the way to the drop point. Barnes's response had been expected—once he had the money, he'd call with the directions to Vicky. Their gamble had paid off. The closed down bed and breakfast out in the middle of nowhere was the perfect place for Barnes to hide. Vicky and St. James had to be inside somewhere.

He punched a number on his cell, and his father answered immediately. "He's here. Call the sheriff."

They had one more play. Callan moved out of the shadows he'd been crouched in and came up behind Barnes. The man reacted fast but not fast enough to stop Callan's punch from landing. His head flew back and banged on the door of his truck. He stumbled forward and Callan grabbed the back of his head and pushed him down to connect with his knee. Barnes slumped to the ground, unmoving.

"You didn't have to knock him out cold before I had a turn." Sly knelt and rolled Barnes to his side. He frisked him quickly and tossed Callan the revolver from the ankle holster.

"Shotgun's in the back." Callan motioned to the truck.

Sly pulled flex cuffs from his pocket and secured Barnes. "Go. I've got this." Callan was already headed into the abandoned B&B.

He ran to the double front doors of the main house. The solid wood wouldn't budge. He used his Maglite to break one of the side windows and crawled through.

"You see that?" Sly's voice in his ear was loud in the quiet night.

"What?" Callan clicked on the flashlight in the dark room. Moonlight was scarce through the covered windows.

The air was dusty and damp and somehow colder than the air outside.

"Smoke. I don't see it, but I smell it." Glass breaking accompanied Sly's terse words.

Shit. Callan slowed, sweeping his light around the room. A wisp of burned something tinged the air and stung the back of his throat. Plastic maybe, or electrical. He forced his shaking legs to move. If something in the old place had caught fire, he had even less time to find Vicky and get the hell out of there.

Sly met him in the foyer. "I've got upstairs, you clear the rest of this floor."

"Vicky!" Callan called her name every few feet. Through two large living areas, an office, and into the kitchen. No answer. No fire. But the smell of smoke was stronger up there. "First floor is clear."

Sly grunted in answer. The earpiece they were using crackled with static before clearing.

Shining his light around the kitchen, he searched for any sign of where the fire was. The pantry door stood ajar and inside was another door. He twisted and pulled on the knob, but the door wouldn't budge.

He kicked at it until it loosened. He found stairs leading down to the basement. The air was warm and thick with smoke.

"Fire's in the basement," he called to Sly before rushing down the stairs.

"Vicky!" Smoke burned his nose and throat. The acrid taste triggered too many memories. The heat. The sting of watering eyes. The roar of his pulse muted any other sounds around him. Stars danced in his vision. He jerked forward, desperate to keep moving through his disorientation. Find Vicky. He had to find Vicky.

Something bumped him and knocked the flashlight out of his hand. Instinct kicked in. The assailant was against the wall, Callan's arm at his neck with little struggle.

"St. James?"

The man slumped against the wall and Callan retrieved his flashlight.

"Where's Vicky?"

St. James's response was muffled over the crack of fire building from the area he'd just been.

"Come on you bastard. As much as I'd like to leave you here, you're going to help me find Vicky."

"She helped me. She was here. Barnes has lost his mind." His words ran together like he was drunk or talking through a swollen mouth.

"Vicky!"

He locked St. James's arm around his shoulders and dragged him away from where the fire was coming for them.

"Where the fuck are you?" Sly's demand cut through the noise.

"In the basement somewhere."

"Go to the east side. There's a stairwell and door that looks clear."

He pulled St. James along. Static sounded through his earpiece. Smoke burned in his lungs. His flashlight did little to illuminate their way.

A flash of light in the distance shined before moving out of sight. Another few feet ahead and he stumbled into the railing to a staircase. He pulled his charge up the narrow path and tried the door. It didn't budge.

"You. Stay." He pushed St. James against the wall between him and the railing and tackled the door, slamming into it with all his strength. Pummeling it again and again until his shoulder was numb from the abuse. One last push and it gave way leading to an outside well filled with debris. He pushed until his body was half in and half out, a light shined on his face.

"Hang on. I need to move some of the wood blocking the door." He'd never been more relieved to hear another man's voice.

Once the doorway was clear enough to push St. James through, Callan raced back down the stairs. Vicky was down there. Somewhere.

The whoosh of oxygen being consumed by flame filled his ears. Flames engulfed the hallway from where he'd entered the basement. He had minutes at the most.

An avalanche of debris fell from the floor above as the floorboards gave way.

"Help!"

He heard the cry from his left. Flames licked at the columns between him and where the voice had come from.

"Vicky?"

"Callan!"

"Keep calling my name."

He followed the sound of her voice into a small room. She huddled by a small window.

"Oh, God." She sobbed and rushed to him. Relief like he'd never experienced in his life washed over him. Her arms tight around his neck, her face buried in his shoulder, he held her. Unable to let her go.

"I left Grayson. I can't find him." Her words caught on

sobs as she pulled out of his arms. "Barnes hurt him. I couldn't carry him."

"I found him. He's safe." He tried to assure her, but she didn't seem to understand him. It was then he saw the blood on her face. She wasn't just sobbing, she was shaking hard enough to rattle her teeth.

"I'm getting you out of here. It's going to be okay." He spoke calmly but firmly. "I need you to hold on to me." She fought him when he pulled her into another hug. "Trust me." He'd seen the damage going into shock could do, but he couldn't help her there. He had to get her out or they'd both die.

"Fire. It's everywhere." She squirmed as he picked her up and laid her over his shoulder. He clamped his forearms over the back of her legs.

They couldn't go out the window. His only bet was to get back to the stairway he'd gotten St. James out of. His mind balked. Moving toward the flames was wrong.

Sparks that hadn't been there seconds before crackled and grew along his intended path.

It's now or never, O'Shea. One-handed, he grabbed a drop-cloth from a pile in the corner and threw it over his shoulder and Vicky and ran toward the burning doorway. Smoke filled his lungs, seizing his airway.

Only a few more feet. He stumbled toward the staircase in blind faith that for once, his need to run and get outside was the only thing that would save Vicky's life.

He didn't stop until he was up the stairs, out the basement door well and a hundred yards away from the house. Only when he was free from the shadow of the fire now engulfing half the building was he able to stop.

Vicky was still, like a rag doll over his shoulder. He laid her gently on the ground.

She didn't move. Didn't speak.

No, no, no, no. She lay bloody and pale in the moonlight. He pressed his ear against her chest. Felt the rise and fall. Thank God.

He knelt next to her and cradled her in his lap and rubbed her hands between his palms, calling on every divine entity he'd ever heard of for help. "Please come back to me."

"Callan?" Her hoarse whisper answered every prayer.

"I'm here. You're safe."

Sirens in the distance raced toward them. Thank God.

He held her as she shook, and, finally, her gut-wrenching sobs eased.

"You saved me." A soft smile tilted the edge of her mouth before her eyelids drifted shut. His heart seized in his chest.

"No, sweetheart. You saved me."

She's okay, he reminded himself, holding onto her until the paramedics pried her from his arms. He tried to follow as she was loaded on to a stretcher and taken to a waiting ambulance, but his world tilted. The crackle and hiss of the fire as it fought to consume the building had retreated into muffled background noise, but now it resurfaced as dark music to his nightmares coming alive. The pain in his chest ached only slightly less than the pain in his head as adrenaline pounded through him, twitching every nerve, every raw spot that fear had exposed. What if he hadn't gotten to her in time? What if Barnes had killed her during his sick game?

Barnes.

Suddenly, his unclear thoughts and stymied need for action found an outlet. He'd kill that bastard once and for all.

Sly appeared in his path. "He's in custody. You need to stand down."

"The fuck I will."

"We've got him. He's not getting away this time. Let the sheriff handle this."

Callan stepped to his left, but Sly moved with him. Wrong choice. He clocked him with a shoulder to his chest and barreled past, straight toward Barnes, who was in cuffs and being led to the sheriff's cruiser. Barnes couldn't run, and the fear on his face stoked Callan's rage until it boiled over.

"Keep him away from me!" Barnes yelled.

Someone grabbed Callan's shoulder from behind. He shrugged it off with ease, but before he reached his target, Callan's father rushed at Barnes from the side, taking Deputy Hayworth by surprise.

No! The smack of fist to face and crunch of bone should have come from Callan, not from his father, but seeing Barnes's face explode in a spray of blood was something, at least. Another grab at his shoulder and Callan finally stopped. The reality of where he was and what he'd been doing solidified with a pop of noise and chaos. Barnes, cowering behind the deputy, covered his face with his cuffed hands. It would have to do.

Vicky was who mattered. Not this guy and not his own fury.

"If you broke one of my fucking ribs, you're going to

owe me big time." Sly came up beside him, wincing and holding his side.

"Sometimes the old man gets a hit in too." His father grimaced and cradled his hand against his chest. "You want a chance at him, I'll take care of it."

Deputy Hayworth ushered Barnes toward the paramedics, keeping himself between Barnes and Callan.

"Aren't you going to arrest him for assault?" Barnes whined.

"Keep walking or you might fall on your face again." Hayworth gave a nod to Callan, his father, and Sly.

"We'll have a talk about this in a few." Hayworth continued, "Go get yourselves checked out. I'll meet you at the hospital. And be ready to tell me what the hell you were doing out here."

"Let's go." Sly nudged him toward his truck. "And your dad too."

Callan nodded, unsure how to speak around the emotions whirling through him.

27

*C*allan paced outside Vicky's hospital room door. He hadn't seen her since she'd been admitted for observation. He'd answered the sheriff's questions, watched her family come in and out of her room, and even checked on St. James, but he couldn't bring himself to face her. All night, he'd stood vigil, ignoring any twinge telling him to get out.

"You going to pace all day or grow a set and go on in?" Annoyance laced his father's tone.

Callan grimaced. "You have a real way with words. Anyone ever tell you that?"

"I didn't stop you from killing Barnes to watch you stand out here. You know what's worse than death? Letting fear stop you from living." He raised his bandaged hand and pointed a finger toward Vicky's door. "In that room is a real life waiting for you to get your head out of your ass."

"What are you still doing here anyway? Don't you have a speech to give or some hands to shake, away from me?"

"I had some things to say to you first, and since I can't

be sure you won't disappear on me again, I'm saying them here."

"I don't want to hear anything except goodbye and good luck." Just because the man had insisted on helping him didn't mean Callan was ready to forgive a lifetime of indifference.

His father sighed heavily and sat in one of the two empty chairs against the wall outside Vicky's door. Nurses and techs passed through the halls occasionally but for all the people that were around, they were alone at that moment. "I'm not too stubborn to realize I owe you more than an apology. You and your mother deserved better. I'm leaving, and I promise not to try to drag you in to my campaign again." He stood and pulled on the coat he'd been holding. "Now do me a favor and don't make the same mistakes I made. Get out of your own damn way and tell that woman that you love her and make sure you do everything you can to show her that every day."

Heat flushed Callan's skin. He'd never thought he'd be talking to his father about something like this, much less considering the man's advice. He didn't even flinch at the pat on his back, nudging him toward the door. "Okay. I'm going."

The door handle was cold and slick in his nervous hand. He rushed in before he could change his mind. Vicky looked small and frail under the covers with a bandage on her temple.

"I was beginning to wonder if you'd ever visit." Her voice was raw but strong. Relief warred with his anxiety.

"I'm sorry." Shame weighted his words, and he began to pace. He avoided looking at her. Didn't want to see the damage his neglect had done. He should have known Barnes would be desperate.

"Callan. Stop. Please."

Her soft request pulled his gaze to hers.

She raised her hand, beckoning him and the simple gesture broke something open from deep inside him. He moved to her side and helped her sit up, keeping her hand clasped in his. Now that he'd touched her, he never wanted to let her go.

"I was an idiot." His breath shaky. "I'm never letting you walk out of my life again."

The cool touch of her fingers on his cheek shook him to his core. "I don't want this to end. Even if you were an idiot." Her smile turned to a grimace and she squeezed her eyes shut.

"Don't move," Callan said.

"I'll be okay." She shifted and patted the bed next to her.

"I can get a job in DC as easily as anywhere else—"

"No." Tears pooled in her eyes as they squeezed shut against the pain again.

Oh, Christ. Had he lost his one chance to be happy? She didn't want him in DC—

"You belong in Home." Her voice grew stronger. Her eyes opened and her gaze steadied on his. "It's your home now too. You're needed there, Callan O'Shea. And I need you too."

"What about DC?" He'd go anywhere, do anything to get another chance to make up for his mistakes.

"Someone has to keep my mom in line. Home needs us and I don't want to be here without you."

He hadn't lost her. Not one bit. "Wherever you want," he said. "I'm yours."

She gripped his shirt and tugged, pulling him to her until his lips met hers. He kissed away her tears, keeping his caresses light and careful.

"I love you, Callan," she said, her voice seeping into his pores.

The lead that had been weighing him down seemed to disintegrate into nothing. "You knew it before I did."

"But now you have to say it," she teased and he knew his world was right. She loved him despite everything. He'd been given another chance at life and love. Nothing would ever come before that again.

"I love you, Vicky Alexander. And Queenie Jones. And Victoria Alexandra Mary Elizabeth Jones."

EPILOGUE

Three Weeks Later

"You ready for this?" Vicky asked as she reached for the door to The Walrus. John and Kaylie stood behind her, arm in arm. Callan smiled at her from behind the couple.

"Your mom has already been so kind to us. I can't wait to meet the rest of the people that Callan and John keep talking about." Kaylie straightened her dress and turned to John at her side. "This is where we're going to raise little Kelsey Grace." Vicky heard the hope, nervousness, and excitement in her new friend's words. She felt the same. This was a new chapter for all of them.

"Everyone is happy to have John home and can't wait to meet you." Vicky assured her.

"But not if we don't get inside. It's not getting any warmer and there's a beer in there with my name on it." Callan said from the back. Vicky suppressed a grin at Callan's affected impatience. It did have the desired effect.

John and Kaylie nodded and motioned for Vicky to open the door.

"Okay, here we go." Vicky held the door open for them to walk through. Music filtered out. She threaded her hand into Callan's, and they followed their friends inside. "You doing okay?" she asked. He squeezed her hand and nodded. "I'll be fine."

Almost immediately, the two couples were separated. Vicky's parents were the first to greet John and Kaylie.

Vicky slipped her arm around Callan's waist and pressed a kiss to his cheek. "You did this. Thank you."

"No," his gaze held hers, "we did this."

"No smooching you two, get over here." The mayor's voice cut through the music. "We've got a party to get started."

Vicky and Callan moved to the center of the dance floor where Kaylie and John were standing in front of a small stage that held a microphone.

The crowd in the bar slowly moved toward the dance floor where tables had been cleared. Her mother stepped up onto the stage. It was like a sign for the rest of the group that it was okay to approach. Rochelle introduced herself first.

"Welcome to Home." She opened her arms to give John a quick hug and then turned to Kaylie for the same. "It's about time this town had more boss-ass women to set things right around here." Leave it to Rochelle to break the ice even further. Kaylie and John laughed, and Vicky could feel Callan relax next to her. She blinked away unexpected tears at the love she had for Callan and the pride she felt for her town.

The way everyone had reacted when John and Kaylie

had moved back to town the week prior eased her own fears about the transition. Most of those who'd come to love the John Callan had portrayed accepted the whole story and embraced the couple as one of their own and forgave Callan for his lie. Without Callan, Blake would have bought the town and they knew it. This was the official welcome to Home celebration, and Vicky could practically feel Callan's nervousness for his friend.

"Excuse me, young man." Mr. Singleton ambled up to stand in front of John.

"Yes, sir." John stood at attention.

"Do you remember me?" Mr. Singleton looked him in the eye as he asked the question. Almost like it was a test. John studied him a minute and nodded.

"I remember you gave the best haircuts and always had my favorite kind of tootsie pop." He ran a hand over his head. "I could probably use another, if you'll have me."

The older man's hoot of laughter resonated around the small crowd. "That's fine. That's fine, indeed. I'll expect you Monday morning, bright and early." He shuffled past John and stopped in front of Callan and Vicky. "And you," he said, "My grandpa used to tell us kids growing up that we'd learn it's better to not interfere with something that ain't bothering us, but I'm glad you came to interfere." Callan accepted Mr. Singleton's outstretched hand for a shake. "You helped when you didn't have to, and that's a good thing."

A few more locals introduced themselves to Kaylie and John. Vicky and Callan stepped to the edge of the crowd, giving Callan more room to breathe. The place wasn't too crowded, but a good portion of the town had shown up. She lightly elbowed Callan and motioned to the bar with her chin. "Who's that with Grayson?"

He looked and then shrugged. "Haven't seen her around."

"They were pretty cozy in my diner last night and here they are again." Jo answered from Vicky's right. She tapped her toe to the music and took a sip of her beer. "Sorry, I couldn't help but overhear the question." She looked at the couple, talking close, sitting on stools at the bar, and back to Vicky. "I should probably warn her he's no good."

"I think he's proved he's okay," Vicky responded, defending him. Callan grumbled something under his breath beside her.

"Behave."

"We'll see." Jo took another sip of beer before moving into the crowd to speak with John and Kaylie.

The mayor cleared her throat in front of the microphone and the crowd hushed and faced her.

"First off, thank you all for coming tonight for a bit of an unusual celebration. There's been a lot of talk the last few weeks since my wedding and everything that happened afterward."

Vicky heard the catch in her mother's voice. It had only been three weeks since her parents' wedding and the night Barnes kidnapped Vicky and Grayson. Only three weeks. She shivered and moved closer to Callan. Without hesitation he pulled her in front of him and wrapped his arms around her, cradling her in his warmth. He'd saved them. His strength had helped bolster her own and push the fear aside.

"Tonight, is a celebration for Home and for everything we've accomplished and will accomplish together." She waited for a round of cheers to die down. "First, we welcome John Pearce and his lovely wife, Kaylie, back to Home. Without Pearce Hardware we wouldn't have been able to do what we did. And that brings me to another man to thank. Callan O'Shea, formerly known as John. We're glad to know you and thank you for saving my baby girl." Her mother choked up and had to pause. Her father, who normally took a back seat at any kind of event where her mother was on a stage, moved up next to her and took her hand in his, giving it a kiss. There was another round of clapping and cheers from the crowd, giving her the time she needed.

"Thank you. Now," She cleared her throat, "this isn't the end of what Home has in store. Weddings are getting booked through the end of the year already and that brings me to my next exciting announcement."

The crowd hushed, and Vicky straightened from Callan's arms. She hadn't heard of any exciting, new announcement, and her warning bells started chiming. What was her mother up to now?

"We can't expect to have weddings without a place for the wedding parties to stay, right?" She nodded as she asked the rhetorical question. "The old bed and breakfast and town hall that has been sitting empty and unused for so long is going to get a facelift. Especially after the fire. The Carlisles have decided to sell their properties now that Blake is out of the picture."

There was a rumble of murmurs in the crowd as everyone tried to figure out what she was getting at. "As the new owner, I believe Mr. St. James will enjoy their home and the land it sits on while they have agreed to deed the other half of their land and the B&B to the town. We have an exciting competition planned for the new prospective owners."

Applause and whistles and whoops filled the air at the potential for the new venture and what it would mean for the town's business owners. Enthusiasm for the future energized the crowd. Their love for Home and each other had carried them through one fight, Vicky knew it would be enough to keep them growing for years to come.

THANK YOU!

Thank you for reading *Home For A Hero*!

If you enjoyed this book, the next story in the series is *Home Sweet Home*. Grayson St. James is used to getting what he wants but when his bid to buy Home's run down B&B is challenged and turned into another marketing opportunity for the town, he is forced to compete with the one woman that might just beat him at his own game. I hope you choose to visit Home and see how the wedding business is going and join Grayson and Emma as they fight their way to a Happily Ever After.

Want more Real Romance At Home? Join me on my exclusive mailing list to get the scoop on upcoming releases, bonus content, and fun giveaways or follow me on social media for updates.

To sign up for my mailing list or find me on social media visit www.chloealan.com/newsletter.

Thanks for reading!

Chloe xoxo

ABOUT THE AUTHOR

Chloe Alan is a romantic at heart who strives to tell stories about the power of true love.

Since a teen, she's loved romances and believes we can all live our happily-ever-after. Always a people watcher, Chloe has combined her natural curiosity (some might say nosiness) with her love of romance for the sake of bringing the movies in her head to life on the page.

Chloe lives in the upper mid-west with her husband, two teens, and a hyper pup named Cocoa. When not writing, she enjoys gardening, cooking, great wine, and sharing a laugh with friends and family.

You can usually find her on Facebook, Instagram, or Twitter. Stop by for a chat.

www.chloealan.com

facebook.com/ChloeAlanBooks

twitter.com/ChloeAlanBooks

instagram.com/chloealanbooks